Phillip Gwynne is the author of acclaimed bestsellers *Deadly, Unna* and *Nukkin Ya* and the AFI-winning screenwriter of *Australian Rules*.

THE BUILD UP

Phillip Gwynne

Pan Macmillan Australia

'Up There, Cazaly' (Mike Brady)
Copyright © Remix Publishing Pty Limited/Origin Network Pty Ltd
Lyrics produced with permission of Albert Music.

First published 2008 in Macmillan by Pan Macmillan Australia Pty Limited
1 Market Street, Sydney

Copyright © Phillip Gwynne 2008

The moral right of the author has been asserted.

All rights reserved. No part of this book may be reproduced or transmitted by any person or entity (including Google, Amazon or similar organisations), in any form or by any means, electronic or mechanical, including photocopying, recording, scanning or by any information storage and retrieval system, without prior permission in writing from the publisher.

National Library of Australia Cataloguing-in-Publication entry

Gwynne, Phillip.
The build up / Phillip Gwynne.

Sydney : Pan Macmillan Australia, 2008.

ISBN: 978 1 405 03849 2 (pbk.)

A823.3

Typeset in 13/16 pt Adobe Garamond by Midland Typesetters, Australia
Printed in Australia by McPherson's Printing Group

Papers used by Pan Macmillan Australia Pty Limited are natural, recyclable products made from wood grown in sustainable forests. The manufacturing processes conform to the environmental regulations of the country of origin.

For Eliza, who else?

Acknowledgements

Thanks go to Ducks – without you there wouldn't be much of a book, my publisher Tom Gilliatt for his faith, my agent Margaret Connolly for her sagacity, Jamie Grant for his edit (no cavalry arrival was ever as timely) and my learned friend Jeremy Kirk for the lawyerly advice.

Chapter 1

4th October 2006

Jimmy casts and he's thirteen again, king of Tathra wharf. Standing in his spot, Jimbo's spot they call it, nobody else game enough to get up there, standing high on the south pylon, below him the other fishermen, a carpet of hats, a thicket of rods. He pulls up fish after fish after fish – salmon, bonita, mackerel, all clean and flapping as he flicks them onto the deck. None of the others catching a thing, glaring at him like he's got voodoo or something.

'What's your fucking secret, kid?' Costa the fat Greek finally asks, pride stuck in his throat, like bad kebab.

Jimmy smiles – home is shit, school not much better, but here on Tathra wharf he's king.

'It's all in the wrist, Costa,' he says, grinning like the cat who drank the dairy dry. 'All in the wrist.'

Forty years later and still it's all in the wrist, Costa. All in the wrist.

The Nilsmaster lure spins blue and white as it arcs slowly through the thick air, towards the other side of the billabong, where the slender paperbarks and spiky-headed pandanus come right down, crowding at the water's edge like cattle to a dam in a drought. Getting off the gear wasn't just about getting off the gear, it was going back to the everyday stuff – a shower every morning, eating breakfast again, and fishing. Jesus, none of the other blokes have caught the fish he's caught.

'The Barramundi Kid,' Barry called him the other day.

And he'd had this feeling, which took him a while to recognise: junkies and pride don't have much to do with each other.

Yesterday, though, Barry had just about bitten his head off.

'Lay off the fishing for a while, Jimmy,' he'd said. 'Keep away from that fucking billabong.'

He'd come, though, sneaking away when nobody was looking. He knew a big barra for tea tonight would change Barry's mind. A big barra'd change anybody's mind.

The lure kisses water and Jimmy smiles – it's exactly where he wanted it to be, just near where the toppled tree, its trunk smooth and white as sand, angles into the water. He lets the lure sink, then starts to retrieve – three winds and a tweak of the rod tip, three winds and a tweak. The lure stops, the line draws taut and for a second he thinks he's on, but Jimmy's caught too many fish in his time to not know that this isn't one. The line is snagged. He tries all the old tricks, moving around the edge of the billabong to work the angles, but all he manages to do is tangle the line around the tree. It's tough on lures, this country, and you've got to expect to lose a few. This is Jimmy's last Nilsmaster, though. He's got a few of those trendy treble-hooked squidgies, but Jimmy prefers it old school. So he shucks off his T-shirt, his shorts, down to his Y-fronts, his torso, his legs, so spindly, so white, mottled with bruising. He steps into the water, the mud squelching between his toes, water lapping his narrow calves.

He thinks about what that blackfella had said. 'A big old boss croc, him name called Sweetheart.'

The Build Up

Jimmy isn't sure, though. That blackfella hadn't stopped smiling, and he knows blackfellas love to wind up whitefellas, especially southerners like him. He's been fishing here for a month and hasn't seen any sign of a croc. That doesn't mean it isn't there, though. That's one thing Jimmy learnt in Vietnam – just because you can't see it doesn't mean it's not there. He scans the perimeter. Nothing. He pushes off, breast-stroking, pushing the lily fronds away from his face. Finds his rhythm, spreading the water with his hands.

Again he's thirteen and king of Tathra wharf. Him and his mates wouldn't think twice about jumping off and swimming to the shore. Jesus, how far had that been? A mile? Probably more. When was the last time he'd gone to the beach? He can't even remember. It's the old things, that's what he has to get right. Fishing. Swimming. Nothing too drastic, just the old things, the simple things.

He reaches the tree, feels for the line. Finding it he pulls. The line gives and then gives no more. A branch, thinks Jimmy, a branch that bends as he pulls. He could pull harder but the line is only five kilo, and he doesn't want to break it – there'd be no chance of finding the lure then.

Again Jimmy scans the area. He has this feeling he's often had here – that somebody, or something, is watching him. He breathes in deep, filling his lungs, and dives, his eyes open. The water is surprisingly clear, the tree trunk disappears into the depths. He follows the line down, his gunked-up lungs burning – all those cigarettes, all that fucking dope – but keeps going. Another big kick. He pulls at the line and it floats up. An anemone, he thinks. A tangle of tentacles. But he knows that can't be right, this is fresh, not salt, water. It's hair. Then a face. Hollow eyes. A lipless grimace. Her body naked. And in her, up her, a white-handled knife.

Chapter 2

27th September
Detective Dusty Buchanon of the NT Police Force wouldn't admit it – a true Top Ender never complained about the Build Up, it came with the territory – but this year she was finding it tough going. Last night she'd hardly slept at all. Naked on her bed, limbs as far away from each other as possible, cruciform beneath a ceiling-high eiderdown of heavy wet air, she watched the ceiling fan as it slowly whirred, admiring its dumb perseverance if not its effectiveness.

Dusty loved her high-set house, loved its wooden floors and shuttered windows, its wide verandahs, its corrugated iron roof. And when her colleagues complained about their astronomical power bills, she felt so smug, so eco-righteous. Lately, however, she'd been thinking that an air conditioner wouldn't be such a bad investment. She had the pool, of course, and three times last night she'd traipsed downstairs for a refreshing plunge, but as she sat on the back verandah, a sarong knotted above her breasts, eating half a papaya anointed with a squeeze of lime for breakfast, her eyes were drawn towards an advertisement for a Fujitsu in yesterday's *Northern Territory News*. The machine itself looked fine, quite stylish actually, and the price was reasonable, but what concerned Dusty was the former Australian cricket team captain standing next to it. She just couldn't see herself buying anything from somebody as gormless as that.

She returned to an article that had earlier piqued her interest. A group of thirty or so Vietnam veterans, described as 'disaffected', were lobbying the territory government to be given ownership to a block of land they'd been camping on during the Dry for the last few years. It'd become a sort of retreat, 'a place of healing', according to spokesman Barry O'Loughlin.

The accompanying photo showed an older man, greying at the temples, standing, incongruously, in front of one of the Territory's iconic termite mounds.

This one was particularly large, making Barry O'Loughlin look particularly small and ineffectual. Wouldn't want to have him as my spokesman, thought Dusty, as she scooped out more of the papaya flesh.

At thirty-three, Dusty was too young to have any memory of Australia's involvement in the Vietnam War. She'd learned little about it at school, but, there again, most of her school years had been spent doing endless laps of a fifty-metre pool or sitting at her desk, half-asleep, recovering from doing endless laps of a fifty-metre pool. What she did know about Vietnam had been gleaned from Hollywood movies: *Apocalypse Now*, *The Deer Hunter*, *Born on the Fourth of July*. As far as movies went, they were pretty good, but Dusty doubted somehow that historical accuracy had been a major concern during their making. She read the article with interest – conscription, Agent Orange, Post Traumatic Stress Syndrome. Poor bastards – it seemed only fair that the government should give them a bit of dirt in the middle of nowhere as compensation. Of course, it was never going to be that straightforward. Some blackfella mob reckoned that they had first dibs, that they'd put in a land claim years ago. But you could say that about almost any part of Australia. Parks and Wildlife were also keen, due to the 'unique nature of the termite mounds found there'. And if that wasn't enough, Rio Tinto, the mining company, were adamant that they had an exploration lease on the land. Again, you could say that about almost any part of Australia. Dusty's money was on Rio Tinto. Australia may once have ridden on the sheep's back, but now it preferred to dig bits of itself up and put them onto large ships and send them overseas. As for the sheep's back, that was now served medium-rare with a glass of Coonawarra shiraz. Still, as Dusty scraped out the last of the papaya, she wished Barry O'Loughlin and his disaffected vets all the best; it seemed to her that they'd been to hell and back in a Hyundai.

Dusty tossed the skin over the rail and into the garden. Though 'garden', with its connotation of neatness and order, was not the right word to describe what was going on down there. James had been the gardener, or, as he'd put it, using his famous lawyer's wit, 'a master of the secateurs', and when he'd left taking both his wit and his secateurs with him Dusty had let the garden go. It hadn't taken long for it to turn feral – Darwin may have been hacked out of the wilderness, but the wilderness was constantly fighting back, reclaiming its territory.

Amongst the plants that Dusty recognised – the frangipani, the bougainvillea, the Carpentaria palms – was other flora of less certain pedigree.

'Weeds', perhaps, but Dusty had decided that was just a term of convenience, a marketing ploy to con people into buying exorbitantly priced weed killers. All plants were welcome in her backyard, irrespective of class, colour or weediness.

After four months of the Dry the garden was looking tired, its glossy leaves dulled by a layer of dust. Dusty knew from experience, however, that it would be instantly revived when the Wet broke, when the monsoonal rains arrived. Whether the same would happen to her remained to be seen.

Checking her watch, a ten-buck Taiwanese special, Dusty

The Build Up

contemplated whether to go for a run before work, whether an hour was enough time for a decent workout. Her two dogs, or 'dawgs' as she liked to call them, Smith and Wesson, were giving her definite c'mon-let's-go looks from their respective positions next to the table and on the Bali seat. Both medium-sized dogs were bitsers. Smithie had a lot of pitbull in her, Wessie not much, and that was as much as Dusty knew about their ancestry. Never a pretty dog, Smithie had got even uglier lately when one of her eyes had become infected and turned milky. She was also getting on now, showing signs of arthritis, and wasn't as alert as she'd once been. Last year Dusty had acquired Wessie. In her open house, backing onto parklands, in her profession, a good watchdog wasn't such a bad idea.

From within Dusty's bedroom came the sound of her mobile ringing, playing 'I Shot The Sheriff'. Fontana had installed it, his idea of a joke.

She rushed into the house and answered it without looking at the caller's name – at this hour it had to be work.

'Detective Buchanon here.'

'Frances?'

Dusty had been Dusty since she was eight years old and in Grade 5 at West Adelaide Primary School. She'd come into the classroom dishevelled after her usual lunchtime wrestle with pooey-pants Tommy Papadopoulos. 'Frances, you really are dusty,' the teacher had said, and that'd been her name ever since. Only one person still persisted in calling her Frances.

'Mum, do you know what time it is?'

Not an unreasonable question, but her mother ignored it. 'Guess what?' she asked, in that annoying way she had – why didn't she just come straight out and tell her the obviously pressing news instead of indulging in these infantile guessing games?

'Another interesting homicide?' queried Dusty.

If there was one thing guaranteed to annoy her mother it was to remind her that genteel Adelaide, the self-proclaimed City of Churches, had a long history of bizarre and unusually cruel murders.

Again Celia chose to ignore her daughter.

'Nat is pregnant, again.'

Nat was the youngest of Dusty's three stepsisters, the daughters of her mother's third husband, Phil. They took it in turns getting pregnant, like some sort of relay race, the fecundity baton being passed from one to the other.

'That's nice.'

'Well, you could be a little more excited.'

'I hardly know her!'

When Dusty had left Adelaide Celia had still been on husband number two, the ineffectual Daryl. Phil had only arrived on the scene about six years ago.

'She's still your sister.'

'Stepsister.'

'Frances!'

'OK, Mum, here we go. Wow, that's really great. I'm so very happy for her.'

'That wasn't too hard, was it now?'

Sarcasm, any form of irony really, was wasted on Celia.

'And have you had any thoughts in that direction, yourself?'

'I really have to get to work.'

'You're not getting any younger, you know.'

'Time's arrow is a concept I'm familiar with, Mum.'

'Well, have you thought about Richard's offer?'

Richard was Dusty's property-developing, Porsche-driving, secretary-shagging younger brother. Actually, Dusty wasn't sure about the secretary-shagging, wasn't even sure if he had a secre-

The Build Up

tary to shag, and as for the Porsche, well maybe his car wasn't technically an example of Germanic engineering excellence, but it did have two doors, no roof and was, according to Richard himself, a chick-magnet. He was most definitely a property developer, though, frequently ringing her with news of his latest sure-fire scheme. His offer? That she quit the Force, come back to Adelaide and he'd help her set up a business – a coffee shop, or a newsagency, or what about a pet shop? She loved animals. Always had. A pet shop would be ideal.

'I have thought about it and I'm not interested.'

'I don't want to sound pushy, darling. But, you know, all I want is the best for you. I just don't think you're going to find Mr Right up there. Mr Really Big Beer Gut, maybe. Or Mr Rough As Bags. But not Mr Right. Mr Right doesn't live in places like Darwin.'

For some reason – perversity was Dusty's guess – Celia insisted on pronouncing Darwin with the stress on the last syllable. Dar-*win*.

'Mum, you know nothing about *Dar*-win,' said Dusty, with a countervailing stress of her own.

In all the years that Dusty had lived in the Top End, Celia had visited her twice. The last time, two years ago, had started off well. James and Dusty had just bought their dream troppo home. Celia was excited by its potential and was full of grand decorating ideas – most of them seemed to involve air conditioning, wall-to-wall carpet and a colour she insisted on calling 'apricot blush'. Then they'd gone to Parap market, a place Dusty thought of as an intriguing microcosm of multicultural Darwin.

'You'll love it here, Celia,' James had said, and as much as Dusty was now determined to despise James and everything he'd ever said, done or intimated, she had to admit he'd really tried his hardest with his prospective mother-in-law. 'It's a real East-meets-West place.'

Just then a couple of Humpty Doo ferals walked past, both of them dreadlocked and barefoot, one of them wearing a grimy sarong with half his arse hanging out. Celia cocked a meticulously plucked eyebrow and Dusty knew that what was coming next wasn't going to be pleasant.

'More like East meets White Trash.'

She wouldn't eat the food. *Surely there must be some sort of health regulations.* She wouldn't drink the coffee. *It's just too hot for coffee.* And when Dusty bought some bok choy from an Asian woman she was aghast. *But surely you know they urinate on it, those Asians.* It didn't get any better after that and it was a relief when they were able to bundle her back onto the redeye, the 1.30 am flight back to Adelaide.

Celia continued. 'I know I've asked this before, but all I want to hear is the truth and you know I'll still love you if you are. You're not one of those, are you?'

'One of what?' asked Dusty, even though she knew exactly what her mother was suggesting.

'You know, one of those lezz-be-annes.'

'Not last time I looked.'

'There's no need to be flippant about it, Frances.'

'I was with James for five years, remember, Mum?'

'Such a lovely man.'

Celia had never liked James. Never liked the fact that he was a Legal Aid lawyer. Never liked the fact that although his cane-farmer parents were from Italy, they were from the south, from Calabria, not somewhere nice, like Tuscany. But since Dusty and James had split up Celia's feelings seemed to have done a complete U-turn.

'Remember Peggy-Down-The-Road's daughter?' she said. 'Not a pretty girl, at all. Absolutely no chin. Well, she left her husband of twelve years and moved in with some barmaid. And

The Build Up

the police force, I know from your father, is overrun by them.'

Celia seldom mentioned Dusty's father, but when she did it was invariably to invoke some sort of parental solidarity.

'Mum, if I do turn, you'll be the first to know, OK?'

Dusty switched to a topic she knew her mother was more comfortable with. 'Had my hair done yesterday,'

'You had it cut?'

'I had my highlights done.'

'There is nothing wrong with your natural hair colour.'

'If I was a mouse, no.'

'So those wispy bits you're forever fidgeting with are still there?'

'Not really,' said Dusty, pushing the wispy bits behind her ears.

'Frances, either you have short hair or long hair. Why do you insist on being so in-between?'

'Bye, Mum.'

As she'd done many times before, usually after a call from her mother, Dusty threw her Nokia at the hammock. This time, however, it hit some sort of sweet spot and trampolined into the air, over the rail and, after performing an inward one-and-a-quarter somersault, dropped into the pool. Dusty watched it sink to the bottom, emitting a pearly trail of air-bubbles.

A Kreepy Krauly does not move quickly, and maybe there was time for Dusty to hurry down the steps, dive in and retrieve her phone. She was mesmerised, though, entranced by the very inevitability of it, like watching one of those David Attenborough documentaries – the ruthless predator closing in on its unsuspecting prey. She could only sit and watch as her phone disappeared into the undulating blue tentacles of the award-winning pool-cleaner. She really did need that run, after all.

Chapter 3

Dawgs bouncing around in the back, Dusty drove to Casuarina Beach in Beastie Boy, her 1978 model Holden HZ ute. She'd personally confiscated it from a bad-cheque merchant when she was in Fraud, kept track of its progress through the system, and managed to get it at the police auction for a song. There was no power-steering. There was no airconditioning. There used to be a radio until some druggie ripped that out, leaving a gaping hole full of raw wires. Beastie Boy was used for two things: taking the dawgs to the beach and, theoretically anyway, old palm fronds to the rubbish tip. The rest of the time Dusty used the police-supplied car, the white VZ Commodore.

Dusty already had her running gear on: a sports bra, shorts, a 'Cheeky Monkey' singlet, and recently-purchased Asics. Without the familiar weight of her mobile in her pocket, however, she felt almost naked.

A mob of Long Grassers, the name given to the itinerant Aborigines who camped in the parklands around Darwin, was near the toilets, sitting cross-legged around the smouldering ashes of last night's fire, passing a flagon of wine around, still in its brown paper bag. Although they were breaking at least two laws – drinking in a public place and breaching a total fire ban – upholding the law wasn't Dusty's major concern at the moment. She ran past them, studiously looking the other way, a

The Build Up

private citizen on her morning run with her dawgs.

'Hey, Broken Arse!' came a familiar voice.

Broken Arse was one of Dusty's most cherished blackfella insults. Basically it had to do with bum cheeks and underpants, and the tendency of the latter to divide the former into two distinct regions.

Dusty stopped and looked around. It was who she thought it would be – Marion. Once a beautiful woman, she was now a wreck – her left eye permanently half-closed, her matted hair full of twigs, her right arm in a filthy sling. Years ago Marion had been raped by some powerful men in her community and Dusty, working in the Sex Crimes unit at the time, had done the investigation. They'd had a strong case, a conviction looked likely so Dusty had persuaded Marion to take it to court. Unfortunately, the combination of a ruthless defence lawyer, Marion's inability to withstand his constant probing and an unsympathetic judge, led to the perpetrators being let off. The shame had been too much, of course. Marion hadn't been able to return to her community. She became a Long Grasser, and an alcoholic.

'Dutty, you got some of them clothes?' she asked.

Dusty was in the habit of giving any old clothes she had to Marion.

'Not today, Auntie.'

Marion wasn't much older than Dusty, technically a 'sister', but Dusty called her 'Auntie'. Maybe it was a recognition of the horrendous ordeal Marion had been through, or maybe, less charitably, it was because she looked about a hundred years older.

Dusty kept on going, jogging across the footbridge that spanned Rapid Creek, one of the many mangrove creeks that drained into Darwin Harbour. The beach wasn't popular during the Build Up. The first, and the most venomous reason, was the box jellyfish, *Chironex fleckeri* to the more scientifically inclined.

An innocuous looking animal, especially when compared to the toothy, and more conspicuously dangerous, crocodile, its sting could cause extensive welting, cardiovascular trauma, heart failure and, worst possible scenario, death. The other reason had to do with the extreme tidal fluctuations of the Top End. It was low tide now, which meant that the Arafura Sea had retreated towards Timor, leaving a vast flat expanse of gritty brown sand. Even if you were foolhardy enough to want to brave *Chironex fleckeri* and take a dip, there was no water to dip into.

Dusty followed the high tide mark as she ran; the sand was more compact there. The only sound was the occasional crunch as she trod on mangrove litter, leaves and twigs, and the ragged panting of Smith and Wesson as they scampered alongside her, tails and tongues working overtime.

Dusty always knew when she'd found her rhythm – the fob chain she wore, her dad's twenty-first birthday present to her, would bounce in time to her stride. The other day Fontana had been blathering on about monitors, about target zones, about maximum pulse rate.

'Don't go anywhere without mine,' he'd said, unbuttoning his shirt to show the strap around his bulky chest.

It'd all sounded very impressive, very scientific, but Dusty knew it wasn't for her. Her legs were working well now, so too her lungs, and the sweat, inevitable when the humidity was close to a hundred percent, was beading her brow. Really, this was all the science she needed, and it'd been like this since when she was a kid. Back then it'd been water polo, swimming, but it was the same feeling, of leaving it all behind, all the shit that went with being a human being, and just becoming muscle and sinew and breath and, eventually, pain.

She pushed it harder, the dawgs easily keeping up with the increase in pace. Up ahead the beach was clear except for an odd

The Build Up

shape on the sand. As she got closer she could see it was two people, one on top of the other. She assumed they were having sex. It wouldn't be the first time she'd encountered a couple *in flagrante delicto* on the gritty sand of Casuarina Beach. Again it was a serious misdemeanour, a blatant contravention of S. 47(a) of the Summary Offences Act, but Dusty averted her gaze, fixing on the horizon to her left, where clouds were gathering like onlookers around a car crash. By evening they would be piled high, tinged with grey, maybe even black, there would even be flashes of lightning, but Dusty knew it was only a tease – there wouldn't be any rain, not yet. That would be too easy, and the Build Up was never easy.

The lovers were speaking in Tiwi, the language from the island to the north of Darwin. Though Dusty didn't understand what was being said, it certainly didn't sound as if sweet nothings were being swapped.

Don't look! Dusty kept admonishing herself, I'm just a private citizen on a private run with her private dawgs.

But had she not also sworn to 'cause her Majesty's peace to be kept and preserved and prevent to the best of my power all offences against the same'? Dusty looked. A very dark, scrawny, bare-chested man with a shaved head was straddling a woman, also very dark, yanking at her hair with one hand while the other pressed against her face.

Dusty didn't hate most crims, not like other cops who hated them the same way a farmer hates vermin, who saw it as their god-given duty to rid the world of them. No, she actually felt almost sorry for most of them; they were just sad fucked-up people with sad fucked-up lives they'd inherited from their sad fucked-up parents – survival of the shittiest. She hated wife-bashers, though, hated them with an intensity that even frightened her sometimes.

'Hey, you,' yelled Dusty. 'Get off her!'

The man looked around.

'Fuck orf,' he said, in a language she clearly understood.

Time to call in some reinforcements. Dusty felt for her phone. It wasn't there! She remembered it disappearing into the tentacular embrace of the Kreepy Krauly. What to do? Wesson was yelping and scratching at the sand where he'd seen a fiddler crab. Of course!

'Wessie, sic 'em!' ordered Dusty. 'Go on, sic 'em!'

Wesson looked up at her, his eyes brown and liquid.

'Do I really have to?' he seemed to be imploring, 'I'm an excellent watchdog, but I'm not really the siccing type. Besides there's a pesky crab here that needs seeing to.'

Dusty turned back to the couple.

'Look, I'm number one copper,' she said, unconsciously reverting to pidgin. 'You in big mobs trouble.'

The man looked Dusty up and down, brought his fist back and punched the woman in the face. Dusty heard the crack – teeth? cheekbone? – and saw the blood. The unsatisfactory conversation with her unsatisfactory mother, the demise of her Nokia, and now this. Dusty had spent too much time kicking a football around with her brother and his mates not to have a good understanding of the mechanics of the tackle. She hit him low and she hit him hard, driving her left shoulder into his midriff, knocking the air out of him. As he lay winded, gulping in air, she rammed his head into the sand and applied a regulation police hammerlock, bending his right arm up behind his back. The woman, her face smeared with tears, with blood and snot, struggled to her feet. She was only a kid, barely into her teens.

'You call police, OK?' said Dusty, making a phone with her thumb and first finger.

The woman looked at Dusty and her make-believe phone. Dusty could see the fear in her eyes. Fear and distrust.

The Build Up

'OK, you call police. We lock-em up this no-good fella.'

The woman took a couple of steps forward and, with some deliberation, stomped on the man's head. She was barefooted, but that didn't seem to matter. The man emitted a sand-muffled scream. Encouraged, the woman stomped again on his head. Another muffled scream. One part of Dusty could see the advantage of this summarily dispensed justice: that would be the end of it and she could walk away. Another part, however, was a police officer. As the woman brought her foot back for a third time Dusty put a hand up and said, 'Stop!'

The woman scowled at Dusty before hitching up her skirt up and staggering back along the beach.

'You make call, OK?' yelled Dusty at the departing figure.

At ten o'clock, the time Dusty was due to start work, she was still sitting on top of her wife-basher. Though he'd stopped struggling, he was a bony fella and didn't make a particularly comfortable seat. She'd yelled out to a couple of joggers, but they'd been too far away and hadn't heard her. Even if somebody did come along there was no guarantee they'd be of assistance. Darwin was a frontier town, the place people ended up in when they'd outstayed their welcome down south; many of its inhabitants were, if not criminal, at least anti-authoritarian. The dawgs weren't happy, either. Thirsty and hungry, they were whimpering, making unsubtle 'let's go' signs. As much as she hated the idea, Dusty decided that she had to let him go free, that she should've let rough justice run its course, after all.

She released her grip and stood up, stepping back quickly. The man remained motionless. Is he playing possum, Dusty asked herself, or is he, in fact, dead? It was possible, a brain aneurism caused by the brace of barefoot stomps or perhaps asphyxiation due to ingestion of a large quantity of gritty brown sand. She gave him a tentative nudge in the ribs with the toe of her Asics.

He stirred. She nudged him again, harder this time. He slowly rolled over onto his side, sand clinging to his face like coconut to a lamington, and scowled at Dusty.

'You big hole.'

Big hole? Dusty tried to recall the last time she'd had sex. That's right, it was eighteen months ago, two nights before James had decided that he wanted out, that their relationship 'was no longer viable'. And now here was this scrawny wife-basher suggesting that she was promiscuous. Really, it was getting to be too much – now she wanted to stomp on his head herself.

As she ran back along the beach, her legs stiff, her rhythm gone, Dusty pictured a pet shop. She could see tanks full of vibrant fish. She could see a window full of adorable puppies. And standing behind the counter she could see herself, pet shop owner, a garrulous cockatoo on her shoulder.

'Dusty wanna cracker?' it squawked. 'Dusty wanna cracker?'

Maybe Dusty did wanna cracker, after all. She'd give Richard a call tonight. Just to talk it over, that's all. Where was the harm in that?

Chapter 4

A naked Tasanee Niratpattanasai, or, as she was more commonly known, Noi, looked at Rob 'Trigger' Tregenza's deflated penis with some dismay; in much the same way, perhaps, as a keen gardener would regard a slug found on their prize cabbage.

'Cazaly, he no good today,' she said, the vowels so broad, with a rising inflexion so exaggerated, it was almost a parody of an ocker accent.

It began as a joke, the Cazaly thing. Trigger's teammates at the Swans, Sydney's famous Australian Rules football team, had started calling him that when the football anthem became famous in the eighties.

Up there Cazaly, in there and fight,
Out there and at 'em, show 'em your might.

It had nothing to do with his football ability, though, and everything to do with his sexual appetite. They reckoned he was just like Cazaly, either 'up there' or trying to get 'up there'. The name hadn't lasted long, though, about as long as his time in the big league, and he'd soon gone back to being what he'd been since he was a kid: Trigger. He'd liked the Cazaly, though, and had decided that he still wanted it around. Right now, however, Cazaly was anything but 'up there'. In fact, he was more like an Italian soccer player collapsed in the penalty box, waiting for the referee to blow his whistle and award him a World Cup-winning penalty kick. Who or what could Trigger blame? Not the heat – the air con at Ruby's was very good. Not the bed either, that was comfortable enough and the bed linen, for a knock-shop, surprisingly clean. Not the grog, he'd only had a couple of beers, or the drugs, it'd been at least a week since he'd done any blow. And he definitely couldn't blame Noi – she'd attended to Cazaly like the true pro she was, both hand and mouth working him over plenty. OK, he still hadn't got used to her new tits, they reminded him of those blister-packs you got your tartare sauce in at the fish and chip shop, and he wasn't sure about the Brazilian, either – Trigger, like Shane Warne, preferred some grass on his wicket. They weren't the reason though. No, the problem, as with most things in Trigger's life, was fucking Darwin.

'OK, Noi get jumper?' said Noi.

'Wait. I wanted to ask you something.'

'Wha?'

'You want to do some work together again?'

Footballer. Pant's man. Dinkum Australian. Mate. These were all words Trigger would use to describe himself. Pimp, however, did not roll so easily off his tongue. Especially not with its connotations of loud clothes and bad bling. He considered himself to be more of a professional facilitator, somebody who arranged for two parties with mutually beneficial interests – sex and money – to come together. Besides, he'd only done it twice before, both times for visiting football teams, and saw it more as freelance work, a means to augment his income, an income that had plummeted since Channel 9 decided not to renew his commentating contract.

'Just seck. Noi no do show!' said Noi, even more shrilly than usual.

Last time, one of the players, the ruckman if Trigger remembered correctly, had produced some ping-pong balls and

The Build Up

suggested that Noi might like to show the boys what she could do with them. She'd refused, of course, she just wasn't that sort of Thai prostitute.

'Of course, Noi no do floor show,' said Trigger.

'More football?' asked Noi.

'No,' said Trigger. 'No football team.'

Unfortunately, thought Trigger. Footy players were a sure thing. They were, almost by definition, blokes who poke. And amateur teams, like the two Trigger had facilitated, who lacked any of the hey-I-seen-you-on-TV cachet that professional players had, were blokes who had to pay to poke. A group of Vietnam vets, however?

'How mutt?' asked Noi.

Tank, Trigger's contact, had made all sorts of reassurances, guaranteeing him at least ten punters. At two hundred a pop, that was two grand.

'At least a thousand.'

Noi was absent-mindedly working at Cazaly, gently moving the foreskin back and forth.

'OK, Noi do it. Buy land in Noi's village for plant rice.'

Trigger had been hearing this for the last five years, as he'd followed Noi from one Top End brothel to another. It was a noble thought, and no doubt it earned Noi plenty of tips – men are often at their most vulnerable post-coital – but Trigger was dubious about Noi and her land for plant rice. Just tonight, for example, he'd seen her stick at least a paddy's worth of white powder up each nostril.

'No problem Noi get time off work?' Trigger asked.

Noi had only been working at Ruby's for a couple of months, and Ruby's had only been operating for a year or so. In that time, however, it had become one of the major players in Darwin's very healthy prostitution scene.

'When?' she asked.

'This Sunday.'

'No ploblem,' said Noi.

Despite Noi's expert ministrations, Cazaly was still supine, still waiting for the referee to blow his whistle.

'Noi get jumper now?'

'OK, get jumper.'

Noi is on her hands and knees and Trigger is behind her. He moves his hands from her hips and grabs two handfuls of jumper. The whiff of perfume doesn't matter, it's brown and it's gold, Hawthorn colours, and his groin is slapping hard against the orbs of her arse and Cazaly's as big as a goalpost.

Up there Cazaly, don't let 'em in

Fly like an angel, you're out there to win

Noi's up to her old tricks, screaming, 'Fucky Noi, yeah fucky Noi hard, yeah fucky Noi hard!' A performance about as genuine as a ten-baht Rolex.

His hands slide up her back until they rest on the plastic numbers, the left hand on the '2' and the right on the '3'.

Hawthorn. Number 23. Dermott Brereton. The man who kicked nine goals on Trigger in two quarters of finals football. The man who'd ended his AFL career. No other club would touch him after that. He had no choice but to go north, to this hick fucking town.

'C'mon fuck Noi,' she screams. 'Fuck Noi good.'

'Shut up!' commands Trigger.

'You no like Noi make jiggy-jiggy music?'

'Just shut up, OK!'

Trigger concentrates, scrunching the numbers harder.

'I'll fuck you, Dermie. The same way you fucked me!'

Finally he lets it all go then; more of a relief than anything else as sperm hits latex.

The Build Up

*

As usual, Trigger's post-coital thoughts turned to his life and its present unsatisfactory state. Trigger's father, Trigger Snr, was a gambler, a boozer, and a womaniser – never a real chance in the Ballarat Father of the Year Award, but there is one thing he'd said to Trigger Jnr, which Trigger Jnr had never forgotten.

'You've got a brain, son, use the cunt.'

Once he got some money together, he'd leave Darwin. Either you're living in Sydney or you're camping out, Keating once said, and he was dead right. A dead-shit prime minister, but dead right. Trigger Tregenza had been camping out for far too long now. He had to go back in style, though, with a fat roll of cash in his pocket. Throw some money around at all those trendy bars, those swanky restaurants. Back to the old watering hole, the Fox and the Lion, and catch up with his old teammates. It'll be just like old times.

'Trigger, you give Noi tip. She buy land to plant rice in village Noi.'

'Fuck off, Noi,' he said, carefully removing the condom from Cazaly.

When he looked up it was to see that Noi, still wearing the Hawthorn jumper, was holding a small gun, a pink-handled Lady Derringer.

'What the fuck is that for?'

'Bad man,' said Noi, taking aim at the door. 'I shoot his dick off!'

Guns made Trigger nervous, even small ones, especially when in the hands of a coke-fiend like Noi.

'For fuck's sake, put that thing away!'

Noi took no notice of Trigger, though, and as he dressed she took aim at various other inanimate targets around the room.

'Sunday, OK?' said Trigger, opening the door. 'I'll ring you.'

'OK,' said Noi, putting the gun back in her purse.

There was debate around the traps as to who was the money behind Ruby's. Some said it was a prominent local politician. Others said it was the Russkie, a well-known criminal.

Whenever Trigger asked Noi, she fobbed him off. 'Big boss say Noi no say.'

Whoever the owner was, he made sure there was always plenty of muscle in the reception/bar area. Sometimes it was impressive, monolithic Islanders, imported, Trigger guessed, from the east coast – Townsville, Cairns, places like that. Other times, like tonight, it wasn't. Although Ned Maleski was a lump of a man, six foot six tall, at least 120 kilos with a head like a Besser brick, and had been, without doubt, the toughest footballer Trigger had ever played against, the *NT News* invariably describing their matchup as a 'titanic struggle', 'a struggle between two titans' or on one occasion 'a titanic struggle between two titans', Trigger still didn't rate him.

Trigger considered walking over and saying gidday, but decided against it. For a start he didn't want Ned Maleski to know that Trigger Tregenza paid for his sex. If only occasionally. And only then because Noi seemed to get such a kick out of having the famous number 23 on her back.

Unlike other establishments where you saw the same old faces night in, night out, Ruby's had a steady supply of new girls, mostly Thai. There was one at the bar now, being entertained by a cartel of Japanese businessmen. In Trigger's eyes all Thai women were beautiful, even the ugly ones, but this girl – and she really was a girl; how old could she be, sixteen? Seventeen? – was an absolute doll.

Trigger Tregenza signed the credit card chit, had his frequent user card stamped, and got out of Ruby's.

Chapter 5

The new police centre was situated on the outskirts of Darwin, on the very busy McMillans Road, one of the main arteries into the city. On the other side was the Croc Pot, 'Darwin's Premier Tourist Attraction' according to the sign outside.

Dusty had only been to the Croc Pot once, with her mother, and they'd only made it as far as the shop. Celia wasn't keen on the reptiles themselves, not in their unprocessed state, but had thought that she might be able to get a bargain handbag, and there was nothing that Celia enjoyed more than a bargain. Unfortunately there hadn't been any available, and Celia had been able to add another item – no bargains to be had at the Croc Pot – to her already comprehensive Things I Detest About Darwin list.

Dusty always thought there was a clever and witty comparison to be made between the Croc Pot on one side of the road and the police complex on the other. In the five years since the complex had been completed, and opened by an Akubra-hatted prime minister, she hadn't come up with one, though, and today didn't look like it was going to be any different. She pulled the Commodore into her parking spot, noticing, with surprise, all the empty places.

Dressed in her usual work attire – a black fitted V-neck T-shirt, wide-legged linen trousers and closed-toe shoes – Dusty walked across the tarmac, spongy in the heat. Even after all these years in the Top End she wasn't quite used to the savagery of the weather at this time of the year. The air wasn't just air any more; supercharged with heat and humidity, it had body, corporeality. You didn't walk through it, you walked against it. Slowly. It was no wonder the crime rate dropped during the Build Up. It was even too much for your average crim.

As she turned the corner Dusty could see Trace, one of the hundred or so Aboriginal Community Police Officers (ACPOs) employed by the NT Police, standing in the shade of a mahogany tree – the Tree of Shame, they called it, a confetti of butts at its trunk – lighting up a cigarette.

'Sis!' yelled Dusty.

Trace looked up, a guilty look on her face, like a school kid caught having a surreptitious puff behind the shelter-shed.

'Thought you said you were giving up.'

'I am,' she replied, sucking hard.

Trace was one of those exotic Territorians whose mixed ancestry had always fascinated Dusty; her own Anglo background seemed so dull in comparison. Trace had light-coloured eyes, dark skin and high cheekbones. Even the jagged scar that bisected her chin seemed to work for her, made her even more intriguing.

Trace's father was a Gurindji man, involved in the famous strike of 1966, when Aboriginal stockmen walked off Victoria Park Station demanding better pay and conditions. Her mother, a mixture of Malay-Chinese and Scottish, went into labour with her third child on Christmas Eve in 1974. With Cyclone Tracy at its height, winds gusting to 200 kilometres per hour, Darwin disintegrating around her, her daughter was born. They called her Tracy, of course.

'Cancer Club's looking pretty thin today,' said Dusty. 'Where is everybody? Dead?'

The Build Up

'Haven't you heard?'

'Heard what?' said Dusty, again thinking of her drowned Nokia.

'They found her.'

'Her' could only be one person, Dianna McVeigh, the biggest case in the Northern Territory since 1980 when a dingo sneaked into a tent and took a ten-week-old baby called Azaria.

'Fuck!'

'Some crusty old prospector wandering around out there found her.'

'Fuck!' repeated Dusty, already on the move, already accelerating.

Dusty had liked the previous police HQ in the old section of Darwin. It had character, it had history, its very walls infused with years of policing, with crimes solved and not, the slow spinning ceiling fans giving it a *noir* charm. Yes, the new centre was supposedly state-of-the-art, yes it had won some architectural award or another, but Dusty couldn't help but think of it as just another beige government office – if it wasn't for the wanted posters on the noticeboard you could be in Centrelink or the Tax Department.

She shared an office with the two other detectives in Homicide. It was open-plan, of course, to 'facilitate the easy traffic of knowledge from one knowledge unit to the other'. This morning, only one other knowledge unit, Fontana, was at his desk. Tall, bald and broad-shouldered, he had the tanned, prematurely lined face of a committed athlete. Though he was thirty-nine, four years older than Dusty, they'd been in the same intake. They'd even gone on a couple of dates in the early days, but any sexual tension between them had long been resolved, and their friendship had settled into one of begrudging professional respect and intense athletic rivalry. Dressed, as usual, in a short-sleeve shirt and chinos, Fontana blanked out the screen as Dusty entered. He'd been doing this a bit, lately. Porn, was Dusty's guess. The Font was using departmental bandwidth to make a few timely deposits in the old wank bank.

'We tried calling you,' he said, almost apologetically.

'You mean . . .?'

'Afraid so.'

Dusty swung her bag against her desk, sending a stack of loose papers flurrying upwards.

'Why didn't you answer your fucking mobile?' said Fontana.

'Don't ask,' said Dusty.

'I got them to wait until nine, but you didn't turn up then, either. Mate, it was out of my hands.'

'So who's on it?'

Not fucking Flick, Dusty told herself.

'Fucking Flick,' said Fontana.

Again Dusty swung her bag against the desk, again papers flurried upwards.

Felicity Roberts-Thomson embodied pretty much everything Dusty hated in a fellow copper.

There was her name for a start. What copper was called Felicity? What copper had a hyphen? And she was from Sydney, from Bondi for fuck's sake – the quintessential southerner. OK, Dusty was from Adelaide and technically Adelaide was further south than Sydney, but southernness was not just measured by degree of latitude, it was also an attitude, an orientation, a state of being. Felicity Roberts-Thomson was also overeducated – as Fontana had put it, employing his customary eloquence, she's got degrees hanging out of her arse.

Apparently, Flick had been some corporate high-flyer but after some personal calamity – her BMW had been assaulted, her labradoodle had been pack-raped, something like that – she'd

The Build Up

decided to get out of Sydney and devote the rest of her life to the pursuit of justice. Of course, everybody thought that was tremendously brave of her. The *NT News* had done its obligatory write-up. What Dusty didn't get was why somebody who had given up their money-grubbing self-serving lifestyle was more worthy than somebody who'd never contemplated one in the first place.

'I better go see the new boss,' said Dusty.

'Fuck me, was she shitty,' said Fontana.

'Even more reason to see her then, isn't it?'

Chapter 6

Apparently, at forty-two, Christine Schneider was the youngest person, man or woman, to be appointed to the position of commander in the Northern Territory. As Dusty sat opposite her, separated by only a metre and a half of government-issue melamine, she wondered about the forty-two, whether it was a figure beneficial to both the appointer and the appointed. Yes, the commander's elegantly coiffured hair was free of grey, her teeth surprisingly white, her skin relatively unlined but Dusty wouldn't be surprised if she'd skipped a few birthdays along the line, disconnected her personal tachometer.

When Geoff was the commander, Dusty had spent a lot of time in this office. Predictably, the scuttlebutt had been that, despite the thirty-year age difference, they'd been fucking each other's brains out. The truth had less to do with concupiscence and more to do with conviviality – they just happened to get on, had quite a few things in common, not the least of which was putting bad guys behind bars. Back then the decor had been all football and fishing, balls and barramundi, but now there was a definite feminine touch.

On the desk was a framed photo showing the commander with two confident-looking children, a boy and a girl. Next to it was a vase of flowers – carnations in a flounce of baby's breath – and next to that a jug of water on top of a doily. Dusty was

The Build Up

surprised – she would never have pegged the new commander as a doily sort of chick, but there was no doubting it – it was round, crocheted and had a lacy edge – it was a doily. Behind her was a bookshelf, in it a slew of management texts, arranged in decreasing order of height.

'Something to drink?' said the commander. 'Tea? Coffee?'

'Water would be fine,' said Dusty.

The commander poured her a glass.

'Let's get straight to the point.'

A very good idea, thought Dusty.

'As you no doubt know, a body has been found. We don't know, for sure, but it's a pretty safe bet it's her.'

The incumbent commander steepled her fingers. Interestingly enough, it was a gesture the erstwhile commander often made, too. Maybe it's a prerequisite for the position, pondered Dusty. Ability of candidate to steeple fingers looked favourably upon.

'I realise how much time and effort you've put into the McVeigh case.'

No you don't, thought Dusty. You wouldn't have a fucking clue.

'And though it was rather unfortunate and somewhat unprofessional that you were unable to be contacted this morning.'

Dusty went to say something in her defence, but the commander unsteepled her fingers and held her palms out as if to say 'not now'. Which perhaps wasn't such a bad thing. 'A Kreepy Krauly ate my phone' probably wasn't going to do her cause a whole lot of good, anyway.

'But to be entirely truthful with you, it was probably for the best. I was going to take you off the case, anyway.'

Dusty could scarcely believe what she was hearing. It was her case and always had been, ever since the day two years ago when the call had come in that a woman had been abducted.

'But . . .' started Dusty, but again she was cut short by the commander. 'There is no discussion about this, Detective Buchanon. My predecessor should've done this after the trial. Well, I'm taking you off it, now. End of story.'

Chapter 7

When Dusty stormed back into the office, Fontana was gone. There was, perhaps, an entirely innocent explanation for his absence – he'd gone on a job, perhaps, or for his morning dump – but Dusty doubted it. Fontana was gone because he knew that when she returned, she'd be spitting chips, and not just ordinary chips either – chips hacked out of anger, frustration and indignation, chips he sensibly didn't want to be anywhere near. He had, however, picked up the papers from the floor and stacked them back on her desk, not a typical Fontana gesture – as the chaotic state of his own desk would attest, he wasn't a particularly tidy unit.

One swipe of her hand, however, and Dusty sent the papers back to where they'd come from.

'Fuck!' she yelled.

'Cunt!' she wanted to yell, but she remembered the pact she'd made with Julien to stop using that appalling word with such abandon.

'Cunt!' she yelled.

She kicked at the papers.

In incandescently angry moments like this it wasn't difficult to understand the impetus to homicide. If she'd had a knife perhaps she would've stabbed the papers; a gun, perhaps she would've shot them. Instead, she kicked them around a bit more.

It simply wasn't possible to take her off this case.

She knew more about it than anybody else. How many other coppers could say that they got a Christmas card from the victim's parents? No, the commander would eventually come to her senses and put her back on it. Consoled by this, Dusty picked up the papers – some were torn, a couple quite severely but they were all still legible.

She then sat at her desk forcing herself to return to the quotidian – powering on her PC, she went through her emails. There wasn't much of interest – a generous offer to increase the size of her penis, departmental rubbish, the usual jokes. Often she enjoyed these, especially the more puerile ones, but not today, today it was delete, delete, and more delete.

There was one from Julien, however, reminding her that they were having dinner on Friday at a new restaurant at East Point called Peewees ('ps. it's posh'). There was also a message from her mum. 'V. sorry about morning,' it said. And then :) :) The 'V' was bad enough – just how long does it take to type 'ery' but the emoticons were too much, like being grinned at by the village idiot. Dusty typed in :(:(, thought about it for a nanosecond, before pressing reply.

Detective Fontana walked in, smelling of freshly applied deodorant, his shaven head still glistening with water.

'Gym,' he said by way of explanation.

Though the chip-spitting urge had abated Dusty still wanted Fontana to understand the extent of her anger, the depth of her resentment.

'Aren't you just pushing shit uphill?' she said.

'What do you mean?'

Once a state-ranked triathlete, Fontana's peak years were well behind him. He still believed he could make the big time, though – all he had to do was set more goals, program his pulse meter more scientifically, push his aging body harder and harder.

The Build Up

'I mean–' started Dusty, but she lost heart. It wasn't Fontana's fault, she shouldn't be having a go at him.

'She's a worry, isn't she?'

'A real big worry.'

Normally, Dusty would cut Fontana off right there – categorising women according to their body type just wasn't on in a modern police force.

'The Big C, eh?' she said, thinking of the satisfied look on the commander's face.

'The Big C,' echoed Fontana.

'I'm going for a coffee. If anybody rings I'm on my mobile,' said Dusty.

'Thought you didn't have a mobile.'

'Oh, shit. OK, I'm going for a mobile. If anybody rings I'm on my coffee.'

Fontana smiled his goofy smile, relieved, no doubt, that his long-time colleague seemed to have regained her sense of humour.

For the time being, anyway.

Chapter 8

As she turned off the main road and into the Parap shopping centre, the car behind her tooted.

Southerner, thought Dusty. OK, maybe I didn't exactly use my indicator, but only somebody from the shoe-wearing states would toot like that. The usually empty car spaces outside the café were occupied by gargantuan four-wheel drives, many with 'Baby On Board' signs affixed to the back window. Ever since an ABC child care centre had opened up nearby it had been like this. Dusty scanned the number-plates; they were relatively cheap in the Northern Territory, and they always made interesting reading. JACQUI. MUM4EVER. SUPERMUM.

Ten years ago, when Café Hanuman first opened, the Balinese theme was considered quite exotic, but now it looked a little tired, a little run-of-the-mill. There was so much of Bali in Darwin now. Which made sense really. Denpasar was only about 1800 kilometres from Darwin, far closer than any of the major Australian cities. Everybody here seemed to holiday in Indonesia, fill a shipping container with cheap teak furniture, stone Buddhas, batik bedspreads, and turn their Wulagi two-bedder into a little piece of tropical paradise. Dusty had been going to the Café Hanuman for a long time and saw no reason to change. The coffee was still good and strong, they had the interstate papers, and there was a bowl of water in case she brought the dawgs.

The Build Up

The Balinese owner, Nyoman, smiled at Dusty as she sat at her usual outside table.

In his fifties, he had the Indo-hippy thing down pat – long hair, drawstring batik trousers, embroidered waistcoat.

'*Apa khabar?*' he said, with that exaggerated rolled 'r' of Bahasa Indonesia, the common language of the many islands of the Indonesian archipelago. How are you?

'*Baik. Baik*,' replied Dusty. Very good.

Her Indonesian was rudimentary, just bits and pieces she'd picked up on her many visits to Bali, but they both pretended that she was some sort of linguistic marvel, her grasp of Bahasa a thing of wonder.

'*Kafe?*' asked Nyoman.

'*Bagus*,' replied Dusty. Sure.

Dusty scanned the cafe. At the other end, under a large painting of the cafe's namesake – the monkey god Hanuman – a group of women sipped lattés. Alongside them were their hi-tech strollers, marginally smaller versions of the Pathfinders, Pajeros and Prados outside. This was obviously Jacqui, Mum4ever, Supermum. 'Yummy mummies,' is what Fontana called women like this and Dusty could see just how apt it was – there was definitely something ripe and yummy about them, like the mangoes that were now heavy on the many trees around Darwin. Dusty had another name for them, however – the Absolutelies.

'Have you booked your two in for swimming lessons yet?'

'Yes, absolutely.'

Dusty turned her attention to the *NT News*. Unusually, there was no croc story. No tourist taken while skinny-dipping off Mindil Beach. No fifteen-foot monster found wandering around the Botanic Gardens. If Dusty remembered correctly this was the fourth day in a row in which *Crocodylus porosus* had not figured on the front page. Some sort of record, surely, and a concern for the bean counters at the *NT News*. Sport sells. Sex sells. But crocs sell more. *Shane Warne in Nude Romp with Top End Croc* would surely break all existing circulation records.

No, it was the croc's reptilian cousin the cane toad that dominated today. *Cane Toads On Relentless March to Darwin* warned the headline. Dusty wondered about the 'march'. Her experience of croakers, and she had an especially friendly one resident in her downstairs toilet, was that they tended to hop. *Cane Toads On Relentless Hop to Darwin,* didn't quite have the same impact, however. Either way, it was an ecological fuck-up of the highest order.

Introduced into Queensland from Hawaii in 1935 to control sugar cane pests, *Buffo marinus* had thrived in Australia's tropics, spreading in all directions, leaving a trail of devastation, Dusty read. And now it was on its way to Darwin; there had already been sightings in Kakadu National Park, 300 kilometres to the east. With an election coming up it had become a political issue, both major parties promising their constituents that they would be tough on cane toads.

'We will decide what toads come into the Territory, and the manner in which they come,' the prominent Liberal politician Ward Johns was quoted as saying.

Dusty turned to the photo on the front page of *The Australian*. A serial rapist, with a jumper pulled over his head – the preferred headwear of bad guys all over the world – was being escorted into a courtroom by two burly coppers.

She tried to concentrate on the article but kept getting distracted by the Absolutelies, by the snatches of their conversation; their talk of interrupted sleep routines, cracked nipples and starting solids.

'What do you think, Jacqui?'

Dusty looked up; it was always interesting to put a face to a

The Build Up

personalised number-plate. Given the tremendous size of her vehicle Jacqui was surprisingly petite. She had a blonde bob and a swollen belly. Yes, Jacqui was pregnant, and given that the Bugaboo next to her was a double, she seemed to be on a personal campaign to arrest the decline in the national birth-rate.

Jacqui hesitated before answering, making sure she had the full attention of the other Absolutelies before making her pronouncement.

'Having babies is the most important thing a woman can do.'

There were murmurs of agreement. Of course it was. Absolutely.

Dusty felt like taking the paper over to these Absolutelies, and telling them straight – anybody can have babies, don't you get that? Anybody. All you have to do is spread your legs a couple of times, nine months apart. But not everybody can do what I do. It takes guts, rat-cunning, persistence, dedication, experience, to stick crooks behind bars, not two sweaty minutes of jiggy-jiggy. I risk my fucking life so you can sit in fucking cafés with your fucking lattés and cracked nipples without some animal busting in here and raping the shit out of you!

Dusty dropped the paper, her outrage disappearing as quickly as it had arrived. Who was she kidding? Sticking crooks behind bars? Protecting yummies from rapists? Standing up, Dusty threw some change on the table.

'*Selamat jalan*,' said Nyoman as she passed the front counter. Good bye.

'*Selamat tinggal*,' replied Dusty.

Chapter 9

Detective Dusty Buchanon and Administrative Officer Alex Vatskalis didn't appear to have much in common. He was Greek, descended from the Kastelorizians who had first migrated to Darwin to work in the meatworks. Dusty wasn't. He was obese. Dusty wasn't. He liked to go to the Erotic Croc on a Thursday night and get gently whipped by Katerina the Russian dominatrix. Dusty didn't. But they both barracked for the same Australian Rules football team, St Kilda. So they had everything in common.

'We gotta get rid of that useless turd of a coach,' said Alex, as Dusty filled in the form he'd given her.

Actually, Dusty was very fond of that useless turd of a coach. She still remembered the thrills his heroic deeds as a player – as well as the heroic bulge in his shorts – had given her as a teenager, and wasn't about to give up on him yet.

'He's not so bad,' she said, and then, 'what do I write here?'

'What happened to it, again?'

'My Kreepy Krauly ate it.'

'One of them pool cleaner things?'

Dusty nodded.

Alex appeared completely unfazed, as if Kreepy Kraulys eating phones was an everyday experience.

'Put "lost in course of duty".'

The Build Up

As Dusty wrote that down the door opened and Sergeant Gerard Bevan from the Exhibit Storage Facility entered. Late thirties, medium build, he was one of those sandy-haired, sandy-complexioned people, who must've been away the day pigmentation was handed out. Meticulous in appearance and nature, it was easy to see how he'd been given the slightly pejorative nickname the Clerk. One of those people, Dusty thought, who would habitually take the second newspaper from the pile even though there was nothing wrong with the first.

'Morning,' he said to Dusty.

'Morning,' she replied.

Then he turned his attention to Alex.

'Has it come in yet?'

'Right here,' said Alex, hefting a parcel onto the table.

Sergeant Bevan took the parcel, signed the book, and was gone.

'Lost his bottle, you know?'

'What?' said Dusty, pushing the form towards Alex, thinking he was still talking about that useless turd of a coach.

'Over in Queensland. Lost his bottle and his partner ended up copping one.'

She realised, then, that it was Sergeant Bevan he was referring to.

Of all the rumourmongers in the Force, and there was no shortage of them, Alex was the most prolific. His office was rumour central: rumours were brought in, processed, sent out again. Dusty had no desire to hear about Sergeant Bevan's reputed loss of bottle, however. In her dealings with him she'd found him to be very cordial and very professional and that's all that mattered to her. She switched the conversation back to football.

'Don't know why they traded Goldie.'

'They had their reasons,' said Alex, obviously a man in the know.

As he set about configuring Dusty's new Nokia, Alex gave a rundown of those reasons. Goldie, apparently, was a party boy. With a liking for the 'nose candy' as Alex called it.

'You're from Adelaide originally, aren't you?' he asked.

'That's right.'

'Then how come you don't go for the Crows? Or Port?'

'My dad went for the Saints.'

'Your inheritance, eh?'

'Yeah, I guess.'

As Dusty made her way back to her office her new mobile rang, playing 'Zorba The Greek'. She laughed – bloody Alex!

It was Felicity Roberts-Thomson. Could they meet later on that day, say four? Discuss the McVeigh case?

Dusty constructed a mental list, in increasing order of onerousness, of the things she'd rather do than meet with Felicity Roberts-Thomson.

Pap smear?

Tick.

Root canal therapy?

Tick.

Partake in a team-building exercise?

Tick.

She couldn't refuse, though – policework was teamwork and all that bullshit.

Flick came bearing coffee, and the right type, too – skim milk flat white. Like the gun detective she supposedly was, she'd done her research.

'No thanks,' said Dusty, as Flick proffered the cup. 'I only have one a day.'

The Build Up

A blatant lie, as Dusty's styrofoam-laden desk would attest – she drank several hundred coffees a day, but she wasn't going to let Flick get the ascendancy, especially not for two dollars eighty.

'I like your hair,' said Flick.

If not the oldest trick in the book, it was of comparable antiquity, and one that Dusty herself often employed with female suspects – start off with some über-girly talk in order to establish a (false) sense of feminine solidarity.

'Thanks,' said Dusty, unconsciously pushing Celia's wispy bits behind her ears.

'Who did it?'

It had taken Dusty years and many dodgy haircuts to find a hairdresser she could grow old with. She'd already decided if Laura of Parap Cuts did leave Darwin, she would have no choice but to go with her. She wasn't about to start sharing her with the likes of Felicity Roberts-Thomson.

'Sam's,' said Dusty, giving the name of a salon in the Casuarina shopping centre which was known as a black hole of hairdressing, the place nobody ever went back to.

'Thanks,' said Flick, with that characteristic half-smile on her face, like all was basically right with the world – lark on the wing, snail on the thorn, God in His heaven – all that crap. When Flick had first arrived, still with the Bondi sand between her toes, Dusty had given the smile six months at the longest. The first major road accident, first double murder, and it'd vanish forever from her face but, to the smile's credit, it had persevered despite the atrocities it had no doubt witnessed.

If Felicity Roberts-Thomson had been an archetypal Bondi glamour with bikini-friendly boobs and swishing blonde hair and legs all the way up to her arse then that would've been the straw that snapped the dromedary's back. She wasn't, though. She had librarian's hips and no tits to speak of, and was really no looker at all. And it wasn't just Dusty who thought so. She'd canvassed several of her male colleagues (well, she'd canvassed one several times).

'She's no looker, is she, Font?'

'No, Dusty, she's definitely no looker.'

'Bushpig, then?' Dusty had suggested tentatively, hopefully.

'I wouldn't go that far.'

'So you'd do her, would you, Fontana?'

'Depends on how many Jim Beams I'd had that night,' had been his not uncharacteristic reply.

Flick pulled up a chair at Dusty's desk.

'Is it her?' Dusty asked.

'As you well know a positive identification is not really possible at this early stage.'

Dusty had spent so long looking for her, thinking about her. She'd even driven down to the desert in her own time, dragging James along one trip. She'd camped down there, spent the days driving around, walking around, following hunches, thinking where he could've put her. Now this southerner was treating her like she was some sort of outsider.

'Is it her or not?' Dusty demanded.

'Well, all indications point in that direction, but we won't be making a public announcement until we're absolutely sure.'

It was her.

'Look, I appreciate you've spent a lot of time and effort on this case and probably resent me for taking it over,' said Flick.

'Not at all,' said Dusty, her words so counterfeit, it's a wonder the Fraud Squad didn't come busting in to arrest them.

'But if you did have any thoughts on the case, then I'd love to discuss them with you.'

'Of course,' said Dusty.

Of course not.

The Build Up

She waited at her desk until half past five, until it was eight in the morning in England, before dialling. She hadn't rehearsed what she was going to say, there was nothing worse than wooden copspeak: 'Madam, it is my duty to inform you that a female person fitting the description . . .' Forget it. She also reminded herself to resist the temptation to use the word 'closure'. Jesus, ten years ago nobody outside the psych community had heard of 'closure', now it was everywhere, a cane toad of a word.

'Hello,' answered Mrs Maxwell almost immediately, as if she'd been waiting by the phone. A small, fragile-looking woman, she'd been very difficult at the beginning of the trial, the weather was too hot, the serviced apartment not good enough. Mr Maxwell, in contrast, had been quintessentially English – polite, reserved. It was only after the trial had been going for a few weeks, when they'd seen the effort Dusty and the prosecution team were making that they started to open up and expose some of their raw pain.

'Mrs Maxwell, it's Detective Buchanon here.'

'Oh, Dusty, it's lovely to hear your voice again.'

In the background Dusty could hear the tweet of budgerigars.

'Is your husband there, Mrs Maxwell?'

'Yes, he's having breakfast.'

Really, there was no gentle way to say this.

'I wanted to tell you before you read it in the papers, but it seems like we may have found your daughter.'

They'd told Dusty that they knew their daughter was dead, that all they wanted now was to bring her body home. Dusty had wondered, though, if a parent could totally give up hope for their child. Surely, somewhere, a particle of hope must persist.

'Where?' said Mrs Maxwell.

'In the desert. Near where we thought she'd be.'

'And was she . . .?'

'I'm not sure of the details, Mrs Maxwell. There'll be an autopsy report pretty soon.'

'When can we come and get her?'

'There's no need for you to come back here. We can make the necessary–'

'My husband and I will come and get our daughter,' said Mrs Maxwell curtly, and Dusty knew her and her husband well enough to know that this is exactly what they'd do.

'And that man, now you can send him to jail.'

That man was Gardner, of course. Mrs Maxwell never referred to him by name, as if allowing such a monster a title would give him a respectability he didn't possess, or deserve.

'I hope so, Mrs Maxwell. But it's not going to be easy. I know in your country the law has changed but here a person can't be charged for an offence they've already been found innocent of.'

A long silence, except for the sound of the budgerigars.

Finally she said: 'I know you'll do your best, Dusty. Both my husband and I know you'll do your best.'

As she put down the phone a feeling of intense shame swept over Dusty. Her dislike of Flick, her anger at getting kicked off the case, what were they compared to the pain of the Maxwells, of their need to see justice finally done?

She rang Flick.

'Dusty, here. Look, there are a couple of things I thought of. Maybe we could get together tomorrow and discuss them.'

Chapter 10

Keep a lid on it. That had been Barry O'Loughlin's motto from the start, when his instincts had told him to keep it small. He'd even started thinking of it acronymically, American military style, KALOI. Keep a lid on it. Or even KAFLOI. Keep a fucking lid on it. When the publicity started, everybody had said it was a good thing. The radio. The newspaper articles. The segment on *Today Tonight*. Hey, it's publicity, it must be good. Barry wasn't so sure. A little bit of publicity? Sure. Let other vets know we're here, let the public know what we're about. A little, but not a lot. KALOI. Keep a lid on it. Keep it small. Don't become a freak show. Step right up. Step right up. Look at the vets. They walk! They talk! They got poisoned by Agent Orange! They got PTSD!

The NT government's decision to consider their request for the land had been a big win, no doubt about that. To tell the truth, despite all the work he and the others had done, Barry hadn't expected it to happen. But there was still a long way to go. All that opposition. From the blackfellas. From Parks and Wildlife. From Rio Tinto. From just about everybody, it seemed.

A big win, but not *the* win. KALOI. Keep a lid on it.

The others had wanted to celebrate, and who was he to say no?

They were leaving their cars everywhere, now. There was a parking area, clearly marked as such – Barry had put up the signs himself – with plenty of space, but they were leaving their cars everywhere.

The ceremony itself, that had gone well. Very simple, unveiling of the plaque, a few words. No, it'd gone really well. But this, this party, it was going to end in shit. Of that, Barry had no doubt. It was the same feeling he'd had that night they'd gone into the Hai Bo forest and Suave Harve had lost his guts. The same fucking feeling.

The anxiety he hadn't felt for years, not since the repat hospital, was coming back at him. Stirring up his insides. Giving his ticker a hurry-up. He had to find Tank and Scotty, and they could put a stop to this. Put a stop to it before it ended in shit.

Who were these people, anyway? They were everywhere. Who were they? What were they doing here, on his camp?

Tank was behind the barbecue, a stupid apron on, pair of tongs in one paw, green can in the other, incinerating sausages.

'Going well, eh?' he beamed when he saw Barry.

'Tank. Tank. We've got to do something about this. There's people parking everywhere. Put an end to it, mate. Tell 'em all to go home. Party's finished. You and me, we've got to tell them all to piss off and go home.'

Tank handed the tongs to somebody else, grabbed his walking stick, took Barry by the elbow and steered him away from the crowd, towards the creek.

'Breathe deep, Bazz.'

'It's gunna end in shit, Tank, it's . . .'

'Shut up and breathe deep.'

Barry did as Tank said. They'd done a lot of breathing in the repat hospital. At first he'd thought it was bullshit, like swimming with fucking dolphins, but it hadn't taken him long to change his mind.

He breathed in deep.

The Build Up

Tank started talking. Barry wasn't able to follow the ebb and flow of his words; only certain phrases finding their way through to him.

Bazz, it's not your responsibility.

These are grown men, Bazz.

It's not Vietnam, Bazz.

After a while, through all the anxiety, he could see that Tank was right.

It wasn't Vietnam; it wasn't his responsibility.

It wasn't Vietnam; people weren't going to die like Suave Harve had died in the Hai Bo forest.

Just a few Diggers and their mates having a few drinks and a laugh.

And why not – look what they'd done, look what they'd achieved.

It wasn't Vietnam and he could go to bed.

Barry let Tank lead him to his honcho. Tank took something from his pocket. A blister pack. Some pills.

'Just a couple of Normison, Bazz. It'll take the edge off it.'

Barry took the pills, glad to cede responsibility, to have someone look after him for a change. He lay down on his swag and closed his eyes.

The cars were still coming, though. More people yelling. It'd all turn to shit. Just like in the Hai Bo forest. He had to get up and stop it. But his legs were lead now and his eyelids nailed shut.

Chapter 11

It used to be the Cage, the toughest pub north of the Tropic of Capricorn. Forget the famously rough Humpty Doo, or the bearpit that was the Tennant Creek – if you wanted to score the drug of your choice, drink yourself comatose, get your head punched in or get friendly with a one-legged grandma, the Cage was the only place to go.

Now it was the Beachfront, all marina views and shiny wood, where the yuppies drank their pinot gris and ate their caesar salads while listening to Norah Fucking Jones.

Trigger felt like a traitor just stepping foot in the place. Drugs? Maybe coke on a good night, but even then it'd be cut to buggery. Comatose? There was a sign at the bar that said 'Anybody showing signs of intoxication will not be served'. In the old Cage they wouldn't let you in if you weren't half-pissed. Fights? You've got to be joking; two yuppies bitch-slapping each other over some share-deal, maybe. As for the one-legged granny, she'd persevered for a year until either the lack of suitably energetic beaus or the Norah Fucking Jones forced her to decamp, as well.

At least Noi was there, sitting at a table, looking every inch the Bangkok whore – too much makeup, not enough clothes and that hungry, hard look they all get, the prostitute's version of a soldier's thousand-yard stare, the thousand-cock glare.

Next to her was the girl Trigger had seen at Ruby's the other day, the absolute doll.

The Build Up

Noi jumped up when Trig arrived at her table, wrapping her arms around him, pressing her silicone tits hard against him.

'Trig, number one boyfriend,' she said loudly. 'Why you butterfly me?'

Trig looked around, worried that even here, in this yuppie hole, somebody might know him. A champion sportsman, he was a role model, after all. He manoeuvred out of Noi's grasp and sat down.

'This my friend, Noi,' said Noi, indicating the other girl.

'Hi, Noi Two,' said Trigger.

She didn't reply, didn't even meet his eyes.

'OK, Trig buy drinks then talk, OK?' said Noi.

Which didn't seem such a bad idea. Noi wanted something silly in a tall glass, the other Noi, apparently, wanted a Coke, while Trig was thinking that a vodka and lime might just improve his mood.

The bar was empty, just some chick looking the other way, so Trigger strolled right up and gave his order to the barman.

'Excuse me,' said the chick. 'I'm pretty sure I was next.'

Mid-thirties, Trigger guessed. Bottle blonde. Tall, but not too tall. A swimmer's shoulders. No glamour, but not bad-looking, either.

'Beauty first,' said Trigger, struggling to get his eyes above her neck; there was nothing plastic about those puppies.

When he did manage to drag his eyes upward, it was to encounter hers. Blue? Grey? An in-between colour.

Trigger was not unused to the ladies giving him the eye. Who could blame them – he was a big, good looking fella who exuded a certain laconic charm. He had to admit though, it hadn't been happening all that much, lately. It was all that metrosexual crap, women seemed to prefer men who didn't look like men any more, pretty boys who sat down to piss.

'I should think so,' she said, and she smiled. Nothing big, but you could tell from the easy way her face relaxed into it that it was something she did a fair bit of.

She was hot to trot, this one. If he had the time, Trigger would've gone hard, released a tsunami of charm. Tonight, however, was about work, not play, and he was trying not to mix the two.

When he returned Nois One and Two were having a heated conversation. As it was in Thai, it was impossible for Trigger to know exactly what was being said, but it certainly didn't sound like they were swapping tom yum goong recipes.

Noi One opened her purse. From it she took a small bottle labelled in Thai. She poured some of its contents into Noi Two's drink.

'Thai medicine,' she said to Trigger, giving the bottle to Noi Two.

Trigger was getting concerned about the time; it was a long drive, including a stretch of dirt, and he was keen to get started.

'We better get going,' he said.

'Noi no can come,' said number one Noi.

Apparently Sod had first come up with it, but Trigger liked to think of it as his own creation, Trig's Law: sometime, somewhere there'll be a fuck-up. You can plan it all out, cross every 't' and dot every 'i', but there's bound to be a fuck-up, especially when you're dealing with a) whores and b) Asians. Trig's law times two.

'Now why would that be?'

'Noi work Ruby.'

'You said you'd arrange it!'

'You take number two Noi.'

Trigger could guess her story – she'd be from some village in the north of Thailand. Family dirt poor. Promised a job overseas working in a café. Tickets, passport, everything arranged for her. When she got to Australia they'd present her with an enormous bill and only one way of paying it off.

The Build Up

Number two Noi was a doll, but Trigger didn't want a doll, he wanted number one Noi. She was a whore's whore, able to take on a whole football team, the playing group plus coaching staff, without batting a mascara-laden eyelid.

'I don't want this Noi!'

'Big Boss say Noi work Ruby.'

She was smart, Noi. Despite all his prodding, she would never tell him who Big Boss actually was. A mysterious Big Boss was bigger, nastier and more likely to break both his legs than a known Big Boss.

'So you explained the deal to her?' said Trigger resignedly.

'No ploblem,' said Noi, dismissively.

'Noi, have you explained it to her? Ten blokes, at least!'

'No ploblem. Noi explain. Noi good girl. Noi from same village like Noi.'

Trigger wasn't convinced, but what choice did he have? He'd given Tank his word. And he needed the money.

They finished their drinks and the three of them walked out together. As they did a taxi pulled up.

'Hey, Noi,' said the driver.

Vietnamese by the looks of him. Hair in a ponytail. Dodgy leather jacket.

'Franky,' said number one Noi, and number two Noi smiled, the first sign of emotion Trigger had seen from her.

'Need a cab?'

'Noi need,' said number one Noi, opening the back door.

Number two Noi went to follow but when the other Noi said something to her in Thai she stopped.

The door closed, Noi said, 'Bye, Trigger', the taxi left and, not for the first time, Trigger wondered how his life had come to this.

His old man's words coming back like a bad curry.

You've got a brain, son, use the cunt.

Chapter 12

Dusty was at yoga, in *adho mukha svanasana*, the downward facing dog position, when it started, scrolling across her consciousness, like a news update on CNN. By the time she'd moved into *sarvangasana* – shoulder stand – it'd become more insistent, but it was during *shavasna*, while she was lying face-up on her purple yoga mat, attempting to relax all those impossible-to-relax muscles, that it became a full-blown exhortation – you need a drink.

'If you have any thoughts,' purred Vashti the teacher, 'then acknowledge them and let them move on.'

It was excellent advice, especially with a thought as tawdry as this one. Dusty dutifully acknowledged it and bade it farewell. The thought, however, did not acknowledge this acknowledgement, refusing to go anywhere, becoming if anything, more adamant – you really do need a drink – and more specific – a Clare riesling or a nice crisp sauvignon blanc from New Zealand.

It was a relief, therefore, when for the third time Vashti chimed her chime, they all rose from the floor, gave their *om shantis* and repaired to the Beachfront.

Only in Darwin would you go to the pub after yoga, thought Dusty as she sat down at an outside table with her fellow yogis. OK, it was a pub-nouveau, there was a cappuccino machine, a kid's playground and even paper in the toilets, but it was a pub nonetheless.

The Build Up

Dusty had been practising yoga for ten years now, six of those with Vashti, and though the regular pub-goers were a disparate group there was an easy familiarity between them, no doubt partly due to the amount of doglike downward facing they did in each other's company.

'Same as usual, Dusty?' asked Sean.

In his fifties, with a grey-flecked beard and Teva hi-tech sandals, he was one of those desk-shy academics who seemed to spend most of the time doing fieldwork. An ecologist, his area of expertise was in mangroves, but Dusty was always impressed by the breadth of his knowledge. He seemed to know something about everything.

Dusty nodded.

'I'll help carry the drinks,' said Vashti, standing up.

As Dusty watched the two of them, the angular Sean and the curvaceous Vashti, disappear into the bar she thought, not for the first time, what a good pair they'd make – both smart unattached people able to go into full-lotus.

'This weather!' said Brenda, a high school teacher.

'It's impossible,' agreed Siobhan, an Irish nurse.

And so it started – chatter, the oil of human interaction. Dusty said nothing. Not because she was averse to meaningless conversation, she could blather with the best of them. But after you've spent hours looking at child pornography or photos of a butchered girl, after a day spent in the company of scumbags, it took a while before you could consider the rest of the world with any equanimity. Eventually, when drinks appeared, Dusty almost had to restrain herself from grabbing hers from the tray Sean was carrying – the glass was so beautifully frosty, the wine in it so deliciously golden. And as she brought its rim to her lips, she stopped herself from downing the entire contents. She sipped. Demurely. Even giving the wine an oenological swirl in her mouth before swallowing. It's almost as if that's what alcohol was designed for: a liquid, available in many pleasing flavours, which made the transition from duty to off-duty less difficult for homicide detectives or front-line soldiers or trauma nurses or any of those other professions where you saw too much shit too quickly.

Yes, alcohol did the trick, but Dusty had worked with too many coppers with cirrhotic livers and litigious wives and kids who wouldn't give them the time of the day not to know that alcohol could also do you in. It was the stuff of every cop show – the detective with a hipflask-sized bulge in his jacket – but that didn't mean it wasn't an occupational hazard.

Dusty kept one day a week, usually Monday, drink-free and every couple of months she'd have a whole week off the booze. Just to prove that she could.

'Well, is it her?' asked Vashti, suddenly turning to Dusty, obviously keen to move on to the criminal.

It'd been on the radio – a body had been found in the desert. And Vashti, like many people, was fascinated with Dusty's job and loved to hear her stories. The bloodier the better. Her all-time favourite, what she fondly referred to as the Gado Gado story, was about an Indonesian deckhand who tipped a wok of boiling oil over his sleeping, and, so it transpired, tyrannical skipper. The skipper survived, amazingly enough, turning up in court with a head like a *krupuk,* a prawn cracker.

'We're not sure, yet,' said Dusty, following the party line.

'Come on, it has to be her,' insisted Vashti.

'Who?' asked Siohban, a recent arrival in Darwin.

'Dianna McVeigh,' offered Sean.

Siobhan shook her head. Obviously, she didn't have a clue who they were talking about. Dusty was surprised – she thought everybody in the English-speaking, internet-connected world had heard of this woman who had gone missing in the Australian

The Build Up

outback. The other yogis were all looking at Dusty, expecting her, no doubt, to explain who Dianna McVeigh was.

'Do I have to?' she said.

'It is your case, dear,' said Bev, at sixty-eight the oldest in the class.

Was my case, thought Dusty, but that wasn't something she was going to divulge.

'Here we go,' she said, taking a hefty swig of wine. 'Dianna and Greg McVeigh. Late twenties. Pommies. Just married, they arrive in Sydney. Hire a campervan. Wander up the east coast. Byron. Gold Coast. Cairns. Usual places. Then across to Darwin. After a week here they head for the big rock, for Uluru. About a hundred clicks past Pine Creek they pull off the road to watch the sunset. Drink some rum. Smoke a couple of joints. Get pretty shit-faced, both of them. Decide that driving's out of the question so they may as well stay where they are, sleep under the stars. About two in the morning, we reckon, somebody turns up. Trusses Greg up. Takes Dianna. Next morning Greg manages to get free. Drives back to Pine Creek. A number of possessions are missing from the van. We go public with a few of them. A week later we get a phone call from a mechanic in Katherine. Says he recognises the backpack in a LandCruiser he's been working on. Belongs to a bloke by the name of Evan Dale Gardner. He's got no shortage of form, mostly property though. We bring him in. Real hard nut. Denies everything. Still, we go to trial. There's no body. Everything's circumstantial. We lose. Gardner walks.'

'I think I saw him the other day,' said Bev, giving an involuntary shudder.

Dusty, too, had seen him the other day. She'd been at Parap market, ordering from the Som Tum lady, when he'd walked past her, dressed, as usual, in King Gee khaki. The continued police surveillance, or what Stan Lavery, his lawyer, called the 'unprecedented harassment of my client' meant that his normal job, interstate drug running, was no longer viable. He'd moved to Howard Springs, about thirty kilometres out of Darwin and had taken on more conventional employment. He was now 'gainfully engaged in the mango industry'. Still, she thought she'd been mistaken, he wouldn't have the audacity to walk around in broad daylight like that, not after all the adverse publicity he'd had, his ugly mug in the *NT News* almost every day, croc-like in its ubiquity. It was him, though – the sloping shoulders, the slightly protruding ears, that mean square face.

'He absolutely radiated evil,' said Bev.

It was Dusty's turn to buy drinks. As she approached the bar she took note of who was waiting – the bald bloke in the noisy shirt was next, then the suit with the tasty butt, then her. When the suit walked off with his drinks Dusty turned around to further check out his assets, certain the barman had clocked her as next in line. When she returned her gaze, however, it was to see that a tall broad-shouldered man had pushed in front of her.

'Excuse me,' said Dusty. 'I'm pretty sure I was next.'

The man turned to look at her. Instantly Dusty knew who he was. You couldn't follow AFL in Darwin and not know Trigger Tregenza. He'd played a few games in the backline for the Sydney Swans before coming to Darwin and reinventing himself as a full-forward. Like a car repaired at a backyard panel-beater's, his features weren't quite straight: his nose kinked twice before it arrived back at the more-or-less vertical, his cheekbones didn't match. It gave him a rugged sort of charm, though, that was further enhanced by his hair. Thick and sandy, it was a young man's hair, the sort women like to run their hands through. He hadn't put on the weight either, his poloshirt was tucked into his shorts and he had the sculpted legs of a sportsman. Apart from flirting quite seriously with him one night at a Grand Final do – she even remembered the year: 1998, the Adelaide Crows had

The Build Up

just won their second flag – Dusty didn't really know Trigger personally very well. She'd heard so many stories, though, and felt as if she was much better acquainted. For a start, there was his dick. Apparently he was one of those blokes who feel obliged to christen their member. In his case it went by the name of Cazaly, as in 'Up there, Cazaly'.

He also liked his ladies to dress up a bit. No schoolgirl outfits, no nurse's uniforms, not even thigh-high patent leather boots and split-crotch panties. No, apparently the champion full-forward preferred them to wear a football jumper, but not any old football jumper, it had to a Hawthorn jumper and it had to be 23, the great Dermott Brereton's number! It was a great story, and Dusty had heard it a few times, but she didn't believe it – nobody was that weird!

Trigger smiled at Dusty, a smile about as genuine as eBay Armani, and continued ogling her breasts.

'Beauty first,' he said, giving no sign that he'd recognised her.

What did that mean? Either, thought Dusty, I've aged so much I no longer resemble the willowy lass of eight mango seasons ago, or the preferred option, he's been with so many women he no longer recognises them individually, they've all just blended into some amorphous mass.

'Beauty's got nothing to do with it,' said Dusty, and, determined that he wasn't the only one who could play the non-recognition game, she added, 'Visiting Darwin, are you?'

'No, actually I live here,' said Trigger, throwing an astonished glance at the barman – she doesn't know who I am! 'You obviously don't.'

'Only the last eleven years.'

Dusty paid for her drinks and walked away. Had she really once flirted with that terrible man, perhaps even considered going home with him? She could see his reflection in the window now, walking the other way, drinks on a tray. He approached a table, where two women were sitting. They were dark-haired. Were they Asian? It was hard to tell. By that time Dusty had turned the corner and Trigger and his reflection had disappeared.

Chapter 13

The car, a red RAV4 Cruiser, belonged to Spida, an ex-teammate who was now residing in one of the Top End's less sought-after residential properties – Berrimah Prison. He was doing six years for importation of a prohibited substance. He had a hotshot new lawyer now, though, and last time Trigger visited him he was talking about getting out before Christmas. Which, of course, would be great and Trigger wished him the best of luck. Well, most of him did. There was a small part that said, fuck it, he's a drug smuggler after all, cutting our kids down in their prime, and should pay his debt to society. Besides, where would he live if Spida got out – he'd been minding Spida's Walsh Bay apartment since he'd booked into Berrimah, and what's more, what would he drive?

Though the car wasn't his, the CDs in the stacker were, and, once again, as he fast-forwarded through the collection, he had cause to congratulate himself on his classic taste – Billy Joel, Dire Straits, Johnny Farnham, Celine Dion. All of it gold, but he was thinking something a bit edgier today, something to get him into the facilitating mood, the right mood to separate those vets from their disability cheques. As if on cue, there it was – Sting. Perfect!

'Noi, you like the Stingster?' asked Trigger.

Noi, however, was already asleep, curled up, catlike, in her seat, one hand holding the Buddha amulet that hung around her neck. It occurred to Trigger that maybe she was on something. He'd heard of that – they'd bring the girls over and dope them up, turn them into addicts, a pharmaceutical ball-and-chain. Trigger felt an unfamiliar cardiac jolt – did she really know what she was in for, had Noi explained it to her properly? This concern was dismissed from his mind as quickly as it came, however – it was a tough world out there and there was nothing Trigger Tregenza could do about that. We all make choices, don't we, and we all have to live with the consequences.

After an hour of driving, just past the Noonamah pub his mobile rang. It was Noi, sounding even more hysterical than usual.

'Trig. You come back now. You bring back Noi now.'

'Slow down, what's your problem?'

'Big Boss, he say to me, Noi belong him. You bring Noi back now.'

Trig's law, yet again. What to do? If Big Boss was as tough as his imagination suggested, then to continue would not be advisable. Trigger tended to think, however, that a fair measure of a boss was the muscle he employed, and Big Boss employed Ned Maleski, a man Trigger would back himself against any day of the week. In fact, it was something he'd look forward to, another 'titanic struggle between two titans'.

'Tank, I hope you've got plenty of Viagra,' said Trigger as he hung up and put his foot down.

Two and a half hours later and he was at the camp. The lights were a surprise – he'd been expecting something more dingy, a couple of gas-lamps throwing off a feeble light, but the camp was lit up like Sydney Harbour Bridge on New Year's Eve. The second surprise was that there were so many people. Trigger should've guessed – Aussies didn't need much excuse for a party, especially Territorians, especially Territorians who

The Build Up

lived in remote areas. Fuck it – that'll do. Let's get together! Let's party!

People had come from all over the general area. Blackfellas from the Pandanus Springs community. Ringers from the cattle stations. Gem prospectors from the gem fields. And vets, of course. Quite a few in uniform, or part-uniform, their chests spangled with medals.

'You stay here,' he said to Noi, but he could've saved his words – she was still asleep.

He got out of the car, making sure to lock it behind him. The thick night air smelled of eucalyptus and burnt sausages and Jimmy Barnes was belting out 'Khe Sahn' over the loudspeakers.

Trigger could remember exactly the last time he'd seen Tank. It was at the Fox and Lion Hotel in Fox Studios, just next to the Sydney Cricket Ground, the Swans' home ground. He'd just been delisted by the Swans and was having a few commiserative drinks – if not drowning his sorrows at least giving them plenty of fluid to splash around in. Tank, who was a trainer at the club, had taken him aside and suggested that he might like to pursue a career up north. He'd even given him a couple of numbers to ring. OK, going to Darwin was the worst decision he'd ever made, but that wasn't Tank's fault, he'd only been trying to help a mate out. Trigger owed him one.

Finding Tank was no problem. As soon as he heard that distinctive kookaburra laugh, Trigger knew he had his man. He hadn't changed much, either. He still had the mane of white hair swept back, the wide, open face, the big, solid gut. Only now he was walking with the aid of a stick. The result, Trigger found out later, of a recent hip replacement.

'Maaaaate!' said Tank, when he spotted Trigger.

He detached himself from his fellow vets and hobbled over to pump Trigger's hand. The usual bullshit ensued – don't look a day older, could still pull on the boots, before Tank lowered his voice and said 'So how'd you go?'

'All sorted.'

'Knew I could rely on you, Champ.'

This was only his third outing as a facilitator, and Trigger was feeling slightly out of his depth. Tank had it all worked out though. First he gave him a quick tour of the camp.

The kitchen was made from saplings with a corrugated iron roof and brick floor. So too the toilet, or 'latrine', as Tank called it. The twenty or so 2-man tents were all neatly laid out, some of them inside A-frames with tarpaulin roofs and mosquito-proof netting enclosing the sides. Water was stored in three polytanks. A diesel generator supplied the power.

Trigger was impressed – no wonder the government was listening to what these vets had to say. There were a few women around, but none of them appeared to be single, let alone on the game. Trigger was starting to feel real good about this – a seller's market and he had the goods. Tank led him along a track, away from the camp proper, through a cluster of termite mounds. Trigger had been ten years in the Top End, he'd seen termite mounds before. Nothing like these, though – they were huge things. Hideous.

'Fucking termites, eh?' said Trigger.

'Fucking termites,' agreed Tank.

The light here wasn't good, but Trigger could make out an old-style army tent.

'The little lady can set herself up in that honcho,' said Tank.

Trigger took a look inside – a thin mattress, a torn sheet, and a smell that would not only wake the dead but give them nightmares for years to come.

'Fuck!' said Trigger, stepping back quickly.

'Detox tent,' explained Tank. 'It's where we put our druggies.'

The Build Up

Trigger had toyed with the idea of going first, testing the goods so to speak, but there was no way he was going to do that now. Not in there, anyway.

'What say we get going at twenty-three hundred hours?' said Tank, looking at his watch.

Trigger had to smile – in all the time he'd spent with Tank back in his Sydney days he hadn't even mentioned Nam, in fact back then he'd only had two topics of conversation, football and fucking. Now, apparently, it was all army-speak.

'No problems,' said Trigger. 'Just one more thing. We've got the all-clear for this, haven't we? I mean the boss is OK with it?'

Tank gave him a conspiratorial wink. 'All Indians here, mate. No chiefs.'

Number two Noi was still asleep. Trigger nudged her gently, but she woke with a start, eyes wide.

'Noi, it's OK, it's me, Trigger, remember?'

'Me feel bad,' she said, and Trigger could see that she wasn't lying.

'Take some medicine,' he said, remembering the bottle Noi had given her.

She did as he suggested, washing it down with some of the Coke Trigger had brought her.

He handed her a sausage in a hammock of bread.

'Thank you,' she said, smiling.

So she can speak English, thought Trigger.

She ate daintily, picking at the bread with the very tips of her fingers.

'How long Noi Australia?' asked Trigger, pronouncing each syllable slowly.

'Three mun,' she said.

'You like Australia?'

'Many kangaroo,' said Noi, and again she smiled.

Fucking kangaroos! They'd almost run into a couple on the way down.

Now it was Noi's turn to ask a question. 'You wife?'

Trigger smiled. Technically, yes. Practically, no. And two kids to boot. But he didn't think Noi's English was up to understanding his complicated marital status.

'No,' he simply said. 'No married.'

'You marry Noi.'

Such an unexpected request, it sneaked past Trigger's guard. For a second, he considered it. Marry Noi. Drive away from here, turn left on the Track and head south. Save Noi. Save himself too, probably. He looked at her face and he could see the hope in it. It would be the most decent thing he'd ever done. Would ever do.

'C'mon, let's get to work,' he said.

He needed money. She needed money. It was as simple as that. He showed Noi the tent and she said nothing. Just as she was about to disappear inside he stopped her. 'Protection. Noi have condom? Rubber?'

'Noi have.'

Not so innocent after all, thought Trig. Bloody good, these girls, a fella's got to have his wits about him. He positioned himself with his back to a termite mound, and waited. The sound of irregular footsteps, a crunch of leaf litter, and Trigger had his first customer. Tank.

'Never big on slops,' he said, taking out his wallet. 'What's the damage?'

'Mate, I feel bad charging you.'

'Bullshit. What's the damage?'

'How does two hundred sound?'

'Fair enough, I reckon,' said Tank, sliding four fifties from his wallet.

The Build Up

'Take your time,' said Trigger, pocketing the money, as Tank awkwardly negotiated the tent entrance, crawling in on hands and knees.

As he took up his position by the termite mound again, he made a mental note – next time bring an iPod. There was going to be a lot of standing around, and John or Celine would be great company out here. Seven-and-a-half minutes later Tank was back.

'Shit, what's wrong?' said Trigger, recalling Tank's stories of all-night shagging sessions.

It would be her fault, of course. Why had he ever brought number two Noi?

'Nothing.'

'The girl?'

'Gorgeous.'

'But–'

'Just a quickie,' said Tank. 'I wanna leave plenty of time for the other fellas.'

'Come back later, then,' said Trigger. 'A root on the house for old time's sake, eh?'

The next customer was Scotty, another vet, a mate of Tank's. Had a bikie look about him, but everything went fine – he paid his money and had his pleasure and even remembered to say 'Thanks'.

To Trigger, anyway.

Chapter 14

Trigger thumbed through the wad of notes.

Two thousand and four hundred bucks.

It wasn't the easiest money he'd ever made – he'd backed a few winning horses in his time, but this, unlike that, was proper work. If prostitution was, as they said, the oldest profession in the world, then pimping must be the next.

What he'd do was get himself a nice four-wheel drive, a Nissan Patrol or a Range Rover, stick a thirty-foot caravan on the back, stick a couple of girls in that, take off around Australia, stopping off at all the vets' camps, servicing their needs. There had to be more vets' camps, didn't there? And why only vets? All those cashed-up baby boomers, sea-changing, tree-changing – doing whatever it is they did, were moving away from the cities, to where the air was clean and the grass was green and the snatch wasn't exactly thick on the ground.

They were gentleman, those vets, a pleasure to do business with. Grateful almost. The only grief he'd had all night had nothing to do with any of them, it was that baby-faced ringer who wanted his money back.

'She just lay there,' he said. 'She didn't do nothing.'

'What did ya expect, a fucking floor show? This ain't Patpong, cowboy.'

The Build Up

That had shut him up, and he'd walked off, all big hat and bandy legs, mumbling to himself.

He'd checked on Noi a couple of times, handed her some Cokes. She'd taken them, but hadn't said anything, just lay there in her darkness.

It was past three and there hadn't been a customer for half an hour. Again, Trigger counted the money. Two thousand four hundred. Split that fifty-fifty and that'd be twelve hundred each. That, however was the deal he'd had with the other Noi, not this Noi. He was thinking more like sixty/forty. Who'd set this thing up? Who'd done all the work?

'Maaate!'

It was Tank, flushed in the face, even more unsteady on his feet.

'Thought I'd take you up on that offer, you know.'

'Go ahead, mate. She's all yours,' said Trigger.

It was the least he could do.

Trigger moved off to get a can of beer – it wasn't as if he hadn't earned himself a drink. As he did a car's headlights switched on. Out of the corner of his eye Trigger could see Tank's silhouette – menacing, almost grotesque, against the canvas of the tent. The car swung around and it all became dark again. At the bar he got talking to another vet by the name of Jimmy. Bit scatty, but not a bad bloke, keen on his fishing. By the time he got back he'd been gone half an hour.

'You still there, big fella?' he yelled, in the direction of the tent.

There was no reply. Tank must've gone already, he told himself.

'Noi! We go home now.'

Suddenly, a man was standing there. Trigger had heard nothing – no footsteps, no crunch of leaf litter. It was as if a giant had placed him there, a chess piece on a chessboard.

He was a small man, rover size – five foot six, seventy kilo, something like that. Wearing thongs, fatigues, a tight green T-shirt, and an SAS beret.

He hadn't been to Vietnam though. He was in his thirties, too young for that. Trigger remembered Tank telling him that all vets were welcome, not just those who'd been to Nam. Afghanistan, Timor, Somalia, Iraq, the Solomons – there was no shortage of wars to pick from.

'Fuck me, mate,' said Trigger. 'Where'd you come from?'

He turned slightly, towards the light, and Trigger could see his dilated pupils, the thin ring of iris. The skin across his cheeks was taut and sheened with sweat. His jaw was working overtime, his face distorting.

Trigger's defence mechanisms clicked in. Sliding his right foot back, he bent his knees slightly, moving his weight to where he wanted it.

'Anything I can help you with?'

'Actually there is,' he said, his slow delivery surprising Trigger, who had expected a flurry of words, speech accelerated by amphetamines.

'Go on,' said Trigger.

'What I'd really like you to help me with is some pussy,' he said with a slight lisp. *Thum puthy*.

'I'm afraid shop's closed for the night,' said Trigger.

'Well, maybe thith will open it.'

A white-handled knife in his hand now. The blade long and worn narrow, a roo-skinner's knife, a fish-filleter's knife. Trigger had been scared before – the old man with his drinking, on the football field, the usual bar fights – but never like this. Now, for the first time, he understood what it was to be 'shit-scared', to be scared to the very marrow, to the very shit, of his being.

'Fuck me!' said Trigger.

The Build Up

'Not exactly what I had in mind,' said the intruder, laughing at his own joke. 'Two hundred they reckon?'

Trigger found some words. 'That's the rate.'

The knife was in his other hand, now. His jaw still working away.

'You know what – I never like to pay up front for pussy.' *For puthy.*

'Mate, fair enough,' said Trigger. 'You go ahead, pay later.'

As the man in the SAS beret entered the tent, a roo-skinner about to skin a roo, fish-filleter about to fillet a fish, Trigger Tregenza, eight-time leading goalkicker, three-time Best and Fairest, took off down the path.

Chapter 15

Barry woke late. It was past seven when he blinked his eyes open to a tent full of light. The chemical taste at the back of his throat reminded him of the pills Tank had given him. Then, his thoughts moving sluggishly, he backtracked from there – people everywhere, cars everywhere, all turning to shit. He pulled on a pair of shorts and hurried outside, expecting the worst.

The fire was still smouldering. Next to it a blackfella slept, his body a question mark. Beer cans were strewn everywhere, a rainbow of colours. There were paper plates, bleeding tomato sauce. A nest of empty Jim Beam bottles. It was a disgrace, but there was a couple of hours' work in it at the most, even less if he found help.

Barry could feel his shoulders drop, his jaw relax. Tank had been right – the celebration had been good for the vets. It had been wrong of him not to trust them – they were grown men, grandfathers some of them.

He set off on his customary morning walk, following the creek – barely a trickle now – for several hundred metres, turning right when it turned left. Upon reaching the track, he swung right again. Passing the scene of the party he came to the patch of termite mounds.

Usually Barry took no notice of the detox tent – it'd become part of the landscape. This morning, however, something – the

The Build Up

smell, the buzz of flies? – made him detour towards it.

He pushed the canvas flap aside with the back of his hand. A twisted sheet. Coke cans. Ruptured condom packets. A woman. A man.

And though somebody else might think they were asleep, or perhaps unconscious, Barry had seen enough death in his time to know that this was more of it.

Still, he squatted down next to her and placed two fingers on her neck. Her skin was cold, her pulse long gone. His eye travelled down her body. Over her dark-nippled breasts. The tuft of pubic hair. A white-handled knife between her legs. As for the man; he had a bullet hole in his head.

Chapter 16

6th October
As Senior Sergeant Dave Kirk drove through Darwin's industrial outskirts, he said nothing. Dusty, in the passenger's seat, wasn't fazed; she'd worked with Kirky before, knew he was always quiet this early in the morning, that what energy he had was devoted to digesting the fry-up, the full coronary disaster, he'd no doubt scoffed for breakfast.

Kirky was every casting agent's idea of Bad Cop – he had the hefty stomach straining hard against the fabric of his khaki shirt, he had the thick neck and deep-set eyes and, just in case all that wasn't enough, he had the Chopper-style handlebar moustache. All he had to do was learn to say 'y'all' instead of 'youse' and Hollywood was his for the taking.

They were on the the Stuart Highway, or the Track as the locals called it – the main road south out of Darwin. An oversized four-wheel-drive towing an oversized caravan – a Tweety Bird painted on the back with the words 'Don't you get too cwose!' underneath it – dawdled along in the right lane, refusing to budge.

'Don't get too cwose,' read Dusty, laughing.

'Fuck that,' said Kirky.

'Saw one the other day – adventure before dementia,' said Dusty.

The Build Up

'Fuck that, too.'

Kirky passed on the inside lane, the elderly silver-haired driver perched high on the seat, seemingly unaware of their presence.

'Fucking grey nomads! Got half a fucking mind to book the older fucker.'

Dusty smiled – it'd been a while since she'd been in Kirky's company, and she'd forgotten the breadth of his eloquence.

'I see you took the commander's recent directive about gratuitous use of profane language onboard, Kirky.'

'Fuck that.'

They passed a sign listing distances to all the major cities in Australia. Alice Springs 1498 km. Brisbane 3429 km. Adelaide 3027 km. Melbourne 3755 km. Sydney 3931 km. Perth 3995 km.

It was for the tourists, of course. Meant to give them some sense of how isolated Darwin was, how authentic their outback experience was. Still, the numbers always surprised Dusty; Darwin really was a long way from anywhere.

Dusty re-read the brief. A call had been received this morning from Pandanus Springs. A couple of their fellas, out hunting, had found one of those vets, a skinny whitefella in the bush. Said he'd spent the night there. Didn't have a clue where he was. Surprisingly enough, he wasn't in such a bad way. They took him back to the community. Gave him food and drink. He kept raving about something he'd seen in the billabong. A body? A gook? A croc?

'So how's my favourite frontbum?' said Kirky as they passed the turnoff to Berry Springs, the eggs and bacon obviously sufficiently digested by now.

In the old days they were all 'frontbums', all the women police, but times had changed, and 'frontbum' was pretty much on top of the list of unacceptable terms. Even the once common 'wopo', a contraction of women police, was frowned upon, now.

If anybody else had used that term, Dusty would've risen to the challenge. Not Kirky, though. He was just looking for a reaction and Dusty wasn't about to provide him with one.

'Heard you're quitting?' she said, instead.

Kirky nodded.

'TJF?' asked Dusty.

TJF – this job's fucked, or senior sergeant's disease.

'Not really,' said Kirky.

'Villains not like they used to be? All druggies these days. No class anymore?'

Now Dusty was the one looking for a rise – despite her own recent thoughts of adorable puppies and garrulous cockatoos she didn't have much time for coppers who quit.

'Not that either.'

'Let me guess – security. You've been headhunted. Off to Afghanistan, one of those hellholes.'

'Fuck that.'

Dusty had only been making conversation but now she was genuinely intrigued. Kirky was a dinosaur, but he hadn't been such a bad cop and he only had about five years until retirement – why didn't he just serve them out?

'What then?'

'Put it this way – I'm a bit fucking particular about who I take my fucking orders from.'

'So you don't like the new commander?' asked Dusty.

She felt strangely vindicated – so she wasn't the only copper having problems with the Big C.

'I'm not saying nothing,' said Kirky.

Which was probably for the best as Dusty suspected that Kirky's dissatisfaction with Commander Schneider had more to do with her gender than any perceived lack of professionalism on her part.

The Build Up

Kirky turned on the radio, hitting the search button until he'd found some music to his liking – Solid Gold Oldies.

After two hours of Elvis, Roy Orbison and the Dave Clark Five they'd reached the mining town of Pine Creek.

'What do you reckon about this case?' Dusty asked.

'Another fucking wild goose chase.'

'So keeping an open mind are we, Kirky?' said Dusty, though she'd been thinking along those lines herself.

On the radio Elvis had just launched into 'Hound Dog'. Somehow, it seemed appropriate.

'You been to the camp before?' asked Dusty.

A terse 'no' was Kirky's only response, until about half an hour later when suddenly he said, 'I was pretty close to going to Nam myself.'

'Really?'

'Missed out by two days.'

'What do you mean you missed out?'

Not for the first time Dusty had cause to regret all those hours she'd spent churning up and down the pool instead of doing her schoolwork.

Kirky explained how the ballot worked: if your twentieth birthday fell in a certain six month period you were required to register. Numbered marbles representing dates of the year were placed in a barrel – the same barrel they used for the Tattersall's lottery – and some were drawn out. If your number came up, you were conscripted.

'Few of my mates went. Half of 'em came back fucked in the head. As a copper you see some terrible things. You know what I mean, a whole fucking family turned into mince because some pissed blackfella's wandered across the road. But at least we get some respect. Not as much as we fucking deserve, but we get some. Those poor buggers, they came back and people spat on them on the street. Literally spat on them.'

They turned off again, onto a small rutted track, gum trees on either side swishing against the side of the car. Dusty wound down the window, breathing in deep. She loved that eucalypt smell, it brought back so many memories – the suburban park where she used to play with her brother, outings to the Adelaide Hills, even camping trips with James.

The atmosphere in the car more convivial now, Dusty and Kirky chatted until they pulled into a clearing and Kirky said, 'This is it, I reckon.'

Chapter 17

Dusty opened the car door and stepped outside. After almost four hours in airconditioning, the humidity was a slap in the face, a punch in the guts.

A man walked towards them. Dusty took a while to recognise him as Barry O'Loughlin. The photo in the *NT News*, dominated by that termite mound, had done him no favours. He was bigger than Dusty had expected – especially in the upper body – and much better looking, the grey in his hair contrasting nicely with his tanned face. There was a definite air of authority about him too, reinforced, no doubt, by the secular uniform he was wearing: khaki shorts, a long-sleeved khaki shirt and boots.

'Welcome,' he said, smiling professionally, offering his hand to Kirky. 'Barry O'Loughlin.'

'Senior Sergeant Kirk, and this is Detective Buchanon,' said Kirky.

'Detective,' he said, shaking Dusty's hand, his grip firm, his gaze steady. 'I'll give you a cook's tour of the camp.'

Dusty had been to bush camps before, belonging to dope-growers, barramundi poachers, and, in one case, radical lesbian separatists but none of those had been as substantial, or well organised, as this one.

'Fancy a brew?' said Barry, when they'd finished. 'I'll put the billy on.'

'Now you're talking,' said Kirky, as they sat down in white plastic chairs arranged in the shade of a pandanus clump.

Dusty could see that Kirky was loving this – it was a man's world, out here. She had to admit, though, that the billy tea, when it came, did taste wonderful – sweet and black – as she sipped it from a chipped enamel mug.

They were joined by two other vets, one walking with the aid of a stick, and another tough-looking fella, who were introduced as Tank and Scotty.

'What's a bloke have to do to get arrested by the likes of you, darl?' Tank said, leering at Dusty.

She was reminded of her uncle Des, her father's thrice-married brother – the white hair swept back, the flashy watch. Tank, like Des, obviously saw himself as bit of a lady's man, a Lothario of the RSL.

As for Scotty, he was obviously the one who had strayed the furthest from the straight and narrow. There was a lot of the bikie about him – both arms were sleeved with tatts, and these were tatts, too, not body art – and he had a sort of cockiness that Dusty instantly recognised as belonging to a certain type who'd had extensive dealings with the law but reckoned they'd come out OK, if not on top.

An unlikely trio, but given that it was a lottery that threw them together in the first place this was not unexpected.

'What those tanks hold, twenty thousand litres?' asked Kirky, noisily draining his tea.

'Sixteen,' replied Barry.

They were off then, the blokes: it was all tanks, pipes and pressure. Dusty was not unused to this – when she'd joined the Force only eight per cent of officers were women. Even now,

The Build Up

eleven years later, it was only seventeen per cent. At one time she would've made a point of joining in on the conversation. Did they think she'd never been to Bunnings, Stratco or Mitre 10? Who did they think did all the maintenance on the pool? Had she not personally extricated her defunct Nokia from the Kreepy Krauly's maw? Today, though, she couldn't be bothered, the boys could have their pvc.

By the time she'd finished her tea, Dusty's good mood, like all good moods, had moved on. Maybe it was the enervating heat, the relentless bloke-speak, or the nagging feeling that she should be back at HQ keeping track of the McVeigh case. Whatever it was, she was sick of the not-so-secret men's business.

'Now, about this body,' she said.

A flash of annoyance crossed Kirky's face. The conversation had moved onto diesel generators, and the senior sergeant considered himself to be somewhat of an expert in this area.

'Body?' said Barry, and he seemed genuinely surprised. 'Oh yes, the body. Look, between you and me, I know Jimmy may have sounded pretty convinced he saw something out there, but our Jimmy's not a well man.'

Barry looked over to his fellow vets. They both shook their heads. No, not a well man at all.

'He's got PTSD. That's post . . .'

Dusty was getting a bit annoyed with Barry O'Loughlin. 'We're all pretty familiar with post traumatic stress disorder. In our line of work, you have to be.'

Barry looked across at his new best mate, Kirky. More secret men's business. Though this wasn't so secret, either. Barry wanted Kirky to overrule Dusty. He was the one in the uniform, after all. Instead, Kirky said, 'Maybe we could talk to Jimmy, anyway.' He took out his pad and pen from his top pocket. 'You know, for the books,' he added almost apologetically.

Dusty could see the first crack in Barry's veneer.

'Tank, go see if you can find Jimmy,' he snapped, throwing the dregs of his tea onto the ground.

Jimmy wasn't Kurtz, Rambo or Travis Bickle, but he was more like what Dusty was expecting. He was thin – the ladder of his ribs was visible through the thin cotton of his T-shirt – and he had long unkempt hair and a bewildering array of chunky jewellery around his neck and wrists. He was also a user. Or an ex-user – the scars on the inside of his arms were freshly healed. After introductions he told his story. Jimmy had a quickfire way of talking, ending almost every sentence with a rhetorical 'You know what I mean?'

'So I'm fishing at the billabong, you know what I mean?'

'What billabong?' asked Dusty.

'I don't know its name, we just call it the billabong.'

'Where is it?'

Jimmy pointed to the road.

'There's a turnoff down there about three k's, you know what I mean? Take that and it's another k or so to the water.'

Dusty waited until Kirky had stopped writing before she said, 'So, Jimmy, you're fishing at the billabong?'

'Like I told you.'

'From the bank or a boat?'

Dusty had noticed the tip of an aluminium dinghy poking out from behind one of the tents.

'Jimmy always fishes from the bank,' said Barry.

'If you don't mind,' admonished Dusty, 'I'd prefer it if Jimmy answered the questions.'

Dusty let Jimmy get to the end of his story without further interruption.

She wasn't sure if it was his staccato delivery or her lack of concentration but it didn't seem to make much sense.

The Build Up

'So you saw a body?' she said finally.

Jimmy looked over at Barry before answering.

'Maybe what I saw was, like, an old body. Like a flashback body. You know what I mean.'

'Either you saw a body or you didn't, mate. Which one is it?' said Dusty, not bothering to disguise the impatience in her voice.

Jimmy shrugged.

'Could you describe it for me?'

'Yeah, well it was, like, you know, a chick. You know what I mean?'

'Anything else?'

'Yeah, it was a gook. You know what I mean?'

'A woman of Asian appearance?' said Dusty.

'Yeah, that's right. A fuckin' gook.'

'OK, then. Thanks for your time, gentlemen. We'll be off,' said Dusty.

Back in the car she asked Kirky, 'What'd you make of Barry?'

'Straight as they come.'

'Not so sure about that.'

'Come on, Dusty.'

'Jimmy?'

'Nerves were shot to pieces. If it wasn't Vietnam it was the fucking smack.'

'You noticed, too?'

'Noticed? You could've ran the fucking Ghan train on those tracks.'

'PTSD?'

'Textbook, the poor bastard.'

'Gook in the billabong?'

'Yeah, right.'

'We better check it out, though. At least then we can say we've done it.'

'It's fucking four o'clock now, which means we don't get back until eight at the earliest. And my missus is gunna have my fucking guts for garters.'

'ps. it's posh' Julien had emailed. It would take Dusty ages to get ready.

'Had to be PTSD, didn't it?' asked Dusty.

'Of course it did.'

'OK, fuck it,' said Dusty.

Kirky didn't need any more encouragement. He started the engine, swung the car around and pressed down hard on the accelerator.

Chapter 18

Dusty pulled up outside Peewees. It was a new restaurant, housed in an old customs building at East Point. She'd once spent a week here on a stake-out. She remembered it well, though not fondly – having to put up with the Plastics, as the Federal Police were known, endless games of euchre, and, in the end, no bust; the bad guys not even bothering to turn up. The building had certainly changed since then, it was all exposed sandstone, pastel colours and subdued lighting.

'Excuse me, do you have a reservation?' demanded the maître d', as Dusty passed the front desk.

She was young and pretty, dressed in black, with beautifully pale skin, skin that definitely didn't come from the Top End.

'A reservation?' said Dusty, momentarily lost.

'Yes, I'm afraid we're fully booked tonight.'

She then gave Dusty the once-over.

It was sneaky, but Dusty knew a once-over when she saw one. After Julien's emailed warning, she'd put on her yellow and black Scanlan & Theodore with the criss-cross back and flippy skirt.

OK, she'd had it for a while, but a Scanlan was a Scanlan and she didn't deserve a once-over, sneaky or not. Especially in Darwin where Territory Rig – which basically meant wear anything you feel comfortable in – had reigned since the town was first hacked out of the mangroves. What was happening to her town!

'In the name of Matthews,' said Dusty, searching for a note of confidence in her voice. 'Table for two.'

As the girl ran her conspicuously manicured finger down the list, Dusty was hoping like hell that Julien had booked. If he hadn't, whitefella English couldn't capture the humiliation she'd suffer. She'd have to borrow an Aboriginal phrase – shame-job. It would be the biggest shame-job, the mother of all shame-jobs.

The girl smiled, displaying teeth that weren't from the Top End either. 'Yes, here we are. Matthews. Table for two. Follow me, please.'

Dusty relaxed. Julien, you beautiful man! She followed the girl outside and onto the patio, smiling complicity at her fellow diners.

'This is your table,' said the girl.

If it wasn't the best table in the restaurant – the table under the red-flowered poinciana tree, sporting the large 'RESERVED' sign, was probably the most coveted – it was still right next to the water, still wonderful.

Julien, you beautiful, beautiful man!

'Can I get you a drink?' asked the girl, after Dusty had sat down.

'Maybe something with a hat,' said Dusty, gaining in confidence.

The girl looked at her blankly.

'You know, the cocktail list?' said Dusty, unsure as to whether she'd just scored a point against Little Miss Paleskin, or said something so egregious it would entertain the staff for weeks to come – 'And this woman, right, goes "maybe something with a hat", like she's starring in her own *Sex and the City*.'

The Build Up

'Certainly,' said the girl, flashing those sparkling non-Territorian teeth, once again.

She returned with the list and Dusty ordered a Mango Mojito, remembering that the 'j' wasn't really a 'j' but a 'h' in disguise.

'Where are you from, by the way?' asked Dusty, curiosity getting the better of her.

'From here, of course.'

'No, originally I mean.'

'I was born in Darwin – grew up in Wangaru.'

Born here! With those teeth. That skin. Darwin was definitely changing, and whether it was for the better was up for debate.

As Dusty sipped her drink, she remembered the first time she arrived in Darwin. June 1994. She'd stepped off the plane and onto the sticky black tarmac that first morning, expecting a tropical paradise – dazzling white beaches, swaying palms, bluer than blue water. She couldn't believe it – dry and dusty, it looked just like South Australia, painted using the same muted palette. And the people! The T-shirts and thongs, beer-guts and sun-fucked skin. She'd thought that she'd last the week. But at night it was different. The darkness cloaked the shabbiness, the air was unbelievably soft, velvety almost, and smelled so sweet.

'Sorry I'm late.'

Dusty looked up to find Julien standing next to her. Like always, she felt a pang, a little emotional stab inside. Even at thirty-six he hadn't lost his naughty-boy good looks. Freckles across the bridge of his nose. The slightly lopsided grin. Dressed in designer jeans and a long sleeved shirt with a subtle floral print, he looked great as usual.

'Julien, you're always late.'

'Yes, but I'm always genuinely sorry.'

Paleskin returned. 'Can I get you a drink, sir?'

'Bubbles!' said Julien expansively. 'I made a big sale to a Euro being,' he said as an aside to Dusty.

'A what?'

'It's what I call them now, Europeans.'

'Very droll,' said Dusty.

Last year Julien had opened his own gallery, specialising in the art of the indigenous people of Maningrida, a coastal settlement on the mouth of the Liverpool River about three hundred and fifty clicks east of Darwin.

'Moet or Krug, sir?'

'Let's see,' said Julien, as he checked the prices on the wine list. 'Actually the Seaview Brut will do fine.' Again, as an aside. 'I only sold a print.'

When the champagne came they clinked glasses, first the bottom then the top, then they looked into each other's eyes. It was one of Julien's rules; if you broke it, ten years of bad sex was guaranteed to follow.

'To the gallery,' said Dusty.

'Fuck the gallery. It doesn't need us, not with the Eurobeings squandering their Euros. To us! How long has it been now?'

'Let's see,' said Dusty, doing the maths in her head. 'Eleven years.'

Dusty had still been in uniform, a probationary constable, when a distraught Julien had burst into the Berrimah station. His car had just been stolen. On the back seat – several Aboriginal paintings that he'd borrowed for his Master's thesis. The duty officer hadn't been taking him seriously – mate, it's only a friggin' Datsun 120Y – so Dusty had taken over, assured him she'd do her best to find the car. She'd driven around for days, mostly on her own time, grilling all the likely suspects, and eventually found the car and, more importantly, the paintings. They'd been friends ever since.

The Build Up

Across the harbour she could see Darwin's city lights. The moon had just risen, too. A huge pale disc throwing light onto the harbour water, silhouetting a clump of palm trees on the beach.

'It's actually quite beautiful, isn't it?' said Dusty, waving her hand at the nightscape.

'What do you mean "quite beautiful"? It's really fucking beautiful! They're palm trees we're looking at. That's moonlight on the water. You kill me, Dusty. You're the first person to defend this town if anybody knocks it, but deep down you still don't think it's as good as other places. Territory cringe, that's what you've got.'

'Maybe,' said Dusty, as she finished her champagne.

Domestic, but it tasted great. It also had the usual desired effect – she could feel herself relaxing, settling into the evening. They talked about their Bali trip for a while, then Dusty said, 'Julien, can I ask you a really personal question?'

'My life is an open book. Well, more like a *Who* magazine, actually.'

'Do you reckon you're always going to be gay?'

'Dusty! Not this again.'

'But what about those times we had sex. Didn't you enjoy it?'

In those eleven years Dusty and Julien had shared a house for three of them, they'd been to twelve weddings and four funerals together, they'd been to Bali eleven times together, Thailand three times, India twice and Hong Kong once, they'd been drunk countless times, stoned a few less, they'd slept in the same room many times, in the same bed quite a few times, and had sex on three separate occasions.

'It was nice. I told you that before Dusty.'

'Nice? C'mon, for a supposedly gay man you didn't seem to have much trouble getting a big ole erection.'

'It's those beautiful tits of yours, darling. They're better than any Viagra.'

Dusty was justifiably proud of her breasts, but she wasn't in the mood for Julien's facile charm.

'And it's not as if you didn't, you know, achieve climax.'

'OK, OK, I came. Taddies all over the show. But do you really want to know the truth?'

'Of course. I'm a police officer. It's my professional responsibility to know the truth.'

'I was thinking of somebody else.'

'Who?'

'Fuck me,' said Julien, getting exasperated. 'The point is, I'm a poof and I'll always be a poof. I know that's hard for you to get your head around but, guess what, I actually like being a poof. End of discussion.'

'Have it your way, but there's no way I'm sharing an entrée with you,' said Dusty, as she splashed some more bubbly into her glass.

By the time they'd finished a second bottle, they were friends again. Dusty was telling Julien about the vet camp, ragged Jimmy and his PTSD.

'But what if there really is a body in the billabong?' he said.

'Jesus, that sounds like the name of a really bad Australian movie.'

Julien put on his sonorous announcer's voice. '*Body in the Billabong* starring Sigrid Thornton as the body.'

'And Bryan Brown as the billabong.'

'Seriously, what if there is a body?'

'Fat chance. I went through the missing persons' reports. Nobody fits that description. It's a classic case of PTSD. So, Julien, you stick to your Eurobeings, and I'll look after the police work, OK?'

'Don't be so patronising.'

The Build Up

'What do you mean?'

'I reckon I'd be a good copper, especially undercover. You know, like Serpico?'

The mains came then, lamb for Julien and chicken for Dusty and there was a lull in the conversation. Dusty was happy to enjoy the food and absorb the view. The moonlight had reached an intensity usually only found in the more obvious romantic comedies. Animals, probably bats, were scrabbling about in the palm trees.

Julien, however, was starting to become agitated. He was rarely like this, or rarely showed it, so when he started sucking his bottom lip and twisting the ring on his finger, Dusty knew something was up.

'OK, what is it? You're making me nervous, too. Out with it.'

Julien sighed.

'You know that couple we met at Mindil Beach markets the other night? Deb and Bree?'

Dusty nodded. Julien's circle of friends was ever expanding and contracting, like some sort of protozoan. He was either telling Dusty that she couldn't have anything to do with so-and-so anymore, or introducing her to his best new friends. But she did have some recollection of Deb and Bree. Deb was tall and Bree was pretty. Or maybe it was the other way around. Anyway, she remembered that they were both public servants, women's health, something like that.

'Lezzies, weren't they?'

Julien rolled his eyes. 'Dusty, not this again.'

A mischievous smile. 'OK, yes I do remember your two friends Bree and Deb, who were an item, I believe, followers of the Sapphic way.'

Julien couldn't help laughing. 'Followers of the Sapphic way? What goes on in that fucking head of yours?'

He finished his drink.

'Well, they're planning to have a baby.'

Dusty screwed up her face.

'Dusty!'

'Well, you know how I feel about dykes and their designer babies?'

'They've asked me to be the biological father.'

'Congratulations. I'm sure the two of you, sorry, three of you, will make wonderful parents.'

'For fuck's sake, Dusty. This is serious!' said Julien, his voice rising. 'You know I've always wanted kids.'

'Well, maybe you should've thought about that before you opted for a gay lifestyle.'

'You are fucking impossible,' said Julien, shaking his head.

'Go on,' said Dusty. 'I'll behave. Promise.'

Julien leaned in close, so that their faces were almost touching, Eurobeing style.

'For a start, I didn't *opt* for a gay lifestyle.'

'OK, I'm sorry. I know you didn't.'

'And I've always wanted to have kids. To be a dad.'

'What's stopping you? They're over there in Fannie Bay warming up the turkey baster as we speak.'

'Dusty!'

'OK. OK. I'm sorry.'

'The point is–'

'For fuck's sake, Julien. Out with it.'

Julien took Dusty's hands in his, and squeezed gently. He looked into her eyes. He was Tom Hanks in *Sleepless in Seattle*, he was Billy Crystal in *When Harry Met Sally*, he was Hugh Grant in *Notting Hill*, as he said, 'I'd rather have a baby with you.'

The waitress arrived, a plate in each hand. 'Your desserts,' she announced. 'The soufflé is for?'

'Him,' replied Dusty, pointing towards Julien.

The Build Up

'Then the ice-cream would be yours,' said the waitress brightly, putting the plate in front of Dusty. 'Enjoy!'

They ate in silence.

Julien picked delicately at his soufflé – Dusty was sure he always ordered it because of its aesthetic rather than its taste – while she scoffed her mango and coconut ice-cream.

'Dusty,' said Julien, finally.

'What?'

'It's not as if we haven't talked about this.'

This was true, they had talked about it many times. Dusty even remembered making a drunken pact one night on Kuta Beach – no babies by forty, then we'll make one together.

'You want kids. I want kids. Let's be pragmatic about this. Dusty, you're not getting any younger.'

Dusty leaned over and stabbed Julien's soufflé with her spoon, causing it to immediately collapse.

'You are such a cunt,' she said.

Julien was genuinely outraged. 'You broke our pact!'

'Just goes to show how big a cunt you are! You don't think I'm going to find anyone, do you?'

No answer.

'You don't, do you? You think I'm going to be left on the shelf, don't you?'

Julien met Dusty's accusations with a blank face.

'You do, don't you?'

Again, nothing but blankness.

You could call Julien a poof, a fag, a shirt-lifter or a knob jockey, and he didn't mind but, for some reason he hated to be likened to a herbaceous plant of the genus *Viola*.

'You pansy,' said Dusty.

It had the desired effect.

'You did a pretty good job of scaring James off, didn't you?'

'You detested James.'
'But I didn't scare him off, you did!'
'Pansy. Pansy. Pansy. Pansy.'
'Honey, let's face it. You scare men.'
'For a start, don't *honey* me,' said Dusty, her voice a wild thing, straining at its leash, until, eventually it got free. 'And I don't scare men!'

The startled bats took off with high-pitched squeals, flying out to sea.

Dusty didn't like public scenes, she'd witnessed too many of those in the last fractious years of her parent's marriage, but one seemed inevitable now.

'Dusty, keep your voice down. People are looking,' implored Julien.

Dusty scanned the room. People *were* looking, some discreetly, others eagerly, like they were occupying ringside seats at Cirque du Soleil. *Messieurs and Mademoiselles there will be no flash photography in the Grande Chapiteau tonight.*

Good, thought Dusty, what's a scene without an audience? She turned back to face her tormentor, ready to provoke, to escalate, to outrage. As she did she noticed that there were now two people seated at the best table in the house under the poinciana tree – Commander Schneider and Detective Roberts-Thomson.

Dusty stood up. 'I'm going to the toilet.'

As soon as she was in the foyer and out of the other diners' sight she ran through the open door and outside.

Chapter 19

'You OK, lady?' asked the driver, as Dusty slid into the back seat of the taxi.

He was Asian, in his mid-twenties, his long hair in a ponytail. Something about him was familiar, but Dusty couldn't quite place him. It was always like that in Darwin, however. It wasn't a big place, and the laws of physics ensured that its particles were always bouncing around, colliding with each other, that you were always running into people you'd met before.

'It's nothing,' said Dusty, dabbing at her eyes with a tissue. 'Got an insect in my eye, that's all.'

Through the window she could see Julien inside, talking to Paleskin, no doubt asking if she knew where his dining partner had gone. Well, screw you, Julien. And good luck with the bill.

'Can we get going now?' said Dusty.

'No probs,' said the driver, as he swung the car around and drove back down East Point.

Dusty looked at the driver's licence affixed to the front window. Franky Ng, it said. Of course, now she knew who he was. During her Drug Squad days she'd done him for cultivation. A big plantation too, out near Rum Jungle. He'd got four years, if she remembered correctly.

She put her head down, pretending to rummage for something in her bag. She knew from experience that conversations between cops and crims, even ex-crims, could be pretty unenlightening.

'Where to, lady?' he asked when they came to a T-junction.

Left was home. A dip in the pool. Some trashy TV. Another sweaty, but chaste, night's sleep.

Julien's words were still bouncing around her in her head. 'Honey, you scare men.' She thought of a recent conversation she'd had with Trace about her non-existent love life.

'Sis, you should go milat-ing,' Trace had said.

Dusty was familiar with the notorious serial killer Ivan Milat – what cop, what Australian, wasn't? – but had never heard his name used as a verb before.

'What do you mean milat-ing?'

'Pick yourself up a backpacker.'

It was a typically tasteless joke, the *lingua franca* of cop-to-cop interaction, and Dusty had laughed before she'd said, 'That's sex, not love.'

'It's backpacker-love, and it'd do you the world of good.'

Trace had then gone on to explain milat-ing in detail – there were definite dos and definite don'ts – but Dusty had only half-listened.

'We going left or right?' asked the driver.

After eleven years in the police, Dusty's mind was nothing if not logical. What would picking up a backpacker prove? That she didn't scare men? Your average backpacker was hardly discerning. Jesus, they'd brought one in a couple of years ago who had been found attempting congress with roadkill. Would it prove that she wasn't going to end up on the shelf? Not likely. Picking up a backpacker would only prove one thing: that she could pick up a backpacker. And what if she couldn't even achieve that? How would her ego, any chick's ego, survive that low blow? Logic insisted that she tell the driver to turn left.

The Build Up

'Right,' said Dusty. 'To Mitchell Street.'

As they passed the casino, 'Zorba The Greek' started playing. She checked her phone – *Julien calling* – before turning it off.

'Anywhere in particular?'

'Yeah, the Duck's Nuts,' replied Dusty, mentioning the first bar that came to mind.

'Should be going off this time of night.'

Dusty could see that Franky Ng was now checking her out in the rear-vision mirror.

'How's business?' he said, finally.

Dusty looked up. 'I'm not in Drugs, if that's what you're asking.'

'Neither am I.'

'Wise move, I'd say. How was Berrimah?'

'Food was crap, but it gave me some thinking time.'

'So you're driving taxis now?'

'Part-time. I'm studying at TAFE as well.'

'What?'

'Horticulture.'

Dusty tried, unsuccessfully, to stifle a giggle.

'Hey, why waste all that experience? If you can grow ganja out there in that country with all those crocs and mosquitoes, you can grow anything.'

The taxi turned into Mitchell Street, backpacker central. On either side of the street were hostels, travel agents, internet cafés, souvenir shops, restaurants and bars. At midnight it was by far the busiest street in Darwin.

They pulled up outside the Duck's Nuts. It was crowded as usual, the outside tables all occupied, people spilling out onto the footpath.

Dusty handed the driver twenty. 'Keep the change, Franky.'

'Hey, you remember my name.'

'It's up there,' said Dusty, pointing to the licence. 'But I would've remembered it, anyway. Professional courtesy, I remember all my favourite clients.'

Franky laughed, and Dusty felt a warm glow inside. Moments like this didn't happen very often, when a crim and a cop could have a laugh, when the justice system, whatever that is, seemed to have worked, where jail wasn't just Crime School, a place for crims to learn new tricks. Or maybe Franky Ng was just having her on. Maybe he was Darwin's new Mr Big, the one responsible for the methamphetamines now flooding the market. That was another problem with being a copper: you could take nothing at face value, always had to mentally flip the coin to see what was on the other side. As she went to close the door Dusty suddenly had a thought.

'Just out of interest, Franky. You wouldn't know of a young woman who's gone missing lately from your – um your – um – community, would you?'

'What community would that be?'

Dusty couldn't see Franky's expression, but she could sense the edge to his voice.

'Well, she was an Asian woman.'

'Oh, an Asian woman. So that's my community, is it? So all us Indonesians and Thais and Japanese and –'

'OK, dumb question. Forget it,' said Dusty, closing the door. 'And good luck with the horticulture.'

Chapter 20

Dusty didn't even bother with the Duck's Nuts – it was a favoured haunt of younger cops, and the last people she wanted to run into were other members of the constabulary. So she started walking, trying to recall which Irish pub Trace went to. Darwin now had five of them – not a bad effort for a tropical town, the self-proclaimed Gateway to Asia. Kitty O'Flanagan's was the oldest, though, it'd been there for at least three years.

It had the usual faux Irish bar decor: low ceilings, dark wood, stained-glass and Guinness on tap. Tuesday, apparently, was 'Tits Out Tuesday' – that ancient Celtic tradition where backpackers were invited on stage to display their mammalian wares. It was Friday night, however, and the entertainment was more conventional – a two-piece band. One piece – the guitar player – looked like a Doobie Brother who'd had one doobie too many, but Dusty was pretty sure that wasn't the only reason he looked familiar. Hadn't she'd busted him once for possession? The other piece, an Islander woman in a floral dress, had a big, gutsy voice.

Dusty ordered a vodka and tonic in a tall glass, received one in a short glass, was about to complain but decided not to, found an empty table next to the pool table and sat down. The bar was half-full, and most of the clientele were English. Dusty remembered what Trace had said about Poms: keep well away from them. She could see why, too. The bony-headed boys with their sallow skin, cropped hair and garish soccer shirts weren't particularly attractive. The girls were even worse. Much fleshier than the boys, all of them seemed to have tandoori tans, generic tattoos and clothes that were at least one size too small.

'Scandos,' Trace had said. Scandinavians. 'They're the go. Get yourself a nice clean Viking.'

Dusty's enthusiasm was starting to falter. She could be on the couch now, watching the 'I'll have what she's having' scene in *When Harry Met Sally*. It had sounded so straightforward when Trace had talked about it – *Pick up a backpacker, eh*, like picking up a slab of green cans at Liquormart. But how did she actually do it? Trace was dark and gorgeous, and maybe that was enough – she just sat there being all dark and gorgeous, the backpackers flocking around her like bats around a figtree ripe with fruit and she took her pick.

Dusty downed her drink, and ordered another vodka and tonic, a double this time. Again she asked for a tall glass. Again it came in a short. This time she did complain, and the barman – he also looked like somebody she'd arrested, a school librarian from Palmerston who'd been caught with a hard disk full of kiddie porn – gracelessly slopped the contents of the short glass into a taller one.

The two-piece had started on Bob Marley's 'Is This Love?' and the backpackers were up and dancing, singing along.

You had to hand it to the Poms, thought Dusty, they know how to have a good time. Or is it the young who know how to have a good time? All those Gen Xers, or whatever they call themselves. Or is it just everybody else, besides me, who knows how to have a good time?

The mojito, the champagne and the vodka were conspiring to affect Dusty in a way she was seldom affected – Detective Dusty Buchanon was starting to feel very sorry for Detective Dusty

The Build Up

Buchanon. What right did James have to leave her like that? Actually, what right did James have to leave her like this? In some scungy bar, watching Pommy backpackers dance badly and, in a couple of cases, openly grope each other. Two weeks it'd taken between the day he'd said, 'Dusty, I don't think this relationship is viable', to the removalist carrying his last possessions, his Radiohead CDs, from the house. Two fucking weeks! Sure, they'd had problems, what couple didn't, but he hadn't even wanted to work on them, to talk about them, to see somebody. A man who spent weeks, months sometimes, negotiating on some small point of law in a land claim, because 'I owe it to the original owners of this land'. But their relationship, forget it. It was 'irretrievable' he'd said. Dusty went to order another drink. Putting a steadying hand on the bar she said, 'A todka and vonic. I mean a vodka and tonic. A double.'

'Are you sure?' asked the paedophile.

'Of course, I'm sure. We're still in Darwin aren't we? You know, drinking capital of Australia?'

The paedophile looked over to where the bouncer, a squat Tongan, was standing, arms crossed, emphasising the preternatural size of his tattooed biceps.

'Look, perhaps you've had enough.'

Dusty leaned over the bar and grabbed him by the sleeve. 'Hey, you fucking kiddie fiddler, bring me a drink or I'll arrest you again, and this time I'll throw away the key.'

Dusty hadn't been kicked out of a bar before, but she'd seen enough heroes with broken heads to know that it was generally better to go obligingly. The squat Tongan was actually very pleasant and once they were outside Dusty congratulated him on his professionalism. She knew from experience that crowd control was never easy, especially when there was alcohol involved.

'You're really good,' she said. 'Have you ever thought of joining the police force?'

'I'm too short, eh?' he replied.

'No, everybody thinks that. Actually, there is no height requirement.'

'No bullshit?'

Dusty did a double-take as five blond men, five tall blond men, walked past. Their faces weren't bony, their skin wasn't sallow, and not one of them seemed to support Arsenal, Chelsea or Man United. She watched with disbelief as they disappeared into Kitty O'Flanagan's.

'What are the chances of you letting me back in?' asked Dusty, concentrating hard on getting her syntax right.

'I'm afraid I can't do that. You've been kicked out, eh?'

'What if I really really really promise to behave really really really well?'

'You seem nice, but I just can't. The barman reckons you called him a "effing kiddie fiddler".'

He really was a very nice bouncer, substituting 'effing' like that so as not to offend the delicate sensibility of the drunk he'd just kicked out.

'I did apologise to him.'

The bouncer shook his head. Dusty took out her wallet and flipped it open. It slipped out of her hand and onto the footpath. The Tongan retrieved it, the NT Police badge now glinting in the streetlight.

'You're a copper?' he asked, his incredulity hardly surprising.

'Undercover,' said Dusty *sotto voce*. 'And I really need to get back in there.'

'OK,' he said, taking a closer look at Dusty's badge before handing it back. 'I guess I better let you back in.'

'Square it with the barman, eh?' said Dusty, putting her wallet

The Build Up

away before straightening her dress and putting Celia's wispy bits back behind her ears where they belonged.

The Vikings were playing pool. The table Dusty had been sitting at was still empty, so she made straight for it. Out of the corner of her eye she could see two of the fleshy Pommy girls also heading in that direction. Dusty increased her pace. The Poms increased theirs. England and Australia arrived at the table simultaneously. Dusty tried her withering stare, the one she used in court when a defence lawyer asked her a moronic question. The Poms didn't seem particularly withered though. In fact one of them, the fleshier and more tandooried of the two, smiled at her and said, 'You by yourself, then?'

Dusty nodded.

'Then we might as well share?'

Dusty smiled. Might as well.

This Pommy's name was Jo. Her friend, who was actually her third cousin on her mother's side, was Fran. Both of them were nurses. They were from a town by the name of Thornton Hough (honest!), and had been in Australia for almost a year. Sydney had been brilliant. Then they'd bought a station wagon and gone up the east coast. To Byron Bay. Brilliant. Cairns. Brilliant. Cape Tribulation. Brilliant. Then some more work in Sydney. Then back in the car. South this time. To Melbourne. Brilliant. Adelaide. Not so brilliant. Uluru. Brilliant. They'd worked on a cattle station for a couple of months. Brilliant, of course. And here they were in Darwin. They'd sold their car. And were flying out to Bali in a couple of days.

'What about you Dusty? What do you do?' asked Fran.

'I . . . um . . . well . . . actually I own a pet shop.'

Of course, that was also brilliant. And got them talking about animals in general, especially the ones in Darwin that were capable of doing unspeakable things to you: the crocodiles, box jellyfish, stonefish, sharks. As one of the Vikings bent over to take his shot, his taut behind close to Dusty's face, Jo elbowed her. 'You fancy a bit of that, then?'

'Now that you mention it,' said Dusty.

'Excuse me,' said Fran, leaning over and tapping the Viking on the elbow.

'Ya?'

'I really like the position of your balls,' she said, with her best nudge-nudge, wink-wink Benny Hill delivery.

The Viking smiled. 'Ya, I think I'm in a good position to score.'

She wasn't sure if Benny Hill was big in Scandinavia, or the innuendo had been unintentional, but Dusty and her two new best friends laughed so much they almost cried.

'So what do we do, wait for them to come over?' asked Dusty, after the game had finished and the Vikings had retreated to their table.

The Poms exchanged glances. 'I think you've been in that pet shop too long, lady,' said Jo.

'This isn't a frickin' Jane Austen novel,' added Fran.

Jo stood up, smoothing her skirt, adjusting her breasts. 'C'mon ladies, grab your drinks. Let's go introduce ourselves.'

The Vikings weren't Vikings at all, but a type of European All-Sorts – two Swiss, one German, one Belgian, and a man from Luxembourg.

They were twitchers, dedicated birdwatchers who had just finished a ten-day tour of the Northern Territory. They were obviously on some sort of ornithological high, determined to celebrate, ordering jug after jug of beer.

It'd been a wonderful trip. Hot, ya, very hot, but wonderful. They'd slept beneath the stars, they'd eaten damper and drunk billy tea, they'd gone swimming in waterholes, they'd met

The Build Up

traditional Aborigines, they'd played the didgeridoo, and, most importantly, they'd twitched. *Scheisse*, had they twitched. In ten days they'd seen 157 species of birds.

Dusty knew nothing about twitching, but 157 seemed like a remarkable total and she was happy to partake in their numerous toasts.

Jo had managed to corral the cute Belgian into one corner, and if Dusty's eyes did not deceive her – quite possible given her alcohol intake – it was Jo's hand that was resting on his thigh, in impressive proximity to his groin. Her third cousin on her mother's side had wasted no time, either. She and the shorter of the Swiss had embarked on a series of arm wrestles. So far the score was one all, but Dusty suspected Fran had thrown the second bout.

That left the quiet German, the taller Swiss and the man from Luxembourg. The taller Swiss was friendly and had an impressive operatic voice – three times already he'd launched into 'Nessun Dorma' – but he was wearing a wedding ring. The man from Luxembourg was also friendly, but Luxembourg worried Dusty – was it the one next to Belgium, or was that Lichtenstein? What did she know about people from Luxembourg? What did anybody know about people from Luxembourg? It was the quiet German, then. Dusty had the sense that he, alone amongst the Vikings, may have resented their intrusion, that he'd been more than happy with the beer and bird talk. It was obvious, too, from the way the others deferred to him that he was some sort of champion bird-watcher, an über-twitcher. He was older than his companions, late thirties, and very tall – almost two metres, Dusty guessed, six foot six in the old language.

Thin but not too thin. Not a swimmer – he didn't have the shoulders for that, but there was something of the athlete about him. A skier, perhaps? A handballer? One of those people in curling who sweep the ice with a broom? In Europe there were so many more ways to be athletic.

He had Pommy-style cropped hair, and he actually wasn't as blond, as Viking-like, as she'd first thought. He was tanned – ten days peering at birds and you're bound to cop some UV– and had strong, open features. Dusty could see how some women would find him very attractive. Not her, though – she preferred men who were shorter, darker, more intense (Julien would say 'tortured') looking. Men like James. Still, this was milat-ing, not match-making. It wasn't for the rest of her life, it was for one night and maybe not even that long. She shuffled her chair closer. That he'd hardly spoken all night, in English anyway, Dusty could understand. She'd done a lot of travelling, and knew how frustrating, how exhausting, it was to try and communicate in a language that wasn't your own. Speak slowly, she reminded herself. Enunciate each syllable.

'What . . . is . . . your . . . name?'

The quiet German smiled before he said, his delivery a facsimile of Dusty's, 'My . . . name . . . is . . . Tomasz. What . . . is . . . your . . . name?'

'My . . . name . . . is . . . Dusty.'

Speak slowly. Enunciate each syllable.

'And . . . what . . . is . . . your . . . job.'

Again that smile. 'I . . . work . . . for . . . government,' he said, filling Dusty's glass from one of the many jugs that crowded the table. 'And . . . what . . . is . . . your . . . job?'

It was tortuous, but Dusty persevered, discovering that Tomasz was from Berlin. No, Dusty had never been. His parents were actually Polish, that's why he had a Polish name. No, explained Dusty, it's not my real name. It's a nickname. It was his first time in Australia, though he'd been to South America. Bali, said Dusty. Many times. Thailand. India.

The Build Up

'Do ... you ... have ... a ... girlfriend?' asked Dusty, gaining in confidence.

'Please?'

'Girlfriend? Fiancée? Wife?'

Tomasz took a while before he answered 'No.'

Professionally, Dusty would've treated this pause with suspicion. Most people are not natural liars, they need time to fabricate. Not here, however – they'd both drunk too much, it wasn't his language; the pause was innocent until proven guilty.

'And ... you ... Dusty?'

'No girlfriend,' she replied, and their eyes locked. 'No boyfriend, either.'

The bar was crowded now and the two-piece were shamelessly belting out 'Crocodile Rock'.

'You ... want ... to ... dance?' Dusty asked, finishing her beer.

Tomasz pointed at himself. 'Me?' he said, rocking his shoulders. 'Dance?'

'Yeah. You,' said Dusty, rocking her shoulders. 'Dance.'

'Sure.'

Dusty got up but her legs stayed where they were. The best thing for her to do was forget any idea of dancing, that was far too ambitious. Instead, she should stay exactly where she was, maybe even accede to the demands of gravity and rest her forehead on the beer-spattered but still surprisingly inviting-looking table.

She looked up at Tomasz. Despite his reluctance to come into focus, she had no doubt he really was sweet. And obviously not scared of her, so fuck you, Julien! Still, he was upright, she wasn't.

Then somebody else came into view – her man, the Tongan. He nodded at Dusty and Dusty knew exactly what that nod meant – they were a team now, and if things got nasty he'd be there to back her up. He really was very sweet, and not scared of her either, so fuck you again, Julien!

She couldn't let them both down, not Tomasz and the Tongan.

Again she tried to stand. Despite a tremendous wobble she managed to stay on her feet. Tomasz took her lightly by the elbow. It wasn't much, but it was enough. Stabilised, she accompanied him onto the dance floor just as 'Crocodile Rock' finished.

The Islander woman said, 'We'd like to slow it down a bit with a song that means a lot to me, "My Island Home".'

There were a few cheers, but most of the dancers drifted away. Those couples that were left immediately went into a clinch. Dusty stood there awkwardly with Tomasz, not quite sure what to do.

Her eyes half-closed, the mike cradled in both hands, the Islander started to sing. Dusty moved in closer to Tomasz, putting one hand on his shoulder and holding the other one out, fingers outstretched.

'Shall we?' she said, amazed that it didn't sound as corny as it should.

His fingers interlocked with hers and she felt his hand on the small of her back. They were dancing. Dancing slow.

Dusty leaned into Tomasz. Tomasz leaned into Dusty. Dancing close.

'Hmmm. That feels nice,' said Dusty, pressing harder against him.

'Ya,' said Tomasz.

At three o'clock, when Dusty and Tomasz walked out of Kitty O'Flanagan's, hand in hand, Mitchell Street was full of people, in varying states of intoxication, all attempting to hail non-existent taxis.

As soon as Dusty raised her hand, however, one seemed to appear from nowhere. She opened the back door. 'In you get.'

The Build Up

Tomasz jack-knifed his lanky frame in, and Dusty followed, pulling the door shut.

'Where to?' drawled the driver.

Dusty remembered what Trace had said, rule number two – get a room. Never, under any circumstances, do you take a backpacker home.

'To the nearest motel, good man,' Dusty was about to say, until she saw who the driver was. Glossy black ponytail. It was Franky Ng!

'Jesus. It's you, the horticulturist.'

Franky flicked his ponytail. 'So where we going?'

There was no way she could say 'to the nearest motel' now. Not with Franky Ng, ex-client, transporting her there. She was a sworn member of the NT's finest, not some desperate skank off for a quick shag in some seedy motel.

'Home,' she said.

'A bit more detail might help, perhaps.'

'Of course,' said Dusty, giving him her address.

Dusty leaned against Tomasz, putting her head against his arm. She felt his arm slide around her shoulder. When she woke up, they were outside her house and the dawgs were jumping up against the gate barking madly.

'How much?' asked Dusty.

'I pay,' said Tomasz, opening the door and getting out. Dusty slid along the seat.

'Wait,' said Franky.

'What is it?' said Dusty.

'You asked me about a missing girl?'

'Did I?'

'Yes. When I picked you up at Peewees. Well, there is somebody.'

Dusty knew this was important, but with all the alcohol she'd had it was hard to concentrate.

'OK, let's talk about it tomorrow.'

'I don't talk about it tomorrow. There is a girl that's gone missing. And she's a Thai girl. Working girl. She went with a man Trigger. That's it, OK?'

'OK,' said Dusty, but she knew it wasn't. When she got out of the taxi, she took a pen from her bag, and wrote two words on the back of her hand. TIE GIRL.

Franky Ng swung the taxi around, and sped off up the street.

Chapter 21

Usually, it was Dusty who complained about the dead rats, the dead birds – the dead stuff her dawgs dragged home. This morning, however, it was the dawgs who were throwing themselves against the chainwire fence, baring their teeth and barking at what Dusty had dragged home.

'Dingoes?' asked Tomasz, taking a couple of steps back.

'Not dingoes. My dawgs,' she replied proudly – it really was an impressive display of canine ferocity.

And Dusty wondered if they were actually trying to tell her something. On the dance floor, 'My Island Home' playing, Dusty only had one thought – take this man somewhere and fuck him stupid. That ardour had cooled now and Dusty was starting to think – with her brain this time – that perhaps this wasn't such a good idea. What did she know about this man? It would be much simpler – not to mention safer – if she just put him in a taxi and sent him back to his hotel. She took out her phone.

'I go hotel,' pronounced Tomasz, nervously eyeing the dingoes.

Dusty put her phone away.

'You'll come inside,' she said. 'Drink some tea. Then you can go to your hotel.'

She turned to the dawgs.

'Smithie! Wessie! Get down!'

Dusty took a still reluctant Tomasz by the hand, opened the gate, and yanked him across the threshold. Now that she was in familiar surroundings Dusty was beginning to realise exactly how inebriated she was. Her house was usually more stationary. The downstairs light switch was usually much easier to locate. As for the monkeys swinging about in her trees – she'd never noticed them before.

'Nice house,' said Tomasz, more relaxed now that the dingoes had returned, skulking, to their lairs.

'Thanks,' said Dusty, though her attention was now on the pool, and more specifically the single frangipani flower floating on its surface.

That, in itself, was not unusual. Dusty's domestic rainforest boasted two frangipani trees, and occasionally their flowers found their way into the pool. Those trees, however, had classic white and yellow *acutifolia* flowers. This flower was the less common pink and yellow *rubra*, and against the spot-lit blue of her pool, the colours glowed neon.

'How did you get there?' she said, moving closer.

Suddenly the frangipani flower became the axis around which the whole world started spinning. Backpacker, skulking dawgs, looming house – all of them spinning faster and faster. Dusty closed her eyes and sat down, hard.

'Are you OK?' asked Tomasz, touching her shoulder.

'Need to swim,' was Dusty's simple reply.

This was something she, as a police officer, would strongly advise against – Don't Mix Alcohol and Water! She knew from experience, however, that when you're spinning-out drunk, a swim is just the thing. She could see her bathers hanging limply over the verandah railing. The steps leading up to them looked precipitous, however, like something you'd only attempt with

The Build Up

ropes, crampons and a brace of Sherpas. What a disaster this night had become. Why had she gone milat-ing? Why had she drunk so much? Why had she combined the two? The best thing to do now, Dusty decided, was just to sit there, say nothing, until the backpacker went away.

'Can I go schwim?' asked Tomasz.

'Why not,' replied Dusty.

Dusty watched as Tomasz, his back towards her, shed his shirt. She continued watching as he struggled out of his jeans. She contemplated not watching as he began to pull down his boxers, but decided against it – she knew that Europeans, especially those from the more northern climes, were very comfortable with their own nudity. Tomasz walked to the edge of the pool and made as if he was going to dive in.

'Don't!' yelled Dusty.

It happened all the time with backpackers – they'd dive into swimming holes, not realising how shallow they were, and end up going home in wheelchairs.

'Sorry,' said Tomasz, turning around.

Instantly Dusty was reminded of the last time she'd had sex. They'd been out celebrating a favourable verdict and had come home, stripped off, and fucked in the pool. James had been unusually quiet. And he'd taken his time. It'd been so long since he'd taken his time. After, the doubts Dusty had been having about their relationship disappeared. The two of them were as solid as they had ever been. Two weeks later James was gone.

'I'll show you,' said Dusty, standing up, stepping out of her clothes.

She walked, naked, to the pool's edge, aware that Tomasz's bird-watching eyes were on her every step, every undulation of the way.

'The water's shallow,' said Dusty. 'Jump, don't dive.'

She did just that – jumping, sinking, clinging starfish-like to the pool's bottom, willing the water to work its customary magic, to sober her up. When she surfaced Tomasz was looking down at her, smiling.

'Water's nice,' she said.

'Noice?' repeated Tomasz.

Was her accent really that broad?

'*Wunderbar*,' she said.

That, he understood.

Two steps and he too, was in the pool. He surfaced right next to Dusty holding the frangipani flower.

'What do you call this?' he said.

'A mystery,' replied Dusty.

Tomasz handed the mystery to Dusty. 'For you,' he said.

Dusty put her arms around Tomasz's neck. She pressed her breasts against his chest. They kissed, a beery kiss. Hands on her hips, he pulled her close. She could feel it now, thudding against her thigh. Her hand went down.

'I know you said you were Polish, but Jesus!' she said.

'*Bitte?*' he said.

'Nothing,' said Dusty, wrapping her legs around him,

The thought of contraception entered her mind but it had no chance against four hundred days of involuntary abstinence and soon exited again.

Dusty guided the Viking into her.

Chapter 22

Dusty could hear the sound of splashing. Footsteps up the stairs. Then a sing-song little voice. 'Auntie? You awake, Auntie?'

She opened her eyes to a whirring fan, to a gecko scurrying across the wall.

'Auntie. Over here.'

Dusty turned her head to the side. It hurt like hell. The inside of her mouth was the bottom of a birdcage. Her tongue a foreign object.

Brown skin, brown eyes and a mini-afro slowly came into focus. It was Saskia, Trace's five-year-old daughter.

'Auntie, there's a fella in your bed.'

Dusty rolled over. A jagged pain in her head. But Saskia was right, there was a fella in her bed. Tomasz (was that his name?) was naked, sprawled out on his stomach.

There was also a smell in her bed. Of sweat. And sex. Lots of sweat. And lots of sex.

'He's a backpacker, honey,' said Dusty.

'Oh,' said Saskia, considering whether this was an adequate explanation. Obviously it was, because she quickly moved on. 'He's got a really white bottom.'

Dusty smiled. He *did* have a very white bottom. It was cute, though.

'Don't tell your mum about the backpacker, OK, Saskia? He can be our little secret.'

Saskia giggled – she loved secrets. 'OK, Auntie. Can we play that game in the pool with the rings?'

'Give me ten minutes, OK?'

'OK.'

Saskia ran back out of the room and bounced down the stairs yelling 'Mummy, Mummy, Auntie and me have got a heaps big secret!'

Dusty retrieved her Speedos from the railing and put them on. She walked gingerly down the stairs and across the pavers. She dived into the pool. Blowing bubbles from her nose, she sank to the bottom. At the shallow end she could see two sets of brown legs – Nath and Dylan, Trace's boys. When her lungs began to burn, she floated to the surface.

Trace was in a sarong, on the banana lounge, the *NT News* spread across her lap, a carton of iced coffee in her hand. Like many Top Enders – and all South Australians – she was addicted to the stuff. Saskia was standing next to her, five brightly coloured rings arranged along one forearm like oversized bangles.

'Hey, Sis,' said Dusty, levering herself out of the pool.

'So who is he?' asked Trace.

'Saskia!' said Dusty, flicking water in the traitor's direction. 'He's a German,' she giggled.

Trace shook her head. 'What did I tell you? Get a room!'

'Yeah, whatever.'

Saskia pointed to Dusty's hand. 'Mummy says you shouldn't write on yourself.'

Dusty looked down, and saw TIE written on the back of her hand. There was another word, too, but it was faded. Dusty was pretty sure it was GIRL though. Tie girl. She kept repeating the

The Build Up

words, trying to jog her memory. Suddenly it all came back. Thai not tie. Franky Ng! The missing girl!

'Sorry, Trace, but I'm going to have to cancel today.'

'That's great, that is. The kids have been looking forward to this all week.'

'I'm sorry. You can hang around here as long as you like. It's just that I've got something to do.'

'Bloody *balanda*.'

Balanda. Whitefella.

'Trace, I'll explain what I'm doing later, OK.'

'Sis, I think I may have a fair idea,' said Trace, pursing her lips, gesturing towards where her boys were playing in the water. 'Where do you reckon this mob come from?'

Chapter 23

Tomasz knew the road – it was the same one they'd taken to Uluru. But then he'd been in an air-conditioned mini-bus, and now he was in Dusty's ancient pickup, her 'ute' as she called it. Actually, he was surprised that such a car was allowed on the road – in Germany it wouldn't pass certification.

When he'd told his colleagues that he was going to Australia for his annual holiday they'd all been envious. It will be so warm! The beaches are wonderful! Australian girls are so sexy! Wiping the sweat from his brow, Tomasz wondered what his colleagues would make of this 'warm'. What would they say if he told them that you couldn't swim in the ocean at this time of the year? That there was a jellyfish, a *qualle*, that could kill a grown man. What would they make of Dusty, for that matter? Was she one of those 'sexy girls'? In the daylight he could see lines on her face he hadn't noticed the night before. She was wearing knee-length shorts, a T-shirt, sunglasses. He liked her body. It was strong, athletic, but still with a woman's curves. Yes, she definitely was one of those 'sexy girls'.

'Hot, eh?' she said.

'Yes,' he replied, remembering the impromptu swearing lessons Denise, their guide, had given them on the bus.

'Fucking oath hot,' he said.

Dusty laughed, and he liked her laugh, too. It was a big laugh. 'You know, for a Squarehead you're pretty funny?'

The Build Up

'Squarehead' he didn't understand, but 'funny' he knew, of course, and he felt pleased. In Germany he was good at making his friends laugh, but in English it was difficult.

'We'll pull into the pub at Noonamah. Have a drink.'

The Noonamah pub he liked, sitting on the side of the road like that, with nothing around it. There were huge trucks parked outside, 'road trains' she called them, and inside was just like *Crocodile Dundee*. The men sitting at the bar, all of them wearing cowboy hats, even said 'gidday' when they came in. 'Gidday,' he replied. The drinks Dusty ordered were delicious.

'What is the name of this?' he asked, tapping the glass.

'Soda, lime and bitters,' she answered.

'It is fucking oath good.'

They laughed. It'd had been an awkward start to the day. Her shaking him awake, telling him that she had to drop him off at his hotel. The dark woman by the pool who'd given him such strange looks. Then, outside the hotel, Dusty suddenly asking if he wanted to come with her.

'It's a billabong,' she'd said. 'And there'll be mobs of birds there.'

Of course, he should've said 'no'.

It'd been a crazy one night stand, to be filed away with the cockatoos and the kangaroos and other improbable examples of Australian exotica.

He'd said 'yes', though. It wasn't the birds, either, it was her. He needed to know more about her. She didn't own a pet shop, that much he knew. In her bedroom he'd glimpsed a khaki uniform hanging in the wardrobe. Was she in the army? Was she a tour guide?

Dusty bought two large bottles of water and they continued the trip south.

'You want to stop for a photo?' she said, pointing ahead where two wedgetail eagles were perched on a roadkill kangaroo.

'No,' he replied.

Ten days ago when he'd seen his first wedgetail he'd been so excited, they all had, to see one of the world's biggest eagles in the wild. It's funny, he thought, how quickly the exotic becomes familiar.

'What do you call it in German, birdwatching?' she asked.

'*Das vögelbeobachten*,' he replied.

'In Polish?'

'*Obserwowanie ptaków.*'

'Jesus, that's a mouthful. Do you know what the Aborigines call birdwatching?'

'No.'

'Dinner.'

It was a good joke and he laughed. The trip was better now, the tension between them had lessened.

'You want to play a game?' she asked.

'A game?'

'Yeah, it'll help with your English.'

'OK. I play.'

'I spy with my little eye something that starts with "a",' she said.

She was right, it was a good game for his English and they played it until they turned off the main road and onto a much rougher track. The vegetation was different here, more like woodland, and he knew the birds would be different, too. He opened his pack, and started checking his gear.

'*Das vögelbeobachten?*' she said.

He looked at her, amazed to hear German come out of her mouth. Her accent wasn't bad, either.

'Fucking oath,' he replied.

Chapter 24

'*Wunderbar*,' said Tomasz, as he stood at the edge of the billabong.

Dusty agreed. Fringed with paperbarks and pandanus plants, its surface scattered with pink-flowered water-lilies, the billabong looked like something lifted straight out of a Tourism NT brochure. There was no wind, and the hot, heavy air seemed to stifle all movement. The only sounds were animal sounds, a low insect buzz, like the crackle of a faulty electrical appliance, and the occasional bird call. Dusty had been worried that there'd be people here. Jimmy, perhaps, over his ordeal, and keen to catch more barra but there appeared to be nobody around. People had been here though – in places the grass was flattened and footprints were visible in the gelatinous mud of the banks.

Tomasz had his Bausch & Lomb binoculars out and was focusing on a nearby tree.

'Azure kingfisher,' he said reverently.

'Can I have a look?' asked Dusty.

'Yes,' he said, handing her the binoculars, taking a camera from his pack.

Beautiful binoculars, much better than the ones issued by the Force, thought Dusty, as she focused on the azure kingfisher. It was blue. It had a big beak.

'Wonderful, eh?' said Tomasz, as he took a photo.

'Truly,' replied Dusty as she trained the binoculars on the other side of the billabong. The vegetation was much thicker here, and several fallen trees, their trunks smooth and white, pierced the still water.

That must be where Jimmy saw the body, Dusty reasoned. Or thought he saw the body. Really there was only one way to check it out properly – she'd have to get wet. She passed the binoculars back to Tomasz.

'Look, a comb-crested jacana,' he said.

She drank some water from the bottle – already lukewarm – and took stock of the situation. Yes, it was a *wunderbar* billabong. Yes, Tomasz was getting very excited about the birdlife. But what the hell was she doing here? A shell-shocked vet had said there was a body. An Asian. An ex-crim taxi-driver had said there was a missing girl. An Asian. And because of that she was considering entering a potentially croc-inhabited billabong. Objectively, it was madness, but her intuition told her that it was the right thing to do. And before she'd been chucked off the McVeigh case, when she was undoubtedly the hottest detective in the NT Police Force, she had trusted her intuition, trusted it without question. What were her options? She could talk to the Big C tomorrow, persuade her to send a unit out here, a proper unit with a boat and divers and a big gun to scare away any croc that turned up, but if she managed to do that, and they subsequently found no body, then where would she be?

Dusty watched Tomasz as he twitched. The clouds had built up earlier than usual and the sky was a ceiling of cumulus. There wasn't much glare from the sun, but the humidity was ridiculous. Tomasz had taken off his shirt exposing a torso slick with sweat. He kept wiping his brow with an already sodden towel. Despite the trying conditions, he was totally absorbed in what he was doing – binoculars, camera, notebook – working quickly and

The Build Up

methodically. Dusty had seen a reference book in his bag – *The Birds Of Northern Australia* – but he didn't refer to it. Did he know all the birds, anyway? Were they all committed to memory?

Dusty was impressed – in a shoddy world that was getting shoddier, she liked to see people do things well.

'You better keep your liquids up,' she said, handing him the bottle.

'Thanks,' he said, taking a swig.

'Look, I'm going for a swim.'

'Swim? But the . . . the . . . crocodile?'

'No, none of those here, mate,' said Dusty, trying to convince herself as well.

She'd inspected the bank for reptilian tracks, but the thick vegetation on the other side made it impossible to get to all of it. And she kept thinking of what Jimmy had said. 'A boss croc called Sweetheart'. Yes, Jimmy wasn't the full quid and Sweetheart was dead and stuffed and the prize exhibit in the Darwin Museum, but you never know. Maybe it was the Son of Sweetheart he was talking about.

'I come schwimming, too,' said Tomasz.

'No, you keep on with the birdwatching.'

'I come,' he insisted, putting his twitching paraphernalia down.

Dusty went behind the ute to change into her bathers. She smiled to herself – such modesty after the intimacy of last night. When she returned Tomasz had stripped down to his boxers.

'You ready?' she said, stepping into the squelchy mud.

'Ya,' replied Tomasz as he followed her.

'Just one thing,' said Dusty, as the water lapped her knees. 'There are no crocs here, but if there was, and if one grabbed you, what you need to do is gouge it in the eyes. You got that, go for the eyes?'

Tomasz nodded.

'OK, let's swim over to that tree,' said Dusty, pointing.

The water was warm, too warm to be refreshing, and had an unpleasant metallic taste. Dusty was surprised at how well Tomasz could swim. Despite all the medals they seemed to win at the Olympics, she never thought of Europeans as being any good in the water.

They came to the first fallen tree. Dusty ducked her head under the water, opening her eyes. The water was much clearer than she'd thought it would be, and the smooth trunk disappeared into the depths. The next tree was much bigger, its branches diverging in all directions.

'What are you looking for?' asked Tomasz when she came back up.

'Nothing, really. Just looking,' she said, as if this was an entirely normal way to spend a Saturday afternoon in the Antipodes.

'Is it that?' he said, pointing towards the back of the tree.

Dusty could see nothing except intertwining branches. 'What?'

'Fishing line,' he said.

Dusty breast-stroked closer to the branch. She could see it now – a piece of fishing line caught around a twig.

She tested the line, feeling the weight on the end. Taking a deep breath she dived, following the line down. At first all she could see was a blur of colour. As she went deeper it became a naked body. Bloated, distorted, but a body. A woman. A blue and white lure caught in her hair. Dusty went deeper. An engine block wired to her ankles. And a white-handled knife in her vagina.

Her breath finished, Dusty surfaced.

'Tomasz, you better go back?'

The Build Up

'Why?'

'There's something down there you shouldn't see.'

Before she could stop him, Tomasz had duckdived.

When he broke the surface there was surprise in his face, but not the shock, the terror you would expect from somebody who had witnessed such a terrible sight.

'I should've told you before,' said Dusty. 'I'm a copper.'

'A copper?'

'I'm in the police force. I'm a detective.'

Tomasz smiled.

'What's so funny?'

'So am I.'

The clouds had darkened now, especially to the north, where they were inky black and host to thin strikes of lightning. It was even stiller than before, and an eerie light suffused the lagoon, making all the colours, the pink of the water-lilies, the green of the pandanus leaves, look rich and saturated.

'Then you can help me drag her back to shore,' said Dusty.

'You definitely can't do that,' said Tomasz.

'What?' said Dusty.

'It's a crime scene – you must leave the body exactly where it is.'

'How come you're suddenly speaking perfect English?'

'It's your fault,' he said.

'What do you mean?

'Vot . . . is . . . your . . . name?' he said, mimicking Dusty's Colonel Klink delivery of last night.

'I didn't say "vot".'

'Yes, you did.'

'So you've been taking the piss all this time?'

'Once I started speaking like that, it was difficult to change.'

Dusty felt as if she should've been outraged – Tomasz had duped her, pretended he was something he wasn't but actually she was relieved. Communication was going to be so much less painful now.

'What sort of copper are you, anyway?' she asked.

'Forensics.'

'I should've guessed,' said Dusty. 'Sanctity of the crime scene and all that bullshit.'

'We must leave her here.'

'A croc might eat her,' said Dusty.

'You said there wasn't any crocodiles!'

Maybe, he's right, thought Dusty. Maybe it is better to leave the body where it is. Sanctity of the crime scene and all that bullshit.

'OK, you win. We leave her there.'

As they swam back to the bank, Dusty did the maths. Darwin was four hours drive from the billabong and it was at least one and a half hours until there was phone service. It would take a Crime Scene Unit at least six, probably more like seven, hours before it got here. Dusty didn't want to leave the body unattended but what choice did she have? She couldn't leave Tomasz to look after it. She believed him when he said he was a copper, but he was also a backpacker in a foreign country and there was a murderer out there somewhere – it was an unacceptable risk.

The lightning was now accompanied by the occasional crack of thunder. 'We should take photos,' said Tomasz, when they were back on the bank.

Dusty knew what he was talking about – the footprints in the mud, the tyre-tracks, all valuable forensic evidence that would be lost if it rained. But this was the Build Up, all tease and no show – there would be no rain. Besides, Dusty was anxious to get going, she wanted the Crime Scene Unit here as soon as possible.

The Build Up

'It won't rain,' she said. 'Not for a couple of weeks.'
Tomasz looked doubtful, his eyes on the darkening sky.
Dusty opened the door of Beastie Boy. 'C'mon, Squarehead. Let's get out of here.'

Chapter 25

As Dusty drove, they talked.

Tomasz's English wasn't just good, it was very good.

He said it was a result of watching so many Hollywood movies, but Dusty knew it took more than movies to learn a language – like all good Germans he'd done some serious study.

'Tell me, Tomasz, how'd you become a walloper?'

Every now and then she'd throw in some slang, just to keep him on his toes.

'A what?'

'Old-fashioned word – means a policeman.'

When two coppers got together, no matter their nationality, this question would inevitably come up.

'In English, it's difficult.'

'Don't give me that.'

Tomasz proceeded to tell her how he'd become a walloper. His parents had emigrated from Poland to give their three children a better education. Tomasz had always wanted to be in the police, but he'd gone along with his parents' wishes and had become an engineer. But when his father had died, he'd joined the police. He'd been in forensics for three years now.

'And you?' asked Tomasz, as Dusty turned back onto the highway.

She'd been a water-polo player, destined to represent Australia

The Build Up

at the Olympics. At fourteen she was a member of the national junior team. But she didn't get any better. She trained and trained and trained but it made no difference: all the girls she used to beat regularly were now literally leaving her in their wake. Suddenly school was finished and she had no idea what she should do. She'd given so much to water polo, she mistakenly thought that it would look after her. A friend had suggested that she give the police force a go. Why not, she had nothing better to do? During the physical examination she casually mentioned an old knee injury. The pig of a doctor considered this a serious liability; she failed. Determined now to become a copper she re-applied in the Territory, this time eschewing any mention of injuries, knee or otherwise, and had been there ever since.

She'd been telling this story for years, but something in her wanted to go further now, wanted to tell the Tomasz the truth.

'You want to know why I really became a copper?' she asked.

There was no reply. Despite the unforgiving suspension of Beastie Boy, the lack of space and the feral smell, a mixture of stale sweat and fecund mud, Tomasz had managed to fall asleep. In repose, his eyes closed, Dusty thought he looked beautiful, angelic almost. She felt a huge surge of affection for this man she hardly knew. I like him, she admitted to herself. This was unexpected. He was a backpacker she'd milat-ed to prove Julien wrong. 'Like' wasn't supposed to come into it.

'Hey, guess what? I like you,' she said softly.

The sound of it was thrilling. It's been so long since she'd felt like this about a man, let alone said it aloud. Actually, she wasn't sure if she'd ever said it aloud. James and her hadn't been big on declarations of love, of like, of any affection, really, neither of them willing to go beyond a half-mocking 'you're OK, I guess' or 'you'll do'. 'Cheap romanticism' James had called it, but now she wondered if it hadn't been more about power – to admit any deeper emotion was to admit a weakness.

'Hey, guess what, I like you,' she repeated, louder, more emphatically, this time.

Beep! Beep! Beep!

Dusty's phone was back in range.

Tomasz woke with a start. *'Wo bin ich? Wo bin ich?'* he said, panic in his voice.

'It's OK,' said Dusty, squeezing his hand. 'Remember me?'

Tomasz smiled. 'Ya. It's OK. I had an *alpdrücken* . . . a nightmare. The poor girl, you know.'

'I know,' said Dusty.

'Can you let me know what happens?'

'Of course,' said Dusty and she suddenly had a thought. Although she kept thinking of him as a backpacker, Tomasz was a copper, like her, with limited holidays and a job to get back to.

'When are you going back to Germany?'

'Today is the sixth?'

'No. The seventh, I think,' said Dusty checking her phone. 'Yes, the seventh.'

'Shit. I fly back tomorrow.'

'What time?'

'Ten in the morning.'

'Fuck!' said Dusty.

She liked him and he was going away. Serves you right for liking somebody, Dusty told herself. But there was something else to consider. Her plan had been to turn around and drive back to the billabong as soon as she'd contacted HQ. This wasn't possible. She couldn't take Tomasz back with her.

Dusty pulled onto the side of the road, dialled and asked to be put through to the duty sergeant.

The Build Up

'Sergeant Kirk here,' came the gruff reply.

'Jesus, Kirky, what are you doing working on a weekend?'

'Last one left. Everybody else is down there on the McVeigh case.'

'I found that body in the billabong,' said Dusty, trying to sound as nonchalant as possible.

'Jimmy's gook?'

'Yes, the Asian woman.' Already Dusty was feeling protective. 'I'll need a unit down here as quick as possible.'

'No chance.'

'Don't shit me.'

'Like I've told you, everybody's on the McVeigh case.'

'You ready for a few tricky questions, Kirky?'

'What do you mean?'

'Like how you went all the way down there and came back with nothing.'

'You? "We", you mean?'

'Yeah, well I went back. I redeemed myself, Kirky.'

Kirky belched. Whether it was an indication of his dyspepsia or his displeasure, Dusty didn't care.

'You're fucking unbelievable, you are?' he said.

'Just sort it, big fella,' said Dusty.

A click, and she was on hold, listening to Norah Jones.

Two whistling kites wheeling high in the sky had captured Tomasz's attention.

'Can I take a photo?' he asked, camera already in his hands.

'It's a free world,' replied Dusty.

Tomasz smiled, and opened the door.

It took the sergeant three songs to get back to Dusty.

'John's just finishing up at the McVeigh scene. He can get there in less than two hours.'

'That wasn't so hard, was it?'

Dusty considered what to do next. She could leave Tomasz here, let him hitchhike back to Darwin. She looked over to where he was standing, intent on the sky. His T-shirt, once white, was sweat-stained, his khaki shorts muddied. What were the chances of him getting a ride on this lonely piece of road? As if to emphasize this, one of the kites emitted a mournful call. No, she couldn't leave him here.

'Come on, Tomasz, let's go.'

An hour later, and they were in a truck-stop café. The same smell of greasy food they all seemed to have, the same bleary-eyed truckers slouched at plastic tables, watching *Australia's Funniest Home Videos* on a wall-mounted television.

Dusty flashed her badge. 'I need a favour from one of you blokes.'

It was an awkward parting, standing in the truck parking area, the air wreathed with diesel fumes, the driver keen to hit the road.

They hugged chastely.

'Keep in touch,' said Dusty.

'I will,' said Tomasz, before he climbed up into the cabin.

It was only as she watched the truck disappear down the Track that she realised that she didn't have his number.

Chapter 26

It had been the worst feeling in John Goode's life, sitting in the courtroom, watching that bastard Gardner walk. He would never forget the look on the faces of McVeigh's family, her mother especially. He'd let them down. They all had. Second chances didn't come along very often in his line of business. In fact, it'd taken nine years as a forensic scientist for one to appear. And he wasn't going to muck it up. He'd taken extraordinary care with each sample – frequently changing his disposable gloves, sealing the bags, double-checking labels. It was looking promising: there was blood that could be Gardner's, there were hairs that could be Gardner's. It was looking promising.

'Could be the old fella's,' a junior constable remarked.

'Don't think so,' had been John's reply.

The old fella had done well.

'It just looked different, you know,' he'd told the police. 'When you've spent your whole life out here peering at dirt looking for gems you know when it's been interfered with.'

He'd marked the place on his map and driven to the nearest station. If only all people treated a crime scene with this sort of respect, thought John. Especially coppers.

John bagged and labelled the last piece of evidence – an empty chewing gum packet, and checked his watch. 3.20pm. The game started at eight. For the first time since he'd received the phone call – 'They've found Dianna McVeigh' – he could relax. He'd make his fifteen-year-old son's basketball game after all, a promise he'd made at the start of the season.

The stocky figure of Senior Sergeant Barry appeared at the tape. A thirty-year veteran of the Force, he had one of those emotionless, seen-it-all faces.

'Mate, you're not going to like this,' he said gruffly.

'Don't tell me it's another job,' John said.

'Afraid so. A dead 'un.'

'Darwin?' John asked hopefully.

'No such luck. Place by the name of . . . actually, I don't know if it's even got a fucking name. Near where those vets set up their camp. Up the Track and then east, towards Kakadu. I've marked it on the map for you.'

Inside the van John rang his son's mobile, but there was no answer. He left a message. It sounded pathetic, of course. What could he say? He'd promised and now he was breaking that promise.

He'd thought about quitting this job many times before, but now he knew he had no choice. Dead 'uns had wrecked his relationship with his wife and now they were wrecking his relationship with his boy as well.

One more, and he'd quit.

John pulled out of the crime scene, popped a couple of No-Doz, washed them down with some tepid Nescafé and adjusted the air-conditioner vent so that the cold air blasted his face. Half an hour later, as he turned onto the Track, the rain started. It didn't last long – only a few minutes – but it was heavy, water sluicing the windscreen. Sixty kilometres of bitumen and he turned right onto another dirt road.

He assumed the fresh tyre tracks belonged to Detective Buchanon – they were a good match for her early-model Holden

The Build Up

ute. As it had only rained forty or so minutes ago he reasoned that she couldn't be too far ahead, either. His logic proved impeccable – he arrived at his destination to find the ute with the detective inside. He pulled up alongside, wound down the window.

'Let me guess,' he said. 'You've been here about twenty minutes.'

'Sherlock, you've done it again,' said Dusty, flashing a smile.

'Elementary, Detective Buchanon.'

'How'd you go down there?' asked Dusty, as she got out of the ute.

'Got some good stuff,' said John, opening the door. 'We'll get that bastard this time.'

'Which bastard would that be?'

'Don't tell me you still don't think Gardner did it?'

'Keeping an open mind, John.'

John felt sorry for Dusty – nobody liked to be taken off a case, especially a big one like the McVeigh case – but he could understand the commander's decision.

'So what we got here?'

'Asian. Twenties. Maybe younger. Homicide, I reckon.'

'Just the way I like them,' said John. 'Where is she?'

'Still in the water where I found her.'

'Floating?'

'No, got a pair of iron Nikes on.'

'Not like you, Detective Buchanon, following protocol like that.'

Dusty ignored that.

'Water's gorgeous by the way,' she said, as if she was contemplating a quick dip at Bondi Beach.

'Can't wait,' said John, undoing the buttons on his shirt. '*Crocodylus porosus?*'

'None that have made themselves known.'

Dusty stripped down to her bathers, John to his underpants.

'Never have pegged you as a Calvin Klein sort of guy,' said Dusty.

'Fake,' said John. 'Bought them on the street in Bali.'

This is better, thought John. More like the relationship we used to have, before the McVeigh case came and fucked everything up. He followed Dusty as she breast-stroked across the billabong, stopping next to where a fallen gumtree angled into the water. The sun had dropped behind the stand of paperbarks and the resident frogs were now in full chorus.

'She's right under us,' said Dusty, treading water. 'You can't miss her.'

'Well, I better see what we've got,' said John.

He filled his lungs with air and dived.

'Not pretty, eh?' said Dusty when he'd resurfaced.

'Right under us?'

'That's right.'

'I couldn't see anybody,' said John.

'Bullshit!'

'I'm not joking, I couldn't see anybody.'

Dusty went under, surfacing soon after.

'Somebody's taken her!' she said.

John checked his watch, did the calculations. He couldn't get there in time for the start of the game, but he could make the last quarter, definitely the award ceremony.

'Dusty, I'm heading back to Darwin.'

'No, you're not. Somebody's taken her!'

John was already swimming, freestyle this time. Reaching the bank he quickly dressed, got back in the van, started the engine and put his foot down.

Chapter 27

In the fading light Dusty scoured the edge of the billabong for clues. The footprints, the tyre tracks – all the gross evidence that Tomasz had wanted to photograph – had been obliterated by the unexpected downpour. There'd be other evidence – a thread caught on a twig, a smidgen of blood on a leaf – but this wasn't as obvious, it had to be found. Unfortunately, this had never been Dusty's forte. She lacked what they called in the business 'an eye' – acuity of vision, attention to detail, whatever it took to pick up those clues. Early on in her career this had worried Dusty greatly. Without 'an eye', how would she ever become the gun Dee she was determined to be? It hadn't taken her long to realise that in the real world, away from books and television, there were no supercops. Police always worked in teams – one cop's weakness was another cop's strength.

By nightfall she'd found nothing. The thought occurred to her that she could sleep in Beastie Boy, continue the search at daybreak. She dismissed it, though. Dusty wasn't particularly superstitious, but she was alone and she was unarmed and somewhere, perhaps nearby, there was a murderer.

There was only one option: she climbed back into Beastie Boy and once more headed towards Darwin. As she drove she tormented herself with 'if onlys'.

If only I'd left Tomasz here.

If only there was mobile reception.

If only we'd taken the body with us.

That out of the way, Dusty moved onto the stuff she could do something about. She'd have to report John, of course – you just can't abandon a crime scene like that. He'd probably lose his job and, you know what, he deserved to. Dusty liked John and considered him to be one of the better scientific officers she'd worked with but today, as the Yanks would say, he'd been out of line. Way out of line.

Dusty stopped at the same truck stop where she'd left Tomasz. She ate some greasy food, drank some execrable coffee, and watched *Australia's Funniest Home Videos*. An obese truck-driver wearing a T-shirt that said 'I beat anorexia' stopped at her table, leering at her.

'You're not looking for a bit of fun are you, sweetheart?' he said.

'Sweetheart?' questioned Dusty. She'd avoided the mirror during her recent visit to the rest rooms but had no doubt how she must look – frightful.

Against her better judgement, she said, 'What did you have in mind?'

'Bit of slap and tickle in the Kenworth? Got some whiz too, if that's your thing.'

He obviously thought that his combination of forthrightness and amphetamines was going to be a winning one, because he was now holding a hefty bunch of keys.

'Look, I'll keep it in mind,' she said.

'Fair enough,' said the ex-anorexic as he waddled off.

Dusty finished her coffee, paid the bill and hit the road again. Just after Pine Creek a nimbus of light appeared in the distance. It could've been many things – one of those enormous cattle trucks, shooters spotlighting for roos – but Dusty's experience

The Build Up

told her one thing, MVA – motor vehicle accident. Half-an-hour later and her experience was vindicated. Portable spotlights blazing. Police cars. An ambulance.

She slowed down, coming to a stop next to a young blond-haired constable in a fluoro green vest. She'd seen him around, wondered what a surfer type was doing in the Force, but didn't know his name.

'What's up?' she said, winding down the window.

'Bad news, Detective Buchanon.'

Dusty was impressed – despite her bedraggled state he'd recognised her.

'Accident?'

'One of our own, I'm afraid.'

It seemed a strange choice of phrase, especially coming from the surfer cop. One of our own, I'm afraid. Like something out of an old English movie.

'John Goodes.'

Dusty was out of the car and running. She could see the forensics van on its back, a dead creature, wheels in the air.

She could see the kangaroo, its broken grey body splotched with blood. She could smell it, too.

An ambulance, the colours gaudy under the spotlights, the back door open. Two ambulance officers sliding in a stretcher.

Fontana's there. He sees Dusty. Shakes his head.

Chapter 28

Tomasz walked quickly across the concrete expanse of Alexanderplatz, looking up to where the Tele-Spargel pierced the low grey sky. Even though Berlin had been re-unified for seventeen years now he still felt a tiny frisson when he was in the old East Germany, like he was trespassing a forbidden land.

He passed the huge polished stone statues of Marx and Engel. They looked so avuncular, those two, it didn't seem possible that so much havoc could've been wreaked in their name. He crossed the river and turned into a small street, stopping in front of a modest shop front. '*Entwickler der Fotos*', said the sign. Developer of Photos.

'Tomasz, good to see you,' said Herr Franz as Tomasz entered his musty shop.

'You, too,' Tomasz replied.

'Have you been away?' inquired Herr Franz.

Tomasz smiled to himself – such old-fashioned courtesy. Herr Franz was the only one in the shop, he'd developed the photos, he knew exactly where Tomasz had been.

'*Australien*,' replied Tomasz.

'Ah, *Australien*,' repeated Herr Franz pinching the bridge of his nose, and for a second Tomasz thought he was going to continue, to reveal some personal connection with *Australien*, perhaps a relative who had immigrated there after the war or a

The Build Up

long-held desire to go there himself, but he said nothing, instead bending down to retrieve a bundle of envelopes from under the counter.

'Do you want to check them now?' inquired Herr Franz. 'While you're still in the shop?'

'No. I'll wait,' said Tomasz.

Herr Franz smiled at him with complicity; he too understood the pleasure in waiting. With the envelopes clutched against his chest, Tomasz headed up the street towards Hackescher Market. The dingy café, as usual, was empty. The coffee, as usual, took forever.

When finally it came he stirred in a sachet of sugar and took a sip. Now that the ritual had been observed he could open the first envelope. The photos, he knew, would be in chronological order; Herr Franz was meticulous like that. The first photo was taken just out of Darwin – a wedgetail eagle atop a roadkill kangaroo. Not a great photo, he had not yet become accustomed to the harsh lighting in Australia, but, oh, what an animal! He remembered how blasé he'd become towards the end of his trip, 'Oh, just another wedgetail.' But sitting in this café, surrounded by thousands of years of settlement, of civilisation, he was almost overwhelmed by the bird's beauty – the magnificent talons, the feathered legs, the cruel hook of the beak crimson with blood. The next photo showed the same bird in flight, its mighty wings outstretched.

'Wingspan of up to two and a half metres in a mature wedgie,' he remembered the guide saying.

Only later did he realise that a 'wedgie' was a wedgetail eagle, that Australians were averse to too many syllables in their words. What had Dusty called her sunglasses again? That's right – 'sunnies'.

And so it went on. Photo after photo, bird after bird. Occasionally the avian parade would be interrupted by a landscape photo – an obligatory shot of Uluru at sunset, for example – or even less frequently, a portrait, one of his fellow twitchers or Jess, the young Aborigine who had taken them on the bush-tucker tour. People, as subjects, didn't interest Tomasz much, though. Why bother, when there are birds around?

He opened the last envelope, took out the contents and placed them on the table. The photo on top was of a flock of magpie geese, silhouetted against a red-streaked sky, taken in Darwin's Botanic Gardens at dusk. This was the last photo he'd taken that day. After that they'd all gone down to the pub to drink beer, then to another pub to drink more beer, and finally to the pub where'd met Dusty.

He removed the magpie geese and she was there, standing at the edge of the billabong, unaware that his camera was on her. She was just like he remembered her and nothing like he remembered her. She was more beautiful and less beautiful. More desirable and less desirable. He could feel his penis rising.

He slammed the table hard with his fist. The rat-faced waiter was suddenly at the table, seemingly having appeared from nowhere.

'*Bitte?*' he inquired.

His eyes took in the photo and he smiled at Tomasz. 'Your wife?' he asked.

Covering the photo with his hand, Tomasz said '*Nein,*' before ordering another coffee.

Throw it into the bin now, Tomasz told himself. Throw the *ficken* photo into the *ficken* bin. No, even better, throw it off the bridge. He imagined Dusty floating down the river, gently undulating with the current. Even better still, put a match to her. Right there under Herr Marx and Herr Engels would be a good place.

Instead he put the photo into the inside pocket of his jacket.

The Build Up

The next photo of the azure kingfisher, was the best photo he'd taken in twenty years of photographing birds. He picked it up, holding it up to the light. Everything about it – the focus, the composition – was perfect. It was the photo that would at last win him the Verga, the award that he had coveted for so long.

Tomasz's mobile rang. He answered it.

'Tomasz, where are you?' demanded Donia, his wife.

'In a café.'

'We have an appointment at the IVF clinic!'

'At three, you said.'

'What time do you think it is now?'

Tomasz checked his watch – it was 3.10.

'I'll be there in ten minutes,' he said, though he knew it would take at least twenty minutes to get there.

As he went to put the photo back on the pile he noticed something. In the background, amongst the foliage, there was a face. An artefact, he thought. A trick of the light. Later at home, however, when he examined the photo with a magnifying glass, he changed his mind – it was a face. Somebody had been there, concealed in the vegetation, watching them.

'Tomasz, what are you doing in there?' Donia asked.

'Nothing,' he said, putting the photos away.

Was it the murderer?

Chapter 29

When he'd left Darwin, throwing as much as would fit into the back of Spida's RAV4 Cruiser, Trigger's intention had been to head bush, into Australia's vast outback. Apparently, there was a resources boom. He'd get a job in a mine – the Pilbara, Coober Pedy, Roxby Downs, somewhere like that – and lie low for a while. As soon as he'd seen that sign, though, Sydney 3931 km, he knew that wasn't going to happen. That prick-tease of a city had her titties out and was flashing him some serious gash.

When he thought about it, Sydney made sense. Turn up in any country town and straightaway they're into you – wanting to know who you are, where you came from. In Sydney, nobody gives a fuck.

He'd done it in less than forty hours. Katherine. Tennant Creek. Mount Isa. Longreach. Moree. Maitland. And, last night, rolling over the bridge – only an idiot would take the tunnel on their first visit to Sydney in ten years – and onto the Cahill Expressway, looking over to his left, the harbour and the quay and Luna Park and the Opera House all seemed to be saying 'Welcome home, Trigger Tregenza'.

All that shit at the vets' camp was the kick up the arse he needed to finally get out of Darwin. There'd been nothing on the radio or in the papers about what had happened there. Maybe

The Build Up

those army boys had done exactly what Trigger had hoped they'd do. Tidied the whole thing up. Maybe.

He'd driven around for a while, just taking it all in, Kings Cross, Oxford Street, then past the Sydney Cricket Ground and Randwick Racecourse and it really started to feel like home. Over the hump and down into the valley of Coogee, past the old apartment on Dolphin Street, then onto the beach. Three in the morning and they were staggering out of the pubs, the Palace at one end, the Coogee View at the other. Trigger sat in the car, taking it in. Jesus, he saw more glamours in five minutes than he'd seen in Darwin in the last ten years.

He drove up Beach Street and turned left, past Wylies Baths, and pulled up on the headland as the sun came up.

He could see now what a disgrace the RAV4 was, the floor awash with Coke bottles, Macca wrappers, hastily scanned newspapers. And after two days in the car he knew that he stank. A shower, thought Trigger. I need a shower. It was then he realised, again, that he'd been too long in Darwin. There, in front of him was the Pacific fucking Ocean and he was thinking about showers. Not the Arafura with its box jellyfish and its crocs, that just lay there like some dud root. This was the Pacific, the heaving, swirling, crashing, foaming, booming Pacific.

He rummaged around in the back until he found his Speedos. A towel. And then down the stairs to Wylies Baths. A man-made rockpool, the water was replenished twice a day by the tide. The Swans had done a lot of their recovery work here, and Trigger would also come here just to hang out, drink coffee, read the papers, check out the talent.

He threw two dollars onto the plate, and walked through the turnstile and onto the deck, perched high above the rocks on legs of wood. They'd spruced it up a bit – apparently it was now heritage-listed – but it was still the same magical place. To the left he could see the golden arc of Coogee Beach; the headland with the memorial to the victims of the Bali bombing; Clovelly jutting out.

It was low tide, the water inside the pool calm. With the early morning sun sparking off it, it looked like the world's biggest gem, fifty yards of princess-cut diamond.

'Hey, Trigger!'

Tall fit-looking bloke. In his sixties, maybe. Towel around his neck. Speedos and goggles dangling from his hand. Face familiar but Trigger couldn't quite place him. He must've seen he was struggling, because he helped him out. 'Joe. Joe Mason. Nathan's father.'

Of course. Cricketer. Fast bowler. Played a few Tests for Australia. His son, Nathan, was the fitness adviser for the Swans.

'Good to see you, Joe,' said Trigger, conscious of how he must look, how he must smell. Jesus, he didn't expect to be running into old mates as soon as he arrived.

'Last time I heard you were heading north,' said Joe.

'Darwin.'

'Back for a visit, then?'

'Back for good,' said Trigger, and the words sounded so good he wanted to say them again, shout them. Trigger Tregenza is back for good!

'So what business you in now?'

'Got a few options,' said Trigger, and why not, he did, didn't he?

'Water's beautiful,' said Joe. 'Be seeing you around a bit, then?'

'You bet,' said Trigger.

Into the changerooms and into his Speedos. Down the stairs and to the pool's edge and into the water. Joe's right: it's beautiful. Cold but beautiful. He can feel the Pacific Ocean work its magic, all the sweat, all the shit, more than ten years' accretion of gunk, washing away.

Chapter 30

'Sis, you're just paranoid,' counselled Trace, as they sat together at a corner table in the staff café, on Dusty's first day back at work after a week off sick. It'd started when she'd got home from the hospital after Fontana had finally persuaded her that there was nothing else she could do – the scratch in her throat, the pressure against her eardrums, the nugget of pain behind the right temple. She'd dosed herself with vitamin C, with echinacea and zinc, with chemist's own brand cold-eze, with just about everything she'd found in the cabinet, but it'd been to no avail, the microbes had found an ideal host – run-down, stressed, sleep-deprived – and had no intention of moving on until they'd done some serious partying.

'I'm not paranoid,' said Dusty.

She could tell by the way they looked at her, or didn't look at her, by the way they talked to her, or didn't talk to her, by their general behaviour towards her, that various other members of the Northern Territory Police Force, thought that she, in some way, was responsible.

'They reckon I killed him.'

'Dusty, he's not even dead!'

Depending on which medical professional you talked to, and in the last week Dusty, despite her sickness, had managed to talk to all of them, he either had 'some chance of pulling through', a 'battler's chance of making it' or 'a 10 percent chance of survival'.

'He's a fighter, that John,' added Trace.

Which, thought Dusty, was what everybody always says in this situation. Always a fighter, never a quitter.

'And it's not as if it was your fault, Dusty.'

Which was also manifestly true. It wasn't Dusty's fault that John chose to use his mobile while driving at excessive speed – 150 km/hr according to the MVA guys – at night, while fatigued, in an area where kangaroos were demonstrably rife.

Back at her desk Dusty focused on the mountain of work she had to get through. A proper mountain, too – something Himalayan or Andean, not some pitiful Kosciuszko. Fontana arrived, wearing chinos and an open neck shirt, looking and smelling, as usual, freshly scrubbed. He really was a splendidly deodorised example of how to maintain personal hygiene despite trying weather conditions.

'You're back,' he said.

'It would appear so,' replied Dusty. 'You've obviously had a busy week?'

'Homicide-wise?'

Business, during the Build Up, was famously slow. It wasn't also called the Suicide Season for nothing. Even if somebody was keen on a spot of homicide, the only person they seemed to muster enough energy to do away with was themselves.

Dusty nodded. Homicide-wise.

'A couple of hangers, that's all.'

Men – why are they so slow on the uptake? Dusty asked herself. The implication – which any woman would have picked up on – was that Fontana must've been busy because he hadn't dropped in, he hadn't called, he hadn't even texted Dusty during her absence.

The Build Up

While Dusty was a strong independent woman who could look after herself, any token of support from a long-time colleague would've been welcome.

She opened her mouth to say something when Flick appeared, wearing a navy blue suit with a skirt that was just above the knee. In her hand, a report.

'You better?' she asked Dusty.

'Much better, thanks,' said Dusty. 'Is that the McVeigh autopsy?'

Flick nodded.

'Can I have a look?'

'Sure,' said Flick, handing Dusty the report, showing no hint of proprietorship.

'Who did it?' Dusty asked.

'Dr Singh.'

Dusty smiled as she thought of the diminutive Dr Singh, he of the cricket statistics and the appalling knock-knock jokes. The smile vanished, however, as she read his report. Even after eleven years in the police force, four of those in Homicide, a lifetime of reading *True Crime* and watching not-so-true cop shows, of being exposed to the full range of atrocious human behaviour, Dusty still experienced a tremor of shock, of disbelief, of disgust – how could one human being possibly do this to another?

Dusty looked up at Flick, tears in her eyes. Flick reached into her pocket and pulled out a handy pack of tissues, passing them to her colleague.

A cop moment, a chick moment, a person moment. Dusty wasn't sure what it was, but she suddenly felt a solidarity with this woman she'd disliked for so long; together they could work to put the man who had done this, who had carved this poor girl up like sashimi, where he belonged.

'DNA not back yet?'

'Tomorrow or the next day, they reckon. I've upped surveillance on Gardner, of course – bastard's likely to do a runner.'

Dusty's desk phone rang. It was the Big C.

'I believe we had a meeting at nine.'

'Shit!'

She went to give the tissues back but Flick held up her hand.

'You might need them,' she said.

As Dusty hurried up the corridor she wondered what Flick meant, what Flick knew.

That image of her tete-a-tete with the Big C under the poinciana tree was still as vivid, as crimson, as the flowers on the tree themselves.

Chapter 31

The Big C, Dusty noticed, had been doing some rearranging. The management texts were no longer arranged vertically but stacked horizontally. The jug of water had gone and the doily was now host to an oil burner. Thankfully, it wasn't lit – in Dusty's opinion there was nothing quite as inessential as essential oil. On the wall behind the Big C was a gilt-framed certificate on which Dusty could make out the words 'Master of Business Administration'.

'You've had some solid outcomes, Detective,' said the Big C tapping a manila folder on the desk.

Solid outcomes? wondered Dusty. What did that mean in the real world?

'Drug Squad. Sex Crimes. Homicide. You've certainly been around.'

Unlike you, thought Dusty.

'Well, I've had a keen interest in all aspects of policing.'

'Seen some shocking things, I guess.'

Unlike you, thought Dusty.

'The usual stuff.'

'Policing is a very stressful job.'

No shit, Sherlock? The Big C was starting to really annoy Dusty – a person had been killed, most probably murdered, and all she could do was state the obvious.

'I've drawn up a plan of action,' said Dusty, taking the sheet of A4 from her briefcase, placing it in front of the Big C. 'I realise we're stretched for resources at the moment, so I've kept it pretty skinny.'

The Big C, however, only gave it a cursory glance.

'As you may know, we sent a team down to the billabong and unfortunately they weren't able to find any corroborative evidence.'

A team? Fontana had told her all about the 'team' – it comprised one person, and that person was Crouch. Everybody knew that as far as forensics went, as far as just about everything went, except winning the football tipping, Crouch was crap.

'There *was* a body there,' Dusty stated.

'I've had people scour the missing person reports, and they haven't found anybody matching your description.'

'There *was* a body there.'

'I'd like you to see the counsellor. Standard procedure after an event like this.'

'Are you saying I didn't see that body?'

'No, I'm saying I'd like you to see the counsellor.'

Dusty hadn't mentioned Tomasz to anybody, but maybe now was the right time to throw him into the mix.

'I wasn't the only one who saw her.'

'Go on,' said the Big C.

'There was somebody else with me at the billabong, a man by the name of Tomasz.'

The Big C picked up a pen.

'Can you spell that for me, please?'

'T-o-m-a-s, then c-h I think, but it might be z.'

'You think? First name?'

'That is the first name.'

'Surname, then?'

The Build Up

'I'm not sure.'

'Phone number?'

'No.'

'Address?'

'No. Look, he was a backpacker. I sort of picked him up at the pub, and then I got the tip-off from a taxi driver, so I took him with me the next day to check it out, but now he's gone back to Germany.'

The Big C put her pen down.

'Detective, a decision has been made to take you out of Homicide.'

Dusty looked at her superior, not quite comprehending what she was saying – this meeting was about the body in the billabong, not her career.

'As you know, with the increase in DNA work there's been an added emphasis on the storage and cataloguing of forensic exhibits so we'd like you to lend a hand there for a while.'

'Work in the Shed?'

'That's right.'

'But that would mean going back to uniform.'

'That's right.'

The Big C's mouth continued to open and shut, sounds issuing forth, but all Dusty could do was focus on the scalloped edge of the doily, in the hope that it would offer an explanation, any explanation, as to what was happening.

Before the McVeigh case she was red-hot, acknowledged as one of the best detectives in the Force, the Frontbum Most Likely. From that to working in the Shed. It was a spectacular fall and Dusty didn't know how it happened. She knew the starting point – Frontbum Most Likely – and the endpoint – busted back to uniform – but couldn't start at the former and arrive at the latter.

It's not possible, Dusty assured herself. This can't be happening.

She realised that the office was quiet, that the Big C's mouth had stopped moving, that her eyebrows were slightly raised as if she was waiting for some sort of answer.

'So how does that sound?' she asked.

Preposterous. Ridiculous. Ludicrous. A number of answers came to mind, but Dusty resisted employing any of them, biting her lip instead. Hours of interrogation had taught her that above all, you must stay calm, let your intellect be master of your emotions.

'Fuck that!'

'Sorry?'

'When would I be expected to start?' asked Dusty.

A tiny smile from the Big C. 'Tomorrow, of course.'

Dusty was just starting to understand how she got to be the youngest commander in Australia.

'And if I didn't accept this job?' inquired Dusty.

'Like I said, it really is an excellent opportunity for a person in your position.'

The Big C closed Dusty's file, the interview obviously over. Except for one thing. 'Detective,' said the Big C as Dusty got up to leave.

'Yes.'

'You don't have to bring your police car back until tomorrow.'

'Thanks,' said Dusty.

Chapter 32

The Long Grassers were in their usual place, most of them sleeping. Empty beer cans, fast-food wrappers, evidence of the previous night's activity were scattered across the ground.

Marion was sitting cross-legged, contemplatively smoking a rollie.

'Hey, Dutty,' she said, smiling her broken-toothed smile.

Both Smithie and Wessie were wheeling about, impatient to get to the beach.

'What them dogs names called, again?'

'That one's Wessie and the ugly mutt's Smithie.'

'Them nice dogs,' said Marion, wiping her nose with the back of her hand. 'Where's that fella of yours?'

James had always made a point of talking to the Long Grassers, listening intently to their stories of abuse and degradation. He never gave in to 'humbug', though – no money, no ciggies, no lifts. His contribution to the welfare of our Indigenous people, he'd say, was best kept to the law courts.

'He fucked off,' said Dusty.

Marion gave a huge laugh – something about James and his fucking off obviously struck a sympathetic chord with her. Dusty sometimes wondered what would have happened if they'd won Marion's case, whether she could've gone back to her community. She knew the answer, though: if the men who'd raped her had been sent to jail, Marion would have been even more ostracised than she now was.

'Hey, Auntie, this is for you,' said Dusty, handing Marion a green enviro-bag stuffed with clothes.

It was a while since Dusty had taken the dogs to the beach, so she went for a long run, all the way to the university. Again the tide was out, the sand stretching towards Timor. Armies of fiddler crabs were scuttling about, their trails forming arabesques. When they returned the dogs had a romp in the creek before crossing the footbridge again.

Dusty knew Marion wouldn't keep her hand-me-downs to herself – such a thing was unthinkable in Aboriginal culture, especially down-and-not-quite-out Aboriginal culture – but she was still surprised at how quickly the spoils had been distributed. Hector, an emaciated old man, a well-known painter, was looking quite resplendent, bare-chested, but in a pair of khaki police trousers. Sophie, Marion's drinking partner, was wearing one of Dusty's police shirts – unbuttoned, of course; there was no way even a polyester/cotton blend could stretch across her enormous bosom. And Dusty's old police hat was now sitting on top of Marion's head at an angle that could only be described as 'rakish'.

Dusty laughed all the way home. She laughed as she had her shower. Laughed as she changed into jeans and a T-shirt. And when she pulled into the carpark at Parap shopping centre, finding a park between SUPERMUM and MUM4EVER, she was still laughing.

'You look very *senang* today, Dusty,' said Nyoman, as he brought her morning coffee.

'*Senang sekali*,' replied Dusty. *Senang* – happy. *Sekali* – very. Happy very.

So *senang* that when Jacqui and her convoy of Absolutelies

invaded, she smiled benevolently, even offering a couple of baby-directed compliments – what beautiful eyes she has, and, to a particularly gruesome-looking blob, isn't he a big strong boy!

'Maybe scratchie?' suggest Nyoman.

As a Hindu, and a polytheist, he'd found room for one more capricious god in his elastic pantheon – Scratchie, able to bring great fortune with a single rub of a coin.

'No,' said Dusty. 'Not scratchie.'

Something much better than that. Handing that resignation letter to the Big C was going to be one of the defining, the most joyous, moments of her life.

Nyoman left and Dusty took out her mobile. She dialled a number.

'Frances!'

'Hi, Mum!'

'This is a surprise!'

'Can you talk?'

'I'm at the Grower's Market with the girls. We go every Tuesday now, it really is fabulous.'

'Girls? What girls?'

'You know. Susie and Beth, and Lana usually comes along, too.'

'Mum, you're all sixty-plus.'

'Well, that doesn't mean we don't feel young. Sixty is the new fifty, after all.'

Dusty had rehearsed the sentence a couple of times in the car, getting a feel for it, so when she said, 'I've decided to quit the police force and come back to Adelaide,' it tripped easily off her tongue.

It was difficult to imagine her mother as one of the 350,000 fans who reportedly lined the streets to greet the Fab Four when they landed in Adelaide on June 12th 1964, her taste now was so emphatically Classical Lite, but what came down the line then could only be described as a squeal Beatlemaniacal in both its pitch and intensity.

'Darling, that is wonderful news. Wonderful news.'

'Isn't it?' said Dusty.

'When, darling. When are you coming?'

'I have to give notice. Tidy things up. Probably a month.'

'You are making me so happy!'

As she hung up Dusty could hear her mother telling the other girls. 'She's coming home! Frances is coming home!'

Dusty ordered another coffee before turning her attention to today's paper. Apparently the cane toads were getting closer – one had been found at McMinn's Lagoon, about forty kilometres southeast of Darwin. There was a photo of the interloper – an amphibian so hideous, that even an indiscriminating animal lover like Dusty couldn't help but give an involuntary shudder.

So what, she thought. It's what Darwin deserves – a pestilence. Cane toads in Casuarina shopping centre. Cane toads hopping down Smith Street Mall.

Dusty flicked to another page.

'Yabooma the Biggest Thing Since Yothu Yindi', the headline trumpeted. 'Top End Rock Comes of Age'.

'Top End Rock', according to the article, was Australia's only truly original music, 'an intoxicating brew of rock, reggae and didgeridoo'.

Another pestilence. Again, exactly what Darwin deserved.

Dusty pushed the *NT News* aside and picked up a copy of *The Advertiser*, that venerable tabloid so beloved by all croweaters.

More Bodies Found in Barrels! Crows Forward to Marry Part-Time Model. Price of Iced Coffee to Rise by Five Cents!

This is more like it, thought Dusty.

*

The Build Up

When she walked into Police HQ clutching her resignation letter, Dusty was an hour late, and out of uniform, but she couldn't care less. That feeling of *senang* that she had been experiencing all morning, had become even more *sekali*. She felt almost euphoric.

As she walked past the mailboxes on the way to the Big C's office, Dusty noticed a large white envelope in hers.

Ignore it, she told herself.

The stamps were German, the postmark Berlin.

Keep on ignoring it, she told herself.

Dusty, of course, had thought of Tomasz during the last week and a bit. These thoughts, however, were cockroach thoughts, pests to be stomped on and destroyed. It had been a one night stand, that's all. Plus some weirdo stuff the next day.

The envelope was addressed to:
DETECTIVE DUSTY
NORTHERN TERRITORY POLICE
DARWIN
AUSTRALIA 0800

Heedful of her own advice, Dusty kept walking until she was in front of the Big C's office. She knocked on the door.

'Yes?' came the Big C's voice.

Dusty turned on her heels and hurried back along the corridor. She snatched the envelope from the mailbox, and ripped it open.

Inside was an A4-sized photo of a bird, the azure kingfisher they'd seen that day at the billabong.

On the photo somebody – Dusty assumed it was Tomasz – had drawn a black square. And next to that square they'd written 'person?'.

What person? Dusty couldn't see a person. Was this Tomasz's idea of a joke? Or was it her old fallibility again, her lack of an eye?

Her immediate thought – that she could take it to Scientific – was soon quashed. She wasn't a Dee, anymore – she couldn't just drop things off and wait for the report to land on her desk. She couldn't rely on a favour, either. Because of John's accident, her name, apparently, was shit in Scientific.

Dusty stood there, resignation letter in one hand, bird photo in the other, her mind vacillating. It seemed like minutes, but it was probably only seconds. In the end she left the decision to chance, tossing a virtual coin in her head – tails I go this way, heads I don't. It came down tails and Dusty left the building and got back into her car. It was only as she pulled up at some traffic lights that she realised the coin had tails on both sides.

Chapter 33

Julien's first gallery had been on Greening Street, wedged between a locksmith and a tattoo parlour. He'd told Dusty that other galleries would follow his lead, that part of Darwin would become an 'Arts Precinct', the Top End equivalent of London's Soho or Sydney's Woollahra. He was half-right – another tattoo parlour opened, and Julien's Art Precinct became a Body Art Precinct instead.

Now, relocated in Mitchell Street, he had an internet café on one side and a travel agent on the other. Both establishments were always busy – it seemed to Julien that backpackers spent more time sending emails about the exotic locale they were in than they did actually exploring it. Similarly, there was no shortage of people wanting to go to Kuta or Koh Samui or any of those destinations where hot chips came with everything.

It was difficult to sell art, especially this art. Even if people liked it, they didn't always trust their own taste. They needed to see an award, a write-up somewhere, they wanted to know that Elton John owned a piece, or Russell Crowe, or the chick who'd come third in *Australian Idol*.

Julien was paying careful attention to the latté he was drinking. They'd changed baristas at Tropicana, his café of choice, and he wasn't sure if the coffee was of the same high standard. The new barista did have other qualities, though – he was very cute and very gay.

The door opened and a thirtysomething couple walked in – tall, well-dressed, well-groomed. It was time for Pick the Passport, a game in which Julien considered himself to excel. There was no denim on denim, no his-and-hers matching of clothes, no dangling cameras – they weren't American. They weren't Poms either: too sophisticated looking, too healthy looking. (Not that sophisticated, healthy Poms didn't exist, of course, Parkinson had them on all the time. They just didn't seem ever to get to the Top End.) No, they were definitely Euro-beings. Sandals, but no socks. Cross out Deutschland. Madame and Monsieur or a Senora and a Senor.

'Morning,' said Julien.

'Morning,' they both replied, in accentless English.

Shit, thought Julien. This is going to be harder than usual.

'Can I help you at all?'

'We'd just like to have a look around the gallery,' answered the man.

Got you! thought Julien. It was barely discernible, but it was enough. 'Da' instead of 'the'. *Da gallery.*

'So you're from the Nederlands?' asked Julien, remembering not to call it Holland.

'Yes, we are,' replied the woman.

It wasn't racism, of course. It was just that Julien found some nationalities more pleasant than others. There wasn't an anti-Semitic bone in his body, but if no Israeli ever set foot in his shop again he wouldn't be that upset. The same for South Africans. But the Dutch – they spoke good English, they tended to be tolerant – i.e. gay-friendly – and their soccer team wore bright orange. What wasn't there to love about them?

'Then I'm sure I could tempt you with a coffee.'

The woman glanced at the man. He nodded.

'Thank you.'

The Build Up

'*Slagroom*?' inquired Julien. He'd been to Amsterdam a few times. Loved it, but was always startled when he ordered a cappuccino and it came with its own mountain of cream, of *slagroom*.

The woman smiled at Julien. 'No *slagroom*.'

As Julien ordered the coffees over the phone the Netherlanders browsed. Ten minutes later the door opened and it was him, the very cute, very gay barista. He was Eurasian – Singaporean or Malaysian, Julien guessed.

'Just put them on the counter, thanks.'

The barista did as Julien asked.

'What's your name, by the way?'

'Stewart,' he replied. 'But you can call me . . .'

Please not Stuey, Julien told himself. I couldn't have *anything* to do with a Stuey.

'Stewart,' said Stewart, with an old-fashioned wink.

'OK, Stewart. I'll see you later.'

Dusty seldom visited Julien's place of work, and if she did it was invariably late in the afternoon, after she'd finished work. It was a surprise, therefore, when she came bursting into the gallery, a large photograph of a bird in her hand.

'Julien,' she said breathlessly, emanating a type of manic energy that was unusual for her – she was usually so gathered, so composed. 'Thank God you're here.'

What's she talking about, thought Julien, I'm always here.

'Coffee, great,' she said, grabbing one of the cups from the counter. She'd poured half of it down her throat before Julien could reclaim it.

'Dusty!' he said, indicating the Netherlanders with a nod of his head. 'What's the matter with you?'

Not only that, had she forgotten their fight, that they weren't talking? This wasn't the way it was done. There had to be tentative text messages, followed by phone calls, before, eventually, they'd meet. Then there'd be a few tears, lots of *mea culpas*, and a final conciliatory hug before they could be friends again.

'I need help,' said Dusty.

'You don't say?'

'You've got a scanner, haven't you?'

The Maningrida Arts Centre had gone online last year and rather than pay somebody a fortune to do it, Julien had done it all himself – bought the equipment, attended a couple of courses at TAFE, and built his own website.

'Yes, I have a scanner.'

'And Photoshop?'

'And Photoshop.'

Julien evened the cups up before turning his attention to his customers. 'Your coffees are here.'

'I need–' started Dusty, but Julien cut her short. 'Just wait. This is business, OK?'

The Netherlanders were interested in a print of a dilly bag from the Maningrida Woman's Co-op.

'I like it because it is so simple,' said the woman.

Julien couldn't agree more. That's what he, too, loved about Maningrida art – its simplicity. Desert blackfellas were always dropping in, asking him to sell their paintings. He looked at it, of course, it would be bad manners not to, but most of it he hated – sacred dreamings turned into canvas nightmares.

The Netherlanders had no shortage of questions. When was it done? From which community is it? How much of the money goes back to the artist? Julien gave comprehensive answers to them all – it was a pleasure to do business with ethical people like these – but as he did so he could hear Dusty behind him, shuffling about, clearing her throat, sighing, making all manner of unsubtle get-on-with-it noises.

The Build Up

'Can you tell me something about the artist?' asked the woman.

It was with some pride that was able to retrieve the artist's file from the cabinet.

'Here's a photo,' he said, holding up a snap.

Dusty stepped forward, still clutching her bird photo, and scrutinised the print.

'That really is exquisite,' she said, putting on an accent that was supposed to be posh, a prerequisite for any serious art buyer, but, like all Dusty's accents, sounded vaguely Indian. 'Is this the only one you have?'

Julien wanted to kill Dusty – bitch-slap her to death. And then put her in a tank full of formaldehyde, Damien Hirst style, and label it 'Bad Friend 2006'. The dummy bidder – the oldest trick in the book. There was no way a couple of sophisticated Eurobeings would fall for something as gauche as that.

'Yes, it is the only one I have,' said Julien, glaring at Dusty. It actually was the only one he had.

'Then I'd like to–' started Dusty before the Netherlander interjected.

'Madam, we were actually already buying it.'

Chapter 34

'Un-fucking-ethical,' said Julien, sitting at his desk in the backroom.

'Give them their money back, then,' said Dusty.

'That's not the point.'

'What is, then?'

'There's enough shonky art dealers out there peddling black-fella art without me becoming one, too.'

'How do you know I wasn't going to buy it?'

'Because your taste is three feet up your arse.'

Dusty knew Julien was right about the shonky art dealers – there was no shortage of those – but she also knew that the higher moral ground wasn't his natural territory, and if she stayed put, didn't become contrite, eventually he'd come back to your level.

'Well, three foot up your arse is certainly something you'd know about,' she said.

The thinnest of smiles from Julien as he powered up his beautiful Mac Pro.

'Surely the police have got all this software and more?' he said.

'I don't get along with the police that well anymore,' said Dusty.

'Darling, I wonder why that is?'

Dusty was impressed at the way Julien confidently scanned Tomasz's photo. She'd never thought of him as being particularly

The Build Up

technology-literate, but he seemed very adept with a mouse in his hand and was using terms such as 'jpeg' and 'pixel' with a surprising familiarity.

'So what is a pixel, is that like a little pixie?' asked Dusty.

It wasn't that funny, but Dusty knew it was the type of joke that Julien enjoyed. What's brown and sticky? A stick. That sort of thing.

'You're a fuckwit,' said Julien.

In most situations 'you're a fuckwit' would not indicate a détente, but this wasn't most situations, this was Julien and Dusty, fag and hag, and in their private language, forged over many years, 'you're a fuckwit' had long ceased to be any sort of insult and had become an open expression of affection, if not love.

'I'm sorry about being shonky,' said Dusty, putting her arm around his shoulders and squeezing.

'So you should be,' said Julien, but the sting was out of his voice now.

The photo was now displayed on the screen of the Mac.

'Can you blow that section there up?' Dusty asked, pointing to the screen, to the rectangle Tomasz had drawn.

A buzz from next door. Somebody had entered the gallery. Julien smoothed back his hair with both hands, adjusted his watch so it sat squarely on his wrist, and departed to do business of the non-shonky variety.

After a while, Dusty could hear a man speaking with a French accent. Then Julien replying, 'Of course, there has been a lot of renewed interest in the art from this area. Frankly, people are getting bit sick of the desert stuff. There's only so many dots one can take.'

Dusty stifled a giggle – only so many dots one can take!

Julien continued.

'You've heard of Russell Crowe, of course?'

'But, of course, *oui*,' said the Frenchman.

'Well, he's recently shown some interest in one.'

Coffees were ordered. The wonders of Paris discussed – the city, not the slut. Now they were talking food. This, Dusty knew, could go on forever. Julien was now even inflicting his schoolboy French on the poor Froggy.

She gazed at the Mac. At the mighty Photoshop. She trembled, and she felt small and worthless.

On the right of the screen a whole lot of symbols were corralled into a skinny rectangle. There was a squidgy-looking hand, an old-fashioned pen nib, an eye-dropper, but the one that caught her attention was a little magnifying glass. She moved the mouse until the cursor was over this symbol and clicked. The cursor, itself, became a little magnifying glass. She moved this into the centre of the rectangle. Again she clicked the mouse. The photo zoomed in. Dusty could not help but feel the flush of triumph. She had vanquished the mighty Photoshop. She kept clicking until the rectangle was as big as the screen.

'Who's that?'

Engrossed in what she was doing, Dusty hadn't realised that Julien had entered.

'Who's who?'

'That person.'

'Don't shit me.'

'No, seriously,' said Julien, pointing to the middle of the black rectangle.

Dusty could see that something was different there – the light, the texture – but that's all she could see – difference, nothing more.

'What does this so-called person look like?'

The Build Up

Julien looked at the screen, rocking his head a little bit to the left and then a little bit to the right.

'Not like somebody I'd go to bed with.'

'Julien!'

'I don't know, it's hard to say, but there's definitely somebody there.'

Chapter 35

Officially it was called the Crime Scene Exhibit Storage Facility, but its common name, the Shed, owed more to its appearance than its function. It looked like any of the other hangar-like warehouses in Darwin's industrial belt where goods were received and dispatched. But here, instead of disposable nappies or washing machines or DVD players, the goods were the artefacts of crime – a bloodied knife, a semen-stained sheet, a single strand of hair – each bagged and tagged, uniquely numbered according to which case, to which crime, they belonged.

Sergeant Gerard Bevan checked the time – it was already past midday. Again he thought about the bet he'd made with Fontana: fifty bucks that Detective Buchanon wouldn't turn up.

'Mate, you don't know her like I do,' Fontana had said. 'There's no way she'd wear a fucking uniform, again.'

Despite the fifty bucks he'd lose, Gerard hoped that Fontana was right, that Dusty Buchanon's pride would prevent her from taking up her new position in the Shed, *his* Shed. When Gerard had started there, the Shed still hadn't recovered from the Azaria Chamberlain fiasco, where exhibits had gone missing or were wrongly destroyed. Gerard had turned it around just at the time when the increasing importance of DNA analysis made the proper storage, and tracking, of crime scene exhibits and the prevention of contamination major issues. Yes, there'd been a couple

The Build Up

of glitches during the McVeigh trial, but they'd sorted those out, so what use did he have for Detective Dusty Buchanon?

He'd heard all the rumours, of course. Though the Shed wasn't connected to the main building, coppers were forever shuttling between the two, every one of them the bearer of gossip: Detective Buchanon had fucked up big time on the Gardner case, John's accident had been Detective Buchanon's fault, Commander Schneider had it in for Detective Buchanon. There were more salacious rumours as well: Detective Buchanon went to Bali for sex, Detective Buchanon was a hermaphrodite, but Gerard really couldn't be bothered with these.

He just didn't buy it, that she'd been busted back to uniform and assigned to the Shed as some form of punishment. Gerard had another theory: Dusty had lost her stomach for police work. Call it PTSD, call it what you like, she couldn't take it anymore – the blood, the guts, the shit. So she was looking for another career behind a desk, behind *his* desk.

At 2.20 pm a determined-looking Detective Buchanon appeared at Gerard's desk, the uniform she was wearing cross-hatched with creases, straight out of its packet.

'Bugger!' he said.
'What's wrong?' said Dusty.
'You just won me fifty bucks.'
'Let me guess, Fontana?'
Gerard nodded.
'He bet you I wouldn't show?'
Again Gerard nodded.
'And you thought that I would.'
'Something like that.'
'But hoped that I wouldn't.'
Gerard shrugged.

'This,' said Dusty tugging at her uniform, 'I can assure you is only temporary.' A sweep of her hand. 'As much as I love what you've done here, I really have no intention of staying very long.'

Gerard had worked with Dusty before. She'd been one of the advisers when they were developing CSETS, the new whizz-bang Crime Scene Exhibit Tracking System. He'd been impressed with her back then – she was smart, articulate, and had that rare ability to cut through the crap to what really mattered. Still, such directness, even in the police force, was unusual. Now, Gerard wasn't sure how to react, or what to say.

It didn't matter. Dusty seemed to have sufficient conversation for both of them.

'What I'd like you to do is stick me somewhere out of the way. You can say I'm doing some bullshit time and movement thing, process transaction analysis, something like that. I keep out of your way. You keep out of mine. And before you know it I'll be out of here.'

Gerard was both relieved – Detective Buchanon, apparently, had no designs on his job – and annoyed – who the hell did she think she was ordering him around like that? This was the Shed – his domain.

'Why should I do that?'

'Because a girl's been murdered. And I'm going to find out who did it.'

There were only two people who really knew what happened that day down the Track but neither Detective Buchanon nor John Goodes – who was still in hospital – was saying much. That left the rumours, and they'd been multiplying like cane toads since then. Though they varied in detail – as rumours, and cane toads, tend to do – they all seemed to agree on one thing – Detective Buchanon had seen something that wasn't there. But here she was standing in front of him, radiating a sort of con-

The Build Up

viction, a certainty, that reminded Gerard of the evangelical preachers of his childhood.

A girl's been murdered. I'm going to find out who did it.

Wasn't this, after all, why he'd joined the police force?

'So?' said Dusty.

It wouldn't be that difficult to do what she asked. The powers-that-be saw the Shed as some sort of black box – as long as it functioned efficiently they weren't too concerned as to what went on inside.

'Somewhere out of the way?' he reiterated.

Dusty nodded.

'OK, follow me.'

Gerard led Dusty past rows and rows of laden shelves to a tiny office in the very bowels of the Shed. There was no natural light, no natural airflow, and the colour scheme was the usual winning combination of beige, beige and beige. The only view, through the window, was onto the contents of the Shed itself – the cardboard boxes of exhibits, many of them, no doubt, containing the artefacts of unnatural death.

'Blokes found it a bit spooky,' said Gerard, explaining its unused state.

Though not superstitious himself he could understand that if you were that way inclined and here by yourself, your imagination might get up to no good.

'No problem,' said Dusty, already at her desk, already unpacking her laptop.

'Look, if there's anything I can do to help,' said Gerard.

'Do you mean that?'

Again Dusty's directness surprised Gerard.

'Sorry?'

'Are you just being polite or do you mean it?'

'No, I really mean it.'

'Then I will definitely need your help.'

'Good, you've got it.'

As Gerard walked back to his office he wondered what he'd got himself in to.

A girl's been murdered. I'm going to find out who did it.

Chapter 36

An office to yourself had its advantages.

There was music for a start. Dusty was able to bring up iTunes on her laptop, then her favourite radio station – Boot Liquor, (Music for Saddle-Weary Cowboys) – without incurring the displeasure of her country-hating colleagues. The sink wasn't full of dirty mugs, Fontana assuming that the ladies would naturally look after that side of things. And there was nobody to eavesdrop on her conversations, which, at this stage, were mostly with herself.

Most police work is grunt work: tracing leads you know are going nowhere, interviewing people you know have nothing to say. Following procedure. Working the lists. All the stuff they don't show on the TV, because, let's face it, one hour – minus ads – of a pimply-faced constable knocking on doors just isn't going to out-rate *Big Brother*. Not yet.

If Dusty had still been a bigshot in Homicide, if she still had the full weight of the NT Police Force behind her, then it would've been straightforward. Grunt work. But she wasn't – she couldn't afford to follow every lead, so she had to rely on something else: experience, intuition, a hunch, whatever.

All three told her she had to go back to the billabong.

Not by herself, that wouldn't achieve much. She had to take somebody with her, somebody with an 'eye'.

Forensics, whitefella magic, was out of the question. With

John still in hospital Dusty couldn't imagine any of them accompanying her to the pub for a free beer and a bowl of wedges, let alone all the way to the billabong. That left the other sort of magic, blackfella magic.

The NT Police Force didn't use black trackers much these days. In fact, most coppers thought of them as yet another romantic myth about the outback – the blackfella with this preternatural, almost supernatural, knowledge of the land, who can detect any rent in its fabric, no matter how minute.

Not Dusty, however. She made a phone call.

'Angagarra Council,' a woman answered.

Dusty had been to the Angagarra community a few times – it was a beautiful place, south of Katherine, situated on the banks of the Roper River. She could picture the council building the woman was in, its architectural drabness alleviated by the spreading gumtrees that shaded it and the wildly coloured mural that ran along its length. She could also picture Teddy's house, a minute's walk away, and Teddy himself sitting out the front, listening to newsradio.

'Detective Dusty Buchanon here, I was wondering if Teddy Daylight is around?'

'In trouble again, is he?' said the woman, laughing.

Dusty was in on the joke: Teddy didn't drink or smoke and was one of the most respected elders in the community.

'No, not this time,' said Dusty.

'Just a minute, OK. I'll go get him.'

After twenty minutes, during which time Dusty could hear people entering and leaving the office, conversations both in English and Language, she figured the woman had forgotten about her, and hung up.

When she rang again the phone was engaged. Half an hour later she managed to get through.

The Build Up

The same woman answered. 'Angagarra Council.'
'Detective Dusty Buchanon here.'
'Hey, what happened to you?'
'I thought you'd forgotten me.'
'He's here.'

Dusty could hear the woman say something in Language – she could guess what it was, too, it's that typically impatient white-fella cop.

'Teddy!'
'Dusty!'

After the usual small talk, Dusty got down to business.

'You want to do some work for me?'
'I retired.'
'You always say this.'
'This time, fair dinkum. Eyes buggered.'

Teddy had trachoma, a preventable form of conjunctivitis that was rife in the communities.

'You saw the doctor, though.'
'I see doctor, he say "eyes buggered".'

There were other trackers but they weren't as good – either they'd lose interest or their English wasn't up to scratch.

'Is there anybody else?' asked Dusty, on the off-chance there was somebody she hadn't heard of.

'Number one good like me?' asked Teddy, laughing.
'Yeah.'
'Nobody.'
'OK, how about almost as good?'
'My son,' said Teddy.
'Tyson?' asked Dusty, remembering the shy lanky boy he'd once brought along on a job.
'No, not 'im. Young Teddy.'

Dusty remembered him too from one of her visits to Angagarra.

Younger than Tyson. Not so shy. A cheeky kid. But that was years ago, he'd be in his late teens by now.

'Is he there? Can I talk to him?'

'No, he's in Darwin.'

Even better – Dusty was getting excited now.

'Is he in school here?'

'Young Teddy, school?' said Teddy, laughing. 'No, he's a big music fella. He's in that band Yabooma.'

Yabooma. The Biggest Thing Since Yothu Yindi!

After finishing the conversation with Teddy, Dusty made a few more calls. It turned out that Young Teddy wasn't in Darwin after all – Yabooma were playing a series of gigs in North Queensland. They'd be back on Saturday night, however, to play at the Troppo Lounge.

Dusty wasn't one of those chicks afraid to fly solo, who couldn't go anywhere, not even the pub toilet, unless accompanied by at least one other member of her gender. Rock 'n' roll was unfamiliar territory, however, and backup seemed a sensible idea. Secondly, and more cynically, if you're aiming to humbug a blackfella, it really helps to have one on your team. She rang Trace and arranged it. Saturday night they were stylin' up.

That was two days away, though. In the meantime there were other leads to follow. Dusty took out her Spirax A4 notebook and went through the copious notes she'd already made. (That was something else that annoyed Dusty about TV cop shows, they never seemed to take any notes!) One name, one lead, seemed to stand out from the others: Franky fucking Ng.

Chapter 37

Dusty sat sweating in Beastie Boy, opposite the depot for Darwin Combined Taxis, eating pad thai from a plastic container with a plastic fork.

It had only taken a couple of calls to find Franky Ng's place of work. Just after six – the time the very helpful Deidre had said he'd start his shift – a taxi pulled onto the road with Franky Ng at the wheel.

Dusty couldn't remember the last time she'd done any tailing. Usually it was the Surveillance Unit, the Dogs, who did this. And as much as she loved Beastie Boy, as far as this sort of work went it was a serious liability. For a start it was slow and cumbersome. And it was one of a kind. Sometimes, when Dusty left it in the car-park at Casuarina, she'd come back to find a couple of bloke's blokes in thongs and singlets, squatting next to it, drooling. 'You don't see many of these around, luv.'

No, there was nothing anonymous about Beastie Boy, but it was all she had. She mashed the gears into first, dropped the clutch and took off after Franky Ng. For the first hour it went well. Franky Ng drove conservatively and she managed to stay glued to his tail. The fares seemed innocuous enough – a couple of suits to the airport, some blackfellas from the Mall out to the Bagot community, tourists to the fish-feeding at Doctor's Gully. By the time it was 10 pm and Franky Ng had pulled into the

Nightcliff McDonald's she was starting to think that she'd be better off following one of her other leads – a background check on all the vets, for example.

She could see Franky Ng sitting at a table, mobile phone and keys in front of him, reading the *NT News*, sipping something toxic from styrofoam. His mobile rang and after a very short conversation, he hurried back to his taxi. Franky Ng the conservative driver then became Franky Ng the racing car driver, tearing up Bagot Road like it was Mount Panorama. If not for a couple of red lights hindering his progress Dusty would've been left far behind.

Franky Ng turned right onto Palmerston Road. Palmerston was where most of the new development in Darwin took place, and was consequently the part of the city Dusty knew least well.

So when the taxi turned left into Jabiru Crescent, she was concerned. She couldn't remember being on this street before, didn't know where it went. The streets were no longer on a grid pattern, but squiggled this way and that, according to some mad developer's whim.

Jabiru the Crescent suddenly became Jabiru the Dirt Track. The houses fewer, and further apart. There were mostly empty blocks, some ready to build on, others uncleared.

This was starting to look like Badlands to Dusty, the sort of place where you'd establish a meth lab, torch a stolen car, or dig a shallow grave.

The taxi pulled up outside one of the houses, leaving Dusty with no choice but to keep going. Slouching in her seat, she tried to make herself as little like Detective Dusty Buchanon, one time arresting officer of Franky Ng, as possible. She was able to pull over further up the road and check out proceedings in the hastily adjusted rear-vision mirror.

Franky Ng got out of his taxi carrying a black briefcase.

The Build Up

He was inside for twelve and a half minutes before returning alone, still carrying his briefcase. Jumping back into his taxi he took off. Dusty waited a couple of minutes before she started Beastie Boy. She did a U-turn, stopping in front of the house. It was a big sprawling place – brick, with huge lug-like air conditioners sticking out either side. There was something not-quite-finished about it, like those houses with an owner–builder sign outside that seem to be in a state of perpetual construction. Dusty had seen enough for now. She took off.

Chapter 38

'I'll go in at seven,' said Dusty, checking her watch.

'Sounds good,' said Gerard from the driver's seat of his unmarked police Commodore, and then, 'Is that really your watch?'

At one level it was a ridiculous question – it was on her wrist, wasn't it? Of course it was her watch. Dusty understood what Gerard meant, though – is that cheap looking plastic timepiece really what you use in your day-to-day work as a detective?

'I've got a better one at home,' she answered.

Which was true – a Tag Heuer, a present from James, languished in the junk drawer in the kitchen, its face reminding her too much of his face, and the years he'd thieved from her, for Dusty to wear it.

'You're about five minutes slow,' said Gerard, referring to his own watch, a substantial-looking Rolex Submariner.

Maybe it was the lack of caffeine – they'd met at six so Dusty could give Gerard a thorough briefing, exchange mobile numbers, that sort of thing and as a result, Dusty hadn't had a coffee – but already the Clerk was starting to annoy her.

'Doesn't really matter,' said Dusty.

She turned her attention back to the house at 242 Jabiru Crescent. There was still no sign of life.

'Maybe you could adjust your watch?' suggested Gerard.

'Synchronise watches you mean?'

The Build Up

'I guess that's one way to put it.'

'You've been watching a little too much TV,' said Dusty gently.

Gerard took this onboard, but Dusty could see that he still wasn't happy.

'I really would feel better if we synchronised watches,' he said, finally.

There was no shortage of stories about how 'anal' Gerard was. As far as managing the Shed went, attention to detail was undoubtedly an advantage, one of the reasons it ran so smoothly, not unlike a Rolex Submariner in fact. But Dusty wasn't sure if 'anal' was going to get them very far this morning.

'If you really want to,' she said.

Gerard seemed pleased with this.

'When I say, you change yours to seven.'

'OK,' said Dusty, taking her watch off.

'Now,' said Gerard.

Dusty made the required adjustment. Both watches, Taiwan cheapie, Rolex Submariner, were now on seven.

'You've got my mobile number?' Dusty asked.

Gerard nodded.

'OK, I'm outta here,' she said, as she cracked open the door and stepped outside.

She strode confidently along the road, through the open gate, and to the front door. There was an intercom, but Dusty decided to knock – a more emphatic statement of her authority. No response. She knocked harder. Still no response. She pressed the button on the intercom.

'Ruby closed,' a woman's voice pronounced.

'It's the police,' said Dusty into the speaker.

'OK, I give you good price. Mate rate, OK? You come back night, OK?'

'No, you don't understand,' said Dusty, 'It's the police.'
'After sick, OK?'

A click, and the voice was gone. Dusty pressed the buzzer again without response. Her suspicions were both confirmed – 242 Jabiru Crescent was a brothel – and deepened, she needed to have a look around. She followed the path that ran along the side of the house and into an unruly backyard dominated by an enormous spreading mango tree. Dusty was prepared for a dog, something brutish – a wet-mouthed rottweiler or a snarling doberman. The pig was a surprise.

It wasn't a huge pig, nothing like those porkers you see squeezed into pens at the Royal Show, but it was a pig nonetheless, its belly slung low, rooting around in the overripe fruit that littered the ground. Though it was Dusty's theory that any animal, no matter how bestial, should be acknowledged, she wasn't quite sure what to do when the pig stopped its snuffling and looked up at her. If it was a dog she would've said something consoling like, 'It's OK, fella', if it was a cat she would've opted for flattery, 'Who's a lovely puss?' but what the hell do you say to a pig? In the end she combined the two, 'It's OK, pretty fella'. The pig seemed reassured by this and returned to its mangoes.

Dusty tried the back door. It was unlocked. She pushed it open, walking into a kitchen. Nothing remarkable here – a ricecooker on the bench, some trashy magazines, a Domino's pizza menu on the refrigerator. On the table was a green A4 diary. Dusty picked it up, flicking through the pages. It appeared to be some sort of ledger: for each day there was a set of numbers ranging from one to ten. What they represented Dusty could only guess as all the writing was in Thai. If it was a summary of the girls' activities then it could be just what she was looking for, evidence of a girl turning tricks one day, turning nothing the next. She took her phone out, changed the setting to macro and

The Build Up

took a photo of the page dated Wednesday 4th October, the day Jimmy had said he'd seen a body in the billabong. Working methodically she took photos of the previous six days. Suddenly 'Zorba the Greek' started playing. Dusty answered her phone.

'There's some people coming,' said Gerard.

'OK, I'm on my way,' she said putting the diary back.

As Dusty hurried back through the doorway she could hear men's voices coming from the side of the house, getting louder, getting closer. 'Check the backyard!'

Though there'd been no mango trees in Adelaide when Dusty was growing up, there'd been plenty of other types, and Dusty, tomboy that she was, had been forever climbing them. Climbing trees, like riding bikes, is a skill not easily forgotten. She tore past the pig, shimmied up the mango tree trunk and wedged herself between two branches, trying to make herself as inconspicuous, as mango-like, as possible. Through the chinks in the foliage she could see a large man, a gun in his hand. Finding an especially delicious mango, the pig snuffled loudly. The man reacted instantly, raising his gun, stepping towards the pig, towards the tree, towards Dusty. She recognised him now. Once an excellent footballer, Ned Maleski was now a very mediocre crim. Though Dusty hadn't had dealings with him professionally – Ned Maleski's CV, though extensive, did not include homicide – his name was mentioned frequently, and derisively, around the station. Dusty didn't think Ned Maleski had the guts, or whatever quality it takes to squeeze the trigger but there was something about a gun, its lack of ambiguity, its absolute gun-ness, that demands respect, even with B-grade villains like Maleski. Dusty tried to make herself even more like a mango.

Another man appeared. Bojan 'Spanners' Spanovic was an altogether more serious proposition than Maleski. He was a kickboxer, a habitué of Darwin's hardcore gyms, and a person of considerable interest in a number of drug-related killings. He was also a well-known womaniser, one of those good-looking bad men who respectable girls find irresistible. He, too, was armed, though his gun was much more imposing than Ned Maleski's.

'What is it?' he asked.

'Nothin',' said Ned Maleski, lowering his gun. 'Reckon Mamasan was hearing things.'

'What's that fucking thing?' said Spanners, waving his gun at the pig.

'That's a pig, Spanners.'

'Yeah, well, I don't like the look of the fucking thing.'

The pig fixed Spanners with a beady stare and snorted.

'Fuck off!' said Spanners.

Undeterred, the pig snorted again, this time taking a couple of dainty steps in Spanners' direction.

Spanners took aim and shot the pig. Ned Maleski, to his credit, was unimpressed.

'Why'd you do that for?'

'Because I fucking could.' Spanners laughed. 'C'mon, let's go.'

The two men disappeared along the side of the house. The pig lay in a glistening pool of its own blood, squealing pitifully, front legs scrabbling in the dirt. It could've been a trap, a ruse to flush her out but Dusty knew that Maleski wasn't that cunning, and doubted very much if Spanners was either. Still, it was better to be sure. She texted Gerard, holding onto the mango tree with one hand.

'haue they gone?'

'haue?' came the reply.

'have.'

'have they gone?'

'yes!'

'yes.'

The Build Up

Dusty jumped down from the tree and ran to the pig. It had stopped squealing, stopped scrabbling but its eyes were still open. It was alive. Its skin slicked with blood, it was difficult to pick up. Dusty managed, though, holding the pig tight against her chest, carrying it along the side of the house and towards the waiting car.

'You'll be OK, Piggy,' she kept repeating. 'You'll be OK.'

Gerard was out of the car.

'He's been shot,' said Dusty. 'Open the back door.'

'It's got blood all over it!'

'Open the door!'

'How about the boot?'

'Open the fucking door!'

Gerard opened the fucking door. Dusty gently slid the pig along the seat before getting in herself.

'Come on, let's go!' she said to Gerard, who was now back behind the wheel.

'Where?'

'The vet, of course. There's one in Casuarina.'

Gerard started the car, put it into drive, cut back onto the road, driving in a safe and responsible manner.

'Gerard, in case you hadn't noticed, I got a dying pig here. Get a fucking move on.'

Gerard took the hint – he got a fucking move on. For a clerk he drove very fast and very well.

Just as they'd reached Casuarina, Dusty said, 'You can slow down now, mate.'

The pig, its head on Dusty's lap, was dead.

'Gone?' asked Gerard.

Tears found their way down Dusty's cheeks.

'Gone.'

Chapter 39

The Saturday Parap market was one of the places where the various tribes of Darwin met – backpackers, tourists in their faux safari suits, young blackfellas blinged-up like their hip-hop heroes, bare-foot ferals who came for the organic fruit and veg, southerners like Jacqui, Top Enders by number-plate only. In the car park two Aboriginal women, one wearing what looked suspiciously like a NT Police shirt, were accosting tourists, competing to sell their paintings.

'Hey, lady you buy my painting!'

'Hey, lady this one 'ere got plenny more dot.'

There were four som tum ladies at the market, all of them from Thailand, of course – nobody of any other nationality would dare attempt to create something that was so quintessentially Thai. Imagine an Inuit trying their hand at haggis, or a Bulgarian whipping up some sushi? Dusty always went to Mrs Pon, and had been doing so for at least the last ten years. As usual she was wearing a vast straw hat and a plastic apron, and was seated on a tiny wooden stool, the large stone mortar positioned between her legs.

'Mrs Dusty!' she said, smiling, revealing her betel-leaf stained teeth.

'Mrs Pon!' replied Dusty, with equal gusto.

'I think you no come today. You go other som tum lady.'

The Build Up

Dusty's supposed infidelity was a standing joke between them.

'No, nobody makes som tum like Mrs Pon.'

And it was true. Som tum only had a few ingredients – grated unripe papaya, peanuts, chilli, lime-juice, sugar, dried shrimp and fish sauce – but somehow Mrs Pon and her magic mortar got the balance right every time.

'How many chilli you like today?'

One was usually enough for Dusty. James had preferred two, but it had never been a pretty sight watching him eat it – the cascading sweat, the blotchy skin. Dusty suspected it had more to do with some misplaced notion of solidarity with the chilli-eating underprivileged of the Third World than because he actually enjoyed it. Today, for some reason, Dusty decided to up the ante.

'*Sarm*,' she said.

'*Sarm?*' Mrs Pon laughed, holding up three fingers.

'*Sarm*,' repeated Dusty, this time trying to mimic Mrs Pon's rising tone.

'*Pedas*,' she added, before remembering that '*pedas*' was the Indonesia word for spicy, not the Thai.

Mrs Pon understood, though. '*Pedas, pedas,*' she said approvingly, before rhythmically pounding the ingredients with the wooden pestle, eventually holding out some on a spoon for Dusty to try. The balance of sweet, sour, spicy, salty and bitter was just perfect.

'Great.'

Mrs Pon scooped the contents of the mortar into a plastic container.

'*Kup khun ca,*' said Dusty as she paid the six dollars.

'*Kup khun ca,*' said Mrs Pon, placing the palms of her hands together.

'One more thing,' said Dusty, as she took out a copy of one of the pages she'd photographed from the diary at Ruby's.

Dusty doubted, somehow, that any document translated by Mrs Pon the som tum lady would hold up in a court of law. Her skills, sublime as they were, probably did not include the required NAATI accreditation. Given Dusty's present busted-back-to-uniform state, however, Mrs Pon the som tum lady would have to do.

'Can you tell me what this means?'

Mrs Pon wiped her hands carefully on a tea-towel and took the paper from Dusty, treating it with great reverence. She studied it closely before pronouncing, with some satisfaction, 'Thai language.'

'Yes, I know that, but what does it say?'

Mrs Pon yelled out something over her shoulder. Soon there were four som tum ladies, each with a vast straw hat and plastic apron, each redolent of the ingredients they used, perusing the paper.

'So what does it say?' asked Dusty finally, conscious of the queue of customers now behind her.

'You know, to stop baby.'

'Condoms?' queried Dusty.

This sent the som tum ladies into paroxysms of laughter. Rivals they may be, but when it came to having a laugh, especially a laugh at the expense of a *farang*, they were in on it together.

'Thanks,' said Dusty, taking the paper back.

She bought a mango shake, sat in the shade of a tamarind tree, and ate her som tum. At the next table the two Aboriginal women, competitors not so long ago, were now sharing a plate of chicken sate. Obviously they'd persuaded somebody that 'plenny dots' was an admirable quality in an artwork.

She was disappointed, but not debilitated. It was so often like this – the most promising leads coming to nothing.

Chapter 40

Dusty pulled up outside Trace's house in Galagi, a suburb dominated by housing commission flats.

She knew these streets well from her days in uniform. Break and enter, domestic violence, car theft – you name it, Galagi had it – rich pickings for a keen junior law enforcer.

If she went inside she'd be ambushed by Trace's kids and it'd be half an hour before she got away so she beeped the horn instead.

Five minutes later Trace appeared. Dressed simply in a figure-hugging black dress and with no hint of product on her person she looked stunning.

She slid into the passenger's seat. 'Hey, you look hot, Detective.'

Dusty was wearing her favourite Diesel jeans, a fitted V-necked singlet, Puma trainers and some chunky beads she'd bought in Bali. She'd also put on lipgloss and a touch of eyeliner.

'And you look like shit.'

'Why, what's wrong?' said a concerned Trace checking her reflection in the rear-vision mirror.

'Hey, I'm kidding. You look gorgeous, as usual. I hate your guts.'

Trace relaxed. 'Yeah, well, look where it's got me. A house full of screaming kids and an arsehole ex-husband.'

Born during a cyclone, Trace's life had always been unsettled. Dusty had first met her playing netball. Fierce opponents on the court, they became good friends off it. Over time, Trace had confided in Dusty that her husband, a respected member of the community, was a tyrant. When they were both picked for the same representative team, and travelled to Alice Springs together, Dusty had experienced this firsthand. Trace's mobile was forever ringing, even at three in the morning, her husband demanding to know where she was and who she was with, how much money she'd spent. With Dusty's support Trace left him. It was Dusty, too, who had persuaded her to apply for the ACPO job.

'Trace, you made some bad choices. We all do. Look at me and James. Doesn't mean you have to keep on making them.'

'Thank you, officer, for your patronising words.'

'Fuck you, Trace.'

Trace leaned into Dusty, kissing her on the cheek.

'And I love you, too, Dusty.'

Not for the first time Dusty asked herself: why aren't men more like women? She got the same answer she always got, though: because they're men. The sound of a child yelling came from within the house. Then another.

'Let's go, before Sis changes her mind,' said Trace.

Dusty took off with a squeal of rubber.

'Do you mind if I have a bit of *yarndi* before we get there?' Trace asked as they passed the Casino, the car park already full.

'Trace, we're police officers!'

'I'll blow the smoke out the window, eh?'

'OK, if you have to,' said Dusty.

The joint Trace extricated from her purse was just a stub of a thing, and gone after a couple of puffs. The results, though, appeared satisfactory.

'Yeooooooooow!' she yelled.

The Build Up

*

The queue to the Troppo Lounge snaked down Mitchell Street and around the corner. Maybe the *NT News* was right and Yabooma *were* the biggest thing since Yothu Yindi. But then, if you allowed them that, you also had to believe that crime was out of control, Long Grassers were taking over the town centre and the introduction of daylight saving would be hell on curtains.

'Show them your badge,' said Trace, giggling.

It occurred to Dusty, too – a discreet flash and they'd be in. She decided against it, though – this wasn't strictly police business, and it wouldn't be fair if they jumped the queue. They attached themselves to the end of it. If anything it seemed to be moving backwards, like a millipede in reverse, pushing them further down Cavenagh Street. Dusty tapped the bony-headed backpacker in front on the shoulder.

'Mate, how long you been waiting?' she asked.

'A fooking hour,' was the reply.

Dusty gave it a second's thought, before taking Trace by the arm and detaching from the queue. An hour was bad enough, but a fooking hour was ridiculous.

At the entrance was the bouncer from Kitty O'Flanagan's, the quadrilateral Tongan.

'Hey, you get around,' Dusty said.

'Yeah, well, I gotta family to support,' replied the Tongan.

'You put in that application?'

'Got the form, eh?'

'Well, what's stopping you?'

The Tongan shrugged.

'We need more fellas like you. What's your name, by the way?'

'Samisoni,' said the Tongan, giving Dusty yet another version of the brother handshake, a knuckle-cruncher with thumbs interlocked. 'But everybody calls me Sam.'

'Mine's Dusty,' said Dusty, shaking some feeling back into her hand. 'And this is my friend Trace.'

'Sis,' said Sam.

'Bro,' said Trace.

'Look, we need to get inside,' said Dusty, as Bro and Sis sized each other up.

'No problem,' said Sam.

While I'm on a good thing, thought Dusty.

'I also need to get backstage after the show.'

'I'll see what I can do,' said Sam, looking around, making sure nobody else was privy to their top-secret conversation.

'Cute,' said Trace as they crossed the threshold.

'Married,' said Dusty.

'Still cute.'

The main room was packed – whitefellas and blackfellas, locals and tourists, the usual Darwin melange – as the band sauntered onto the stage and took up their positions. They started up, the ba-do ba-do ba-do of the bassline reverberating around the room, and the crowd began to press forward. The drummer and the keyboard player were whitefellas, the bass player looked Indo, but the rest of the band – the didge player, the singer and the guitarist, the fella Dusty had come to see – were blackfellas.

Dressed in lurid yellow-and-blue-tracksuit pants, a Tupac T-shirt and wrap-around sunglasses and sporting some serious bling, Teddy's son looked pretty much like a pimp. Though not the pimps Dusty had had past dealings with; they actually looked more like real-estate salesmen. Though, again, not like the real estate salesmen of her acquaintance, who looked more like doctors. And so it went on. But that was the Top End for you, where nobody looked, or behaved, like they were really supposed to. Still, he looked a lot like his father, but whereas old Teddy had

The Build Up

a bushy grey beard young Teddy had dreadlocks, dreadlocks that bounced as he skipped across the stage, hammering away at his low-slung Telecaster.

It wasn't Dusty's type of music but Trace was already into her Beyonce thing: hey, I'm black, I'm a babe, I'm bootilicious. A bit obvious, thought Dusty, but she had to admit that for a mother of three, Trace could still bust some moves. The next song was a cover – Bob Marley's 'Get Up, Stand Up' – and even a country-loving *balanda* like Dusty couldn't help but sway discreetly to the beat.

'Shit!' said Trace, stopping mid-song.

'What is it?'

Trace indicated a group of blackfellas on the other side of the room.

'Lonnie's mob.'

Lonnie was Trace's ex-husband. His 'mob' was his extended family, his skin group, his clan, his tribe.

'Ignore them,' said Dusty.

'I'm going to the Duck's Nuts,' said Trace. 'Call me if you need me.'

Dusty didn't understand blackfella business – she wasn't sure if blackfellas even understood blackfella business – but she knew it was no use trying to persuade Trace to stay. When the band went off after the last song, there were obligatory cries of 'more!' 'more!'. As usual, it worked and they were soon back for the obligatory encore. The whole band came to the front of the stage, the three blackfellas each with a didge, the other band members each a set of clapping sticks. As they started, creating a simple *da-da da-da da-da* rthythym, the didges joined in, playing the same low drone, but soon the three instruments were weaving sinuously in and out of each other. The Troppo Lounge was quiet now, even the homies had stopped practicing the moves they'd seen on MTV. Dusty closed her eyes, surrendering to the music. Like some bad 80s video clip, she was skimming across the red sand of the Top End, until she was at the billabong with its fringing paperbarks, its muddy banks, its lily-strewn water.

'Hey Dusty, you OK?'

She opened her eyes to see Sam standing there, a concerned look on his face. The band had gone, Sting was playing over the PA and people were moving quickly out.

'Sure, I'm fine.'

'You wanna meet the band?'

'I'd love to.'

'Hey, those boys not in trouble, are they?'

'No, of course not. Nothing like that.'

Dusty followed Sam down a passage that smelled like stale beer and fresh vomit, into the packed green room.

'I got to get back to work,' Sam said.

Dusty thanked him, then stood with her back against the wall, slouching slightly, adopting what she hoped was a convincing rock-chick pose. It was a while since she'd done any undercover work – the last time was when she'd gone to Kanulla, Gardner's hometown, with Fontana – and she couldn't help thinking that it had to be obvious that she was both a copper and a country music fan. Slumped on tattered vinyl couches, band members drank green cans, ate Domino pizzas. The talk, however, was more upmarket. Imagine playing in New York? Or LA? Around them were a couple of smarmy-looking types, record execs Dusty guessed, a baby-faced journo and two Hiltonesque blondes. When Young Teddy got up and made for the esky of beer she intercepted him.

'Teddy?'

'Jamarra,' he replied.

'You're Teddy's son?'

The Build Up

'Yo,' he said. 'But my handle's Jamarra, you know what I mean?'

'Well, Jamarra, I loved the show,' she said, which wasn't strictly a lie – she'd loved the last song, and the rest wasn't that bad.

'Yo.'

Yo? What sort of answer was that?

It was time to get to the point. Yo.

'Look, I'm a copper,' she said.

'No, you gammin' me?'

It was difficult to tell whether he was taking the piss – it was obvious she was a copper – or he was genuinely surprised.

'I've worked with your dad, a bit,' said Dusty. 'It's a shame about his eyes.'

'Yeah, well. Shit happens, you know what I mean?'

Dusty nodded. She knew exactly what he meant. Shit does happen. Especially if you're a blackfella.

'He reckons you're as good as he is.'

'I don't do that shit,' he replied, an edge to his voice now.

'I'll pay you top dollar,' said Dusty, and as soon as she did she knew it was an instant candidate for the stupidest thing that had ever come out of her mouth.

'I'm sure you would,' said Teddy. 'But I ain't no mother fucking tea-towel, you know what I mean?'

Again, Dusty knew exactly what he meant – that classic tea-towel image, the noble savage standing on one leg, spear in hand, staring into the distance.

'See ya later, Constable.'

'Yeah, see ya,' replied Dusty, not bothering to correct him.

Right now she wasn't feeling much like a detective.

Chapter 41

'Dad, you have to see a doctor.'

The 'dad' still came as a surprise to Tank. What had he done to deserve that title? Treated her mother like shit. Walked out on them when she was only a little girl. Yes, he'd paid the maintenance but, really, he'd had nothing to do with her upbringing. And then, ten years ago, she comes looking for him. This gorgeous, educated young woman, his daughter. She wants *him* to be part of *her* life. She's read a lot about Vietnam, she doesn't know – how could you know if you weren't there – but she has some idea what he went through. She's willing to forgive, to put the past behind, to move on.

'Dad, you really have to see a doctor,' she repeated. 'I'll come with you, if you like.'

The eczema had come back, his arms afire with it. His hip wasn't mending like the specialist said it would, either. There was the other stuff, too. Stuff she didn't know about – the night-sweats, the blackouts, the sitting inside all day afraid to come out. All the stuff he thought had gone away for good.

'Pop!' cried Hayley, Tank's nine-year-old granddaughter.

'Look I can do third position,' she said, all hair flicks and ballet pumps.

The Build Up

Tank had this theory: some men, like him, were meant to be grandfathers, but not fathers. 'Dad' was never going to feel right, but 'Pop' was where he belonged.

'Is that right, sweetie?' he said

'Pop, are we going to the beach?' asked Bella.

Six years old, the tomboy, she'd outgrown the boogie board he'd bought her and now wanted a proper surfboard.

'Bit windy for the beach, today,' said Tank.

A stiff southerly, blow a dog off a chain. The disappointment in the girls' faces, especially Bella's, sent a jolt through Tank's heart.

'But I tell you what, we can go to Wylies Baths – it's protected there. Have a snorkel, check out the fish.'

'I'm not sure where the girls' snorkelling gear is,' said their mother.

'Don't worry,' said Tank. 'We'll sort that out.'

Tank wasn't surprised to see Trigger there – he'd heard that he was back in town, and the big fella had always loved his Wylies. He was surprised at how good he looked, however, fit and tanned, and how good he sounded – 'Hey, Tank, great to see you, mate!' – as if that stuff in the Territory had never happened.

'These are my grandkids, Hayley and Bella.'

'Never took you for the grandfatherly type,' said Trigger.

Tank wanted to knock him out of his boardshorts – what would he know about being a grandfather, the prick?

He sorted the kids out, rubbed sunblock into their shoulders, adjusted their new masks, their fins, before he went back up on the deck. Trigger did all the talking. He'd found some digs in a boarding house in Randwick. The other tenants were either very short, jockeys from the nearby racecourse, or very Asian – the university was also nearby. It was a bit of a dive. Trigger had forgotten just how expensive Sydney was, so he spent most of his free time here. He'd found a job as well. Nathan Mason's father, Joe, had helped him out there – security guard at the Coogee View hotel. Nothing flash, but nightshift suited him, and the money was just enough.

'Have you heard anything at all?' Tank blurted.

'Fuck me, Tank,' said Trigger, looking around. 'Keep a lid on it.'

'How come we haven't heard anything? It's not right.'

'What's that shit all over your arms?'

'Fucking eczema, that's what it is. Every time I pass a cop shop, I want to go inside.'

Trigger grabbed Tank by the sleeve of his poloshirt, pulling him in closer.

'Listen to me, Tank,' he said, through clenched teeth. 'You keep away from the fucking cops, OK. Girls, like that, they're not in the system. You got that? They go missing and no one cares. I didn't do her. You didn't do her. Don't fuck up a whole lot of lives for no reason.'

'Pop!'

Both girls, faces wet with water.

'Can we have a paddlepop?'

'Tell you what, kids,' said Tank, 'let's go to that joint on Coogee Bay Road, have us a proper ice-cream.'

Trigger watched as Tank fussed about his grandkids like a clucky old chook. Who would've thought it, eh? Trigger didn't even know the old bastard had any kids, let alone grandkids. Still, he was a worry. If he went to the cops, they were all fucked. Trigger borrowed a pen and paper from the kiosk and wrote down his new mobile number.

'If you ever need to talk,' he said, handing it to Tank.

He pocketed the paper before guiding his grandkids through the exit.

The Build Up

Trigger grabbed his goggles and walked down to the pool's edge. He wasn't a fish-sticker-on-your-bumper-bar sort of guy but he did believe in a higher power. And although his god was a punitive god – He'd turn you to fucking dust if He felt like it – He was also a reasonable god, in other words, He'd cut you a deal. The deal was straightforward: if He could give him some slack about that night – and so far He had – then Trigger Tregenza would get back onto the reasonably straight and the reasonably narrow. Swimming, somehow, had become part of the deal. Since that first morning when he'd dived into the water, washing the road trip from his body, he hadn't stopped swimming. Lap after lap after lap of Wylies Baths.

In the beginning it'd taken him half an hour to swim a kilometre. Now he had it down to twenty. Eighteen by the end of the year was his target.

Trigger set his stopwatch to zero and dived in.

Chapter 42

Dusty had offered to pick him up at his house, but he'd refused. And who could blame him if he didn't want the Filth to know where he lived?

'Eight o'clock at Rapid Creek shopping centre?' Dusty had then suggested over the phone.

'Six,' Jamarra had countered.

Six suited Dusty: The sooner they got to the billabong the better, but she wasn't sure how serious Jamarra was.

'You sure?' she'd asked, but he'd already hung up.

Dusty had hired a Subaru Forrester for the trip – there was no dignity for either party in a whitefella picking up a blackfella in a blackfella car. Right now, sitting outside a deserted Rapid Creek shopping centre, Dusty wished she hadn't bothered. It was half past six and there was no Jamarra. And maybe, thought Dusty, no Jamarra is exactly what I deserve.

It'd seemed so straightforward – she needed a gun tracker and she would've done almost anything to get one, play as dirty as necessary. Blackmail, the means, would justify the end – finding the body and, ultimately, the killer.

Jesus, she hadn't planted drugs on him, she hadn't verballed him, she hadn't given him a clip over the ear – she hadn't used any of those effective but ethically questionable techniques they

The Build Up

were so fond of in the southern states. All she'd done was suggest that if he helped her then she could help him.

Dusty's thinking was interrupted by a boisterous 'Constable!'

As Jamara got in, Dusty could smell beer, she could smell *yarndi*, she could smell a real good night out. She could smell sex, too, but that wasn't something she wanted to think too much about. As soon as Dusty pulled out of the car park, Jamarra was asleep.

With nobody to talk to, Dusty concentrated on the driving. Not that it was that difficult, the traffic was sparse and the Subaru's air con, power steering, cruise control and ABS braking made it a much different proposition to Beastie Boy.

Dusty stopped twice on the long drive south. The first was at the scene of the accident, the painted yellow hieroglyphics of the MVA guys still visible on the bitumen. John was now expected to make 'a good recovery'. There was even talk that he could be back at work sooner rather than later.

The second stop was at Noonamah. Not for fuel, she'd filled up before she'd left. Not for the toilet, either. And it wasn't a hankering for chips, chocolate or chewing gum. It was Tomasz. The photo had legitimised the dead girl's existence and doing so had done the same with Tomasz. He'd become flesh again. Or the memory of flesh. Dusty wandered around the roadhouse, then the pub. Locard's exchange principle – every contact leaves a trace – the basis of all forensics, was true of all relationships, too, no matter how fleeting. She remembered him asking the name of the drink she'd bought him.

'Soda, lime and bitters.'

She smiled when she thought of his reply – 'It is fucking oath good.'

Smiled when she thought of him speaking with that Colonel Klink accent for all that time. Dusty wasn't sure if she believed in the 'one'. Wasn't that just the stuff of romantic comedies? Surely it was just a matter of finding somebody who is a fairly good fit and then learn to live with them? But what if there was a 'one' and, even worse, what if that 'one' were Tomasz. A copper. A Squarehead. A birdwatcher! It was not a great thought. Dusty binned it and returned to the car and the sleeping Jamarra.

Dusty could feel her heart rate increase, her muscles tense as she turned off the Track and onto the dirt road. What was her body warning her about? The killer? This time she'd come prepared – as well as iced water, sandwiches and fruit she'd brought Smith & Wesson. The gun, not the dogs. In fact, it was a 40 cal self-loading Glock, but Dusty still thought of it as a Smith & Wesson, the gun the Force had used when she'd joined.

Dusty tapped on the brakes, the Subaru skidding slightly. Jamarra pitched forward, straining against his seatbelt.

'What the fuck!'

'Bloody roo,' lied Dusty.

Now that Jamarra was awake Dusty intended to keep him that way. She hit play on the CD player. Turned up the volume. Lucinda Williams.

'You like country music?' she asked.

'Fuck off.'

'So you don't like this.'

Jamarra listened for a while.

'Gnarly guitar,' he said.

'Real gnarly,' said Dusty. 'Look, I better fill you in.'

As Dusty talked, Jamarra started slapping the dash, bongo-style. Then he played some air guitar, presumably of the gnarly variety. She finished her explanation just as they were arriving at the billabong.

'Any questions?'

'What's this album called?'

The Build Up

'*Car Wheels on a Country Road.* I'll burn you a copy.'

'Isn't that against the law, Constable?'

'OK, you can have this copy. Whatever. Get with it, Jamarra. You ready for this, or not?'

'Who's that?' he said, pointing through the passenger window.

Dusty's premonitory fear had been justified, there was somebody at the billabong. They didn't look much like killers, though. More like nomads. Of the grey variety. A pair of them sitting in matching fold-up chairs under a striped awning attached to a caravan. Him reading a newspaper spread across his lap. Her reading a newspaper spread across her lap. In front, on a small table, were porcelain cups atop porcelain saucers.

'Don't know,' said Dusty.

That's all she needed, Ma and Pa tramping all over her crime scene.

'You hungry?' she asked Jamarra.

'S'pose Maccas is out of the question?'

Dusty couldn't help smiling. 'I can do you a sandwich.'

'Sounds good.'

Dusty got out of the car, receiving the usual slap in the face from the humidity. The weather bureau had predicted that the Wet would break later this week. The weather bureau wasn't always right. Dusty went over to introduce herself to the nomads. As she walked around the back of the caravan she saw the Tweety Bird. Don't you get too cwose! Dusty smiled to herself, recalling Kirky's words: Got half a fucking mind to book the old fucker. The old fucker was Wes, his wife Bette. They were from Bellingen, on the North Coast of New South Wales. They'd sold their dairy farm (bloody kids weren't interested in getting up at four every morning), bought the caravan and were doing the Big Loop. They were tough-looking, both of them wiry and weather-beaten, and there was something endearing about their enthusiasm for their new lifestyle.

'How'd you end up here, then?' asked Dusty.

'Got lost, actually,' said Bette, with a sideways glance at Wes.

'Geographically challenged,' said Wes, with a sheepish grin.

Bette continued. 'Liked it so much, we decided to stay for a while.'

'What about you, what brings you here?' asked Bette.

'Work,' said Dusty, taking out her badge. 'NT Police.'

'Nothing serious, I hope,' said Bette.

'Routine stuff.'

'Anything we can do to help?' asked Wes eagerly.

'You seen anybody around?'

No, they hadn't seen anybody around, but they were keen to keep an eye open. Especially Wes. When Dusty returned to the car, Jamarra had finished the sandwiches, all the sandwiches.

'Good?' inquired Dusty, grabbing an apple before that disappeared as well.

'OK. Needed some pickles, or something, I reckon.'

One generation, that's all it had taken. From Teddy to Jamarra. From gentleman to fuckwit.

'Time to get started,' said Dusty.

Jamarra took his shoes and socks off, carefully rolled his tracksuit bottoms to above the knees, peeled off his T-shirt. He had two raised scars across his chest. Initiation scars. Jamarra was so rock 'n' roll, it came as a surprise to think of him as belonging to this other world as well. He reached into his pocket and brought out an iPod. Dusty could hear the muffled thump of the bass as she followed Jamarra towards the billabong. He had the same precise, almost dainty, way of moving as his father. As he squatted down next to the mud bank, Dusty stood beside him.

'What ya doing, Constable?' he yelled.

'Just tagging along,' said Dusty.

'Eh?'

The Build Up

Dusty gently removed one of the earplugs.

'I said I'm tagging along.'

'No, you aren't. I don't need another *balanda* treading all over the place, you know what I mean?'

Dusty did know what he meant. So she sat in the car and did what she always did: she made copious notes.

'You like a cuppa and a chinwag?' yelled Bette after a while, as if hailing her neighbour over a suburban fence.

Why not, thought Dusty, putting down her pencil and notebook. The tea was very good, though both Bette and Wes were concerned that Dusty took neither milk nor sugar with hers. There were also biscuits on offer, homemade Anzacs.

'A caravan is no excuse to stop baking,' Bette stated.

Dusty agreed, guiltily thinking of the last time she'd baked. Maybe some muffins, about six years ago. And they were out of a packet. The chinwag too, was good, and helped pass the next two hours.

'So what, exactly, is he looking for?' asked Wes, eventually.

Dusty had noticed that Wes was a bit edgy, a bit twitchy. She guessed that he hadn't really settled into retirement and after a lifetime of working hard probably never would.

'Somebody went missing in this area,' said Dusty.

'They're good, aren't they?' said Bette.

'Who?'

'You know, your Indigenous people. Incredible what they can do. That guide we had on the bush tucker tour, he was marvellous,' said Bette, looking to her husband for support.

Just then Jamarra re-appeared next to the Subaru.

'Hey, you wanna cuppa?' yelled Bette.

'Love one,' said Jamarra, skipping towards them.

His demeanour hadn't changed. Had he found anything or not?

'How'd you take it?' asked Bette.

'White. Three sugars,' said Jamarra, taking the chair offered by Wes.

Bette smiled – now that was a proper cup of tea.

It was, said Jamarra, the best cuppa he'd had in years. As for the Anzacs, they were absolutely delicious – on a par with, if not better than, his own mother's. And so it went on, Jamarra holding court, talking about his upbringing, his mob, his music laying it on with a trowel. Bette and Wes were captivated. Especially Bette. And why not – Jamarra was charming, he was funny, he was self-deprecatory. He was making Ernie Dingo, the genial host of *The Great Outdoors*, look like a black separatist.

He can't have found anything, thought Dusty. He wouldn't just sit there spouting bullshit if he had. Or would he? Just to wind her up. And wound up she was. 'Excuse me,' she interrupted, 'but I really need to talk to my colleague in private.'

'So you didn't find anything?' demanded Dusty, as they walked back to the car.

'Didn't I?'

'Don't be stupid, Jamarra. Either you found something or you didn't. This is not a game. Somebody got murdered here.'

'You know, you got real nice eyes, Constable?'

One generation, that's all it'd taken. From gentleman to fuckwit. The sooner she got back to Darwin, the better. There were other leads to follow. Dusty reached the car and opened the door, when something occurred to her.

'Hey, you told them you busked in Central Park?'

'Did I?'

'So you've been to New York?'

'Is that where Central Park is?'

'Don't be a dick.'

'Couple of years ago, playing didge with White Cockatoo.

White Cockatoo was a well-known Indigenous dance troupe.

The Build Up

'So you knew I was bullshitting about them not giving you a visa because you've got that possession charge?'

Jamarra nodded. Dusty felt ashamed. It was as low as she'd gone in her eleven years as a copper. But she was also confused, why had he strung her along, like that?

'Why'd you come?'

'The old man. Don't know why, but he reckons you're OK.'

'Yeah, well I was OK until I met you. Get in the car.'

Jamarra got in the car. So did Dusty.

As she started the engine, Lucinda started singing about not missing him much. Again Dusty had cause to marvel at the uncanny ability of country music to nail the moment. As they passed Wes and Bette, Jamarra wound down the window.

'Hey, I wouldn't stay here if I were you,' he said.

'Why's that?' Wes asked.

'Bad spirits,' said Jamarra. He wound up the window.

'Jesus!' said Dusty. 'Why'd you go scare them like that for?'

'There's dead people buried here.'

Dusty stopped the car, looked over at Jamarra. Once again, she found him impossible to read.

'Are you serious?'

'Ask nicely and I can even show you where.'

Jamarra moved fast, and a couple of times Dusty had to break into a jog to keep up. He skirted the billabong before wending through a paperbark forest, eventually stopping.

'Well?' Dusty said.

'There,' he said, pointing, and even Dusty could see that the ground had been disturbed.

She dropped onto her knees, and started digging, scratching at the soil with her hands.

'Here, use this,' said Jamarra, handing Dusty a pointed stick.

'Aren't you going to help me?'

'Woman's work, digging,' he said, before removing himself, sitting cross-legged under a nearby paperbark, plugging back into his iPod.

Dusty used the stick to loosen the earth, before scooping it out with her hands. Under the low black sky the sweat poured off her face. It dribbled down her neck, drenching her shirt, her bra. Dusty didn't mind: she enjoyed manual jobs like this where you could see immediately what you'd accomplished. It was so different from so much police work where you could toil for months, sometimes years, without a result. When Lance Dykstra appeared Dusty wasn't surprised, he had the habit of popping up unexpectedly. She'd first met him during her time as a probationary constable, three days after he'd committed suicide. His girlfriend had dumped him so he'd run a hose from the exhaust pipe into his car. Dusty had volunteered to look for a suicide note – better to face your demons, she'd reasoned – and had got in the car with Lance Dykstra. Bloated, flyblown Lance Dykstra.

Dusty kept going with the stick, shovelling with her hands, ignoring her visitor. Then, Therese Napangardi appeared. She was Dusty's first homicide. A Long Grasser. According to the coroner her body had '32 fresh external injuries' including removal of both her nipples and an eye.

'Fuck, what's that smell?' said Jamarra.

At first Dusty assumed he must be repeating the chorus, something by Snoop Doggy Dog perhaps, or his hero Tupac. Then it hit her. The smell, the stench, of rotting flesh. Now Dusty understood – this is what had brought Lance and Therese back, caused them to loom large again. Dusty scraped away at the soil with her hands. There was flesh. Bone. Fingers. A hand. It was her. That's all she needed to know. It was her. Dusty kicked the soil back into the hole, smoothing it over.

'Good work,' she said to Jamarra. 'Let's go.'

The Build Up

He hesitated. 'What's the time?'
'Just after three.'
'What time we get back?
'Seven, I guess. Something like that. You playing tonight?"
Jamarra nodded.
'Let's go, then.'
Again he hesitated before smiling. 'OK'.

Chapter 43

Sunday, and the whole day had been planned – kids to be dropped off, kids to be picked up, the usual mad shuffle – but when Dusty had texted suggesting she 'come over for a dip', Trace had shuffled some more. She knew Dusty well enough – they'd been friends for ten years now – to know that 'come over for a dip' was her code for saying 'I need to talk.'

'Hey, I'm in the pool,' yelled Dusty, as they walked through the gate.

Wessie bounded up, in her mouth a limp rat. Saskia screamed, hugging her mother's leg.

'What's wrong?' Dusty asked.

'Bloody Wessie's got a rat,' answered Trace.

'Yeah, she finds them in the garden,' yelled Dusty from the pool. 'Wessie, get out of there!'

Wessie did what she was told, taking herself and her prey into the laundry.

The rat no longer a threat, Saskia gave full expression to her excitement, breaking into a run, yelling, 'I'm coming, Auntie!'

When Trace arrived at the pool's edge, following the trail of her daughter's discarded clothes, Saskia was already in the water. And Dusty, well, Dusty was swimming around, stark bloody naked!

'Where your bathers, girl?' said Trace, averting her gaze.

The Build Up

'Don't need any, nobody can see us here,' said Dusty.

'I can,' said Trace.

She picked up a faded one-piece that lay crumpled on the pavers and threw it at her friend.

'Biggest shame-job!'

Dusty, smiling, slipped the bathers on.

Trace had been expecting a different Dusty, the Dusty of the previous week: peeved, pissed off, even angry.

'Auntie, throw the rings,' said Saskia.

While Dusty tossed the different coloured rings to various parts of the pool for Saskia to retrieve, Trace changed into her bikini.

'They new?' asked Dusty.

'Yeah, Zimmerman, got them on special last week.'

'What do you reckon?'

'Broken arse!' said Dusty.

For a *balanda* she did a pretty good blackfella accent, and Trace couldn't help laughing. No, it really wasn't the Dusty of the previous week. Something had happened, and Trace could hardly wait to find out what it was. She dived into the pool, and paddled over to where Dusty was sitting on the stairs, waist-deep in water.

'OK, out with it,' she said. 'It's that backpacker, eh? He come back?'

'Sort of,' said Dusty. 'Well, he sent me a letter, but that's not it.'

Dusty proceeded to tell Trace exactly what had happened, her monologue only interrupted by Saskia returning the coloured rings for Dusty to throw 'one more time, Auntie'.

'I'm going to the commander on Monday,' said Dusty, sliding deeper into the water.

The old Trace, the cyclonic Trace, who had left school when

she was fifteen, because she had 'learning difficulties' – would've nodded then and said, 'Good idea, Dusty.'

But this Trace was different. 'Learning difficulties, my white arse,' Mr McFarlane, her Adult Ed teacher, had said, 'Teaching difficulties more like it.'

'Why would you do that?' asked this Trace.

'Why do you think?' snapped Dusty.

Trace went underwater, stroking to the other end and back. Thinking, getting her reasons sorted out. When she resurfaced, Dusty was waiting for an answer.

'All this stuff, it's all amazing, but only if you believe there was a body there in the first place,' said Trace, worried that Dusty would find a flaw in her reasoning and snap at her again.

'And you don't?' demanded Dusty.

'Sis, of course I do, but it's not about me, eh? It's about the commander. And the only way you'll convince her that there was a body is by shoving it under her nose.'

It was Dusty's turn to go underwater then. She surfaced at the deep end, and freestyled back, legs, arms, threshing. Shaking the water from her hair she glared at Trace.

'Show me the body, eh?'

'Well, show me some body,' said Trace.

'Throw the ring, Auntie!'

Chapter 44

Unlike on her previous visit to the Big C's office, the oil burner was on. Dusty hoped that whatever was in it had calmative properties because the Big C's rage seemed barely constrained.

'What are these?' she demanded, slamming some photos on the desk before Dusty even had a chance to settle in her seat.

Dusty picked up the photos.

Long Grassers. Wearing various articles of police clothing. Amongst them, Marion.

Now she understood why the Big C had seemed so surprised when Dusty had knocked on her door this morning, why she'd said, 'Just the person I wanted to see.'

Dusty had some fast thinking to do. Had they actually traced the uniforms back to her? Or had the Big C simply assumed it was her – Queen of Fuck-ups, and all that?

'I'd very much like you to explain how these uniforms which were originally issued to a certain Detective F. Buchanon ended up here.'

Dusty smiled to herself. The Big C may have had an MBA on her wall and a bookcase full of management texts but she hadn't spent hour upon hour in the interview room, honing her interrogatory skills. She'd just played a trump card when there was no reason to.

'Well?' she said. 'I'm waiting for your answer.'

Dusty, like every other member of her profession had heard many lies in her time. Some were plausible, most were not. Of all the professional liars – advertising executives, real-estate salesman, lawyers, con men – it was politicians she had the most sneaking admiration for. They had an armoury of techniques. Repeat the same lie often enough and it will start to acquire the glaze of truth was one. Or, the one Dusty intended to use, give an answer that obliquely relates to the question but possesses its own internal legitimacy.

'They must've been taken from my house,' said Dusty.

Which indeed they had. By her.

'Do you think I'm a fucking idiot?'

It was a shock to hear the Big C swear, especially when you considered the number of directives she'd sent out decrying the gratuitous use of profane language. The 'fucking' was either a measure of her hypocrisy or her anger; Dusty was inclined to think it was mostly the latter.

'No, of course not,' said Dusty.

'We have talked to these people, you know?' she said, waving a hand at the photos.

Was the Big C bluffing? Grassers by name, were they grassers by nature? Had Marion given her up? If so, her career was gone.

'They must've been taken from my house,' repeated Dusty, which is also something she'd picked up from the pollies – never resile from your original statement, no matter how much evidence is presented to the contrary.

'Then why didn't you report this?'

So predictable, thought Dusty, her answer already prepared. 'Because I didn't know they'd been taken.'

'So you're telling me that somebody has broken into your house and stolen some police uniforms and nothing else?'

The Build Up

'It's the Build Up,' said Dusty. 'People do crazy things.'

The Big C was now glaring at Dusty.

Is she really trying to stare me down, thought Dusty. When you've looked into the black and pitiless eyes of a serial killer the gaze of a middle-aged bureaucrat doesn't hold many terrors.

Eventually, it was the Big C who broke off eye contact.

'That's all,' she said.

You wish, thought Dusty.

'I've found her body,' she said.

The Big C looked lost.

Dusty helped her out. 'The girl at the billabong.'

I don't believe you. It was in the Big C's face, her body, her entire being. I think you see things. Gruesome things. You've got PTSD. You're quite possibly mad.

Dusty took out a labelled plastic exhibit bag from her briefcase and handed it to the Big C.

'What's this?'

'Her.'

The Big C recoiled, dropping the bag, pushing back hard against her chair.

'Well, some of her,' corrected Dusty.

It didn't take long to organise – a unit would leave at ten for the billabong. And Dusty would be one of them.

'Better get this back to the fridge,' she said, picking up the exhibit bag.

As she entered the women's toilet she sent Trace a text – 'it worked!'.

Dusty dropped the exhibit bag, with its contents, into the nearest toilet and hit the flush button.

It had been grisly work, dissecting the dead rat, even if Trace had done most of it, but it had been worth it. Nobody with any experience of dead human beings, of decaying human flesh, would mistake their concoction for the real thing, but Dusty had gambled that Commander Christine Schneider MBA wasn't one of those people, and she'd won.

As she was about to leave the door opened and Flick entered.

'Your hair looks great,' said Dusty. 'Who did it?'

'That one you recommended – Sam's.'

She'd lost weight, too. And in the right places.

It'd been Dusty's observation that when pear-shaped chicks lost weight many ended up looking even more pear-shaped. Not Flick, though.

'You've lost too, haven't you?' said Dusty.

'A bit,' said Flick. 'How are you coping back in uniform?'

Dusty couldn't tell if the concern in her voice was faux or not. 'You know what, I realised I actually missed the feeling of polyester against my skin.'

Flick laughed, and she looked almost pretty. It really was a good haircut.

'Got the DNA report,' said Flick.

'And?'

'Gardner's there,' she said smiling.

It was the result, or 'outcome' as the Big C would call it, that everybody had been hoping for, herself included at one stage, and made the case against Gardner so strong it was almost *fait accompli*. Even the lawyers couldn't screw this one up. Chalk up another win up for the all-conquering DNA.

'Vaginal?' Dusty asked casually.

Flick shook her head. 'Nothing.'

'Anal?'

'Actually, there's a bit of an issue there. We're thinking there might be some contamination.'

Like hell, thought Dusty.

The Build Up

'Could I have a copy?'
'Sure,' said Flick. 'Come by. I'll be at my desk all afternoon.'
With that Flick and her haircut disappeared into a cubicle.

Chapter 45

The glade of paperbarks, alive with white and yellow butterflies, seemed more a place for a lepidopterist than a criminologist. Dusty had done some research. Well, she'd googled. The Aborigines, she'd read, had many uses for the papery bark of the *melaleuca* – as a lining in a coolamon to make a baby's cradle, as a disposable raincoat, a shroud for the dead. Now four *melaleuca*s served as the corners of a rough square, the yellow Crime Scene tape strung between them, looped around their flaking trunks.

From her position outside the perimeter Dusty watched Craig Schmidt, senior crime scene examiner, his poloshirt and cargo trousers already darkened with sweat, start to dig. The air was so dense you felt you could grab a handful of it and squeeze out the moisture.

'She's about a metre-and-a-half down,' said Dusty.

'So you said.'

It was clear that Craig had the shits with her. Obviously he blamed her, in some part, for John Goode's accident. The Department had tried to find a replacement, but experienced crime scene investigators, unlike windfall mangoes, weren't thick on the ground in the Top End, and Craig's workload, already insane, had become insaner.

The soil had been turned twice so the actual digging was easy.

The Build Up

Craig took it slowly, though, meticulously sifting each shovel-load through a sieve, making sure he didn't miss any clues. As he did so, he and Senior Sergeant Barry talked fishing and footy, and all those other subjects blokes tend to explore when they're exhuming the dead.

Forensic pathologist Dr Monty Singh joined Dusty.

'Knock, knock,' he said.

Dusty liked the diminutive and loquacious Dr Singh. She admired his professionalism, was entertained by his archaic English and didn't even mind his appalling jokes. But right now she really wanted him to shut the fuck up.

Actually, she wanted everybody at the crime scene to shut the fuck up. To stop making talk so small it crawled on its belly, stop cracking the same bad jokes. Of course, it was what you did when death was around, especially if the death, like this one, was sudden and violent. When your own mortality was up and at you, snapping like a croc. You fed it, distracted it with small talk, bad jokes – whatever it took.

Dusty knew this but today was different, today she wanted everybody to concentrate on the job at hand, persuade the crime scene to give up all its clues, get her out of the ground and back to Darwin and, ultimately, jail the bastard responsible for this.

'Can we not do this today, Singhie?' said Dusty gently.

'Jesus, that's ripe,' said Craig, smiling. He wore disposable gloves, but no face mask, or nose cream – like most experienced crime scene examiners he seemed immune to the stench of human decay. Dr Singh, too, seemed unaffected, sniffing at the air as if it bore some exotic fragrance.

'For how long do you say she's been there, again?' he asked.

'More than four weeks, by my calculations.'

'Hmmm, extremely odiferous.'

'But she was in the water before, remember?'

'Oh, that's right. Quite.'

Dusty had already told Dr Singh the whole story. Why hadn't he remembered? What was wrong with him today? What was wrong with everybody today? Craig had stopped digging, and was sipping water from a plastic cup.

'Craig, you want me to dig for a while?' asked Dusty, impatiently.

'I'll be right,' he said, looking hard at her.

He slowly finished the water before returning to work. Aware, now, that the body must be close, he swapped the spade for a trowel. Dusty found herself moving closer to the makeshift grave, the tape now taut across her midriff.

Craig was on his haunches, using the tip of the trowel to clear the soil from around something.

'What is it?' Dusty asked eagerly.

No response.

'Craig, I asked you a question!'

Craig looked up at Dusty. 'Can you just let me do my fucking job?'

'Detective, maybe it's better you back off a bit,' Senior Sergeant Barry suggested. 'Give Schmitty some breathing space.'

He was right – she was too wound up. Retreating to the same paperbark that Jamarra had used, she sat down in semi-lotus, the trunk as a backrest, and closed her eyes.

'Monkey thoughts,' Vashti called them, and it was a good description – they were swinging around in her head now, eating bananas and scratching their nit-infested arses. The idea, apparently, was to get them to stay put. Dusty tried, but it was no good – if anything they became more frenetic, taunting her.

'Detective!'

Dusty's eyes snapped opened. She jumped up and joined Dr Singh.

The Build Up

'Is this her?' said Craig, smirking.

The body wasn't in great shape. It took her a while to get everything into context. Even when it became clear what she was looking at, she kept looking at it, willing it to be anything other than what it was – a distended, discoloured penis.

'Maybe *katoey*?' said Craig. The Thai word for a transvestite.

Dusty had seen her naked, she was no *katoey*.

'It's not her,' said Dusty.

'No kidding?' said Craig.

'Quite,' said Dr Singh.

Craig picked up something with his gloved hands, a beret, shaking the soil from it.

'Jesus!' he said.

'What?'

'SAS.'

Chapter 46

Dusty rang pathology. The man himself, answered. You had to admire that about Dr Singh – up to his elbows in blood and guts but still took calls.

'Any luck?' asked Dusty.

'I have calculated his age to be thirty-eight.'

'That's pretty exact.'

'As you know modern pathology offers a number of techniques to ascertain the age of the human body.'

'Quite,' said Dusty, borrowing one of the doctor's favourite words.

'Besides, I have his driver's licence right here in front of me.'

The doctor found this funny. Dusty found it funny, too, but not quite as much as the doctor did. She had to wait for him to finish laughing.

'So you've got a name, then?'

A pause.

'Actually,' said Singhie, 'I might have to resort to more conventional means for age determination. I think this licence is a phoney, isn't it?'

'What makes you say that?'

'Not my area of expertise, but something not quite right about it.'

'What name is on it?'

'I'm not sure I'm able to go into that.'

Dusty could understand his reluctance, one of the Big C's recent directives had been about the wrongful dissemination – her phrase – of pathology results.

'Knock, knock,' said Dusty.

'Who's there?'

'The commander.'

'The commander who?'

'Exactly.'

Another burst of Dr Singh's patented laughter.

'James Wells,' he said.

Dusty scribbled that down on a pad.

'What about the address?'

'Kanulla Street, Brisbane. Number five.'

'Kay. Aye. En. You. Double Ell. Aye. Kanulla?'

'That is correct.'

Dusty wrote the address down, underlining the word 'Kanulla' several times.

'Owe you one, Singhie.'

'Quite.'

Something else occurred to Dusty.

'Before you go.'

'What now, Detective?'

'Does Mr Wells have tatts?'

'Several.'

'One wouldn't say KKK would it?'

'Not that I can see.'

'Shit!'

'But . . .'

'Yes?'

'He does had a rather peculiar tattoo of a hanging man, isn't it?'

'A black man?'

'You could say that.'

There was a rap on the glass. After the visit to Ruby's, Gerard had been in the habit of dropping by for a chat, updates on the case. Today, bless his sensible shoes, he was bearing styrofoam.

'Flat white, isn't it?'

'You're a good man, Gerry,' said Dusty taking the coffee.

'No big deal, but I do prefer Gerard.'

'Gerard, you want to come for a drive?'

'Where to?'

'Kanulla.'

'Kanulla in Western Australia.'

'Kanulla in Western Australia.'

'Yeah, OK!'

'Great, let's go then,' said Dusty, getting up from her desk.

'Hey, I thought you were joking.'

Dusty shook her head. 'I never joke about Kanulla.'

'But why do you want to go there?'

'It's complicated, I'll fill you in on the way.'

Gerard looked unconvinced.

'Trust me, Gerry.'

'Gerard!'

'Sorry, Gerard. Trust me, Gerard.'

'I can't just leave here.'

'Tell me, when's the last time you had a sickie?'

'I don't know. A couple of years ago, maybe longer.'

Dusty placed her palm against Gerard's forehead.

'Look, I'm no doctor but I reckon you've got a temperature. You need to go home, grab a change of clothes and a toothbrush, pick me up at my place, and then we can drive to Kanulla.'

'You want to go in my car?'

Dusty smiled.

'You've seen mine, haven't you?'

Chapter 47

It didn't take long – the car had just passed Noonamah – for Gerard to conclude that this was the craziest thing he'd ever done. This was not, as most of his colleagues would've assumed, an indication of how dull his life had been, but a measure of just how crazy this trip was. For a start, he'd pulled a sickie, something he'd never done before and now his car – OK, it was a police car, but he was ultimately responsible for it – was being driven by somebody who gave all the signs of being, as office scuttlebutt had suggested for a while now, slightly unhinged. Not only that, it was heading at a rapid speed – the speedometer needle was glued to 160 km/hr – to a town that Gerard had never been to, in a state Gerard had never been to. Why?

A girl's been murdered and I'm going to find out who did it was sounding rather grandiose now. Dusty had said that when people invent – a name, a street, anything – they usually go with what's available to them, access their internal database. She also mentioned something about a tattoo. That's about as far as it went, explanation-wise.

Maybe it's always like this, thought Gerard. I've become so used to the mundane world of the Shed that I've lost touch with this sort of speculative detective work. Maybe they're right – I'm just a clerk.

Dusty's phone started playing 'Zorba the Greek'. She'd already asked if she could put it in the hands-free. Gerard had agreed, of course – he knew all about John's accident. Dusty checked the number before looking over at Gerard. 'Do you mind?'

'No, go ahead.'

'Hello.'

'Frances.'

'Mum, this isn't your usual number.'

Dusty looked over at Gerard and mouthed 'Sorry'.

'I'm at Susie's, but I just had to call you about your room.'

Her plummy accent surprised Gerard – he knew Dusty was from Adelaide, but not this Adelaide.

'I don't expect you'll be staying with me forever, but until you find your feet it'll be a perfect base.'

Gerard would've liked to have discreetly stepped outside, given mother and daughter some privacy. Not at 160 km/hr, though.

'And I've had your old bedroom painted in a lovely apricotty colour.'

Gerard could sense Dusty's growing discomfort. Once more she mouthed 'Sorry'.

'I've cleared most of the stuff from your wardrobes.'

'Mum,' Dusty interrupted, 'I'm not coming back to Adelaide.'

'It's only a single bed but I'm sure–'

'Mum, listen to me,' said Dusty, more forcefully this time. 'I've changed my mind. I'm not leaving the police force and I'm not leaving Darwin.'

There was breathing on the other end, and then, click!

'After John's accident I thought about going back to Adelaide,' said Dusty, by way of explanation.

'You must've been in a bad way,' said Gerard.

He'd been to Adelaide many times and always found it to be

The Build Up

a pleasant place, a very *liveable* place, but he'd been in the Top End long enough to know the etiquette – if it was below the Tropic of Capricorn, it was shite.

They stopped at Katherine to fill up and change drivers. Then, instead of following the Track south to Alice Springs, Gerard took the road west, the Victoria Highway.

'Do you mind?' said Dusty, taking out some well-thumbed notebooks. 'Want to check up on a couple of things.'

'Not at all.'

A zipper of bitumen cut through the treeless plain. Maybe a scientist, or an artist, or a mystic, could find interest in this landscape, but not Gerard. To him it looked either unfinished or worn right away. Oncoming drivers were cocking a finger or two, some of them raising a hand. Obviously they were in the outback proper, now, where it was necessary to acknowledge the daring of your fellow explorer. Gerard noticed that Dusty was looking at a photo, the one that had been in all the papers, the smiling newly-weds, Dianna and Greg McVeigh, arms linked, standing on Bondi Beach, about to embark on the trip of a lifetime.

'Where's he now?'

'Greg?'

Gerard nodded.

'He came back for Gardner's trial but since then we've lost touch. Last we heard he was in Africa.'

Dusty put the photo away.

'You want a rest?'

'No, I'm fine,' said Gerard, putting on sunglasses.

Out here the monsoonal trough had no influence; there was no Build Up. The sky was cloudless and they were heading straight into the descending sun.

'OK, so why'd you become a copper?' Dusty suddenly asked.

'My old man was a copper.'

'So was mine.'

'No shit?'

'Actually, a lot of shit.'

They both laughed at this.

'How'd you end up in the Shed, anyway?' Dusty asked.

'Anterior prolapse of L4/L5 lumbar disc.'

'You did your back?'

'Completely.'

'It seems OK, now.'

'Only because I look after my core strength.'

'Pilates?'

Gerard nodded.

They crossed into Western Australia as the sun was setting – the sky a slit throat, pumping red. Gerard dropped his speed back to the limit, one ten. They'd already seen quite a few roos. At 9.25 pm they pulled in front of the Kanulla Motel.

'Seven and a half hours,' said Gerard, checking his Rolex Submariner.

Dusty smiled, looking at her Taiwan cheapie.

'Exactly what I got.'

Chapter 48

He was one of those overly-cheerful, overly-familiar people who seem only to exist in the dingy offices of second-rate country motels.

'How are we all tonight?' he said.

And he had dandruff.

'We'd like two rooms,' said Dusty.

'I'm afraid I can't help you. Got a whole lot of mine people booked in tonight.'

The mine was the Carlyle Diamond Mine, thirty clicks to the north, and the reason for Kanulla's existence. In the 1880s, gold was discovered in the area and the town boomed, but when that ran out and the miners decamped to California, Kanulla, like so many other boom-and-bust towns, began its slow decline. Then they found diamonds. Though Kanulla's second boom was much less frenetic than its first, the town was still relatively prosperous. There was the hotel–motel, a supermarket, a service station and a primary school.

'So you've got nothing?' said Dusty.

'Well, we've got the honeymoon suite, but you're paying top dollar for that.'

'Does it have two beds?'

'The sofa folds out.'

'OK, we'll take that.'

'Did you want the package, then? Free bottle of bubbly and dinner at Tiffany's thrown in?'

Do I look like I want the fucking package, Snowcone? Dusty wanted to say.

'Just the room, thanks. For one night.'

Though Gerard kept insisting that he would sleep in the car, Dusty eventually persuaded him to take the sofa.

'You know what I don't understand,' said Gerard, as they entered the honeymoon suite with its grime-ringed spa and lop-sided bed.

'What?' said Dusty.

'What sort of place must you come from to spend your honeymoon here?'

Dusty laughed. 'Whyalla.'

'Rough?'

'Put it this way, the dogs bark out of their arses.'

After showers they ate at Tiffany's. The steak was good. The coffee wasn't. While inviting Gerard along had been a spur-of-the-moment thing, Dusty had done so knowing that he brought with him two wonderful qualities – a car, and the ability to drive it. That he was also good company was an unexpected bonus. He didn't have the most scintillating reputation in the Top End – get some mud, put a stick in it, that's Gerard. That phone call from Celia had been so embarrassing but the revelation, and it was a revelation – Dusty had never told anybody in the Force this before – that both their fathers had been cops had forged a bond between them. Cops' kids, unlike those of doctors, farmers and Kerry Packer, do not tend to follow in their parent's footsteps. Why would they, when they know firsthand what goes with the job? After paying the bill – Dusty insisting they put it on her card – they returned to the honeymoon suite to get ready.

The easiest thing to do would be to barge into the pub, badges

The Build Up

blazing, and start firing off questions. Dusty was reluctant to do this, however. She remembered the conversation with Fontana when they drove back from Kanulla last time.

'You know what,' he'd said, stretching his long legs out. 'I actually feel bad.'

'So would I if I fucked a barmaid,' Dusty had answered.

Fontana shook his head.

'And a redhead, at that,' she'd added.

'They were such nice people, and we shat all over them.'

'We were undercover gathering intel. Or in your case, a disease.'

'I feel bad.'

'Gonorrhoea is like that.'

If somebody like Fontana, with Fontana's questionable ethics, could 'feel bad', then blowing the cover, even a year or so later, wasn't the way to go.

'Gerard, you ever done any undercover work?'

'Can't say I have.'

'Then this is your lucky day.'

'Do I need to wear anything special?' he asked.

Lilac poloshirt. Hungry-arse shorts. Jesus sandals.

'No, that'll do,' said Dusty.

Dusty pushed open the door to the pub. Miners, still in their workclothes, stood at the bar. No blackened faces or hobnailed boots here, though, just neat khaki uniforms adorned with the Carlyle Diamond logo. These were open-cut miners, operators of diggers, dumptrucks, and their air-conditioned like.

Dusty had dressed conservatively in fitted shirt and jeans, but she could sense the eyes following her, fondling her, as she made for a table. Diamonds may be a girl's best friend, but she figured not many made their way out here to look for them.

A group of blackfellas was at the back of the room. Dusty had forgotten the name of the mob out here, but she knew that the mine was on their land. From the way they fed the pokies it was clear that they intended on keeping their royalties in circulation. Dusty remembered how James used to go on about self-determination, economic independence. It'd seemed fair enough, but now she wasn't so sure – welfare was welfare, it was all sit-down money, and it didn't really matter whether it was private or public enterprise signing the cheque.

She couldn't see any of the people she'd met with Fontana the last time. Although Belinda, the red-haired barmaid, smiled when she saw Dusty. 'Back already, eh?'

Dusty wasn't sure whether the irony was intentional or eighteen months wasn't considered such a long time in Kanulla terms.

'Couldn't stay away. How you been?'

'Can't complain. Big fella with you?'

'No,' said Dusty, and she saw the flicker of disappointment pass across Belinda's face.

'Not many locals around tonight?'

'They'll be here directly. Don't worry about that.'

Dusty ordered two glasses of white wine and returned to the table.

'You married?' she asked Gerard, realising she knew nothing about his private life.

'No.'

'Got a partner?'

'Still looking.'

Dusty was about to pop another, more impertinent question when Tissues and Beefy turned up. Both were wearing jeans and rock 'n' roll T-shirts – Tissues, it seemed, was a fan of the seminal heavy metal group Black Sabbath, while Beefy preferred the Australian proto-rockers AC/DC. They were happy to see Dusty,

The Build Up

pleased to meet Gerard and disappointed that Fontana hadn't been able to make it.

'Fucking character,' said Tissues, who wasn't a bad example of that species himself.

Big and boxy – which is where the nickname came from, Tissues, as in tissue box, and not, as Dusty had first assumed, from any masturbatory practice – he was the local postman. Beefy's nickname also derived from his physique, though in his case it was pure irony; he was a ferret of a fella, and the local odds-job man – dog-catching, grave-digging, marriage celebrancy. Apparently he could turn his hand to anything.

It intrigued Dusty to hear them reminisce about her last visit. The drinking. The bets on the gee-gees. The visit out to the mine. It had become bubblewrapped in nostalgia, as if it belonged to a distant, more carefree past.

'Ron around?' said Dusty.

He'd been the one to bite when Dusty had casually – and quite artfully, she thought – dropped Gardner into the conversation.

'Went to school with him,' he'd said. 'Always was a scumbag.'

'So you reckon he done that Pommy sheila?' Fontana had added, perhaps not so artfully.

Ron hadn't even hesitated.

'Nah. He was a scumbag, but not that sort of a scumbag. More of a follower, you know?'

Ron had also spent much of the weekend making goo-goo eyes at Dusty, even suggesting that he'd look her up next time he was in Darwin.

'He'll be here any minute,' said Tissues. 'Footy thing would've finished by now.'

Ron, Dusty had gathered, was not so much a pillar of the local community as its very foundation. A school teacher, he seemed to be involved in everything from the footy club to the Tidy Town committee.

Two minutes later, Ron walked in.

How could you ever get away with a murder in a country town? thought Dusty. You couldn't even fart in the bath without everybody knowing. Ron was mid-forties, not handsome, not ugly, carrying a bit too much weight. Sandy complexion – a bit like Gerard, actually. If he was glad to see Dusty he didn't show it. He joined the table but seemed diffident, pissed-off almost, and took no part in the conversation. This wasn't the chatty Ron Dusty had met last time.

'I got to go,' he said, finishing his drink, getting up from his chair. 'Essays to mark.'

'What's his problem?' Dusty asked as she watched him disappear through the door.

'Dunno, maybe you better ask him,' said Tissues.

Taking his advice, Dusty hurried outside, running to catch up with Ron.

'Ron, you OK?' she asked.

He stopped, turned around, and looked at her – if eyes were knives she was mincemeat.

' I drove to Darwin, you know. Couple of weekends after you were here.'

Dusty knew what was coming next.

'Rang that number you gave me. Didn't work.'

'Maybe you copied it down wrong.'

'Yeah, well, that's what I thought, too. Anyway, I remember you mentioned the Nightcliff Footy Club so I go over there, ask if anybody knows Dusty. Sure, everybody knows Dusty. The copper, you mean? No, I said. This Dusty runs a pet shop. I show them the photo I took on my mobile. No, that's Dusty all right, they said. That's the copper. Then it all falls into place. Those questions about Gardner.'

Dusty wanted to disappear. Evaporate. Disintegrate.

The Build Up

'I'm really sorry, Ron.'

'Forget it, Detective. You had a job to do. So do I. Now if you'll excuse me, I need to get home.'

Dusty watched Ron get into his car and drive off. The undercover caper was now over. Ron would've told his mates and Tissues and Beefy were just stringing them along, giving the filthy pigs back a bit of their own. But when Dusty returned, Gerard and his two new best mates seemed to be hitting it off famously.

'This bloke's a freak!' said Tissues, admiringly.

'Nineteen eighty-three?' asked Beefy.

'Winner was Kiwi,' Gerard said. 'Ridden by Johnny Cassidy. Carried fifty-three kilo.'

'Sorry to break up the party, but I'm going to hit the sack. Gerard?'

'Gerard's going nowhere, are you, mate? We're just getting started,' insisted Beefy.

'Two thousand and two?' asked Tissues.

'Media Puzzle,' said Gerard.

Dusty didn't hear the rest.

She went back to her room where she had another shower, brushed her teeth and got into bed. It was difficult to sleep – the unfamiliar bed in the unfamiliar room, the clatter of the air conditioner, the blare from a TV from one side and a couple having sex on the other, and, most of all, the guilt.

Ron hadn't been the only one making goo-goo eyes that weekend – Dusty, too, had flirted. It was strictly professional, she could argue; she was trying to get him to open up in the hope that he would offer something on Gardner. But did the ends justify the means, especially when the ends were so meagre? They hadn't got much on Gardner at all before they were urgently called back to Darwin – there'd been a murder out at Humpty Doo. And was it really strictly professional? James had just left, taking not only his Radiohead CDs but Dusty's self-esteem as well. It had felt good to flirt again, to be the object of somebody else's goo-goo eyes. Fontana was right – they, she, really had *shat all over them*.

Eventually she did sleep only to be woken by the scratch of a key trying to locate a keyhole, again and again. Then the door being pulled the wrong way, again and again. Then Gerard lurching in, collapsing on the sofa.

At seven, when Dusty went for breakfast the overly-familiar manager was now the overly-familiar waiter.

'How are we this morning?'

'I'll have the eggs with bacon,' said Dusty.

'Jezza had a big one, eh?'

'Who?'

'Your room-mate.'

'And a really strong flat white,' said Dusty.

Again the food was good. Again, the coffee wasn't. Dusty returned to the room where the man formerly known as Gerard hadn't moved. She now noticed that he was wearing a several sizes-too-small AC/DC T-shirt instead of the lilac number she'd last seen him in. He also had a boomerang tucked into the waistband of his hungry-arse shorts. It made sense, now – the L4/L5 anterior disc prolapse explanation had been, as Dusty had suspected, bullshit. So was Alex's he-lost-his-bottle story. Gerard had an issue – drink, drugs, whatever and that's the reason he'd been knocked sideways out of active service and into the Shed.

'Gerard!' she said.

No response.

'Jezza! she said, giving his shoulder a none-too-gentle shake.

He stirred, his eyes blinking open. Dusty knew that there was no use being angry. Lots of people had issues – they were alcoholics, they were addicts, they were fucked-up. Maybe it was

The Build Up

their fault, maybe it wasn't, but either way getting angry got you nowhere.

'I'll be back at lunch, OK. You sleep it off, mate.'

There'd be no undercover today, only old-fashioned grunt police-work – knocking on doors, asking questions. Gerard muttered something unintelligible.

'What?' snapped Dusty, reminding herself not to get angry.

Gerard rolled off the sofa and stumbled into the bathroom. A variety of hoicking noises ensued. When he reappeared, his face glistening with water, he'd regained the power of speech.

'Brian Jonsberg,' he said.

'What?'

'Gardner's best mate at school. His name was Brian Jonsberg.'

'Who told you that?'

'Ali.'

'And who would Ali be?'

Gerard held up the boomerang. 'Blackfella who gave me this.'

'Mate, they were onto us. There was no cover. This Ali fella was just having a bit of fun with you.'

'So you don't want to hear any more?'

'Of course I want to hear.'

Before he could continue Gerard had to revisit the bathroom, do some more hoiking, drink some more water.

'Around the mid-eighties a lot of real weird shit went on in Kanulla. Cats found dead. Dogs with their eyes out. Houses set alight. Then sexual stuff. Young girls, mostly black, assaulted in the playground. It was Gardner who got blamed for most of it. But Ali reckons Gardner was never into sex. While him and his mates were wanking over *Playboys* Gardner'd be doing the milk round, ripping off people's milk money. Brian Jonsberg was into sex, though. Obsessed with it, Ali reckons. Sex and violence. But Jonsberg was a whole lot smarter than Gardner. He never got caught.'

'Gardner was never into sex,' repeated Dusty. 'That's what he said?'

'That's what he said.'

Two years ago Dusty had stood in the commander's office and told Geoff much the same thing.

'I don't think Gardner did it,' she'd said.

'Why not?'

'He's no sexual predator.'

Dusty had done four years in Sex Crimes; she knew predators. She knew what it was like to listen to their dirty dirty talk – every utterance an innuendo. Knew what it was like to be undressed by their eyes, fucked by their eyes, while they stroked themselves moist under the table.

Gardner was none of this.

Now Dusty's whole body was tingling – was this the break she'd been hoping for?

'Let's go find out some more about Brian Jonsberg.'

'His mother still lives here,' said Gerard. 'Left at the servo, third street on the right, and then the house with EH Holden in the front yard. Can't miss is, apparently.'

Dusty was already moving.

'Come on, Gerard, let's go!'

As they turned left at the servo Dusty asked, 'How do you remember all that, with all the beer you drank?'

'Actually, I didn't drink that much.'

'So it was all an act?'

Gerard shook his head.

'No, it was the bongs that did me in.'

'You smoke *yarndi*?'

'I do now.'

It wouldn't have been shitty old leaf either. These miners got paid big money, these blackfellas got paid big royalties, they

The Build Up

could afford the best: nasty hydro skunk that took your brain apart neuron by neuron. Dusty's estimation of Gerard ratcheted up a couple of notches.

They turned down the third street on the left. This was old Kanulla here, rundown and decrepit. None of the mine's largesse got this far. Most of the stone houses were uninhabited, reduced to shells or else boarded up.

At number 7, however, there were signs of habitation – the EH Holden in the front drive, and, incongruously, the satellite dish tacked to an iron roof scabbed with rust.

Dusty and Gerard got out of the car and approached the house. The Holden's tyres were flat but a girl's face (she was maybe five or six) appeared at one of its windows. Her lips were smeared with lipstick, her eyes darkened with mascara, and she was wearing a two dollar store tiara on her head.

'Hello,' she said. 'I'm a princess and this is my castle.'

'That's a very nice castle and you're a very pretty princess,' said Dusty.

'What's your name?' the girl asked.

'My name's Dusty and this is my friend Jezza.'

The girl got out of the car, smiling at Dusty. She was wearing a tattered fairy dress, a tattered set of fairy wings. The sun caught her jewellery. The cheap sparkle of the plastic jewels in her tiara. The flash of her bangles. And, around her neck, a gold necklace. It was too big for her, dangling down, the small cross almost at the level of her stomach.

'That's a pretty necklace,' said Dusty.

'So's yours,' said the girl, pointing to the fob chain around Dusty's neck.

'I tell you what, let's swap'? said Dusty.

The girl smiled broadly, showing lipstick-stained teeth. 'OK,' she said, slipping the necklace over her head.

'Chantay, who's there?' came a voice from behind the house.
'Some nice people, Nana.'

A woman appeared, dressed in black leggings, an over-sized T-shirt, ciggie in her hand. Instantly, Dusty recognised her. A 'battler', in the language of an older Australia; a 'loser' in the new. She looked sixty, she'd be less than fifty.

Fontana reckoned that poeple like this came from the same family – Ruggling. They even had the same initials: S.T. *S.T Ruggling.*

'Who the fuck are you?' You could see the wariness in her face – this woman trusted nobody.

Gerard stepped forward, in front of Dusty, in front of the girl.
'I'm Detective Bevan and this is Detective Buchanon.'
'You got a search warrant, copper?'
'No.'
'Then get off my fucking property.'
'We just wanted to ask–'
'Get off my fucking property!'
'Nana, the nice lady gave me–' said Chantay.
'Chantay, git in the house!'

Chantay smiled again. Getting scolded by Nana was obviously not a novel event, but she obeyed, scurrying off behind the house, Dusty's fob chain clutched in her hand.

'Just a couple of–' started Gerard, before he was again cut short.

'Get off *now*!' said Nana.
'Let's go,' said Dusty.
'Detective Bevan?' Dusty inquired as she got back into the car.
'Jezza?' countered Gerard. 'Did you get it?'
Dusty nodded.
'What is–'
'I'll explain later, let's just get our stuff and get out of here.'

Chapter 49

Dusty had often thought that Julien would like the morgue. He, who was forever railing against Darwin's architecture, complaining how unsuitable most of it was for the tropics, would surely approve of its cool, uncluttered surfaces, its clean uninterrupted lines.

'Brought you a coffee,' said Dusty to Bethany, the thirty-something morgue attendant renowned for her surliness. Once Dusty had attributed this to her occupation – constant exposure to the dead had done ugly things to her psyche. In fact, for a while there Dusty saw Bethany as an examplar: what we'd all be like if we weren't constantly shielded from death. Lately, though, she'd changed her mind – Bethany was just one of those grumpy lesbians.

'How many sugars?' she demanded, looking at the proffered cup with suspicion.

Dusty had been caught out before. 'None,' she said, fishing in her pocket for the sugar sachets. 'I know you like to put your own in.'

'Well, OK. Thanks, I suppose,' said Bethany, tentatively taking the coffee, as if there were, literally, strings attached.

'So that's our fella?' said Dusty, indicating the sheet-covered body on top of the stainless steel gurney.

Bethany nodded.

'Don't know how the fuck you pulled this off,' she said, and you could hear the relief in her voice – she had a legitimate excuse to become grumpy again.

Dusty knew exactly what she was on about. Bodies were meant to be viewed in the viewing room, a pane of glass between the viewer and the viewed. There was no shortage of reasons for this – health, legal, moral. A pane of glass between the viewer and the viewed did not suit Dusty's purposes, however. It'd taken her two frenetic days on the phone – trading favours like a Wall Street stockbroker, bullying, begging – until eventually, theoretically, she'd arranged it. Dusty checked her watch – she still had fifteen minutes until ten, the time she'd arranged to meet Flick.

'Singhie in today?'

Bethany shrugged. How would I know? I only work here.

The door to his office was open. Dr Singh was sitting at his desk.

'Knock, knock,' said Dusty.

'Who's there?' said the doctor, not looking up from the report he was engrossed in.

'No, I really mean "knock, knock".'

'Come in, by all means.'

Despite its location, Singhie's office was actually quite cosy. It smelled like the *chai* he was forever drinking, like cinnamon and cardamom.

'You seen this?' he said, waving the report at Dusty.

'No.'

'Ballistics.'

Unlike other pathologists, who took no further interest once they'd shoved the innards back in, sewn the body up and written up their report, Singhie liked to keep track of his customers as they progressed through the system. It could get annoying,

The Build Up

Singhie ringing up offering all sorts of exotic theories, and Dusty did sometimes wonder whether he'd read one too many Patricia Cornwell novels.

'Makarov,' said Singhie. 'Russian made. You don't see those very often.'

Dusty's knowledge of firearms only extended as far as her first-hand experience of them – the one she carried herself and the ones that had been used in the cases she'd worked on. A Makarov meant nothing to her.

Singhie was at his computer, typing 'Makarov' into Google. He hit return, clicked on one of the search results.

From the next door the sound of a buzzer. A door being opened. The voices of her former Homicide colleagues, their words bouncing off the tiled surfaces.

'I'm up,' said Dusty to Dr Singh, and that's how it felt: as if she were the one being scrutinised, not the dead person on the gurney.

Bethany was sipping her coffee, Flick was on her mobile and Fontana was looking pissed-off.

'This better be good, Buchanon,' he said, 'I've got work up to the eyeballs.'

'Just keep close to Gardner, OK,' said Dusty. 'If I've got this right, he could do anything.'

The buzzer buzzed again, Bethany opened the door and lawyer Stan Lavery appeared. Gruff and grizzled, he was an old Darwin hand who knew where the skeletons were buried, who'd buried them and what football teams they barracked for. With him was the prime suspect in the murder of Dianna McVeigh, Evan Dale Gardner.

'Evan, how are you today?' asked Dusty, pleasantly.

He grunted.

Some things never change, she thought. Hours and hours of questioning and that's all she'd ever got from Gardner – grunts.

'Owe you one,' she said, shaking Stan Lavery's hand.

'One?' he replied.

Dusty, Bethany and Flick stood on one side of the gurney while Stan Lavey and his client stood on the other, Fontana hovering behind them.

'Mr Gardner, just wondered if you knew this person,' said Dusty, motioning to Bethany.

She pulled the edge of the sheet back, exposing Jonsberg's face.

Gardner didn't react.

Dusty had half-expected that. Jonsberg had been shot, buried, disinterred and autopsied – he probably wasn't looking his best. She could see the satisfaction on Bethany's face, Flick's face, maybe even Fontana's face – Dusty's fucked up again.

'More,' said Dusty to Bethany.

'This is bullshit,' she said.

Moving forward Dusty grabbed the sheet and yanked it down revealing the tattoo of a lynched blackfella on the mottled skin of Jonsberg's right shoulder.

It wasn't a scream, it wasn't a bellow, but whatever it was it came from the very pit of Gardner's being. And while it was not enough to stir the dead – they remained recumbent on their gurneys – it did bring one of their attendants, Omar, running in from the next room yelling, 'What is matter?'

Gardner lunged at Jonsberg, digging his fingers into the waxy flesh of his face. Fontana moved quickly, grabbing him from behind, handfuls of King Gee, pulling him away. Stan Lavery got in on the act too, enveloping his client in a bear hug.

Dusty handed Flick two sheets of paper, on each of them a DNA profile. The first was from the report Flick had given her detailing the unidentified DNA from McVeigh's body, the so-called contamination. The second was from the body in front of them. They were identical. Dusty knew she was grandstanding

The Build Up

and would probably make Detective Roberts-Thomson hate her forever, but she couldn't help herself. She took out a plastic exhibit bag. Inside was the necklace Chantay had been wearing, the one she'd swapped her own fob chain for.

'What's that?' asked Flick.

Dusty pointed to the cadaver.

'His daughter was wearing it.'

Flick shrugged. And?

Dusty held out a photo. The honeymooners about to embark on the trip of a lifetime. Flick took the photo, looking at it closely. At the necklace around Dianna McVeigh's neck. She took the bag containing the necklace. Looked at it closely. They were the same.

'This doesn't mean he killed her,' said Flick.

'He fucking killed her all right,' said Gardner, the words Dusty had been waiting more than two years to hear.

'My client has nothing more to say here,' said Stan Lavery, but he was mistaken, his client had plenty more to say.

Dusty was so accustomed to a Gardner that was mute, monosyllabic at best, that when he started talking – words, phrases, sentences spinning from his mouth – she thought it must be some trick of ventriloquism. That quickly passed, though, as she began to enjoy – and appreciate – this new garrulous version of the man who had caused her so much frustration.

'Jonno was in one of those fucking moods, you know. His missus had shot through, left him with the kid. Usually, when we were working, we'd mix it up – a few beers, a few cones, a bit of whiz. Jonno was doing line after fucking line of goey. I told him, "All that chemical's gunna fuck you up, mate. You need some of the green, as well." He didn't take no notice. On and on about how he was gunna find her. Track her down. Slice her up good. Then he gets it into his head he wants to go over to this other camp we seen earlier. Make ourselves known. "Go to bed you silly cunt," I tell him. Couple more cones and I've had enough. I crawl into the back of the LandCruiser and I'm out like a fucking light. When I wake up, there's this dead chick there. Just fucking lying there, you know. I freak, of course. I don't want nothin' to do with this shit. But Jonno's out of his fucking tree. Waving this gun around. If I don't help him get rid of her he's gunna blow me fucking head off. I don't have no choice in the matter.'

When he'd finished, the only sound was the thrum of the air conditioner, then Fontana clearing his throat. Dusty could see the shock in Bethany's face. Death she was familiar with but perhaps not the casual way it was delivered. Gardner had been so matter-of-fact, like he'd been describing a recent picnic he'd been on. Dusty felt strangely elated. After so long imagining what had happened that night in the desert at last she knew. And the truth – she had no doubt that Gardner had told exactly that – wasn't dissimilar to what she'd thought.

Stan Lavery broke the silence. 'My client has nothing more to say here.'

Bethany wheeled Jonsberg back into storage. Flick and Fontana took Stan Lavery and his client to the station to make a more formal statement. Dusty went back to the Shed.

Though she received a few congratulatory phone calls, nobody suggested that they should all go down the pub, customary practice after bringing a big case home. Go down the pub and drink litres of beer and drunkenly tell everybody how great they'd been, how this fucker of a case couldn't possibly have been solved without them.

So Dusty invited Trace and Gerard for a drink at the Sailing Club instead.

They sat outside and watched the sun set over Fannie Bay. Nearby a gaggle of tourists were excitedly snapping away with their

The Build Up

cameras, tracking the sun's inexorable descent with their video cameras.

Dusty didn't really get the sunset thing. Yes, inevitably, at the end of the day the sun did set, and that setting was often, like tonight, accompanied by an ostentatious display of colours, but didn't these people have their own sunsets to go gaga at? Was Korea bereft of such things? Wasn't Japan, in fact, the land of the rising sun?

'Guess you won't be in the Shed much longer,' said Gerard.

'Not so sure about that,' said Dusty, pouring riesling into the three glasses on the table.

'Anyway, here's to you, Gerard, king of the *yarndi*.'

As they toasted Gerard, Dusty thought again of what Alex had said. Maybe it was true, maybe Gerard had lost his bottle. There had to be a very good reason why somebody with his undoubted skills wasn't a Dee. Gerard deserved another crack at it. That much she knew. This was Darwin, after all, Capital of the Second Chance.

'I reckon you should get back on the street,' said Dusty.

'Yeah, so do I,' said Trace, giggling. 'Get us some of that *yarndi*.'

Dusty had hesitated before inviting both Gerard and Trace – she'd thought that apart from their place of employment they didn't have much in common. They seemed to be getting along well, however. Really well.

'Dusty, can I ask you a question?' said Gerard.

'Sure.'

'On the way to Kanulla, you said there was other stuff besides the phoney licence that linked Jonsberg to Kanulla.'

Dusty nodded. 'Their tatts – I knew Gardner had a Ku Klux Klan tatt, and Singhie told me about Jonsberg's tatt, the blackfella getting lynched.'

'So they both hated blackfellas?'

'Exactly.'

'But so do a lot of people.'

'Yeah, but they don't get tatts.'

Dusty could see that Gerard was still struggling to understand.

'You've been to Kanulla, you've seen how much money those blackfellas throw around. You can sort of understand why somebody, especially a battler, would resent them so much.'

'It still seems, a bit, I don't know . . . thin,' said Gerard.

'It was a lead, Gerard. That's what policework is all about, following leads.'

'I've gotta go,' said Tracy, looking at the time on her mobile. 'Kids, and that.'

'I can give you a lift back to your car, if you like,' Gerard said.

'Great,' said Trace, standing to leave. 'Sis, you're a star. Let's have lunch tomorrow.'

Dusty was left by herself. For a moment she contemplated drinking litres of beer and drunkenly telling herself how great she was, how this fucker of a case couldn't possibly have been solved without her, but she decided against it and went home, fed the dogs, and went to bed.

Chapter 50

It was during *surya namaskar*, the salute to the sun, that the thunder started. The weather bureau had predicted that the Build Up would end soon, but from Dusty's experience the Build Up ended when it wanted to and not because some meteorologist with a pointy head and a computer model decided it should. As the yoga class continued, the thunder got louder and louder, filling the room. By *shavasna* time, as Dusty lay on her back, eyes closed, Vashti needed to yell to be heard.

'Relax all those hard-to-relax muscles in your body.'

'I said relax them!'

It was easy to understand how Zeus, and Thor, those rumbling gods of thunder were so revered, so feared. If you were going to believe in a higher power, then why not one with some attitude.

But as suddenly as it had started, the thunder stopped. Dusty smiled to herself. Pointy heads. Computer models. The silence left behind was so crystalline that at the end of the class, when Vashti sounded her miniscule chimes, they tolled like cathedral bells.

Everybody was going to the pub – they all wanted to hear about Jonsberg. It had made front page of today's *NT News*, relegating Shane Warne in Nude Croc Romp to page two, which in turn relegated Cane Toad Found in Casuarina Shopping Centre to page three. The story had come from the Media Unit, but it had the Big C's managerial DNA all over it – *best practice, desired outcome,* all of them, of course, *going forward.* That she was only mentioned in passing did not upset Dusty. She understood the rules: police work was teamwork, there were no stars.

Against a sky that was a mountainscape of cloud, peaked and troughed, capped in black, the Beachfront blazed like a fun-palace. Drinks were ordered, small talk was talked, until Vashti looked at Dusty and said 'Well?'

'Well, what?'

'Well, what's the real story?'

Dusty often thought that modesty, as far as virtues went, was a touch over-rated. Usually she'd have no problem allowing herself credit if she felt she'd earned it. Tonight, however, she felt no such desire, a case had been solved, but it wasn't *the* case. So Dusty followed the party line – *dogged police work, procedure, process* – enlivening the story with some choice titbits (she did have some responsibility as a storyteller, after all) but she made no mention of Kanulla.

'So who shot Jonsberg?' asked the ever-logical Sean.

Dusty was about to answer, but Zeus, Thor, whoever was on duty tonight, had other ideas. There a prolonged crack of thunder, the sky burst open and the rain came.

The Build Up could build up no more. The Wet had broken.

The patrons of the Beachfront Hotel, crowded under the available shelter, drank their drinks and watched. Old hands made old hand comments: I knew it'd break soon, eh?; while the newbies – as newbies tend to do – reiterated the everyday: there's just so much fucking water! The downpour lasted an hour during which time dinners went cold, favourite TV programs went unwatched and babies' shitty nappies remained unchanged as all over Darwin people tuned into the water-

The Build Up

and-gravity extravaganza. After, Dusty joined the many people milling around the Nightcliff foreshore. For the first time in weeks the air felt, and smelled, fresh. Wet roads glistened under streetlights. Gutters burbled with water. There was a sense of celebration in the air. The Wet has broken! The Wet has broken! Long live the Wet!

Dusty sat on a damp bench seat, facing the sea. Having grown up in Adelaide, known as the City of Chuches, but more usefully described as the City of Jetties, Dusty was very fond of a jetty. The one in front of her was relatively short, made of steel, and couldn't hope to compete against the Grange Jetty, the Glenelg Jetty, the Semaphore Jetty, or any of the stately wooden structures of her birth city. It still possessed, however, some of the same pleasing qualities – it poked out into the water, lights twinkled along its length, fisherman fished from it.

Dusty checked her watch. It was almost nine, around midday in London. She took out her mobile and dialled the number – she knew it by heart.

This time Mr Maxwell answered.

'Yes.'

'It's Detective Buchanon, Mr Maxwell.'

'I was hoping to hear from you, Dusty.'

Though the Maxwells no longer read the papers or watched the news – they'd had enough misery, they'd told Dusty – it would be impossible, in this information age, not to hear something.

'So you know?' Dusty asked.

'I'd like to hear it from you.'

Dusty explained what had happened.

'So there will be no trial?' Mr Maxwell asked when she'd finished.

'An inquest, not a trial.'

There was more talk, more explanation until eventually Dusty said, 'Mr Maxwell, can I ask a favour from you?'

'Of course,' he said. 'Anything I can do to help.'

Chapter 51

The commander had underestimated Detective Buchanon – she was a much more formidable opponent than she'd first thought. Not that she was an opponent, of course. They were both *on the same page*, sharing the same mission statement, working to, if not exactly *grow the business*, at least achieve the target outcomes – *to reduce crime and protect the community*.

A knock on the door.

'Come in.'

As the commander expected, it was Detective Buchanon.

In plainclothes!

Who had given her permission to go back to plainclothes?

'You asked to see me,' said Detective Buchanon, and again she had that look on her face.

The commander didn't know how to describe it – it wasn't a smile, it wasn't a smirk – but whatever it was it irked the commander and had so since the first day she'd seen it. Her predecessor had been patronising, bordering on misogynistic, in his attitude towards her, and snidely dismissive of her management background. That Detective Buchanon was his protégé had soon become apparent – he'd described her as being 'a special talent'. The commander had been determined to treat all her detectives equally – police work was about teamwork. Obviously 'special talent' did have its place, intuition should be acknowledged and rewarded, but not to the detriment of process.

'I've had a phone call from Mr Maxwell,' said the commander.

She had talked to Mr Maxwell previously and had found him to be polite and reasonable, the epitome of English reserve. There had been none of that English reserve in evidence during this call, however. He had suggested, no stated, that without the efforts of Detective Buchanon, the case would still be unsolved, or, even worse, the wrong man would've been convicted of his daughter's murder. He'd also insisted that it was Detective Buchanon who had kept he and his wife informed, *in the loop* was the phrase he'd used. He'd finished with a threat: if Detective Buchanon wasn't given *due recognition* for her efforts then he would have no recourse but to go to the press and *air his grievances* as to what he saw as *irregularities* and *deficiencies* in the case management.

'You two seem pretty chummy,' said the commander.

'That tends to happen when you spend a long time on a homicide,' said Dusty.

She was a smartarse, too.

'Let's not beat around the bush here, Detective. What is it that you want?'

After the Chamberlain case, after the Falconio case, neither of which had reflected well on the Northern Territory Police Force, she could not afford to have the press let off the leash again, especially the junkyard dog that was the British tabloid press. She could imagine the headlines: Another Ocker Cop Shocker!

'I want to go back to plainclothes,' said Detective Buchanon.

'Well, it seems you've already made some steps in that direction.'

'And I'll need my car.'

'Now, let me guess,' said the commander, wresting back the initiative. 'You'd like to continue to search for this mysterious woman, despite there being absolutely no evidence that she exists or ever did.'

The Build Up

Dusty shook her head.

'So, you'll finish this case,' said the commander. 'Find out who killed Jonsberg. Prepare for the inquest.'

These were statements, not questions, progeny of the commander's authority. This is not, however, how the detective chose to interpret them.

'No, I want to be taken off this case immediately. Detective Roberts-Thomson can bring it home.'

'And what, may I ask, do you intend to do with you time?'

'I'll take the floater,' she said, referring to the body that had recently been found in the harbour, under Stokes Wharf.

The commander looked towards her bookshelf, as if to garner inspiration from the management gurus assembled there. There wasn't a lot forthcoming, however. Not that the gurus were wrong, rather it was Detective Buchanon who was wrong. Supposedly rational human beings were not meant to behave in such bizarre and unpredictable ways.

'It's yours,' said the commander, taking the brief from the pile on her desk, handing it over.

'One more thing,' said Dusty, putting a sheaf of receipts on the desk. 'I'd like to be reimbursed for expenses incurred in the Jonsberg case.'

'Expenses you had absolutely no authorisation for!'

Detective Buchanon said nothing. Just that non-smile, non-smirk again before she turned around and walked out. Angrily, the commander took the receipts, scrunched them into a ball, and threw them into the wastepaper bin. As she did the image of the junkyard dog loomed again.

Another Ocker Cop Shocker!

She retrieved the receipts, smoothing them out on the edge of the desk.

A formidable opponent, all right.

Chapter 52

'Welcome back,' said Flick, her desk laden with notes, folder stacked upon folder, and other bits and pieces from the McVeigh case, as Dusty made a triumphant return to her former office.

'Yeah,' said Fontana, less enthusiastically.

Yes, she would miss 'Music for Saddle-Weary Cowboys', Gerard's impromptu visits, and an uncluttered sink, but it sure did feel good to sit back down at her desk again. To celebrate her return to plainclothes she'd taken a couple of old friends – the lovely Ms Visa and the delightful Ms Mastercard – out shopping last night. She was wearing the spoils – a lightweight chocolate-brown jersey wrap dress and latté-coloured peep-toe flats – and feeling pretty good about it.

'Just been talking to Rex,' said Flick, referring to Rex Tamblin, the Territory's chief prosecutor.

If Flick held any animosity towards Dusty for the spectacular way in which she'd solved what was technically her case, she wasn't showing it. In fact, she seemed to have become friendlier, more at ease.

'What's he want?'
'Accessory.'
'After the fact?'
'No, to murder.'
'No chance.'

The Build Up

'So you believe Gardner's story?'

'That part of it, I do.'

'Rex couldn't understand how somebody could sleep while a girl was being "butchered" – his word – outside his door,' said Flick.

'Rex probably hasn't spent the whole day drinking tinnies, punching cones and doing whiz,' said Dusty.

That image, the honourable Rex getting down and druggy, made them both laugh.

'Gardner's DNA's all over her!' said Fontana from his desk.

'All over her, but not in her.'

'So he didn't fuck her. Doesn't mean he didn't kill her.'

'Yeah, well, I don't think he did.'

'Fuck me, Dusty, you still on his side?' said Fontana.

'I'm not on anybody's side, mate. Gardner can rot in Berrimah for all I care. I'm just interested in what actually happened out there.'

Out of the corner of her eye, Dusty noticed the handgun that was on Flick's desk.

'What's that shooter?'

'A Makarov,' said Flick. 'The type that killed Jonsberg.'

Flick held it up so Dusty could have a better look.

'They're pretty rare, you haven't seen one on your travels, have you?'

'No,' said Dusty.

Lied Dusty.

Chapter 53

Though a lover of animals, Dusty was no sentimentalist. She'd left no gravestone, no cross, nothing to mark where she and Gerard had buried the pig. It was between the two frangipani trees, that much she remembered. With the onset of the Wet, though, the now-daily downpour had destroyed any evidence of recent ingression.

'I reckon it's about here,' said Dusty, marking a spot with her shoe.

'You reckon?' queried an unimpressed Fontana, handing her the spade.

Already he was giving her the shits and Dusty questioned her decision to bring him along. She'd mentioned a pig and its exhumation, but he'd still insisted on coming. Got nothing better to do, he'd said.

Dusty jammed the spade into the soft earth causing Smith and Wesson to release a volley of appreciative barking. Another dull morning had been unexpectedly enlivened by the early return of their mistress.

She worked slowly, not wanting to break into a sweat. Though the Wet had officially started, each day was like the Build Up in miniature, the heat and humidity increasing steadily until the afternoon deluge knocked it on the head. Dusty was starting to regret that they'd dug such an extravagant hole in the first place.

The Build Up

But, there again, she'd poked around too many shallow graves in her time to even consider being responsible for one herself, even if it was for a porker.

Fontana fetched a chair from by the pool, placed it under a frangipani tree and sat down. Dusty glared at him, feeling the first beads of sweat coalesce on her brow. She didn't expect blokes to open doors for her, didn't expect them to give up their seats on buses, and, granted, this was her gig – her garden, her dead pig, her reason for digging it up – but you'd think he'd at least offer, wouldn't you, bloody great lump of gym-buffed musculature that he was?

'You know what they're saying about you and the Clerk?' said Fontana.

'I can guess.'

'Come on, you did go to Kanulla with him, stayed in the honeymoon suite, they reckon.'

'That's right, and we just happened to nail the McVeigh case.'

'We?'

'Yes, me and Gerard. We.'

'You know how he ended up in the Shed, don't you?'

'Yeah, I know all about it. Saw Belinda, by the way.'

'How was she?'

'OK, but it's not easy for her, you know, working at the pub and looking after a little one.'

'Didn't know she had a baby.'

'She does now.'

The concern big in his voice, big on his face as Fontana said, 'She does?'

'Got you!' said Dusty.

'Fucking grow up, Buchanon!'

'Touchy,' said Dusty, tossing a spadeful of soil over Fontana's shoes.

'It's not all up for grabs, you know?' he said kicking it off.

'So I'm the one who makes all the rock spider jokes, am I?'

That quietened Fontana. For a while anyway.

'It was my birthday last week.'

'Sorry, I forgot. Happy birthday to you. Happy birthday, dear Fontana. Happy birthday to you.'

'I was forty,' said Fontana, a pitiful look on his face.

'It's not the end of the world, for chrissakes.'

'By forty I thought I'd have, you know, kids and that?'

'You blokes have got nothing to worry about,' said Dusty dismissively. 'Sperm machines, you are. Look at Rupert Murdoch.'

Fontana smiled his goofy smile, the first one of the morning.

'I'd rather not.'

'I'd cut back on the porn if I were you, though. The taddies get confused.'

'It's not porn.'

'Yeah, right. Then how come the screen goes blank whenever I come near?'

Fontana hesitated before he said, 'RSVP.'

'That internet dating thing?'

Fontana nodded.

Dusty smiled. She sure got that wrong.

'You going to ask me how it's going?' he said, with more than a touch of coyness.

Dusty decided that he couldn't have it both ways – expect her to do the digging as well as provide a sympathetic feminine ear.

'You don't feel like doing some spadework do you?'

'Not really.'

Dusty gave him another chance.

'Save you going to the gym tonight.'

'I'm on lower body tonight, mate. Glutes. Quads. Hammies. That sort of thing.'

The Build Up

'Good for you.'

'So I had a date with this wellness coach last week.'

'Fontana?' Dusty frowned.

'What?'

'I think you may have confused me with somebody who actually gives a stuff.'

As soon as Dusty said this, she felt bad. She shouldn't have. It worked.

'OK, give me the shovel,' sighed Fontana.

'It's a spade, actually.'

'Just give me the fucking thing!'

Dusty handed it over and Fontana, shirt off, was in the hole and into his work.

'So tell me about it,' said Dusty, lowering herself into the chair.

Fontana told her about the wellness coach, about the other dates he'd been on, and Dusty responded with her usual sage advice: don't talk about your gun all the time and if you do get around to having sex it's probably a good idea to remove your pulse meter first.

'Got something!' exclaimed Fontana.

Both Smith and Wesson had seen some things in their canine time but really nothing had been as exciting, as barkworthy as the removal of the hairless mutt from its hole, the laying of it on the pavers next to the pool, and the squirting down of it with the garden hose.

'For chrissakes, can you stop those mongrels barking?' said Fontana.

The pig was bloated and discoloured and – to use Dr Singh's words – slightly odiferous, but it was in surprisingly good nick.

'Bullet must've gone in here, eh?' said Fontana on his haunches, pointing to a wound on the pig's right shoulder, the skin around it tattooed with gunpowder. 'Can't see any exit wound. Must still be in there I reckon.'

Exactly what Dusty had hoped.

'OK, then,' said Fontana. 'We'll load Babe here into the boot and get her to Scientific.'

'No chance.'

'What?'

'You know what it's like in there, everything's got to be in triplicate. Too many questions, Font. Bound to get back to the Big C.'

'OK, how about the local X-ray centre, then. "Sorry, our pig's looking a bit peaky today. Do you mind doing a couple of pictures for us?"'

Which wasn't as ridiculous as it sounded – Singhie had an X-ray, didn't he? Dusty rang the doctor and explained her predicament. Though he was sympathetic, he couldn't help. It just wasn't possible to bring a pig into the morgue.

'Occupational health and safety?' asked Dusty.

'No, Omar. He's a Muslim.'

The doctor did have some advice, though, about tracing bullet trajectory paths in human tissue – which, he pointed out, was very similar to pig tissue.

Dusty relayed this to Fontana.

'Operate, Dr Buchanon?'

'Operate, Dr Fontana.'

After assembling a rudimentary autopsy kit comprising a hacksaw, a fishing knife, a plastic bucket, various kitchen utensils, some long-nosed pliers and locking the now over-excited dogs in the laundry, the two detectives set to work.

'Bucket, please, Doctor Buchanon.'

Fontana's autopsy technique, though unconventional, was effective – he systematically hacksawed portions of the pig off,

The Build Up

and then, ensuring they were bullet-free, dumped them into the bucket. After about an hour – during which time Dusty had to twice to empty the contents into the grave – Fontana cried, 'Got it!'

In the trade of favours between Dusty and Shotgun Rick at Ballistics, it was Dusty who enjoyed a healthy surplus. She'd spent several hours coaching Megan, Rick's fourteen-year-old daughter, an aspiring water polo player. So when Dusty turned up bearing a bullet in a Glad bag, he was ready for her.

'Well, it's the same calibre,' he said, holding the bag up to the light. 'That's promising.'

The bullet found in Jonsberg's head was already in place on one side of the comparison microscope. Rick put the new bullet on the other side. Some focusing, a few adjustments, then 'Bingo!' Even Dusty's inexpert eyes could see that the striations, the unique marks left on the bullet by the rifling of the gun barrel, were identical. The same gun that had shot Jonsberg had shot the pig.

As Dusty drove home all she could think of was Ruby's and the clues that seemed to aggregate around that establishment.

Franky Ng had gone to Ruby's.

Spanners worked at Ruby's.

Spanners, or Spanners's gun, had killed Jonsberg.

Coincidence?

Not likely.

Chapter 54

Julien drove slowly down the poorly lit Jabiru Crescent in his black Golf GTi, Café del Mar in the CD player, his eyes flicking nervously from left to right. He'd never enjoyed Darwin's feral margins; had no love of mangroves or the creatures to be found therein. Yes, he'd been to Kakadu and Litchfield, all those places, but he became anxious away from concrete, glass, and the reassuring hum of an espresso machine. He preferred his nature rendered as art, tastefully framed, greatly admired, and hopefully purchased at extravagant prices by Eurobeings.

The night before he'd dropped around at Dusty's as arranged.

The dogs had been nervous, the place had smelled strange, and Dusty had seemed distracted. As for the home-cooked dinner she'd promised him, they'd ordered pizza.

They'd eaten that on the balcony, drinking beer from stubbies. Julien's several attempts at conversation had gone nowhere.

'OK, you're weird tonight,' he'd finally said.

'Sorry, it's work.'

'You want to share?'

'I shouldn't really.'

'Come on, you know me? Model of discretion.'

Dusty had sketched an outline of the case, not mentioning any people by name.

'You need to return to the house of ill-repute,' he'd said

The Build Up

when she'd finished, offering what he hoped was sound fag to hag advice.

'I can't.'

'I mean "you" as in you coppers. Send somebody there undercover.'

'I already explained that the only person on the case is me.'

Julien had hesitated, then leaned forward and said, 'Maybe I could go for you?'

Dusty had giggled, the first sign of levity she'd shown all night.

'What's so funny?'

The giggle became a cackle.

It was then that Julien had decided that he'd show her, that he, a gay man, an art dealer, could, would, go undercover at Ruby's.

The first thing Julien noticed was the subdued lighting. Tasteful, he thought. A quick survey of the walls – a reflex action when you're an art dealer – revealed a velvet painting of a demure Tahitian beauty and on the other wall a poster of a naked woman with breasts so unfeasibly large and unaffected by gravity that you could almost see the maker's mark.

At one end of the room a bar constructed from varnished bamboo gave the room a vaguely tropical feel. A couple of barely dressed girls, both of them Asian, sat on a sofa leafing through magazines. A woman broke off talking to them to approach Julien. Asian. Middle-aged. Face so hard you could slice mangoes on it.

'Welcome to Ruby,' she said in that love-you-long-time delivery so beloved of all bad impersonators of Asian accents. Wel-come to Ru-bee.

Julien had been to various saunas, S&M parlours and suckatoriums, but this was his first visit to a straight brothel and his customary social ease deserted him.

'Love what you've done here,' he said, resorting to the commonplace.

'Thank you very mutt,' said Mamasan Ruby, graciously. 'You velly handsome man. You wan drink firt or mebbe girl?'

'Oh, I'd love a drink,' trilled Julien, sounding a thousand times more camp than he intended to. 'Man's not a fucking camel,' he quickly added.

Mamasan Ruby's smile dropped off her face. 'Please no bad word in Ruby.'

Julien suppressed a smile. A supermarket of fuck and you weren't allowed to name the product. If nothing else he was going to have some good stories to tell. He moved to the bar. There was only one other person there, perched on a stool, his legs crossed. An older man, petite, dapper in chinos and a short-sleeved shirt, dyed hair, neatly parted.

As Julien sat on the stool an older version of Mamasan Ruby said, 'What can you want?'

'Sorry?' said Julien, confused by the unorthodox syntax.

'You wan green can or red can?'

'Do you have any vodka?'

She looked at him quizzically. 'Vodka can?'

The older man said something to her in Thai. At first Julien thought he must be hearing things, but no, the man was speaking fluently.

'Oh. Vokka Tony,' she said. 'You wan Vokka Tony?'

'Sure,' said Julien.

Turning to the older man he said, 'Thanks.'

'My pleasure,' he answered. 'The name's Harold.'

'And mine's–,' began Julien. 'Mine's Dusty.'

'I haven't see you in here before have I, Dusty?' said Harold.

'Heard some good things,' said Julien.

'Vokka Tony,' said the woman, putting his drink on the bar, a welcome interruption.

The Build Up

'How much?' asked Julien, reaching for his wallet.

She waved his question away. 'Pay later. No ploblem.'

Julien took a hefty gulp. The drink was surprisingly good and Julien immediately felt himself relax. At the other end of the bar was a plasma screen showing porn, a blonde sucking a large black penis. Julien watched her technique with some interest. Though he'd had sex with women – well, mostly with Dusty – it had never been of the oral variety and he occasionally wondered who was more adept, males or females, at the fellatory arts. The black penis ejaculated all over the poor woman's face, and Julien turned away. Really, it was a bit much, even for him.

Besides, he now had company. A woman, wearing more make-up than clothes, was standing so close that her spangled crotch was pressing against his thigh.

'Gidday, mate,' she said in an accent so Ocker it made Crocodile Dundee's seem mid-Atlantic.

'Hi,' said Julien.

Her hand was now resting on his thigh, disconcertingly close to his crotch.

'What's your name, mate?' she said.

This time she overcooked the delivery, and the 'mate' sounded more like 'mite' – even Crocodile Dundee didn't say 'mite'.

'Dusty.'

'Dusty?' inquired the girl.

'That's right,' said Julien. 'What's yours?'

'Noi.'

'Noi,' echoed Julien.

'You speak Thai number one,' said Noi.

A professional compliment, but Julien couldn't help but feel chuffed – with its five tones Thai was a notoriously difficult language to speak.

'*Kop khun krap*,' he said, eager to impress further.

Impressed she obviously was, because her crotch was now gyrating against his thigh. Julien had no doubt that if he were more heterosexually inclined, blood would be rapidly making its way southwards.

'You like perfume Noi?' said Noi, pressing her breasts against Julien's shoulder.

Julien did like the perfume. It was *L'air du temps*, Dusty's favourite. She'd put too much on, however. And there were other intermingling smells of less certain provenance.

'Very nice,' Julien replied.

Noi pressed closer and grabbed his cock. At first he thought that he'd imagined it, but when he looked down at his lap he could see that the hand with its violent pink fingernails was exactly where he thought it was. Not only that, it was performing a palpating action, not unlike what Julien imagined a dairy farmer would do to coax milk from a cow's teat. Julien took Noi's hand and moved it away.

'You no like Noi?' she said, petulantly. Turning to Ruby's sister she said something in Thai.

Julien only understood one word – *katoey*.

'You no want Noi?' asked Ruby's sister.

Now Julien was feeling sorry for Noi. Sorry that she was a prostitute. Sorry that inequalities in global economics meant that she had to come here to sell her body. Like his Nikes or the T-shirt he was wearing, she was just another commodity conveniently imported from the developing world. He responded with what he thought of as his Gallic shrug.

'No ploblem,' Ruby's sister said diplomatically, 'Plenny pretty girl at Ruby.'

She dismissed Noi with a wave of her hand and signalled to Ruby.

Julien finished his drink.

The Build Up

'What sort of work you do, Dusty?' Harold asked, with a hint of an accent. South African, thought Julien.

'Work for the government,' he replied. 'Just shuffle papers really.'

Harold, brow furrowed, opened his mouth to say something when Mamasan Ruby appeared with a Thai girl in tow, this one wearing clothes.

'Nice girl this girl. Young. Name Nim,' said Ruby, nudging her in Julien's direction.

Julien had a theory: gay men are often better judges of feminine beauty than straight men, whose judgment is compromised by other more carnal considerations. Nim was young – seventeen or eighteen, Julien estimated. She had high cheekbones, limpid brown eyes, flawless skin. Her long hair was tied back. She was absolutely beautiful. What's more she sat demurely on her stool and made no attempt to rub her crotch against Julien's thigh, press her breasts against his shoulder or touch his private parts.

More customers had arrived – a buck's party determined to give the groom a memorable last night of bachelorhood. Julien was no economist, but he did run his own business, and knew enough about supply and demand to realise that the latter was soon going to exceed the former.

'You go with me?' he asked Nim.

She didn't understand.

'You,' he repeated, pointing at Nim and then to himself, 'go with me?'

'Seck?' said Nim timidly, and Julien's heart was a puddle in his chest. Such a sweet, sweet girl!

Taking his hand she led him down a hallway that had numbered doors leading off on both sides. Nim giggled as she opened the door to number two and let Julien step inside. It was sparse, more public hospital than plush bordello. There was a built-in wardrobe, the door partly open. Julien could see a yellow-and-brown striped football jumper hanging inside. He turned his attention to the double bed. He doubted if the pale pink sheets were Egyptian cotton but they looked clean enough. On a raw pine bedside table was a box of home-brand tissues, a glass bowl containing an assortment of condoms, and a jar of Glyde lubricant.

Nim started to take off her dress.

'Wait,' said Julien.

Nim looked perplexed. 'You no love Nim?'

'Of course, I love you. I love you very much.' Julien perched on the side of the bed. 'Sit here,' he said, patting a spot next to him.

Nim did as she was asked.

'Was there another girl who worked here?' he said, speaking slowly, enunciating each syllable.

'You want other girl?'

Julien was starting to think that he'd made a mistake choosing the gorgeous Nim instead of the vulgar, but fluent, Noi. Suddenly, he had an idea: why just stick with English? These girls get around. Maybe she speaks another language.

'You speak French?' he asked. *Parle vous Francais?*

'You want Frent, no problem,' said Nim, reaching over to undo Julien's fly.

Julien gently removed her hand.

'Listen Nim. Thai girl. Work here. Now gone. Understand? Thai girl. Work here. Go away.'

A look of comprehension appeared on Nim's face.

'Noi!' she exclaimed.

'No, not Noi.'

Nim pointed at Julien's watch. 'Time go.'

The Build Up

Of course – market forces, limited resources, bucks with bucks to burn lining up.

Nim smiled. 'Jiggy jug?'

'French?' said Julien.

'OK,' said Nim, leaning over to grab the bowl. 'You wear condom, OK?'

'OK,' said Julien, inspecting the impressive range available. Everybody likes strawberry, he thought.

Chapter 55

Julien didn't understand Dusty's loyalty to Hanumans – there were much better cafés in Darwin now. The decor was shabby, the owner looked like he'd stepped out of an Ubud batik shop circa 1982, the place was overrun by mums and bubs and the coffee was average.

'You're late!' said Julien, as Dusty appeared, fifteen minutes after their arranged time of 8 am.

'No, I'm not – you're on time!'

Julien waited until Dusty ordered her coffee before making his big pronouncement.

'I went to Ruby's last night.'

'You did what?' she said loudly, causing several of the Absolutelies to look around.

Dusty was concerned. Dusty was outraged. Dusty was appalled. 'Tell me about it,' she then said.

Julien told his story, and it was a story, too. Not that he'd made anything up, he just omitted certain scenes. When he'd finished Dusty said nothing, in fact she seemed more interested in her coffee. Eventually she looked up at him and said, somewhat matter-of-factly. 'You fucked her.'

'I did not fuck that woman,' Julien said, his tone Clinton-esque in its defiance.

The Build Up

'She sucked your pathetic little cock, then.'

'She did not,' he said, more a refutation of 'pathetic little cock' than 'she sucked'.

'I'm going to the toilet. When I come back we're going to start again, OK?'

With that Dusty got up and left.

She returned with a pen and paper borrowed from the Indo-hippy, sat down and fixed Julien with a schoolmarm stare. 'I don't care if you think it's inconsequential. I don't care if you think it's not important. That's not your decision to make, OK? I want to know what your eyes saw. What your ears heard. Basically, what you are is a video camera.'

Julien wasn't going to give in without a fight. 'Sony or Panasonic?'

'Fuck off, Julien, this is a murder investigation.'

'Fuck off, Dusty, I don't have to tell you anything. Sony or Panasonic?'

'A girl was killed.'

'Girls get killed all the time, what's so important about this particular one?'

Dusty sighed. 'Panasonic.'

'OK, here we go. I'm a Panasonic video camera, latest model, of course. Hard Disk. High Definition.'

Dusty glared at him.

'And I walk into Ruby's. The lighting is subdued. One of those velvet paintings on one wall. Girl with huge tits on the other. There's a bar at one end, made from bamboo . . .'

This time Julien told Dusty everything, every detail. She sat, taking notes.

'. . . It's a pretty bare room, bowl of condoms on the bedside table. A football jumper hanging up in the built-in wardrobe.'

'What team?' Dusty interrupted.

'How would I know?'
'What colour?'
'Very nasty shade of brown and yellow, like a gold, I guess.'
'Stripes?'
'Vertical.'
'Number?'
'Didn't see it.'
Trigger? Dusty wrote in her notes.
When Julien had finished, Dusty put the pen down, put away her schoolmarm stare, and smiled.
'You did good, Panasonic.'
'Really?'
'Really.'
'So where do we go from here, bring that Harold character in?'
'Don't you worry about that.'
Dusty's patronising tone annoyed the hell out of Julien. He'd gone deep undercover and come back with gold, great big nuggets of it.
'Promise me something, though?' said Dusty.
'What?'
'That you'll never do anything like that again?'
'I promise,' said Julien, his hand behind his back, fingers crossed.

Chapter 56

Deidre, the woman Dusty had talked to last time, answered the phone.

'Pickup address?'

'Parap shopping centre,' replied Dusty, disguising her voice, dropping it an octave – she didn't want Franky getting tipped off that the cops were after him. 'Outside of Café Hanuman.'

'Going where?'

'Airport,' said Dusty, going with the first place that came to mind.

'How many people?'

'Just the one.'

'Ready now?'

'Yes,' said Dusty. 'Is Franky Ng on today?'

'He sure is.'

'Do you mind if he picks me up? I've always found him to be the most courteous driver.'

'No, of course not. We get a lot of requests for Franky. He might be a while, though. I just sent him out to Berrimah.'

'I don't mind waiting.'

Twenty minutes later Franky Ng pulled up, and Dusty got into the back seat, on the driver's side.

'Airport?' Franky said.

'You got it.'

Dusty didn't think Franky had recognised her, but as they turned onto Bagot Road he said, 'How's your boyfriend, Detective?'

'Not really my boyfriend, Franky.'

'You seemed to be getting along pretty well that night.'

Franky's cheekiness surprised Dusty. Generally ex-jailbirds were more respectful in their dealings with the constabulary, even those who occasionally got shitfaced.

'I got some questions about that night, as well,' said Dusty. 'You said a girl went missing.'

'No I didn't.'

'Don't muck me about, Franky.'

'No offence, but you were pissed.'

'You said a girl went missing.'

'Really pissed.'

'You said she went with a man.'

'You imagine this.'

'What was his name?'

'I don't know what you're talking about.'

Franky had been got at – that much was obvious. Told to keep his mouth shut, or else.

They turned right into McMillan's Road, the airport only a few minutes away. The briefcase was where Dusty had hoped it would be – under the driver's seat. She hooked the toe of her shoe through the handle and pulled it towards her. Again they turned right, this time against the traffic, and into Henry Wrigley Road, named after the pilot who had made the first transcontinental flight from Adelaide to Darwin.

This time of day the airport wasn't busy and Franky had no trouble finding a park in the drop-off zone. There was excavation work going on nearby and a dump truck, loaded with rubble, rumbled past.

The Build Up

'That's nineteen-twenty,' said Franky.

Dusty paid him and shuffled across to the passenger's side.

'Well, see you around,' she said, opening the door.

'Hey, wait. That's mine!'

Dusty, feigning surprise, looked at the black briefcase in her hand.

'Really.'

She stepped onto the footpath, closing the door. Franky, too, was out of the cab.

'It's mine, you must've took it by mistake,' he said hurrying towards her, ponytail swinging.

'Funny, I've got one exactly like this,' said Dusty, also walking, keeping him at a distance. 'Tell you what, let's check inside, that'll sort it out.'

Dusty went to open the briefcase, a thumb on each of the two latches.

'Stop!'

Funny, Franky Ng didn't seem so cheeky now.

'Who did she go with?' Dusty demanded, both of them stationary now.

'Trigger, OK. She went with a man called Trigger.'

'Did you see him?'

'Yeah, I see him.'

'Describe him.'

'I don't know. Tall. Broken nose. Light hair.'

'Where is he now?'

'I don't know.'

'Where does he live?'

'I don't know.'

'That wasn't too hard, was it, Franky?'

Dusty had a fair idea what would be inside the briefcase – grass, coke, speed, pills – the wares of a small-time drug dealer.

One call to Drugs, and Franky was fucked, back in Berrimah for another lengthy stint. And she would spend the rest of the day typing up reports. Franky Ng probably didn't think so, but this was his lucky day.

'Now can I have my briefcase back?' he said.

Another dump truck rumbled past. With a deft toss Dusty deposited the briefcase amongst the rubble.

She smiled sweetly at Franky. 'Do you mind driving me back to Parap, now?'

Chapter 57

It'd always been full of itself, Sydney.

But ever since that morning in September 1993 when ex-fascist and Olympic chief Juan Antonio Samaranch famously announced 'The winner is . . . Sydanee', it'd become insufferable. Take away the harbour and take away the beaches and what was Sydney? It was overpriced real-estate and touchy-feely waiters and coppers so bent they could peer up their own arses.

As Dusty stepped out of the terminal, backpack slung over her shoulder, there was no slap in the face, no knee to the guts. In fact it was around eighteen degrees Celsius, even a bit chilly by Darwin's standards. She turned on her mobile – beep, beep – two text messages, both from Julien. 'Did you talk to Harold?' 'How is the case going?'

'Sell art', she texted back.

'Coogee,' she told the taxi driver.

'Which way do you want me to go?' he asked.

'The cheapest way,' replied Dusty, in no mood to put up with any of your typical Sydney shonkiness.

Last night she'd Wotif-ed herself a hotel. It was surprisingly close to the beach and the room much better than she'd expected. She allowed herself a minute or two of admiration for her Wotif prowess before showering. After changing into jeans and T-shirt, she went off in search of breakfast. As she walked up Coogee Bay

Road, it occurred to Dusty that Coogee must be Aboriginal for 'place of many cafés'. They were everywhere, opening out onto the street, tables and chairs spilling onto the footpath. Dusty could feel the power she had as a consumer (so much choice) but also the dilemma (what if I get it wrong?).

She chose the Globe. It seemed to be full of locals, always a good sign, and, unlike the competing 'Big Brekkie for $5.95' greasy-spooners nearer to the beach, there were no backpackers and, more importantly, no overpowering smell of fatty bacon. Ever since the backyard autopsy, she hadn't been comfortable in the presence of any sort of *charcuterie*.

It was a good choice. The Darwin-style ceiling fans made Dusty feel at ease. The waitress kept her touchy-feely hands to herself. The coffee was sensational and the ricotta pancakes, likewise.

Breakfast over, it was time for work. She took out a Spirax A4 notebook and the photocopies inserted within – a copy of Trigger's latest bank statement, his latest mobile bill. If only all detective work was so easy. Dusty had gone to Trigger's last known address, an apartment in Walsh Bay. His letterbox was stuffed full. Everybody knows this is a green light for any crim – nobody home, rob me please – so Dusty, good citizen that she was, had collected Trigger's mail for him. She'd also taken it back to the office, and gone through it at her leisure. On Monday the 2nd October he'd bought fuel at Darwin. Then at Three Ways, Mount Isa. All the way to Sydney. Since then most of his withdrawals had been made in the Coogee–Randwick area. He'd also deposited a couple of cheques at the Commonwealth Bank on Coogee Bay Road, the drawer a company by the name of Associated Hotel Holdings, which, further investigation revealed, was the owner of the Coogee View Hotel. It took Dusty one phone call to ascertain that a certain Robert

The Build Up

Tregenza was now working as a security guard at that very establishment.

Finding Trigger wasn't going to be a problem. Getting him to talk, however, was a different matter. Even with the full backing of the police force, getting people to talk was never easy.

Hence the hard seats and harsh lights.

Hence the Good Cop and Bad Cop.

Hence the biff.

The bash.

All those techniques they used so effectively in the shoe-wearing states. None of these, however, was available to Dusty. She'd have to come up with something else.

At ten in the morning there was a surprising number of patrons in the Beach Bar of the Coogee View Hotel. A couple of old codgers with roadmap noses and trembling hands and a ragged group of twenty-somethings who looked like they'd put in an all-nighter.

'Good morning,' said Dusty to the barman, all cheekbones and ponytail.

'It is, isn't it?' he replied.

'I was looking for a friend of mine, Rob Tregenza. Works here as a bouncer.'

'Crowd control, you mean?' he said smiling, flashing teeth to go with the cheekbones and ponytail.

'Sorry,' said Dusty. 'Crowd control.'

'Don't know that name, what's he look like?'

'Nowhere as good as you,' said Dusty.

The things you say when you're undercover. Dusty held her hand above her head. 'He's about yay tall.'

'They're all about yay tall, that's why they do what they do.'

'Bent nose?' offered Dusty, thinking that probably wasn't going to narrow the field a whole lot either.

'Trigger, you mean?'

'You know him?'

'Sure, everybody knows Trigger. Hasn't been here long, but he's made a big impression.'

'He's like that, Trig. You know when he's on?'

'Nightshift. It starts at seven.'

If only all police work was so scenic.

There was nothing left to do until tonight. Dusty thought of all the things she could do in the Emerald City. Go shopping. Do the famous Coogee–Bondi walk. Visit a museum, an art gallery. Lie on the beach. Or she could go back to her hotel. Which she did. Take off her clothes. Which she did. Watch an hour or so of crap TV. Which she did. Before going to sleep.

Chapter 58

It'd been a shit night. Too many kids, too many backpackers, too many three-beer fucking heroes.

Trigger checked his watch: 2 am. Time to start looking around, see what's left. The babes had gone – they got snapped up before midnight. So basically what you were looking at was slappers – mostly Pommy, a few Irish, a few Aussies. Or grab-a-granny, mutton dressed up as mutton.

Trigger had been clocking one table for a while, now. Nurses from the Prince of Wales, which meant they had a fair understanding of the human anatomy. He'd already introduced himself, taken the opportunity to inform the ladies that if anybody gave them a hard time all they had to do was tell him and he'd sort it out, quick-smart. Got a squeeze of the bicep and a pinch on his arse for that, and that was two hours and about a thousand chardonnays ago.

'Trigger?'

He swivelled around.

Bottle blonde. Brown eyes. Nice tits. Mid-thirties, but good nick. Sort of familiar, but sort of not.

'Yeah?'

'Darwin?'

A nervous laugh from Trigger. He hadn't heard that word in a while.

'Sorry, do I know you?'

'Dusty.'

'Look, I'm sorry but–'

'You fucked me once.'

It wasn't the first time this had happened to Trigger – but he wasn't going to give in just yet.

'I don't think–'

'Nightcliff footy club.'

'I don't think–'

'How's Cazaly going these days?'

Trigger shot a glance to his right. The nurses had been set upon by a scrum of no-neck rugby players.

'So what are you doing in Sydney?'

'Conference,' she said.

His earpiece crackled. *Help needed at the Aquarium bar.*

Trigger's brain was telling him that something wasn't quite fair dinkum with this chick – she didn't look like the conference type – but his dick, as usual, was having none of it.

'Sorry, I gotta work. Look, I knock off at three. You wanna go somewhere, then? Hit the clubs or something?'

'Sounds good.'

'See ya out front then?'

'OK.'

At knock-off time the boss called him over. 'Hey, big fella, you want some blow?'

The 'big fella', was pure irony; the boss, a Samoan, had at least five cm and ten kilos on Trigger.

The Build Up

'The blow', however, was an invitation into the inner sanctum. After only a few weeks on the job, Trigger knew this was quite the coup. Besides, when did he ever knock back some grade-A narcotic?

'Sure,' replied Trig, and he was ushered into the office.

Four, five other people in there. The lines were on the desk, one above the other, equidistant, equal length – the 100 metres track at the Olympics, razorblade art.

'You first,' said the boss, handing Trigger a fifty rolled into a tube.

He felt self-conscious, reminding him of the first time he did coke. He'd never touched drugs, not even a joint, but a year after he retired, a year that was as fucked-up as 365 days could get, Spida had offered him a good reason to start: 'Trig, it'll make you feel like you're kicking goals, again.' Which wasn't quite true, but true enough. Now Trigger could sense eyes on him, eyes keen to judge. He took the fifty and he took the line, and straightaway he knew that this shit was the business – his nostril hairs, his membranes, his synapses all singing the same song. Went to hand the note back. 'Take another one, bro.' Trigger didn't need another one, bro, but knew he couldn't decline, so he did that, too.

Although it was almost three thirty by the time he made it outside, she was there. Looking like a movie star. Looking like a model. Sparks flying off her like a Catherine wheel.

'So whatta ya wanna do? Hit the Cross?' Trigger asked.

'How about somewhere more private?' she said.

'Like a swim?'

'At the beach?'

'Got my own private pool.'

'That could work.'

They walked up the hill, the life savers' club on the left, kids' playground on the right.

Phillip Gwynne

Stopping in front of Wylie's locked gate. 'Wylie's Baths – Open 365 days a year' said the sign.

'Isn't it locked?' she asked.

Trigger pulled out his keys. 'Not to all of us.'

Chapter 59

His pupils dilated, his nose running like a greyhound, Trigger was exhibiting textbook signs of narcotic intoxication. Dusty was sure that neither her nor Julien, even in their worst moments, had ever talked so much shit, though. An unrelenting stream of it was pouring from Trigger's mouth. Coked to the eyeballs? He was coked to the stars twinkling above. The irony was not lost on Dusty – she'd come all the way here to make him talk and now she couldn't shut him up.

She followed him and his blather down a sloping path past a weatherboard cottage with a sign that said 'Caretaker', through a turnstile and onto a broad wooden deck. Floodlights switched on.

'This way,' said Trigger, shielding his eyes.

Down a flight of stairs and they were on concrete, at the same level as the pool.

'Beautiful, eh?' said Trigger proudly with a sweep of his hand.

Maybe during the day, though Dusty, but now there was something menacing about this place. The deck with its spindly wooden legs. The shadowy tumble of boulders at the edge of the concrete. The pool itself with its dark-coloured water. And the sound of the ocean, the gurgle of water as it percolated through rocks.

Trigger sat down on a step.

'You a swimmer?' he asked.

'A bit,' said Dusty.

'It's all in the roll, you know,' he said, and it started again.

It was as if she wasn't there, now. Trigger moving deeper and deeper into a vortex of self-absorption.

'Hey, what happened to that swim?' said Dusty.

'It's like Ian Thorpe. Always talking about how big his feet are . . .'

Dusty took off her jeans, then she took off her shirt.

'You coming in or what?' she said, standing in front of Trigger.

Is it appropriate to get naked in front of a Person of Interest? Dusty was away the day they studied that at the Academy. It worked, though. Trigger's eyes were all over her, crabs scurrying across the terrain of her body. He, too, stripped off. Dusty noticed with interest, both professional and not, the tented front of his boxers.

Dusty had no desire for a swim, the water looked so forbidding. But as Trigger and his tent came towards her, Dusty took three quick steps and dived into what she hoped was the deep end of the pool. The water was cold, but not the ice-melt she'd expected. It was the salt that surprised her. It'd been so long since Dusty had been in the ocean, she'd forgotten the vigour of its tang. She swam underwater, opening her eyes. She'd expected a pool, concrete-rendered, smooth-bottomed, but this was a piece of the wild Pacific, tentatively sequestered by a wall – there were jutting rocks and tangled seaweed and shapes flitting about. Though Dusty knew there could be no crocodiles she wondered what these other creatures could be.

She surfaced, and swam, a clumsy crawl – she didn't want to give too much away – to the other darker end of the pool. She stopped there, back against the rough-hewn wall, treading water. From here, Dusty reasoned, she had Trigger Tregenza covered.

The Build Up

She watched as fifty metres away he shucked his boxers. Naked, he stood at the other end. Dived in. Dusty scanned the surface, now a grid of intersecting ripples, waiting for him to appear. When he did it was right in front of her

'That's pretty impressive,' said Dusty.

'So's this,' he said, pressing his dick against her.

A hand against the wall either side of her, his body her cage, he went to kiss her. Twisting her head to one side, Dusty averted her face.

'Playing hard to fuck, eh?' Trigger said, leering.

Again he pushed against her, his dick prodding her stomach, prodding lower.

'Cazaly, remember?'

Dusty pressed back against the wall, making herself small. Both hands walked down, finding fissures, something to dig fingers into. When she'd found them, she brought her knee up hard. There was only glancing contact, but it was enough to send him back. She pulled herself down, blowing air hard from her nostrils, the wall, rough with shellfish, ripping at the flesh of her back. Planting her feet against the wall she kicked off. Something speared deep into the meat of her left foot, but Dusty was away from Trigger now.

'Hey, nice move!' he said, pushing hard off the wall, lunging for her.

Dusty was ready, easily moving out of his reach.

'Even nicer,' he said.

Again he lunged for her, but with no wall for leverage, his movement was sluggish, and Dusty had plenty of time to sink to the bottom. Using clumps of seaweed like rungs of a ladder she pulled herself back to the wall. Her foot throbbed, radiating hot pain. She felt it with her hand. The one, two, three, four protruding sea-urchin quills.

Trigger was coming at her again and though no technician, he swam powerfully, swam fast, building momentum. Again Dusty waited until he was almost upon her before pushing off, away from his grasp.

Again he came at her.

And again.

If it were a sprint of fifty, a hundred metres, perhaps he would've caught her, but this was evasion, elusion, this was water polo and Dusty, one-time member of the Australian Junior Women's Squad, had Trigger's measure. Eventually he stopped mid-pool, standing up, his chest heaving, chasing oxygen.

'Why'd you kill the Thai girl, Trigger?' Dusty said, her voice travelling easily across the still water.

'Who the fuck are you?'

'Never mind that. Why'd you kill her?'

'I could throttle you, you know?'

Dusty smiled. 'Mate, you can't even catch me.'

'Fuck off.'

'Let me guess what happened. Trig's forgotten his Dermie jumper. Can't get it up. So whose fault is that? The girl's of course. So you kill her. Stick a knife in her. Then drive her south and dump her in a billabong.'

Trigger closed his eyes. This must be the drugs. This has to be the drugs. He dipped his head into the water. Shook it. But when he brought it up again, opened his eyes, she was still there.

'Who the fuck are you?'

'Detective Dusty Buchanon, Northern Territory Police, at your service.'

A silhouetted head appeared over the railing above. A voice, a German accent, said, 'Is everythink OK, there?'

Dusty's mind, irrationally, imagined the following: Tomasz has made a trans-Pacific dash in order to save the woman he loves!

The Build Up

But Dusty knew she wasn't in danger. Not from Trigger Tregenza, anyway. And, of course, the German accent did not belong to Tomasz. Its owner, the pool's caretaker, a short man in baggy shorts with a salt-and pepper-moustache, appeared on the steps.

'You vant me to call the police?' he asked.

'What do you reckon, Trig?' asked Dusty.

'OK, OK, let's talk.'

'No, we're fine,' said Dusty.

'Then maybe it's time to go home.'

Dusty liked his style – forceful, but polite. The caretaker watched as they got out of his pool, got back into their clothes and, in Dusty's case, hobbled back up the steps.

Dusty knew she needed to do something about her foot. Not now, however. Trigger wanted to talk and as any copper knows, when a suspect wants to talk you don't let a few embedded sea-urchin spines get in the way.

She took out her mobile. Dialled a number.

'Detective Buchanon here,' she said loudly, so Trigger could hear every word. 'I'm just leaving Wylie's Baths with the suspect Tregenza.'

'What the fuck?' responded Trace, four thousand kilometres away, still half-asleep.

Chapter 60

Trigger felt underneath the driver's seat. The gun was where Spida had said it was. He checked the breech. It was loaded. Again, just as Spida said it was. He shoved it into his waistband.

He closed the RAV4's door to find the man once described by the *NT News* as a 'behemoth of the game', Ned Maleski standing in front of him. Alongside him a man Trigger knew only by reputation – Bojan 'Spanners' Spanovic.

'Reckon you might have something that belongs to us,' said Maleski, sounding, as always, in need of a half-decent scriptwriter.

'Yeah, and somebody's about to kill her,' said Trigger, going to move past.

The two men stood there, an impenetrable wall of thug. And though Trigger had a gun, he guessed he wasn't the only one. Besides, guns had never been his thing, even as a kid growing up in the country. While his mates had been blasting holes in bunnies with twenty-twos he'd been kicking a footy, or playing stinkfinger with their sisters.

'If she dies, meathead, it's fucking on you,' said Trigger.

This was getting too complicated for Ned – he turned to his more experienced partner.

'You carrying?' Spanners demanded.

The Build Up

Though obviously, in thug terms, Ned's superior, his lines didn't seem much better.

Trigger nodded. When Spanners held out his hand, Trigger handed the gun over.

'OK, let's all go have a look-see, shall we?' said Spanners.

The generator wasn't running now. The floodlights were turned off, and beyond the termite mounds it was much darker than before. Occasionally, however, the area was illuminated by a passing car's headlights.

'She was in there when I left,' said Trigger, pointing to the detox tent.

No noise came from inside.

'You better go check it out, then,' said Spanners to Maleski.

Trigger knew a power-play when he saw one, Spanners was flexing his thug muscle here, asserting his seniority.

'Go on,' said Spanners. 'What the fuck you waiting for?'

Trigger couldn't help smiling – poor dumb Ned Maleski.

'Maybe you should be the one to check it out, Trigger,' said poor dumb Ned Maleski his gun pointed at Trigger's heart.

Trigger looked at Spanners – surely he wasn't going to let his underling get away with this?

Spanners smiled. 'In our organisation we encourage initiative.'

'Noi?' queried Trigger, outside the tent.

There was no answer. Trigger glanced behind. The gun was still pointed at him.

'Go on,' its owner insisted.

Bending down, Trigger stepped through the opening and into the tent. It smelt like beer and sex and sweat. Old sweat. Fresh sweat. It took his eyes a while to become accustomed to the dim light but when they did he could see that Noi was naked, on her back, her legs spread wide, her head thrown back. Noi was dead.

'Fuck,' said Trigger.

A narrow blade bit into his throat.

'Steady, now. We can sort this out,' said Trigger.

The blade bit deeper. Car lights swept across the tent. The retort of a gun. Fabric tearing. The spatter of liquid against the back of Trigger's head. A body dropping. He stumbled out of the tent. Spanners, with the Makarov still in his hand.

'Shot, eh?' he said, blowing imaginary smoke from the elongated barrel like a Hollywood cowboy.

'You could've fucking killed me!'

Spanners shrugged, holding out his hand.

'Money.'

Trigger didn't hesitate, handing over the stash.

Spanners thrust the money into his pocket.

'Now tell me why I shouldn't do you, too?'

Trigger could think of a thousand reasons, but he couldn't think of one. Finally he said, 'I've got kids.'

Spanner laughed, pointing his gun at Trigger's head. 'Yeah, right. When's the last time you saw your fucking kids?'

Trigger closed his eyes and waited for oblivion.

It didn't come.

He opened his eyes.

Spanners's gun was now by his side.

'Why?' Trigger asked.

Spanners turned his arm over. Even in this light Trigger recognised the tattoo – a water buffalo, emblem of the Nightcliff Football Club, Trigger's club.

'You're a useless cunt, Trigger. But, fuck me, you were some football player.'

Trigger wasn't sure how to react. Drop to his knees and say thanks? Offer his eternal gratitude? Kiss his arse? His body, however, had other ideas – Trigger pissed himself.

The Build Up

'You never seen us, OK, champ. If the cops come knocking on our door, then we come knocking yours down.'

Trigger nodded. 'So what do I do now?'

Spanners smiled.

'How about you get in that shitbox car of yours and start driving.'

'And a change of daks mightn't be such a bad idea,' sniggered Ned Maleski.

Chapter 61

'So you passed this with the Big C,' said Fontana from the driver's seat, as they turned into the Esplanade.

Technically Fontana had made a statement, not a question. Technically it didn't require an answer.

'I really like this part of Darwin,' said Dusty.

Nestled within the gentle loop of the Esplanade, the old stone buildings – the Court House, Admiralty House – gave it a sense of history, that much of the city, bombed by the Japanese, flattened by Cyclone Tracy, done-over by developers, didn't possess. It was also the administrative hub of the Northern Territory – the Supreme Court and Government House were situated here, in architecturally ambitious new buildings.

'So we wait outside the court?' asked Fontana.

'No, Maria's going to text me when they're out. Let's have a coffee.'

Maria, the court officer, was a friend of Dusty's. Another thing she'd learnt from Geoff, the previous commander – either the court officer is your friend or you're up shit creek.

'Roma's?'

'Where else?'

Roma's was a Darwin institution, its position on the Esplanade meaning it was the café of choice for many of the Top End's powerbrokers, the pollies, the journos, the beaks, wigs and spin-doctors, a place of macchiatos and machinations.

'I'll drop you outside, Hopalong,' said Fontana. 'Find a park.'

Though the young doctor at Casualty in Sydney had done her best to remove every last fragment of sea-urchin quill, digging away in Dusty's anaesthetised foot with what had felt like a crowbar, it had become infected. She'd dispensed with the crutches but her foot still ached, sometimes intensely, not letting her forget the ordeal she'd put it through.

The powerbrokers were currently broking power elsewhere because there were plenty of tables available. Dusty chose one near the window. There was a fire at Mandorah, on the other side of the harbour. A curl of smoke rising, joining the gathering clouds. Fontana didn't take long – parking was seldom an issue in Darwin – and soon they were both sipping coffees.

'Look I wanted to tell you something,' he said. 'Thought you should be the first to know.'

Fontana looked so intent, so earnest, that Dusty couldn't help herself. 'You're pregnant, I knew it. Please tell me you've brought an ultrasound. You know how much I love an ultrasound.'

Fontana ignored his colleague.

'I'm quitting.'

'You don't smoke.'

'The police.'

That a police officer was quitting the police force did not surprise Dusty. At least 60 percent of the coppers she'd graduated with were no longer members of the constabulary. That it was Fontana was a surprise, however. She'd always thought that he was in it for the long haul.

'Got head-hunted,' he said.

'Don't tell me – security.'

It was such a well-trodden path – from public to the private. Fontana nodded.

'Don't tell me – Afghanistan?' said Dusty.

'No, Iraq, actually.'

'Fuck, Fontana, you'll get killed!'

'Yeah, well, ask Mac about that.'

Mac had graduated in the same class as Dusty and Fontana. They were godparents to his kids. It'd been a routine call, a domestic out at Palmerston. The husband had come out blazing and that was the end of poor Mac.

'When?' asked Dusty.

'Already put in my notice.'

Dusty's phone beeped: 'they're out'.

'We're on,' she said, finishing her coffee.

Given the newly established climate of truth and transparency that existed between her and her long-time colleague, Dusty felt obliged to confess.

'Fontana, I didn't really get the Big C's OK on this,' she said as they crossed the road.

'I sort of guessed that.'

'Then how come you're here?'

'Don't know, really. Old time's sake. See if Dusty Buchanon's still got it. Blaze of glory and all that crap.'

'Oh,' said Dusty, feeling vaguely flattered.

'Besides, I've already quit. What's she going to do – sack me?'

The Supreme Court foyer was a cavernous space, lined with marble, filled with light, Indigenous artwork adorning the walls. A group of men, half a dozen or so, stood outside the entrance to Courtroom 4. They were all smiles, handshakes and manly backslaps. Dusty only recognised one of them as a vet. Barry O'Loughlin was wearing a well-cut suit, there were medals on his chest. She'd been hoping that Tank would've turned up too but wasn't surprised that he hadn't; the camp had disbanded for the Wet.

The Build Up

'We need to get him back at the station,' Dusty reminded Fontana.

Barry detached himself from the group, hurrying across the polished floor to intercept them.

'Detective Buchanon,' he said cordially, almost as if he was expecting her.

'Mr O'Loughlin,' said Dusty. 'This is Detective Fontana.'

'Went well, then?' said Fontana, shaking Barry's hand.

'Couldn't have gone better,' said Barry. 'We've got our sanctuary now.'

Another of the group, wearing jeans and a short-sleeved shirt, approached.

It was only when he came closer that Dusty recognised him as Jimmy. He'd put on weight, had a haircut, lost all the bling.

'You remember Jimmy?' said Barry.

'How's the fishing going?' asked Dusty, taking in his arms – the scars were barely visible.

'He's doing it for a job now,' said Barry, the pride in his voice unmistakable.

'Working on a trawler,' added Jimmy. 'Is everything OK here, boss?'

'Just give us a minute,' said Barry.

Jimmy rejoined the other men.

'Sorry to do this to you at a moment like this,' said Dusty. 'But I wonder if you'd have time to answer a few questions?'

'Could you just give me a minute with my lawyer?'

Guilty, thought Dusty. Up to his neck in it.

'If you have to,' she said.

'Fuck!' muttered Fontana.

In the old days it was straightforward – you'd ask somebody if they'd answer a few questions and they'd comply. Now, they all wanted to lawyer up. The guiltless, the guilty, the smart and the dumb – every one of them, lawyering up, just like they saw on the TV. Which didn't help anybody. Except the lawyers, of course. And the Porsche dealerships. And the Rolex salesman. When Barry returned fifteen minutes later, a set look on his face, it was without counsel, however.

'We could find a quiet spot somewhere,' he said to Dusty.

'Maybe it'd be a good idea if we went to the station,' she suggested.

'Actually, I don't think so,' said Barry. 'It's been a real big day.'

'Put it this way, Barry,' said Fontana. 'I think it'd be in your interests if we went to the station.'

Barry's eyes flicked between the two cops, the burly Fontana and the much slighter Dusty.

'Yeah, maybe you're right,' he said.

Dusty smiled at her colleague. The Chick Cop/Bloke Cop routine was based on a very simple psychological premise – men don't like women telling them what to do. Once again, it'd worked a treat.

Chapter 62

Barry had worn the stripes, but that was only because he was the one who'd finished high school.

Over there Scotty had been the go-to man.

He still was.

Tank found him at the bar, talking to some other vets.

'This bloke in a SAS cap was mouthing off, telling all and fuckin' sundry he'd been to Afghanistan. Been to Somalia. We've all seen 'em, eh? Turning up on Anzac Day wearing medals that don't belong to 'em. So I ask him a few questions. Just like I thought, he doesn't have a fucking clue. I tell him he's full of shit and he wants to take me on. Mean looking fucker he is too, eyes like a fish. Anyway, me and some other blokes suggest he might like to take a hike. Reckons he's gunna come back and do us. What's he say, again? That's right – you're all fucking meat to me.'

'Scotty, I need to talk to you,' interrupted Tank.

'Go ahead.'

'In private.'

They moved away into the scrub.

Tank explained it all to him. How Trig had offered him one on the house. How he'd taken a Viagra, gone back for seconds. How he'd had a few too many drinks by then. How he'd gone hard at her. Too hard.

'So you hurt her?' Scotty asked.

'Mate, she's dead.'

'So what you telling me, Tank? You fucked her to death?' said Scotty.

'Something like that.'

'Well, that's one more gook than you ever wasted in Nam.'

'I'm fucking serious, mate.'

'Tank, you're pissed. Come on, let's go check her out. I'm sure she's as right as fucking rain. Drugged up or something. You know what these whores are like?'

Scotty, the go-to man. Already Tank was feeling better. Of course, she wasn't dead. Drugged-up. Right as rain, just like Scotty said.

As they moved around the termite mounds and the tent came into view, Scotty put his hand up. Stop!

Two men were standing outside the tent.

A gun went off.

Trigger stumbled out of the tent.

The men talked, something was handed over, before the three hurried off.

'What the fuck was that?' whispered Tank.

Scotty, silent, moved ahead. Tank followed him towards the tent. Into the tent. The girl was where he left her, and another man, dead.

'Jesus,' said Scotty. 'That's the arsehole we kicked out.'

'What about her?' Tank asked.

'I'd say she's kaput, mate. Just like you said.'

'Then we've got to get rid of her.'

'Steady, Tank. Let's just think this through,' said Scotty, squatting on his haunches.

He'd been like that in Vietnam, too. Everybody panicking, including Barry, and he'd be calm and collected, working through the problem.

The Build Up

'OK, what we've got here is your dead fucking gook. And what we've got over here is your dead fucking scumbag. Seems pretty straightforward to me. He's done her. What's-his-name, Trig's, done him. Game, set and fucking match.'

'But she'd stopped breathing, Scotty. I'm sure she had.'

'Cops are like anybody else, Tank. They don't like to do any more work than they have to.'

'What about the forensics, all that stuff?'

'This is the Territory, mate. Dingo stole my baby. Remember how bad they fucked that?'

Tank nodded.

'We do have one problem, but,' said Scotty.

'What?'

'There's not a mark on her.'

Scotty put his hand on Tank's shoulder.

'Seems to me you've got yourself a job, mate.'

It took Tank a moment to understand what Scotty was suggesting, and when he did, he recoiled.

'I can't.'

'No sweat, then, Tank. I reckon you'll like it up there in Berrimah. Taking it up the arse.'

'You do it, Scotty.'

'I'm not the stud, mate. I'm not the one who fucked her to death.'

It was payback. Back in Vietnam he was Tank the Shank, the Tripod, the Grunt with the permanent hard-on. One night he'd fucked five different girls, the last one – the last one! – on the stage with all the blokes cheering him on. And Scotty, nobody would ever say this to his face, but Scotty was pencildick.

'I'll pay you.'

'You're starting to piss me off, Tank.'

Scotty, he knew, was enjoying this. But he also knew that logically, rationally, he was right – apart from them both being dead and in the detox tent, there was nothing that connected the SAS guy to the girl.

Tank bent down, went to pick up the white-handled knife.

'Fingerprints!' cautioned Scotty.

Tank took out a handkerchief and wrapped it around his hand.

'I'll stand guard outside,' said Scotty. 'And Tank?'

'What?'

'Do it with feeling, mate.'

Chapter 63

Interview rooms one to five were generic. They were the same shape, the same size, had the same smell of government cleaning product – vaguely citric, unmistakably chemical – and contained the same type of equipment: table, chairs, one-way mirror, recording apparatus. Dusty had spent so many hours in Room 4, however, trying to coax information from the then taciturn Gardner that its minor blemishes – the kidney-shaped coffee stain on the carpet, the dead insects interred within the overhead light fitting – had become major, giving the room a character it didn't deserve.

If Barry O'Loughlin was intimidated by his surroundings he didn't show it. There again, why would he be? There were cups of tea ('How many sugars, Barry?') and Fontana talking fishing and football and the size of those bloody termite mounds, eh?

Dusty took her time before she said, 'Well, Barry, maybe you'd like to tell us about the events that occurred at the vets' camp on and around the first of October.'

Barry, still wearing medals, sat straight in his chair. On the other side of the table, the two coppers.

'As you can see I've come here today in good faith without legal representation,' he said, doing a fair impersonation of legal representation himself.

'We're aware of that,' said Dusty elbows on the table, fingers interlocked. 'Now, if you'd like to tell us what happened.'

Barry started, his delivery smooth and practiced, '... *I* found the two bodies in the tent that morning ... it was *my* decision not to inform the police ... *I* dropped the weighted bodies into the billabong ... *I* removed the bodies from the billabong and buried them ...' It soon became obvious that he knew this story back to front, like the yarn you've told down the pub a thousand times.

'Do you really expect us to believe that you did all this by yourself?' Dusty asked when he'd finished.

'That's what I've told you, isn't it?'

'Lifted those bodies all by yourself?'

'That's right.'

'Buried two bodies all by yourself?'

'By myself.'

Dusty knew exactly what Barry O'Loughlin was doing. But when he said, 'Well I suppose you'll have to arrest me, now?' she'd had enough of his sanctimony, his phoney martyrdom.

'Just a couple of issues I'd like to clear up first,' said Dusty.

Barry nodded.

'It was you who buried the young woman?'

'That's what I said.'

'In that case, if we were to take you to the billabong you could show me exactly where she is?'

'I can do much better than that,' said Barry, taking out his wallet, extracting a piece of paper, putting it on the table.

On it were two numbers – latitude, longitude.

'Portable GPS,' he said, smugly.

'You've got it all worked out, haven't you, Barry?' said Dusty. 'All nice and neat, isn't it?'

'I think what my colleague is suggesting, but is perhaps too polite to say, is that you're full of shit,' said Fontana, leaning back in his chair.

After more than an hour in Interview Room 4 with Barry

The Build Up

O'Loughlin, Dusty was starting to read his body language. When he straightened in his seat and fidgeted with his tie, she guessed that another big speech was coming on. She was right.

'How could you understand? You weren't there in Vietnam. I made a wrong decision there, and because of that one of my men died and others had their lives ruined. I made a promise I'd never let them down again. I feel sorry for that poor girl, of course I do, but she was already gone, and there was nothing we could do about that. My responsibility was to my men. I couldn't let them down. Not for the second time.'

'Got another question for you, Barry.'

'Yes?'

'Who killed her, the girl?'

'What's-his-name? Jonsberg, of course.'

'You saw him do it?'

'No, of course not.'

'Then how can you be so sure?'

'I saw them. In the tent, together. And it was his knife that was . . . that was . . .'

'Rammed up her cunt, Barry?'

Barry looked at Fontana as if to say: is she for real?

Fontana shrugged – she's a loose cannon, mate. Nothing I can do about it.

'Do you know who the last person to have sex with her was?'

'Him, I suppose. Jonsberg. Before he killed her.'

'Not sure about that,' said Fontana.

Dusty was standing now. 'Maybe it was one of your men, Barry. One of your mates.'

'That's bullshit.'

'Is it?'

'Tell me who, then.'

'Tank, for instance,' said Fontana.

Barry smiled.

'What's so funny, Barry?' Dusty asked.

'You people don't know anything about my men. Tank's impotent, has been for years.'

From what Trigger had told her, and her own investigation, she'd suspected as much. Now Barry had confirmed it. It was Dusty's turn to smile.

'Even better, Barry. Tank tries to have sex with her. For the second time. And when he can't he loses it. He becomes violent. Think of all that frustration, Barry. Years and years of it. A lady's man like Tank, and he can't get it up. He strangles her. He suffocates her. And then, later, at last he gets to stick something hard up her. Jonsberg's knife.'

Again Barry looked over to Fontana. Again Fontana shrugged. Loose cannon, mate.

'Are you going to arrest me?" he demanded.

Dusty looked at her partner.

'What do you reckon, should we arrest Mr O'Loughlin, here?'

'I don't really feel like it. Do you?'

'Nah, not really.'

Barry pushed his chair out. 'Then I'm leaving.'

'Interview concluded at fourteen-twenty,' said Fontana, before he turned off the recorder.

As soon as the door closed Dusty picked up the phone, dialled the Dogs.

'How'd you go?'

'Too easy.'

'And his mobile?'

'Got that sorted as well.'

From now on Barry O'Loughlin's car would be tracked, his mobile calls monitored.

Fontana picked up the paper with the coordinates written on it.

'Fair dinkum, you reckon?'

Dusty nodded.

'He's got his sanctuary. He's got nothing to hide, now. Probably even wants to do a stint in jail – show his men what a hero he is.'

'We better go see the boss.'

As they walked down the corridor together towards the commander's office Fontana said, 'How come you're so sure Tank did her?'

'I'm not, I just wanted to get at Barry. Knock him off-kilter.'

'So it *was* Jonsberg?'

'Not so sure about that, either. Jonsberg was a cutter, you've seen the photos of McVeigh.'

Fontana grimaced.

'Trigger reckons that when he got there she was dead, no blood, no nothing and Jonsberg still had his knife.'

'And you believe Trigger?'

'I do, actually.'

Chapter 64

She was exactly where Barry O'Loughlin had said she'd be, ten metres further into the paperbarks from Jonsberg. Which didn't mean he'd buried her, of course. She was buried east–west, Jonsberg north–south; her grave was deep, Jonsberg's shallow.

Dusty imagined how it'd gone – Barry delegating a detail to bury her, a detail to bury him. *You men, you own the problem, OK. I don't care how you do it, as long as you do it well.* Jamarra had known that there were two bodies. He'd probably even known that it was a male in the grave he'd shown Dusty. And, maybe, if she'd treated him with more – to use his own word – respect, he would've told her about the other grave. Or maybe not. He had a gig to get to, after all. That was his world, his imperative. Dead people, that was hers.

If Dusty did not have the full weight of the NT Police Force behind her now – a murder–suicide at Malak was now the case célèbre – at least she had Fontana. Well, a week's worth of Fontana – Friday was his last day on the job. The rumours that had been circulating the airless corridors of police headquarters – *Buchanon's mad, Buchanon's got PTSD* – were now dormant. Not dead, though; rumours like that only needed the breath of another scandal to resuscitate them. And Dusty had regained her former position as Homicide's gun Dee. Now it was expected that as such she'd wrap up both cases – Jonsberg and Noi – quick-smart.

The Build Up

'Progress' was the term the Big C had used, as in 'I expect you to progress these cases, Detective.'

The phone rang. As expected, it was Dr Singh.

'And?' Dusty asked.

'Respiratory failure,' replied the doctor. 'The knife was post-mortem.'

'I knew it!' said Dusty, thinking of Tank, the bulk of the man.

'It's a bit more complicated than that – I think you better come over.'

The morgue was a fifteen-minute drive from HQ. Dusty did it in twelve. Again that smell, of cinnamon and cardamom.

In Dr Singh's hand, a piece of paper.

'Toxicology report.'

Heroin was Dusty's first thought. Heroin. Coke. Speed. My sweet innocent girl's a junkie, she's OD'd.

'And?'

'Significant levels of Gamma-hydroxy-butyramine, otherwise known as–'

'Fantasy.'

'Very good.'

'Remember, I did four years in Sex Crimes, Doctor. Also known as GBH, Scoop, Liquid E, Liquid X, Salty Water, Cherry Meth.'

'Such names they give these things.'

'Along with Rohypnol and ketamine, the date-rape drug of choice.'

'Effects?'

'In moderate doses, relaxation, drowsiness, and loss of sexual inhibition.'

'So not such a bad drug for a prostitute, especially a reluctant one,' remarked Dr Singh putting down the report. 'Higher doses?'

'Dizziness, vomiting, tremors, seizures, hallucinations, coma, respiratory arrest, and death.'

'Terrible way to die, isn't it,' said the doctor.

Death *was* terrible, no matter how it got you. Still, Dusty could understand what the doctor was getting at.

Alone in that rank-smelling tent, fucked by a procession of strangers, her mind going haywire, her body shutting down. It was a terrible way to die. But who was responsible? Who had given her the Fantasy?

Chapter 65

Legs, feet, kick hard, hands reach for water, dragging it back. As Trigger turns he checks his watch: 16.14, with two laps to go. He's on track to break eighteen minutes. He turns again, pushing hard off the wall. He's hurting bad now, his blood demanding oxygen. Running, you gobble as much air as you want, but with swimming you are slave to your stroke. Head left. Breathe. Left arm. Right arm. Left arm. Head right. Breathe. His stroke turning ragged, he feels like he's drowning. Right arm, left arm, right arm. Breathe. He touches the wall. 17.58!

Later, as he lay on his towel, chest heaving, he was feeling good about himself. For the first time in ages he was feeling good about himself. Then his mobile rang.

'Trigger, Detective Buchanon here.'

She'd rung him a couple of times since that night. Questions about his story, clarifications.

'Morning, Detective.'

Again that image – they'd been invoking it a bit lately, him and Cazaly – her standing naked next to the pool. The swell of her breasts. The sweet curve of her arse.

'Been in the water yet?'

'Have actually.'

'Do a few?'

'Twenty.'

'Time?'

'Less than eighteen.'

'That's pretty impressive, Trigger. Hey, maybe you'll catch me next time.'

'I doubt it.'

'Actually, so do I.'

It was her tone that got him, Trigger had decided. Made him drop his guard. That sort of intimate but take-the-piss tone she had. It reminded him of Donna, his older sister's best friend at high school.

'Aren't you turning into a big handsome boy, Trig?' she'd purr. 'Can't wait until you're old enough to take me out.'

Intimate but take-the-piss. Made him think that despite everything, Detective Buchanon actually liked him.

'You know how I said I didn't think you killed her?' she said.

'Yeah.'

'Well I've changed my mind.'

Then she'd floor you with a haymaker.

'I don't want to talk about this over the phone,' said Trigger.

'Neither do I, Trigger. But we don't have much choice, do we? I used up all my frequent flyer points last trip south.'

'Where are you?'

'The morgue, hanging out with some old friends.'

She was funny, too. In a way that chicks weren't usually funny.

'But it's a bit dead here so I'm off to Roma's for a coffee.'

'OK, I'll meet you there.'

'Ten minutes?' mocked Dusty.

'Fifteen,' said Trigger, and he hung up.

Trigger was quite partial to a sporting analogy; often it was the only way to make any sense of the world. The way he saw it, in the game Buchanon vs. Tregenza, she had what most commentators would refer to as a 'commanding lead'. The surprised look

The Build Up

on her face, however, as he walked into Roma's was worth at least a couple of goals to his team. And her comment – 'I thought you were being an idiot' – one more.

Her hair was blonder than he remembered it – she must've had it done. She was wearing long pants, a white T-shirt. She looked good. Fuckable. Trigger sat down.

'You smell like my childhood,' she said, after ordering coffees.

'What do you mean?'

'Chlorine,' she said. 'Did you really crack eighteen?'

Trigger nodded, but he had his guard up this time. Don't get lulled, he told himself. Get ready for the haymaker, he told himself.

'When you get back, champ?' she asked.

'Couple of days ago.'

After that night at Wylie's he'd got into the RAV4 and started driving, his intention to head west, to the Pilbara. He'd make himself small there. He'd disappear. Two days later, in the middle of a dark night, in the middle of nowhere, he'd pulled over, got out, and had a piss. A road train had torn past and then there was nothing but an immense silence. He felt like the starless sky was pressing down on him. He squatted on his haunches, feet planted wide, and did something he hadn't done in years: he cried. For the man he'd been? For the girl who'd died? He wasn't sure but he cried and he cried and he cried, the red earth absorbing his tears. When he'd finished, his thighs burning, he stood up, got in the car and turned it around. Darwin didn't have her titties out. There was no serious gash. No major come-on. Darwin was his mother. His big sister. His primary schoool teacher. Darwin was Dusty. And that's where he was headed.

'Any particular reason for your return?'

'Had to get the car back to a mate,' answered Trigger.

Spida's lawyer turned out to be a hotshot, after all. He'd be out in time for turkey.

'You heard of Fantasy?' Dusty asked, stirring sugar into her coffee.

'I've been around,' said Trigger, taking a gulp of his.

'Did you give any to Noi?'

'No.'

'Do you know who did?'

'No.'

The caffeine wasn't a good idea, not after all that exercise, Trigger's mind was galloping, his mouth keen to join it. Don't get lulled, he reminded himself. Watch out for the haymaker.

'What did she drink when she was with you?'

'I bought her a couple of cans of Coke.'

'Last of the big spenders, eh, Trigger?'

It was like something Donna would've said to him. *Aren't you turning into a big handsome boy, Trig?*

'You do your best, Detective.'

'So you didn't see her take anything apart from a couple of Cokes all that time she was with you?'

'No,' said Trigger, thinking of that little brown bottle.

He'd already told her enough. He'd come back to Darwin to get himself out of the shit not sink further into it.

Dusty looked away, through the window.

'There's always a fire at Mandorah. You ever noticed that? Even in the Wet there's a friggin' fire.'

'Not really,' said Trigger, pouring himself some water.

Keep your guard up. Don't get lulled. Watch out for the haymaker. Dusty turned her attention back to the table. She took a sip of coffee and grimaced.

'Yours no good either?' she said, indicating his cup.

'No, it's fine.'

The Build Up

Dusty waved the waitress over, ordered a mineral water.

'In a tall glass with plenty of ice and slice of lemon,' she said.

'You got a boyfriend?' Trigger asked.

Dusty ignored his question. 'I was there that day you kicked twenty-two goals, you know?'

It'd been one of those days, the ball had just seemed to follow him. Twenty-two was still the Territory record. Still some sort of national record, too, apparently.

Trigger smiled.

'What's so funny?'

'The amount of people who told me they were there that day, the MCG wouldn't hold them all, let alone Marrara Oval.'

'No, I really was there. You didn't kick your first goal until the second quarter. Snap from the pocket.'

'OK, maybe you were there.'

'You were a really good footballer, Trig. Hard at the ball. But never dirty. Tough but fair, that's the usual cliché, isn't it?'

Four-hundred-and-twenty-seven games of senior football, and he'd never been reported. Not once.

'Why'd you come back to Darwin?'

'Like I said, to get the car back to me mate.'

'That's bullshit, Trigger. The result of that appeal was the day before yesterday. You left Sydney five days ago.'

He knew the haymaker had to come, but it still set him back on his heels.

'So you knew I was in Darwin all along?' he asked.

'Of course, I knew. You're a suspect. It's my job to know. I even know how you got here. It wasn't pretty, either, was it? What'd you do, lose your map, or something?'

Trigger shrugged.

'Here's a tip, Trigger. If you're going to disappear, lose the mobile. You might as well have stuck a GPS up your arse.'

The waitress arrived with the mineral water.

'I'll tell you why you came back. Because you're tough but fair. OK, maybe not so much of the tough. What are you Trigger – six-four, a hundred kilos? And what's Jonsberg? Five-four, five-five, seventy kilos if that.'

'He had a fucking knife!' protested Trigger.

Dusty held up one hand as if to say: I'm doing the talking here.

'Deep down Trigger you feel bad about what happened to Noi. Deep down you want to do something about it. That's why you came back.'

There were flecks in her eyes. He hadn't noticed those before. Dark flecks just like Donna.

She'd come around one night, nobody home except Trigger. Started asking him all these questions. Intimate. Taking the piss. Did he get big stiffys? Did he like to wank off? Did he think of her when he did? He'd lost his virginity then, her straddling him on the couch, *Hey Hey, it's Saturday* on the telly, Daryl and Ossie Ostrich looking on. A week later she left school, left town. He never saw her again.

'Isn't it, Trig?' prompted Dusty.

'She had this stuff.'

It was noisy in Roma's now, the lunchtime crowd arriving. The clatter of dishes, the prattle of conversation, the persistent hiss of the espresso machine.

Dusty leaned in towards him, as if to catch his words before they got lost.

'It was in this little brown bottle, like a medicine bottle, but with Thai writing all over it. That's what I thought it was, some sort of medicine. I didn't know it was drugs.'

'Do you know who gave it to her?'

'Can I get another coffee?'

The Build Up

A galloping mouth didn't seem like such a bad thing now.

'And something to eat?' added Trigger.

'What do you want, a focaccia or something?'

'Just something.'

Dusty ordered for him, and Trigger continued.

'Noi gave it to her at the pub.'

He could see the confusion on Dusty's face.

'The other Noi, the one from Ruby's.'

'Tell me about this other Noi.'

'She's been around a bit. Pretty much worked at every knock-shop in Darwin. At Ruby's she was like the main girl, kept the younger ones in line. She was supposed to come to the vets' camp, but she pulled the pin on it at the last second. Sent the other girl instead.'

'So who actually owns Ruby's, who's the big boss?'

'Nobody knows.'

Dusty let Trigger eat his focaccia, while she digested this information. 'By the way, we didn't find any money on Noi. How much did she make that night?'

'I don't remember.'

'Have a guess.'

'A grand, something like that.'

'What was the split?'

'Fifty-fifty.'

'So basically, you owe her two grand.'

'Two?'

'Her thousand and your thousand. It's pretty straightforward, Trig. A pimp – well a good one, anyway – protects his girls. You didn't, so you pay.'

'I've already told you, Spanners took it all.'

'Your fault, not hers.'

'Hers? She'd dead, remember?'

'OK, you owe her family two thousand.'
'I don't know who her family is.'
'Leave that to me.'
'I'm broke.'
'Plenty of mangoes out there that need picking, big fella. Might keep you out of trouble until the court case.'

She finished her mineral water.

'It's been a pleasure, as usual,' she said. 'But some of us have got work to do.'

'Just one more thing,' said Trigger.

'What?'

'That night outside the pub, you said I'd fucked you.'

'Professional lie.'

'Then how did you know about . . . you know?'

Dusty smiled. Again that tone. Sort of intimate. Taking the piss.

'You're famous, Trigger. Or your dick is.'

She turned around and walked away then, whistling.

Up there Cazaly, in there and fight,
Out there and at 'em, show 'em your might.

Chapter 66

Dusty could understand how on your last week as a member of the Northern Territory Police Force you might be tempted to take your foot off the pedal – why risk getting killed here when you could go somewhere faraway and exotic like Iraq and get killed there – but she really needed Fontana's help. The murder in Malak had turned into a double-murder–suicide – a child's body had been found stuffed into a Samsonite – and was claiming more of Homicide's limited resources.

'Come on, Font. We'll just drop in there and say hello,' said Dusty, picking up a piece of paper from her desk, the search warrant which gave her the right to *enter the premises at 242 Jabiru Crescent* and *search for any prohibited substance*. The Big C had okayed it with surprising equanimity, even if she had used that phrase again – *progress the case*.

'I got a search warrant and everything.'

They'd arrested Spanners, bursting in on him while he was in the middle of a deep squat, 220 kilo on the bar, and there'd been no chance of him pulling his Makarov. He wasn't talking, though. His junior partner Ned Maleski wouldn't stop talking, but he wasn't telling Dusty anything she didn't already know.

She had to go back to Ruby's.

'Come on, you might even get a headjob on the house.'

'No can do,' said Fontana. 'Got that debrief thing happening, the commander wanted some of the younger fellas to access my experience, you know, pick my brains.'

A couple of smartarse comments instantly came to mind – slim pickings, what brains – but Dusty desisted. 'Do it another day.'

'Booked the room and everything.'

'No problem, I'll find some hat to take your place.'

The insinuation – that an inexperienced constable was the equal of a veteran like Fontana was entirely intentional. If he was insulted he gave no indication of it, though.

'I'll come with you.'

Dusty hadn't even realised that Flick was in the room, hidden as she was behind a wall of paperwork.

'Really?'

'Sure, give me a break from the Gardner brief,' she said, standing up.

Dusty could think of a thousand reasons why Felicity Roberts-Thomson shouldn't come, but right now, in the face of Fontana's indifference, some chick solidarity didn't seem such a bad idea.

'Fantastic,' said Dusty, throwing a look at Fontana. 'It'll be great to have you along.'

On the way to Ruby's, Dusty driving, Flick filled her in on the latest in the Gardner case. Rex Tamblin, the prosecutor, had changed his tack, he wanted Accessory After The Fact now.

'That's my boy?' said Dusty.

Flick laughed at that and then she said, 'Was it like a gay thing between Gardner and Jonsberg?'

'It was an arse thing, but I don't know if it was exactly gay.'

Flick looked perplexed.

'Blokes like Gardner are like barnacles, they need to attach to the arse of something bigger and meaner than they are in order to survive.'

The Build Up

'Like Jonsberg?'

'Like Jonsberg.'

Despite herself, Dusty was starting to warm to Flick. She wanted to learn and was willing to ask questions, to expose her own ignorance, in order to do so. Dusty knew from her own experience that in the you-show-me-your-weakness-and-I'll-exploit-it world of the police, this wasn't easy. She still worried about Flick's relationship to the Big C, however. That image of them under the poinciana tree kept reappearing.

This time when Dusty, briefcase in hand, buzzed the buzzer at 242 Jabiru Crescent, the door swung open to reveal – as Dusty was to later write in her report – a female person of Asian appearance. Mid-forties, Dusty guessed, maybe nudging fifty. She was light-skinned, looked more Chinese than Thai. On a chain around her neck was an image of the Buddha. No, she was definitely Thai. She was casually dressed in a T-shirt, leggings and plastic sandals.

As Dusty did the introductions – Detective Buchanon, Detective Roberts-Thomson – she studied the woman's face closely, could see the wariness come into it. The bang crash of a search warrant sanctioned entry wasn't the way to go. She wanted the people inside to open up, to talk, not clam up.

'We've come about the pig,' she said.

'Pig?' said the woman, though her 'p' had a lot of 'b' in it. Bpig.

'Yes, the pig that went missing.'

'You find my bpig?'

'Not exactly,' said Dusty. 'But we'd like to discuss it.'

Dusty knew it was a longshot – why would two detectives bother to inquire about a pig, especially one that wasn't even reported missing? But it was worth a punt. If it didn't work, there was always the bang crash.

'You come inside,' said the woman, opening the door wider. 'My name is Ruby.'

Dusty looked over at Flick, a slight raise of her eyebrows. You OK with this? Flick responded with a minuscule nod of her head. Sure. As soon as Dusty stepped inside she could smell Thai food, that heavenly alchemy of lemongrass and lime leaves and coconut milk and fish sauce and chilli.

'You eat firt,' said Ruby, making that pan-Asian gesture for food, a cupped hand as the bowl, two fingers on the other hand becoming chopsticks, scooping rice.

'Love to,' said Dusty.

One of those velvet paintings on the wall. Girl with huge tits on the other. Bar made from bamboo. Julien the Panasonic's description had been very accurate.

They followed Ruby along the hallway, past rooms one to four. Dusty thought of Julien in room two, Julien with his pants down, Julien being fellated; such unbecoming behaviour for a poofter. Still, without the revelation of the Hawthorn jumper, Dusty didn't know how progressed – thank you, Big C – this case would now be.

The kitchen Dusty knew from her last, more clandestine, visit to Ruby's. Thai pop music was coming from a CD player on the bench and there were five people sitting around the rectangular table. Dusty recognised Harold from Julien's description. She'd already asked the boys in Vice about him. Not a player, they'd said. But when she'd looked up the licence for Ruby's it was to find that the licensee was a Harold La Roux. Noi, Dusty assumed, was the one with the tits. The woman sitting next to her, gold on her fingers, gold around her neck, had to be Ruby's sister. Five years older, five kilos heavier, but the same light skin. And next to her a girl – she couldn't have been twenty – of surpassing beauty.

The Build Up

No formal introductions were made, as if two Dees turning up for lunch at a suburban brothel was an everyday event. The only person who seemed unhappy with their presence was Noi – the scowl on her face was straight out of *The Bold and the Beautiful*. She said something sharp to Ruby in Thai and a conversation ensued. Dusty had the sense that Noi was being put in her place.

Chairs were found, spaces was made, plates proffered. Dusty could see green chicken curry. She could see tom yum goong. She could see another dish she didn't recognise. She looked across the table at Flick wondering how she was coping with this aspect of detective work. Very well by the looks of it as she was piling rice onto her plate.

The first mouthful of green chicken curry and Dusty realised that the previous green chicken curries of her life had been charlatans, base concoctions of inferior ingredients. The same for the tom yum goong, she had never tasted one that was so, well, goongy.

'What's this?' she asked, pointing to the third unknown dish.

'Bpig,' said Ruby's sister.

'Bpig that go away,' added Ruby.

This, apparently, was quite a joke and as such was rewarded with appreciative laughter, especially from the two sisters and Noi. Dusty realised that she hadn't been as half as clever as she'd thought she had. Ruby had seen straight through her flimsy pretext. Why she had indulged her, invited her in, Dusty wasn't sure. Maybe because she knew, ultimately, that the power was with the police? Or was it because she had nothing to hide?

It was time to find out.

'I want to ask some questions about a girl called Noi who worked here?' Dusty said to Ruby.

'Her Noi,' said Ruby's sister, pointing to the woman next to her.

'No, another Noi. A younger one,' said Dusty, noticing that Noi hadn't touched her food.

'We are not obliged to answer any of your questions,' said Harold with an authority that belied his unassuming appearance.

So Julien was right, thought Dusty, Harold is the big boss. It's his name, after all, on the licence.

'I realise—' started Dusty, but she was cut off by Ruby's sister saying something to Harold in Thai.

An argument ensued, one in which all the original occupants of the table, excluding Nim, joined in. It ended when Harold abruptly got up from his chair and left the room.

'Husband Rosy,' said Ruby, pointing at her sister.

Then she gave another gesture – she wagged her little finger – the symbol for a small penis, for male inadequacy the world over. Again there was appreciative laughter, especially from Noi this time.

'So who owns this place?' asked Flick.

'Big boss owns Ruby's,' recited Noi.

Dusty noticed how twitchy she was, moving around in her chair like she had ants in her G-string.

'And who, exactly, would the big boss be?' Dusty asked.

The sisters looked fondly at each other.

'Partners,' they chimed.

Dusty smiled to herself. So Ruby was the half-owner of Ruby's. Sometimes the truth is right there in front of you. She couldn't help but be impressed, too. The brothel proprietors she'd encountered during her one-and-a-half years in Vice had invariably been men and had invariably been scum. Sisters really were doing it for themselves.

'Me partner, too,' said Noi.

'Junior partner,' said Ruby, somewhat dismissively.

'You had another girl called Noi who worked here?' said Dusty.

'My friend,' said Nim, the first time she'd spoken.

The Build Up

'You know her well?'

'She from same village me.'

'Noi went away,' said Ruby, talking over Nim.

Dusty's phone beeped with a text message. She ignored it, not wanting to break the momentum.

'Where did she go?'

'She go with customer,' said Ruby's sister.

Dusty took the photo of Noi from her briefcase – on a gurney, her face ravaged, her body an abomination, the knife still in her. She threw it on the table, next to the bowl of green chicken curry.

'Is this the Noi who worked here?'

Nim leaned forward. She screamed, her hand clamped over her mouth. She pushed back from the table and hurried across the room, stumbling outside, vomiting as she did. Dramatic, but authentic, thought Dusty. There was something about the shocked expression on both sisters' faces that looked staged, however; Noi's death was no news to them.

'You not polite!' said Noi shrilly, taking the photo, throwing it on the floor.

'Did you give her Fantasy?' said Dusty, hands on the table, leaning towards Noi.

'What Fantasy?' Ruby demanded.

'Drugs,' said Dusty. 'The drugs that killed her.'

'Not polite!' she screamed.

'On the night you took her to the Beachfront did you give her a bottle with Fantasy in it?'

'Not polite!'

Noi's face was twisted with rage. Spittle flecked the corners of her mouth.

Dusty hammered away – 'Did you give her Fantasy? Did you give her Fantasy?' – one part part of her advising caution – this woman is unstable – while the other part said 'Fuck it! Somebody has to take some responsibility for this girl's death.'

Ruby joined in, yelling at Noi in Thai. Noi reached down and picked up a tote bag, a Louis Vuitton rip-off. A hand went in and came out with a small pink-handled gun. A report, a shattering sound, and Dusty could feel the liquid on her face. Another report, and Noi toppled from her chair. The backdoor opened and Fontana, big and boofy, gun drawn, was standing there.

'Fuck!' he said. 'I had a bad feeling about this.'

The two sisters were screaming. Noi was writhing on the floor, blood leaking from her shattered arm onto the lino. Flick was looking at the gun in her hand, not quite believing that she'd actually shot somebody. Dusty brought fingers to her face, then in front of her eyes – they were covered in green chicken curry.

Chapter 67

It was raining but only slightly. The sprinkle of water against her face felt good. Dusty walked past a park, green and glossy, all evidence of the Dry having now disappeared.

There would be an inquest into Noi's death but no trial. Even if they could prove that Tasanee Niratpattanasai, the older Noi, had given her drugs, she hadn't made her drink it. And while it was likely that Noi didn't know what she was taking, they couldn't possibly prove that. Not that Tasanee Niratpattanasai wasn't in trouble. Apart from the arm, which had required major surgery, her and her pink-handled gun were facing serious charges.

An hour of walking and Dusty wasn't feeling any better. The Beachfront was just ahead and a soda, lime and bitters didn't seem such a bad idea.

'Broken Arse!'

Even by her questionable standards Marion was looking wrecked. Her good eye was half-closed and her hair was matted with what looked like blood.

'Auntie,' replied Dusty.

'Hey, maybe you got five dollar for me?' Marion asked, straight down to business.

'What do you want it for, Auntie?' Dusty asked.

Marion thought about this for a while.

'Buy some of that tzatziki?'

'Some what?'

'Tzatziki.'

'You mean that dip stuff?'

'Yeah, that tzatziki. Me and Sophie we love that fucking tzatziki.'

Of course, Marion wouldn't buy tzatziki. She'd walk straight around to the bottle-shop and buy a flagon of port – another instalment in her imminent demise. Dusty would be the one who'd have to identify her, too. She could imagine herself at the morgue, Marion on the gurney, Bethany typically impatient. 'Is is her, or not? I haven't got all friggin' day you know.'

Dusty gave Marion a ten dollar note. Who was she to judge?

'Get some Jatz or something to go with it,' she suggested.

'Thank you, eh,' said Marion, tucking the money into the front of her tattered dress before walking off.

Dusty ordered the drink, drank about a quarter of it, watched some cricket on the TV, before deciding she'd catch a taxi home. Opposite the bottle-shop, sitting on a bench, was Marion. She'd lied – there was no Sophie. Marion was eating by herself, dipping Jatz into a plastic tub of tzatziki. A classic Darwin moment, thought Dusty. Where else in Australia, where else in the world, would a homeless indigene beg for money to buy a Greek yoghurt and garlic dip?

'Hey!' said Marion when she saw Dusty, waving a Jatz at her. 'You want some tzatziki?'

Dusty was more a hummus sort of chick, taramasalata at a pinch. She sat down next to Marion, though – it seemed like the polite thing to do – took a Jatz and nibbled at that.

'You sure you don't want any?'

'No, not feeling so good,' said Dusty.

'Where you crook?' said Marion, peering into Dusty's eyes with her half-eye.

The Build Up

Dusty patted her stomach.

'Let me feel,' said Marion.

Dusty had little patience for blackfella hocus-pocus. She remembered one of Julien's arty friends saying that she'd come north to study Aboriginal healing. Dusty had let loose – life expectancy twenty years below the national average, double the rate of heart disease, diabetes rampant – what healing? Still, she let Marion spread her scarred hands on her stomach.

Though the sensation wasn't unpleasant – Marion's hands were surprisingly warm – there were people walking past and Dusty was starting to feel self-conscious.

'Is that the time?' she said, checking her watch.

'Baby,' pronounced Marion.

Dusty laughed so hard fragments of Jatz flew out of her mouth. Apart from one well documented but scientifically unverified case the chances of falling pregnant while celibate weren't great.

'What so funny?'

'Auntie, to get pregnant you need to have had sex.'

'Just one fuck,' said Marion.

Chapter 68

Bella had been easy. Tank had walked into the one of those swish-looking surf shops with the loud music in Bondi and told the blond-haired young fella working there what he wanted. He hadn't shut up, talking about fins and rails and rockers – until Tank had cut him off.

'Son, I just want the best money can buy, OK?'

She'd died from drugs, Barry had said. Just another druggie. There would be no trial. No murder. No manslaughter. As for the other stuff, the lawyer was confident he'd get off that, too. PTSD was going to help them a lot with that. And the fact that she was a gook.

Hayley, had been more difficult. There was only so much ballet gear that you could buy, especially for a nine-year-old, so he'd bought her an iPod, as well. Then he'd felt bad – maybe the younger girl would get jealous – so he'd bought one for her, too.

Do it with feeling, Scotty had said, and he'd listened. Where was Scotty now, though? Disappeared, Barry had said. Nobody can find him, not even the police. Maybe Barry was the go-to man, after all. Maybe Barry had always been the go-to man.

He'd done his will – Veterans' Affairs had helped him there, they were good with that sort of thing – and his daughter was the sole beneficiary. He had thought about leaving something to the

The Build Up

vets' camp, but she should have it all. His super, the house, everything.

It's that woman copper, Barry said. The blonde piece who had come to the camp that day. She must've gone to the papers. Tank, it doesn't matter what they write, Barry had said. We didn't kill her. Remember that, Tank, we didn't kill her.

Tank looked at the bottles crowding the kitchen table: forty years worth of pills. How many doctors had he seen? How many prescriptions had they written? Antibiotics, anti-inflammatories, antidepressants – a different one every week, it seemed. And he'd never thrown out a bottle, not one. Methodically he emptied the bottles into a glass salad bowl. Running his hand through the pills, mixing them up. Bella would like all those colours, she liked pretty colours, the youngest one.

He took some ice from the freezer, put it into a glass. Sloshed some Johnnie Walker into it. Scooped up some pills, washing them down with the whiskey.

Back in Vietnam he was Tank the Shank, the Tripod, the Grunt with the permanent hard-on. One night he'd fucked five different girls, the last one – the last one! – on the stage with blokes cheering him on.

Another handful of pills, another slug of whiskey.

Do it with feeling, Scotty had said, but he hadn't said do that. He couldn't blame Scotty for that.

He'd done that all by himself.

Taken that knife and done that to that poor, poor girl.

Chapter 69

'Come quick', the text had said, so Trace had done just that, piling the kids into the car.

'Geddown,' she said to Smith and Wesson, barking, tails flailing, as she opened the gate.

'Geddown,' echoed Saskia.

Nath and Dylan made straight for the pool.

'Dusty!' yelled Trace.

'Upstairs,' came the reply.

It was a relief to hear her voice – who knows, with what she's been through lately. Trace took the stairs two at a time. Dusty wasn't on the verandah, she wasn't in the kitchen.

'Where are you, Sis?'

'Bathroom.'

Dusty, in her underwear, was sitting on the toilet. In one had her phone, in the other hand a plastic wand.

'It says I'm pregnant,' she said.

'Oh, shit!'

'I need to do another one.'

Trace noticed the three other wands littering the floor. They all had the same positive result.

'No, you don't,' said Trace, taking Dusty's hand.

Epilogue

Northeast Thailand.

The three of them sit outside the house – a bamboo hut, raised on stumps. Behind them is an open sewer. Around their feet, scrawny chickens peck.

Nim was a girl when she left the village – now she's a woman. *Farang* clothes. *Farang* perfume.

In her lap a simple cardboard box.

'How did you find out?' Nim asks.

She tells her.

Last month a fat man from the government had come all the way from Bangkok to tell them that their daughter was dead.

'How did she die?' she'd asked.

'Drugs,' he'd said. 'Your daughter was a prostitute and a drug addict.'

'When will she come home?'

'It will cost twenty thousand baht to repatriate her body,' he'd said.

Twenty thousand baht! More money than the entire village had.

'Noi wasn't a drug addict,' Nim says, her eyes wet.

'Then how did she die?'

'I'm not sure. It was complicated.'

'Is there any money?' Noi's father demands.

Phillip Gwynne

Not yet midday but already his breath smells of Mekong whiskey. Nim takes out a plain white envelope from her handbag and hands it to him. When the smiling couple from Chiang Mai had come in their shiny car looking for pretty girls to recruit it was he who had taken Noi along. We can't afford to send her to school any longer, he'd said. She's a burden.

He rips open the envelope. Inside are four US$50 bills.

'Good,' he says, and he takes the money, two months' wages in their village, to spend on alcohol, to gamble, to visit prostitutes.

'And these are some of your daughter's things,' says Nim, handing her the cardboard box.

They talk a bit longer. Nim tells her how her daughter loved pop music, how she'd been learning English, how she prayed to the Lord Buddha every day. Then Nim has to leave. She's studying at university now in Bangkok.

Noi's mother cooks the evening meal. There's not much – rice, some fish, and the children go to sleep hungry. She opens the cardboard box by the light of the lamp.

Inside is the Buddha amulet she gave her daughter the night before she'd gone with the smiling couple from Chiang Mai. Her mother had given it to her when she'd gone to live in her husband's village. Inside is a plastic hairbrush. She brings it to her face, desperate to smell her again. Noi is her firstborn. There were four more after her, three boys and a girl, but Noi is her firstborn. There are *farang* books. She looks inside one. There is a picture of a kangaroo. Noi had always been a good student, if only they could've kept her at school. There is a small cylinder of paper wrapped tightly with a rubber band. She unloosens the band, removes the paper. A roll of US$50 bills. She counts them. There are forty. She counts them again. There are still forty. Two thousand dollars – more money than she has even seen in her life.

The Build Up

With this money she will leave him.
Go back to the village of her parents.
Buy land to plant rice.
With this money she will keep her children at school.

And she would pay the fat man from the government the twenty thousand baht to bring Sumalee Noppachorn, her first-born, home.